PRAISE FOR

Touch Me

"Monroe brings a fresh voice to historical romance."
—*USA Today* bestselling author Stef Ann Holm

"A light read with many classic touches . . . highly enjoyable."
—*Romantic Times*

"Extremely romantic."
—*Fresh Fiction*

"The quintessential historical romance with exceptionally drawn characters and a unique, absorbing plot. This is the historical romance you want to read when you long for the best of the best."
—*Romance Reviews Today*

"Another winner for Lucy Monroe."
—*Romance Junkies*

"Fans of historical tales will want to journey with Lucy Monroe as her wonderful tale will touch readers' hearts."
—*Midwest Book Review*

continued . . .

Take Me

Lucy Monroe

BERKLEY SENSATION, NEW YORK

THE BERKLEY PUBLISHING GROUP
Published by the Penguin Group
Penguin Group (USA) Inc.
375 Hudson Street, New York, New York 10014, USA
Penguin Group (Canada), 90 Eglinton Avenue East, Suite 700, Toronto, Ontario M4P 2Y3, Canada
(a division of Pearson Penguin Canada Inc.)
Penguin Books Ltd., 80 Strand, London WC2R 0RL, England
Penguin Group Ireland, 25 St. Stephen's Green, Dublin 2, Ireland (a division of Penguin Books Ltd.)
Penguin Group (Australia), 250 Camberwell Road, Camberwell, Victoria 3124, Australia
(a division of Pearson Australia Group Pty. Ltd.)
Penguin Books India Pvt. Ltd., 11 Community Centre, Panchsheel Park, New Delhi—110 017, India
Penguin Group (NZ), Cnr. Airborne and Rosedale Roads, Albany, Auckland 1310, New Zealand
(a division of Pearson New Zealand Ltd.)
Penguin Books (South Africa) (Pty.) Ltd., 24 Sturdee Avenue, Rosebank, Johannesburg 2196, South
Africa

Penguin Books Ltd., Registered Offices: 80 Strand, London WC2R 0RL, England

This is a work of fiction. Names, characters, places, and incidents either are the product of the author's imagination or are used fictitiously, and any resemblance to actual persons, living or dead, business establishments, events, or locales is entirely coincidental. The publisher does not have any control over and does not assume any responsibility for author or third-party websites or their content.

TAKE ME

A Berkley Sensation Book / published by arrangement with the author

PRINTING HISTORY
Berkley Sensation mass-market edition / October 2006

Copyright © 2006 by Lucy Monroe.
Cover art by Franco Accornero.
Cover design by Annette Fiore.
Interior text design by Kristin del Rosario.

ISBN: 0-425-21221-1

BERKLEY SENSATION®
Berkley Sensation Books are published by The Berkley Publishing Group,
a division of Penguin Group (USA) Inc.,
375 Hudson Street, New York, New York 10014.
BERKLEY SENSATION is a registered trademark of Penguin Group (USA) Inc.
The "B" design is a trademark belonging to Penguin Group (USA) Inc.

PRINTED IN THE UNITED STATES OF AMERICA

10   9   8   7   6   5   4   3   2   1

For Louisa Edwards, a very special editor, who sees into my head and helps me make each book better than anything I could imagine on my own. Thank you for taking a chance on a new author, for caring about the books, but most of all for sharing my artistic vision and making it better. You are truly a special person, and I'm grateful for the opportunity to work with you.

Prologue

"Is my mama goin' to be with the angels?"

At the sound of Hannah's voice, Jared's hands stilled in the act of pruning the seven-foot rosebush that towered over his own six-foot frame. He turned to face the child and gave her the only honest answer he could. "I don't know."

Hannah's small hands clutched her pinafore, the temperamental English sun glaring off the white fabric. "I don't want her to go to the angels. I want her to stay here."

Wide brown eyes filled with tears, and Jared bent down to scoop her small form into his arms. He brushed the straight, black strands of hair, very like his own, away from her face and tried to comfort her without words. Hannah resembled him in other superficial ways as well. They shared the same deep brown eyes, and their identical glares had been known to send more than one housemaid running. In fact, they looked so much alike that he knew the villagers and workers on his estates were convinced that he was Hannah's father.

He wasn't.

That honor belonged to the blackhearted monster who had raped and impregnated Mary while she lived far from Jared in the monster's household, as paid companion to his mother.

"My lord, Mary's asking for you."

Not bothering to answer the servant, Jared turned on his heel and headed back into the house, his hold on Hannah firm. His footman stepped back quickly as Jared passed him. When he reached his young housekeeper's rooms, he stepped through the sitting room and knocked twice on the solid wood of the bedchamber door.

It swung open to reveal a maid's anxious face. "Come in, milord. Mary's been asking for you." She didn't look at his face, but spoke in the direction of his cravat. Twisting her hands together, she added, "Maybe you'll let me take the little mite to the kitchen for a cookie and some tea, milord?"

Looking past the housemaid to the woman lying on the bed, Jared concurred. Mary's skin had the look of dry parchment, while dark bruises marred the skin below her eyes. The scent of illness hung in the air of the normally cheerful room. Although the sun shone brightly outside, the drapes had been pulled so the room was cast in shadows.

He handed Hannah to the maid. The sturdy little girl was almost as big as the woman who carried her, and despite his dampened spirits due to Mary's illness, Jared found himself smiling at the picture. His maid, who looked about to say something, shut her mouth with a pop and fled down the hall with Hannah.

Jared sighed. Although he had grown accustomed to the servants' reactions long ago, sometimes it still irritated him. Like now. Pushing aside the frustration and hoping the maid had not meant to say anything important, he approached the bed. "You were asking for me."

"Yes." The one word seemed to sap Mary's strength,

and she didn't speak again for almost a full minute. When she did, her dry lips barely moved. "I need your help."

"Tell me, and I'll do it for you." Mary was more than his housekeeper; she was his friend.

She had been daughter to the vicar in the village near Langley Hall. They had met for the first time not long after he got the hideous scar that marred his face. Even as a child, she had been bright and caring. She had never once shrunk from him in fear, not even that first time.

He'd repaid her friendship by doing all that he could to see her bright ambition realized, including paying for a lady's education for her. He'd long since learned to regret that choice, for she would never have been taken on as companion to the Dowager Duchess of Clairborne without it. He could never forget that, in one respect, her rape and subsequent pregnancy could be laid directly at his door.

Jared had provided the means by which Mary had entered the sphere of the blackguard Duke of Clairborne. She'd never blamed him, but he could not help blaming himself.

A parody of her former smile crossed her face now, and she labored to speak. "Take Hannah to the Angel."

The request so shocked him that at first Jared didn't respond. Damn it. Was Mary hallucinating?

She couldn't really want him to take her innocent little girl to that monster's widow. "No."

Mary moved her head restlessly on the pillow. "You don't understand . . ." She broke off speaking with a spasm of dry coughing. After taking several shallow breaths, she continued. "She's not like him."

The words came out whispered and barely audible, but Jared understood them, and they made him angry. "She was married to him when he raped you. She did nothing to protect you. She's no better than he was."

"No. Different. Please. *Promise*." Each word was spoken with such effort that he could not ignore the plea.

"You expect her to want to raise Hannah? Do you believe she'll feel some obligation to her dead husband's illegitimate daughter?" He reached for Mary's hand and gently held it. "Don't worry about Hannah. I'll take care of her. I'll raise her." He meant it.

He cared for the little girl, just as he'd cared for the mother. Perhaps even more so. Mary was his friend, but Hannah had always felt like his daughter. The bond was unnaturally strong, but it was one he had never questioned. Mary had been very sick after Hannah's birth, and he had cared for the infant, growing attached to her in a way he would never allow himself to become attached to an adult.

Even if he thought the monster's widow was the angel the *beau monde* claimed, he would not give up Hannah.

Mary's eyes closed, and her breathing grew shallow, but when he moved away to call a servant to fetch the doctor, her grip on his hand tightened. He waited, without speaking, for several minutes. Finally, her eyelashes fluttered and her eyes opened again. Their usually clear blue depths were hazy with pain and the fever that had not left her in two weeks, despite the doctor's efforts and Jared's rose hip tea.

"Promise me. Take her to the Angel."

He could not withstand the desperation in Mary's eyes. "I'll tell her grace about Hannah."

He wouldn't, couldn't, promise anything else.

Mary's head moved in a semblance of a nod. "Good." Her eyes closed again, and she slipped into sleep.

She awoke only once more, to say good-bye to her daughter.

The curate would not allow her burial in the church's cemetery, because she had been an unwed mother.

Jared would not tolerate her final resting place to be amidst cutthroats and thieves, so he had her buried in a small grotto at one end of his rose garden.

Hannah wanted to plant a bright red rosebush at the

head of the grave. Jared promised to take a cutting from his prized *Apothecary's Rose*. Medicines made from its hips had not been able to save Mary's life, but it was fitting that the beautiful bloodred flowers would mark her memory.

One

LORD BEAST.
Viscount Ravenswood.
A very dangerous man.

Calantha watched the huge man cross the small ballroom toward her with both anticipation and dread. His black and white evening clothes clung alarmingly to his well-muscled, oversized body, and he carried himself with an easy grace that belied his size. Watching him move demanded all of her attention. The play of muscles under his tight-fitting breeches fascinated her, as did the way others hastened to move aside as he approached.

This inexplicable reaction to him had so startled her on the first night of Lady Ashton's house party that Calantha had fled with the flimsy excuse of a headache as soon as the ladies left the gentlemen to their port after dinner. She had not returned since. Until tonight.

She had promised Lady Ashton that she would attend tonight's ball, and Calantha always kept her promises.

Besides, she liked the friendly Lady Ashton. So, she had

come. And now she watched the man the *ton* referred to as Lord Beast with the same absorption she reserved for her studies, her painting, and her gardening. Yet, none of those things made her tremble with pleasure-laced dread at the thought of being in the same room with them. Nor did they make her pulse race.

In truth, nothing made her pulse race. For such a reaction was an emotional one, and she had long ago learned that life was safer if lived without emotional excesses and turmoil. Her heart was a frozen ball of ice in a soul that shivered from the cold winds that howled across it . . . if she had a soul at all.

"Oh, no. He's coming this way. He has not forgotten our dance. Oh, what shall I do? *What shall I do?*" A young debutante standing directly in front of Calantha spoke.

Ah, so he was coming over to dance with the deb. A mixture of relief and disappointment flowed over Calantha. Of course he would not be desirous of making her acquaintance. She was beautiful, but boring. She had overheard herself referred to as such, and thought it accurate. A woman who hid her true self could not be interesting, but she could be safe.

Everyone knew that Lord Beast spoke only to people who interested him. It was rumored that he gave his own father, the Earl of Langley, the cut direct. And now he intended to dance with the simpering chit in front of Calantha.

She would not have to talk to him. She would not be required to refuse his offer of a dance, or even worse, as she very much feared she might accept.

"Calm yourself, Beatrice. 'Tis only one dance. Lord Beast isn't going to eat you on the ballroom floor," replied another young lady, sounding not in the least sympathetic to her friend's plight.

"That's easy for you to say. *You* don't have to dance with him. I'm at sixes and sevens at the thought of him touching me," complained the silly Beatrice. "I mean that awful scar. And he's so *big*."

Calantha understood her own fear of Ravenswood, but why would the debutante fear him?

Could she not see that under the brute size and glaring demeanor was a man who knew gentleness? Calantha had taught herself to watch others closely in order to assess their true natures after making the colossal mistake of marrying a duke who had been well named after the devil.

It was not difficult. Not really. She was quiet. She remained in the background, another protective behavior she had learned during the years of her marriage. From her vantage point on the periphery of any gathering, she collected and analyzed information on the people around her.

The first night she had seen Ravenswood, she had been unable to focus on anyone else, and her intent regard had revealed some unexpected facts.

He cared deeply for his sisters and respected the men they had married. In his own way, he was even quite patient. It did not seem so at first, but he had an incredible ability to ignore the rudeness of the many who responded to his scar rather than to his person or his position.

Rumor had it that Ravenswood had fought with a wolf as a very young man to save his sister's life, and that is how he had become scarred. Could not the foolish Beatrice and the rest of the *ton* see the beauty in that, the courage and selflessness that such an action would require?

Even the servants were very nervous around him. However, at one point during the previous dinner party, a maid had come close to spilling a tureen of soup on him. He had not berated her, or demanded her punishment as many of the *ton* would do. Instead, he had saved her, and so very carefully that he had not added to her upset.

He was not infinitely patient, however. She had also seen him send footmen running with a look and had heard him raise his voice in argument with a local squire she found particularly set in his outmoded opinions.

Beyond everything else she had noticed about him was the truth that he was a man of power . . . perhaps even enough power to melt the ice that encased Calantha's own heart. The thought sent chills of fear skating down her spine. If that were to happen, there would be pain, great rushing waves of it that would drown her once and for all.

Perhaps the debutante feared Ravenswood because she, too, could sense this power, though Calantha had difficulty crediting the chit with such insight. After all, her voiced complaints amounted to nothing more than window dressing. Like so many others, she was bothered by the scar. Foolish child.

Calantha could have told her that true evil lurked within, and had nothing to do with physical imperfection. That sort of evil had the power to hurt beyond bearing. Her dead husband had taught Calantha that lesson very well.

Ravenswood stopped in front of Beatrice and put out his hand. "Come."

Beatrice's companion's eyes widened at the peremptory command. Gentlemen of the *ton* did not order their partners to the dance floor. They made suitably bland comments and requests, to which a lady could easily respond in the negative.

Beatrice gasped, and Calantha watched with interest as her face drained of all color. "I couldn't possibly, my lord. I've . . . I've . . . I already promised this dance. My partner is over there." She waved her fan in the direction of the other side of the room. "He's waiting for me."

Had Calantha seen hurt in his gaze before his eyes narrowed? Had the hastily made-up excuse pricked his pride or damaged his ego? For some reason she could not fathom, she could not bear the thought. She tried to ignore the stirrings of compassion she felt—compassion toward a man who logic said would not be touched by such a silly girl's foolishness.

Calantha had pushed away such reactions early in her

marriage, when she realized that allowing herself to care for others put them at risk. It gave her husband further opportunities to punish her many imperfections by hurting those she loved. She tried, but failed, to suppress the memory of her one dear friend, Mary.

Calantha had befriended the girl in the first months of her marriage only to discover that when her husband's anger burned brightly toward her, he was capable of all manner of evil toward those she held dear. She still believed her husband was responsible for Mary's disappearance the second year they were married. She did not believe her friend would have left without a word, otherwise.

She still regretted her lack of vigilance on Mary's behalf, just as she bitterly repented so many of the weaknesses that haunted her.

It was definitely a weakness of mind that made her feet move forward and caused her to say, "Excuse me, please," as she stepped around Beatrice to face Ravenswood directly.

"If you are not otherwise engaged, my lord, perhaps you would consent to escort me onto the floor. I am weary of stillness." *Liar. Liar.* Her brain screamed at her, but she could not pay it any heed. She danced rarely and never grew weary of motionlessness. It was a condition of excellence when one existed on the perimeters of life.

His eyes widened, and once again the deb gasped, this time with clear surprise. Calantha waited in frozen silence for him to answer. She had learned not to shift nervously when confronted with a potentially explosive situation, and that training came into play now. She waited.

And waited.

Finally, convinced he would refuse, she began to step back toward the outskirts of the room, as embarrassed by her behavior as she was confused by it. She could feel heat stealing up her cheeks, and she wanted to cover them with her gloved hands. This man of power would have no interest in dancing with a weakling like herself.

But he was willing to escort that brainless twit, Beatrice, her mind taunted her.

Calantha could not believe how that knowledge had the ability to hurt her. She forced away the pain and summoned a smile that meant nothing, just as she had done so many times in the past. She did not remember the last time she had smiled with any true feeling behind it. She opened her mouth to speak.

JARED WATCHED THE ANGEL'S FACE TAKE ON THE QUALITY of a porcelain doll, the little emotion that had been revealed, now wiped clean from her features. She was backing away, not because she feared him as so many others had, but because she believed he would refuse her invitation to dance. He had seen the knowledge in her eyes, and it seared him because he instinctively knew it had caused her pain.

He hadn't meant to stay silent, but he, who was used to shocking others, had been completely taken aback by the actions of the Angel. Ladies *did not* ask gentlemen to dance, and yet she had asked him. She had opened her mouth to speak again, but nothing had yet emerged.

He forestalled her speech by bowing low toward her and said, "I would be delighted by the honor, your grace."

Blue eyes, the exact shade of an English summer sky, widened, and she stopped edging away. Mary had had blue eyes, but even after what she had gone through with the duke, they had never shimmered with quite the wariness the Angel's did.

Beatrice, the simpering miss his sister had arranged for him to partner, stared at them with fascinated awe. She no doubt could not believe that any lady would willingly partner with him. With her trumped-up story of another partner, she'd made it clear she wouldn't.

The Angel's willingness to do so surprised him as well.

As did his fierce urge to hold her, even if it was for something as fleeting as a country dance. He had not expected anything resembling this response to the woman when he had made his promise to Mary.

He reached out to take her arm, unsurprised but disappointed when she flinched from his touch before seeming to gather her courage and allow him to pull her toward him. He led her to the other dancers as the musicians began to play. They joined a set, and she went into the dance steps with polished style.

But then, that was no less than what he expected of the Angel. She looked and acted like the epitome of feminine perfection, her beauty ethereal in its flawlessness. Tall for a woman, she still gave the appearance of fragility.

Her blond hair had been dressed in a Grecian knot, accentuating the slender column of her neck and further encouraging the perception of her as an otherworldly creature. Along with her translucent skin and composed features, it gave the impression of a marble statue of a Greek goddess, rather than of a mere mortal woman.

Her blue silk gown matched the shade of her eyes perfectly, and it exposed the upper swell of her small breasts without being vulgar.

Perfection.

Why had she asked him to dance? It did not fit with his image of her, neither the coldhearted bitch he had assumed she must be, nor the angel the *ton* believed her to be. After all, an angel did not dance with a beast.

He knew what the *ton* called him and did not care. He was used to the reaction of others to his scars. As he'd grown older and bigger, much bigger than most gentlemen amidst the *ton*, that reaction had only intensified.

Hell, the only two men of his acquaintance that approached him for size were his sisters' husbands, and they were unique in other ways as well. Neither one had ever shown the slightest fear of him, and they'd both been coura-

geous enough to marry strong-willed women. His sisters
had stubborn streaks that matched his own.

Why had the Angel asked him to dance?

He frowned in thought, and the lady now facing him forgot the complicated steps involved in this portion of the
dance and tripped. Jared's hand shot out to steady her. Her
eyes flew to his, and he read surprise in her gaze as he gently righted her and continued the pattern of the dance. When
he once again faced the duchess, he did so with relief.

"You are not staying at Ashton Manor?" he asked her,
knowing the answer, but wanting once again to hear the
melodic voice that had asked him to dance.

"No. I live nearby, and your sister graciously invited me
to attend tonight."

He knew that Irisa had invited the Angel to come for all
of her planned entertainments, but the duchess had only
shown up for two. She had come to dinner the first night of
the house party, and Jared had covertly studied her, making
plans to corner her and talk to her after the gentlemen re-
joined the ladies. However, he'd been disappointed to learn
that she had left early with a headache.

He had waited for her to appear again, but she hadn't,
and he'd resigned himself to seeking her out at her home.
He wanted to discern what kind of person she was before
he kept his promise to Mary. His original plan had been to
attend the tail end of the Season and meet her then, but Hannah'd had a small accident playing in the garden and had
not been able to travel.

When he had learned his brother-in-law's primary
country estate was near the duchess's home, and that his
sister planned to invite her to the house party, Jared had
shocked Irisa by accepting his own invitation. Although he
was always happy to see both of his sisters and their families, he preferred his own estates, as his sister was well
aware.

He found the *ton* and its superficial ways irritating. It

wasn't just the way people reacted to his appearance, thinking him a beast because he didn't fit the *beau monde*'s idea of a gentleman. He hated the way truth and honor got shoved aside in order to maintain appearances. It had happened in his own family, and he couldn't stand the sight of his father because of it. He hated the fact that both of his sisters and the mother he had never been allowed to know had been hurt by his father's cowardly actions.

The country dance ended, and the Angel followed him off the floor.

"Would you like a glass of champagne or punch?" he asked her, wanting to prolong their encounter, needing some answers to the questions that continued to grow in his mind.

"A glass of champagne would be lovely." The musical quality of her voice washed over him, and he wanted to keep her talking, but he had to find the footman with the champagne tray.

CALANTHA SAT IN THE CHAIR RAVENSWOOD HAD EScorted her to, her back ramrod straight. She feared that if she let even one muscle relax, she would lose control completely. Dancing with Ravenswood had been more dangerous than she'd anticipated. Much more.

Human touch was something she had avoided as much as possible during her marriage, and completely since her husband's death. Yet there was no comparison between the revolted fear she used to experience whenever her husband so much as brushed against her and the reaction she'd had to Jared's nearness.

She'd found herself terribly jealous of the time he spent facing the other ladies in their set. She wanted him all to herself. At one point, the gentlemen had been required to place their hands on the waists of their current lady partners. She had wanted to shove the woman next to Ravenswood aside and take her place.

It had taken every ounce of her considerable self-control to stifle that urge.

He did not engage in the inane chatter her other partners found necessary and had in fact only asked one question—if she were staying for the house party. She had been relieved he did not ask more, that he had not wanted her direction, because she knew she must not see him again after tonight. She could not afford the risk to her hard-won peace.

Looking around the room, she wondered at how bright the colors seemed. It was as if everything had become more vivid, and that frightened her. It was so much safer in the shadows and away from the vitality of life. She was content with her studies, with her flowers and her painting. She could not allow herself to become enthralled with a man like Ravenswood.

And yet a part of her recognized that she already was.

She wanted to get up and run. Her legs had actually tensed to do so, but he returned.

"Your champagne, your grace."

"Please, call me Calantha." She hated the title that reminded her of all she had failed to be and of a marriage full of hellish memories. For some reason, she despised it all the more on Ravenswood's lips.

"Very well, Calantha. I am Jared." He said it with the same authority one might announce royal bloodlines.

"I'm pleased to meet you, Jared."

"I knew who you were before we danced."

"Yes." She'd known who he was as well, but now they had *met*. There was something intimate in a meeting like this, without someone to introduce them and intrude in the sharing of their first names. "You are Lady Ashton's brother."

He nodded. "Calantha is Greek."

She liked the bluntness of his speech. She did not have to expend effort discerning subtle nuances and double meanings.

She did not smile, but she felt like it, and that surprised

her. "My father was a vicar who spent most of his spare hours doing translations of the Bible from Greek and Hebrew. My mother helped him."

They had both been shocked by the birth of a daughter so late in their lives.

"It means beautiful blossom. Did they know you would grow to such beauty, I wonder?"

"I suspect it was hopeful thinking on their part."

"Their hope was rewarded."

"They thought so," she admitted.

They had believed her beauty a blessing and gift from the Almighty. Having died of the flu the first year of her marriage, her parents had never discovered her husband's true nature and the curse her physical beauty had actually wreaked in her life. For that, she was very grateful—even if their deaths had left her feeling more isolated than ever.

Jared took a sip of his champagne, and she watched his throat move as he swallowed. Extremely masculine, even this small behavior on his part fascinated her. He did not wear the high-pointed collars popular among gentlemen of the *ton*, and she was glad. She would never get to look into his eyes if he could not bend his head. He was too tall.

She liked his eyes. They were filled with life. Not necessarily joy, but life. Jared felt, and Jared lived.

Calantha envied him his courage to do so.

"Why haven't you come to more of the events my sister planned?" he asked.

"I've been busy. It's a delicate time for the flowers in my conservatory. They require continuous care."

He nodded, and she felt the most shocking desire to reach out and touch the black silkiness of his hair. Most men would have tied it back with a ribbon, but Jared let his hang free to brush his shoulders. It added to the wildness of his appearance, despite his gentleman's garb.

She gripped her hands together tightly in case she found

them doing something foolish, as her mouth had done earlier when asking him to dance.

"I didn't like leaving my rose garden, but I left strict instructions for its care," he said.

"You grow roses?" Her voice came out faint, but she could not help it. Everything about this man drew her further into his web, and she felt like a butterfly fascinated by a spider.

"Yes. I specialize in gallicas and damasks."

Gallicas.

"Do you have an *Apothecary's Rose*?" Her voice had risen above her usually well-modulated tones in her excitement.

The *Apothecary's Rose* did not grow well in a conservatory, and though she also kept an outdoor garden, she had not been able to acquire a good cutting. Several of the recipes her mother had left her called for the hips of this particular plant, and Calantha was eager to try them out.

His face turned hard, his gaze shuttered, but not before she saw an inexplicable fury blaze to life in dark eyes. "Yes."

She wanted to shrink against the wall at the rage he had hidden so quickly. She didn't. She knew from experience that to show weakness made one doubly vulnerable. She forced herself to sit straighter and face him squarely, and reminded herself that she had done nothing wrong.

Even if he divined her purpose in asking for a cutting and did not wish to give one, he need only say no. And now, she would not venture to ask.

Nevertheless, anger did not require justification she could comprehend, as she well knew. So she chose to remain silent in the face of Jared's. Taking a small sip of her champagne, she waited for him to speak again.

"I take it you are interested in roses?" He didn't sound angry, but she could not trust his mild response.

Her husband had often gone from mild inquiry to blazing rage in the space of a heartbeat.

"Yes."

"Do you grow them in your conservatory?" he asked, his eyes filled with what appeared to be genuine interest.

Still, she took no chances. "Yes."

"And you are interested in my *Apothecary's Rose*?"

She inclined her head in answer, giving neither a confirmation nor a rebuttal. It seemed safest.

"You are aware they do not grow to their potential in a consistently warm environment or confined to a pot?"

"Yes."

"Damn it, Calantha, don't talk to me in monosyllables. My sisters can tell you that is my domain. You are a woman. You are supposed to talk in sentences, in whole damn paragraphs, even. They train you for it from birth, or so it seems." He glowered at her, sounding affronted.

Startled laughter erupted from her, and she covered her mouth with her gloved hand, stifling the mirth almost immediately. The sound of her own amusement so surprised her that she did not respond for several seconds.

If dancing with him had been dangerous, conversing with him was lethal to her peace of mind. "I'm sorry. I will try to do better." She took a deep breath, wracking her mind for something of interest to add. "I grow small China roses in the conservatory, and some tea roses as well. They're quite lovely and terribly fragile. They make me feel needed."

She hadn't meant to say that last bit. It had slipped out in her effort to talk in paragraphs. She wasn't used to it. One word answers were safer, and silence was safest. There was less chance of words being taken out of context that way, or her comments being misinterpreted by others.

"Will you dance with me again?"

His question caught her by surprise, and she stared at him in stunned shock, much as he had reacted to her earlier.

His black brow rose in sardonic query. "Is the idea of repeating the experience so appalling?"

"*No*." It was much, much too appealing.

He put his hand out in peremptory demand. "Then, come."

She stared at his hand and felt the seductive draw of his warmth and vitality. What could it hurt? She would not return to Lady Ashton's during the house party. She would not see Jared again. Surely, she could withstand one more dance with him.

Reaching out, she placed her hand in his, her fingers trembling as his warmth enveloped them through the two layers of their gloves. He pulled her into his arms and onto the ballroom floor as the orchestra struck up a waltz. A waltz. She had been prepared for a country dance, but not this. This holding of her person, his large body so close to her own.

Her trembling increased.

He squeezed her hand. "An angel need not fear a mere mortal, even if he is a beast."

Her head snapped up, and unaccustomed anger flared inside her. "I am not an angel, and you are no beast. Please do not refer to yourself in such a fashion in my company."

His thumb moved in a strangely affecting caress against the indentation of her waist, and she shivered. Did he have any idea the impact his nearness had on her? She felt that tiny movement of his thumb with every fiber of her being.

His lips quirked in mockery. "The rest of the *ton* sees me as such. Why are you so sure they are wrong?"

"I know a beast when I see one . . . now."

He did not ask how or even what she meant, for which she was grateful. He merely nodded. "But *you* fit the role of angel to perfection."

Despair washed over her. That hated word . . . *perfection*. She was not perfect, as her husband and the rest of his family had taken pains to point out. Others had paid the price for her inability to attain the ideal.

She hated the sight of herself in a looking glass. Her

own outward beauty served as a mocking reminder of how far short of perfection she fell where it counted . . . inside. She was weak, a coward. She had let others be hurt because she had withdrawn behind her walls of icy reserve, her only defense against the slights and cruelties Clairborne had been so good at serving up.

She could have made stronger efforts to protect her servants from his wrath, but she had been terrified of standing up to him. The final price of her own cowardice had been too high, the lesson of her own fallibility too well learned. Because of her, a young girl—a sweet child full of vitality and joy—had died. She could never forgive herself or forget that she was more sinner than angel.

"Appearances are deceptive."

Two

JARED READ BLEAK DESPAIR IN CALANTHA'S eyes before it disappeared behind a composed façade.

What did she mean? Was she as much a monster as her dead husband? Jared had been prepared to accept that as truth before, but now he questioned the probability.

She radiated a vulnerability that did not seem indicative of a cruel nature. Had she been as much a victim of her husband as Mary had been? The thought left him filled with cold rage.

"Have I said something to anger you?" she asked quietly, her eyes once again mirroring nervous fear before she hid it.

He glared at her, finding the workings of her feminine mind incomprehensible. Why should he be angry with her? "Of course not," he growled.

She tried to step out of his grasp, but he tightened his hold and continued to dance. "The music has not ended."

She ceased her struggles, but her body remained stiff in his arms, and her movements had grown jerky as she tried to follow him through the waltz.

"Have you decided I'm a beast after all?"

She shook her head, making another useless attempt to pull away from his arms. "I am sorry. I'm merely tired. Perhaps it is time I found my carriage and went home."

The ball was not half over. Damn it. She *was* afraid of him. "Perhaps if I left, you would be willing to stay," he said with sarcastic honesty.

Her hand against his arm tightened in what seemed like a reflexive gesture, and her gaze flew to his. "No. Please. I don't want you to go."

"But you want to escape me."

She didn't deny it.

"Why did you ask me to dance, Calantha?"

"I don't know."

"It seems out of character for an angel."

She winced. "Yes."

"So why did you do it?"

She shook her head as if trying to dislodge the question from her mind, but he wasn't going to let her go until she answered. He needed to know.

He squeezed her small waist with his hand. "Tell me."

"Why does it matter?"

"I want to know."

Her gaze locked with his. "The chit, Beatrice, lied. She was afraid to dance with you, and it made me angry."

"You're afraid of me, too."

Once again she didn't deny his accusation.

"Say it, damn you. Tell me you are afraid of me."

Her gaze did not so much as waver. "Yes. I am afraid of you," she all but whispered.

"But you asked me to dance anyway."

"Yes."

"Why? Bloody hell. Tell me why."

"I've told you. Because Beatrice lied."

"Why do you care? You don't know me. You're afraid of me, the same as she is."

"No."

"Yes. You bloody well admitted it." He hated liars, and it twisted his guts for her to resort to being one.

"No. I did not admit to fearing you like she does. She's a fool who only sees the outer man, and she fears that man. I'm afraid of who you are on the inside."

Did she think he harbored the same sort of inner depravity as her deceased husband? "You do think I'm a beast, but more than just in appearance, is that it?"

"*Stop it.*" She looked as shocked by her nearly shouted words as he was.

She kept her emotions tightly controlled. When he had first seen her, she had put him in mind of a beautiful marble statue. But now she trembled with her feelings.

Other dancers turned their heads to stare. Jared stopped dancing and pulled her out through a set of French doors into the darkness of the garden. Although it was summer, the air had cooled. It felt good after the heat of the ballroom.

"Stop what? Stop trying to understand the workings of an angel's mind?"

"*I'm not an angel.* I've said it before, but clearly you did not understand. Angels are perfect, and I fall far short of such a standard. I don't think you are a beast, either, and I want you to stop saying that. *I can't stand it.*"

She sounded almost hysterical, and Heaven alone knew why, but he pulled her to him in an effort to comfort her, just as he would have Hannah.

Pressing her head against one shoulder, he soothed her shaking with a light caress up and down her back. "Shh."

Her hand fisted in the fabric of his coat, crushing it. "*This* is what I'm afraid of. *This gentleness* I sensed the first night I saw you. You're a very strong man, Jared, and you frighten me because of it."

He didn't laugh at her description of him because her feelings were too fragile right now, but her assessment was ridiculous. He agreed that he was strong, stronger than most men. But gentle? No. He was rough. Forceful. Impatient.

Anything but gentle. Not only were her words laughable, they made no sense. How could his strength frighten her if she believed him to be gentle? Even if it was an erroneous belief, it should have calmed her fears.

"Explain to me again why you are afraid."

"Combined with your sort of power, your gentleness is terrifying." He could tell she found that difficult to admit, but he was still far from understanding.

"What kind of power is that?"

"The power to make me feel."

She might as well have landed a punch with the force of Gentleman Jackson to his midsection, her words slammed into him so hard. *He made her feel?* She was afraid of him because of what he made her *feel*?

"You are not afraid I will hurt your person?" he asked, just to clarify, his arms almost slack around her, his shock was so great.

"No, of course not."

She honestly did not think he was a monster. Far from it, she thought he was a man of power. A man. Not a beast.

For the first time since Mary's death, another person besides his family looked on him with acceptance. It soothed some of the pain at the loss of his friend, though he did not understand why. That he found comfort in the company of the widow of a man he could not help but hate confused him, too.

Calantha pushed against him, this time succeeding in breaking his weakened hold. "I have to leave."

He looked down at her, his face set. "No."

"Please, Jared. You must realize that I cannot stay here with you. Not now." The light from the house illuminated the troubled, almost desperate, expression on her face.

"Because you've spoken the truth?" And it struck him that she had not lied about anything . . . yet.

"Please. Surely, I've answered enough of your questions. Let me go home now that you understand."

"But I *don't* understand you. Not yet. Though I fully intend to." He reached out and took her shoulders in a light grip and began to pull her toward him, noting again her instant flinching at his touch.

However, she did not look frightened, nor did she pull against his hold. He knew, from somewhere deep inside him, it was not him personally that made her shy from the physical contact. It was something else, and one day she would explain it; he would see to that.

He lowered his head until his mouth was a breath away from hers, inhaling the scent of roses and her own sweet feminine fragrance. "There's so much more I have to learn."

"Please . . ."

He didn't know if it was a plea to release her, or kiss her. He chose to do the latter.

As Jared's lips tenderly caressed her own, Calantha feared she would faint from the feelings coursing through her. She had never experienced a sensation so exquisite, had never had her lips treated with such reverence.

This was insanity, the stuff of fantasy. She could not truly be standing in a darkened garden, allowing a gentleman she had met less than an hour ago to kiss her. It was preposterous, and yet she felt as if she would give a year of her life, nay, five years, for the opportunity to experience a few more moments of such utter bliss.

His hands moved up from her shoulders to cup her neck and face, and she raised her own to grip his wrists. The heat of his skin seared her, and she wanted to tear off his gloves and her own so she could feel the warmth of his fingers, the sinewy strength of his hands.

She heard a moan and realized with shock it had come from her. Her brain registered that her behavior was not at all proper, but she could not make herself care. For just this moment in time, she wanted to *feel*.

And feel she did.

Jared's lips, oh such talented lips, moved against her own in a soft caress that she instinctively felt she should emulate, but she didn't know how. So, she just experienced and reveled in the connection with another human being—with Jared.

Allowing him to nibble at her mouth was its own reward as it caused shivers of pleasure to rush down to her most private, feminine place in a wholly unexpected way. *Heavens*. Had other women felt this way before? Had her mother? No one had told her that she could experience such things.

And she had definitely not done so at her husband's hand. But she would not think of him now. He had no place in this moment of beauty.

Jared pulled his head away from hers, and she tried to follow it, to bring their lips back into contact, but he wouldn't let her. She wanted to cry. Was it over, then? This was all she would have of such heaven?

"Kiss me back," he demanded in a guttural voice.

She stared at him, and all the inadequacies that had plagued her since her wedding night came rushing forward to torment her. She had not been enough of a woman for Clairborne, and she was not woman enough for Jared either. She couldn't do what he asked, because she didn't know how. She felt tears that she had not allowed herself to shed since very early in her marriage prick at her eyes.

"I don't know how," she admitted in a shamed whisper. "I'm sorry."

He said something very foul in a voice rough with fury, and she tried to pull away from the hands that held her face so gently. His thumbs pressed against the underside of her chin and forced her to lift her head, so she had no choice but to meet his gaze.

Even in the shadows, she could not mistake the intensity in his dark eyes. "Do you trust me?"

She felt herself nod, even as her brain screamed that no man, no matter how gentle and strong, could be trusted. But her heart would not listen.

"Let me show you how."

"Yes." She wanted that. Very much.

He brushed her lips with his own, a light caress that made her want more, not just for the physical sensations it brought, but for the way it fed her frozen, hungry soul.

He let go of her, dropping his hands to his sides. "Now you do it."

She did not think of denying him. She would do anything for just one more soul-stirring kiss. Cautiously, she took his face in her hands, feeling the rough skin of his scar through the thin covering of her glove. It reminded her of his sacrifice on his sister's behalf, and another kind of pleasure altogether burned through her. The pleasure of knowing a human being capable of and willing to sacrifice for those he loved.

She pulled his head down so that her lips could meet his. As she brushed them, incredible heat seared deep inside where she had been cold for so very long. He put his hands over hers, holding them against his cheeks, and he kissed her again, this time nibbling gently at her lower lip for several seconds. She felt her body sway toward him, but his hold against her hands stopped her from actually coming close enough to touch him.

Lifting his mouth a fraction of an inch from hers, he said, "It's your turn again."

He wanted her to nibble his lip? Did she have the courage to do it? He waited patiently as she made up her mind.

Then she pulled him down that last bit and pressed her lips to his before taking his lower lip between her teeth and nibbling as if tasting a marvelous new treat. Indeed, that was exactly how he tasted. Rare and wonderful.

She had never tasted another human being before, and

that he should make himself available for her pleasure added indescribable delight to the experience. She nibbled far longer than he had, allowing herself the luxury of tasting every bit of his bottom lip and going back to press her full mouth against his every few seconds.

He made a growling noise deep in his throat and pushed against her hand, forcing her to release her hold on his lips.

She did not want to let go. "Was I doing it wrong?"

"No, *mon ange*, you were doing very well."

For the first time in six years, she felt as if the hated name, *Angel*, was actually an endearment—not a reminder that she must live up to an unattainable standard of perfection. Perhaps because he made it possessive and had called her *his* angel. Regardless, it sent another wave of warmth cascading through her.

"Oh," she replied.

He lowered his mouth to hers before she finished uttering the word and he . . . Oh, my goodness. *His tongue was inside her mouth.* It was improper. No lady should allow such a thing and yet . . . Yet, it felt good. Very, very good. He probed her mouth, as if inviting her to play. She wanted to. Yes. She definitely wanted to, but how?

She experimentally touched the tip of her tongue to his and he shuddered, his grip on her hands against his face tightening. Emboldened by his response, she tried it again, and then she was lost in sensation after sensation as he tasted her and invited her to taste him in every possible way.

Warm tears tracked down her cheeks as the sheer enormity of her feelings and the beauty of the moment overwhelmed her. She had not known such intimacy existed, that a man could accept her faltering efforts and make them something wonderful. Something . . . almost perfect.

But then he was withdrawing again, and this time she wanted to scream out in frustration, in denial. She did not want this kiss to end.

His breath came in warm gasps against the skin of her cheek. "Your turn."

Her eyes, which had fluttered shut, flew open. "You want me to kiss you that way?"

"Yes. You want it, too, little angel. Don't pretend to me that you don't." His eyes burned into hers. "Do not ever lie to me. In any way."

"No," she whispered, "I won't."

"Kiss me. Now." Although he spoke the command with his customary arrogance, she sensed an underlying need that gave her the courage to act in such a bold manner.

She let her mouth pressing against his be her answer. He parted his lips, and after only a brief hesitation, she tentatively slipped her tongue inside. He was hot. So very hot, and he tasted like champagne and spice.

She emulated his actions in inviting him to kiss her back. He accepted the invitation with alacrity, and she felt the excitement all the way to her most secret place. She deepened the kiss just as he'd shown her, and they both groaned.

The sound of music filled her head and at first, she thought it was part of the amazing results of kissing Jared, but then reality intruded in the sound of voices. Someone had opened the French doors and joined them in the garden.

Jared broke the kiss and swore softly as he pulled her hands from his face. "Go back inside," he said with typical brusqueness. "I'll walk around the house and reenter the ballroom from the interior."

She wanted to protest, to say she didn't care about reputations or being caught in a flagrant embrace, not if it meant she could experience his kiss for a little longer. She said nothing, however. It would not be fair to Jared.

He was an honorable man, and she sensed that if he were caught in a compromising situation, he would insist on doing the *right thing*. The very thought of marrying again was enough to cool her raging emotions. That was a risk she could never repeat.

She nodded, but realized that in the shadowed light, he might not have seen it and whispered, "All right."

"Come to the musicale tomorrow night."

At the intense demand radiating from him, she was tempted to agree and then send her excuses the following evening, but she had promised not to lie to him. "No."

He swore. "Then I'll call on you tomorrow."

"No, Jared. Please." She had to say good-bye, no matter how much she wanted to agree to see him again.

It was the only path to safety . . . to a life without risk, a life without pain.

And a life without joy, her mind insisted on reminding her.

He squeezed her shoulders. "I'll see you tomorrow."

Then he was gone, melting away into the shadows as silently as if he'd never been there. But her lips still felt his touch. She pulled off one of her gloves and touched her lips with her fingertip in awe. They felt warm, softer and fuller than usual, and her body still vibrated with sensations brought by his kiss. He had given her an incredible gift tonight.

She had believed Clairborne when he called her frigid and useless as a woman. Jared had shown her that somewhere deep inside her, fire burned. Perhaps it was not warm enough to melt the ice in her soul, but it had warmed her for a little while.

Taking a shuddering breath, she realized she was crying. She found her handkerchief and wiped the wetness from her cheeks. She mourned the loss of warmth that Jared had brought, but she was not fool enough to believe he would desire to continue their association . . . not once he got to know her.

Once he realized how weak she truly was, he would reject her in disgust.

Much safer to maintain her distance now, than to have her heart broken later.

THE NEXT MORNING, JARED WENT IN SEARCH OF IRISA. As Calantha's neighbor, she should have some idea of the type of person the duchess was. He found her keeping his other sister, Thea, company in the nursery with the children.

Hannah came rushing forward when she saw him. "Jared, we're playin' queens and kings. Want to play wif us?"

He smiled down at the sweet little face, incredibly relieved the other children had been able to coax her into playing. She had taken Mary's death hard, her normally pragmatic but sunny nature clouded by sadness and silent grief.

"Who's the king?" he asked.

Hannah pointed to his nephew, Thea's son. "David. I'm a queen and so is Deanna. Her mama and the other lady are princesses."

Jared smiled at his sisters. "I guess that makes me a prince, then."

Hannah frowned, showing a glimmer of her old assertiveness. "No. You're the big king."

David, a sturdy five-year-old with blond hair and gray eyes, shrugged. "You can be king with me if you want, Uncle Jared."

Thea's eyes filled with mischief, and she shook her head, one chestnut curl slipping loose. "I think he'd make a much better page."

Irisa laughed. "Yes. Let's have Jared be our page."

Jared glared at his sisters, but Hannah was the one who spoke. "Is a page bigger 'an a king?"

"Not exactly, little one," Thea replied, her lips curved in a playful smile.

It amazed him how alike his sisters were, since they had been raised separately and had different mothers, but they both had the same mischievous sense of humor. They were also equally kind to Hannah. He hadn't told them anything about her father being the late Duke of Clairborne.

It struck him for the first time that they might think she was his. He shrugged away the thought. It didn't matter. In all the ways that mattered, the little girl did belong to him.

A bird chirped outside the window, and Hannah's head came up at the sound. Prior to Mary's death, that telling little reaction would have been followed by an immediate demand to go outside; however, Hannah said nothing now.

He swung her up into his arms. "Would you like to go outside, sweet?"

She regarded him solemnly. "Will you come?"

"Yes."

"What an excellent idea. Women who are carrying need exercise," Thea said, with a significant look at Irisa.

Irisa and Ashton had returned from visiting relatives in France with the news that she was pregnant. His new niece or nephew was due in only a few months, but Jared could barely tell that his sister carried a child. The fact that she chose to throw a house party during her pregnancy mystified him. Why she wanted to go to all that effort in her current condition, he couldn't fathom. But then he didn't understand her desire to invite a bunch of people to her house at all.

Once they got outside, Jared lagged back with his sisters while the little ones raced ahead. David and Deanna each had one of Hannah's hands and carried her along despite the uncertain glance she sent back at him.

"She's worried you'll leave her," Irisa said with a sigh.

Thea nodded. "I remember feeling so very afraid I would lose everyone I loved after Mama's death, and I was much older. Jared is the only constant left in Hannah's life, now that her mother is gone."

"I'm not going anywhere," Jared vowed.

"She'll come to accept that, and come out of the shell grief has built around her," Thea predicted.

Jared hoped she was right. He missed Mary and her friendship, but he missed Hannah's sunny smiles even more. "Tell me what you know about Calantha Clairborne."

"Oh ho, so you *are* interested," Irisa said, gloating. "I tried to tell Thea, but she didn't see you two dancing and would not believe me."

Jared felt unaccustomed heat rise in his neck and tried to glare his sister into submission, but it failed. Miserably. She smiled back with unrepentant glee.

Thea's face had lost its playful look, however, and she considered him with a concerned air. "You're interested in courting the Angel?"

"No." Damn it, didn't they think he knew how hopeless that would be? "I'm just curious. She asked me to dance last night." Which was as good an excuse as any to interrogate his sisters about the duchess.

"*She* asked *you* to dance?" Irisa, who had spent the first twenty years of her life living up to the strictest standards of the *ton*, was clearly shocked.

"Yes."

Thea's gaze took on a speculative quality. "I wouldn't have expected that of her. She seems so proper, almost inhuman, if you want the truth."

He did. All of it. He wanted to know everything they thought or had heard about Calantha.

"Why did she do it?" Thea asked.

"Because she wanted to get to know Jared, of course, and he's so withdrawn around the ladies. It's no wonder she felt it necessary to take bold action," Irisa replied for him.

Jared grimaced. "She stepped in to save my masculine ego." He could not remember the last time anyone had thought he needed protecting.

"What do you mean?" Thea asked.

"Beatrice was *otherwise engaged* when I came to claim her for our dance."

"The little twit," Irisa said.

Jared shrugged. "I'm used to that sort of thing," he said, dismissing the young woman's actions as unimportant, because they were. "Now, tell me about the Angel."

"You called her Calantha a moment ago," Thea said, apropos of nothing.

"She asked me to."

Both of his sisters stopped walking to stare at him. They acted as if using Calantha's name were as intimate as taking her to bed. He frowned. He wanted to do that, too, but he wasn't about to give into the urge, and they could stop looking like he already had.

"She asked you to use her first name? I don't understand. The duchess's conduct is always above reproach," Irisa had resumed walking, but she sounded astonished. "I can't believe this. My brother's going to marry the Angel."

"I'm not going to marry anyone at the moment." When his sisters gave him identical skeptical looks, he added, "I mean it."

"But you have to marry sometime, Jared," Thea said.

"When I do, it won't be to Calantha. Bloody hell, angels do not marry beasts."

Irisa's eyes filled with tears, and Jared groaned. Even knowing they were more a result of her pregnancy than his comment, he felt terrible.

"You aren't a beast. You're a hero. You saved my life."

Thea patted Irisa's shoulder and glared at her brother. Although he'd only met this sister five years ago, she behaved if she had known him all her life. "A few scars don't make a man into a monster, and there is no reason why the duchess shouldn't want to marry you. You are the best of men, Jared."

Hell. How had the conversation gotten so off track? All he wanted was a little information. Exasperated, he said, "Maybe I don't want to marry a marble statue. Now will you just answer my question?"

The women seemed to realize that he meant it and fell silent in contemplation.

Thea spoke first. "She does rather remind me of a statue. I don't think I've ever seen so much as a flicker of genuine emotion on her face. She always looks so serene."

She hadn't looked serene last night, not after he'd kissed her. She'd looked dazed and wanton. His body reacted to the memory, and he forced his attention back to the conversation at hand before things got embarrassing.

"I met her the first year of my marriage," Thea went on, stopping to scoop up her tiny daughter, who had fallen behind the more boisterous David, who was still dragging Hannah in his wake. "The duke was still alive at that time. He played the perfect gentleman, but I never liked him. He acted above associating with Pierson."

Jared knew his sister had absolutely no tolerance for anyone who judged Drake by the circumstances of his birth. She was fiercely protective of those she loved.

"What about Calantha? Did she behave that way around Drake?" If she were offended by his brother-in-law's illegitimacy, she would not accept Hannah.

Thea shook her head as her daughter patted her cheek. "No. She treated him with the same distant politeness she extended to all gentlemen. She was careful not to give one man more attention than another, but she never cut Pierson in any way. I wondered once or twice if the duke were a violently jealous man."

Irisa nodded. "That would explain a lot. I don't get the impression that she wants to remarry. She doesn't encourage the attention of gentlemen at all."

She had certainly encouraged him last night, and she hadn't been at all distant, but he wasn't about to admit as much to his already overly interested sisters. "Would you say she was a kind person?"

Thea stared at him blankly. "I don't know. She isn't cruel. I've never seen her so much as frown at a servant, but she doesn't extend herself toward others either. It's almost as if she's there, but not. I've always thought her nickname suited her well. She is rather otherworldly."

Irisa's eyes narrowed in thought. "Actually, she is kind, but in a very subtle way. She provides all sorts of tinctures and medicines from her garden for anyone who wants them, but she does it through her housekeeper. She doesn't gush, but I think she cares. I'm not sure she even realizes it, but her actions speak for themselves. She even sent me a remedy for seasickness when she learned I planned to cross the channel to France. She mentioned it was safe for pregnancy. I always wondered if she knew about my condition somehow."

Jared nodded. Irisa had waited until she was onboard the ship to tell Ashton. His brother-in-law had been furious, but she had justified her actions by saying she knew he wouldn't have allowed her to make the trip otherwise. Jared dismissed the idea that Calantha had somehow guessed about the pregnancy as a foolish thought, but considered Irisa's other revelations. A woman who did that could not have turned a blind eye to her husband's depravity. Could she?

"When you say she helps anyone, do you mean anyone in the nobility or anyone at all?" he asked.

"Anyone at all. She even provided fever-reducing tea for a camp of gypsies that came down ill while in the district."

"That's very interesting. I cannot imagine the former duke allowing her to associate with others of lesser birth than herself," Thea mused.

Irisa shrugged. "I don't know what she was like in her marriage. I only know what she's like now, and I do think she's kind. I also think she is lonely. She doesn't allow anyone to get very close. We've met for tea several times, but she withholds herself. But I like her, for all that."

Jared contemplated the possibility Calantha had been a different person married to the duke. As much as he might be tempted to, particularly after the passion of last night and the vulnerability he had sensed in her, he could not ignore the fact that she had been mistress of the house when

Mary was raped. Nor could he dismiss the fact that she had pulled away from her friendship with Mary prior to that. Mary had mentioned it, explaining that was why she had not gone to Calantha for help when the duke had first begun giving her lascivious looks.

She'd planned to leave the household, but the duke had made sure she did not have the resources to do so, holding on to her wages, ostensibly for safekeeping. Desperate, Mary had written to Jared, asking for help. His help had come too late to prevent the horror of the rape, but it had made it possible for her to come to him afterward.

When she had first arrived at his home, she'd insisted on working for her keep and taken the position of housemaid. He'd hated that, but in some ways Mary had been every bit as stubborn as he was. She'd been so ashamed, so devastated by what happened with Clairborne, that it had taken a long time for her to tell Jared what sent her running in the first place. By then, she'd known she was pregnant.

Once her condition became apparent, his housekeeper had rebelled at the idea of employing a "dirty whore" as she called the already terrorized Mary. Jared had fired his housekeeper with a few choice words and hired Mary to take her place. It had been a situation that ultimately suited them both.

However, he could not forget the bright future she had had before she took the position of companion to Clairborne's mother. The duchess was as responsible as Clairborne for Mary's desperate predicament. Jared could not forget that, no matter how bloody innocent she seemed.

No matter how much he wanted her.

Three

"I MUST NOT ALLOW JARED TO KISS ME AGAIN," Calantha muttered under her breath to her *Parson's Pink* rosebush.

Feeling no more certain of her self-control, she cut several rose hips and dropped them into the basket hanging on her left arm. Saying the words again for good measure, she moved on to the next potted rosebush and looked for the seeds necessary for the medicinal recipes she concocted.

The early afternoon sun beat in through the conservatory's glass roof and walls, making her glad that she had donned only a light muslin gown and India cotton apron that morning. Open doors at either side of the indoor garden and several windows propped outward allowed a slight breeze, but did not completely ease the impact of the summer's heat.

No more than her self-remonstrating could eradicate her memories from last night. Unfortunately, even spoken aloud, the words had no more impact than they did as a silent litany in her head.

She had been repeating them in her mind throughout a sleepless night and restless morning, but every time she thought of the rather uncivilized viscount, her lips tingled and her body throbbed.

She could not help wondering what would have happened next if their rendezvous in the garden had not been interrupted. Would Jared have continued to kiss her? Would he have allowed her to continue kissing him? Would he have touched her in some intimate fashion?

After her experiences in that regard with Clairborne, the very idea should be sufficient to halt her curious musings. It was not. Jared's kisses had been unlike anything she had ever known, and she couldn't help believing his touch would have an even stronger impact on her senses.

Which was the last thing she could allow, she reminded herself.

She had given up on tender emotion in order to survive her marriage. She did not think she was even capable of love, but if she were . . . if she committed the ultimate folly of falling in love with the powerful viscount, she had no doubt it would only lead to more emotional pain for herself.

She would disappoint him, just as she had disappointed Clairborne. Only the hurt from doing so would be much greater.

Clairborne had been a true beast, a monster in gentleman's garb. His opinion of her person had ceased to matter to her after the first two months of their marriage, but she instinctively knew that with Jared—it would be different. Losing his regard would lead to an agony of spirit that she could not withstand.

And he *would* come to despise her. It was inevitable, once he learned the truth of her culpability in her former maid's death.

She peeled off one of her gloves and pressed her forefinger into the soil of one of her pots. It felt a little dry, and she watered the rosebush. Unable to concentrate on her studies that morning, she had come into the conservatory in an effort to push thoughts of Jared from her mind, but it had been a dismal failure. Each lovely bloom reminded her of him, perhaps because of his admission the evening before that he maintained an outdoor rose garden.

She would like to see such a thing very much, certain that his garden would be as fascinating as the man himself. Roses were not nearly as popular in England for ornamentation as they were in France. By all accounts, the Empress Josephine had had a truly spectacular collection, one unparalleled in all of Europe. It was gone now, along with any record of the grounds or the specific bushes planted. The amazing garden remained only in the memory of those who had been privileged to see it.

Calantha's mother had grown roses, but only to harvest them for her medicines. Unable to maintain a purely practical approach to the beautiful flowers, Calantha grew them for both harvest and pleasure. She wished she knew why her interest in Jared's *Apothecary's* bush had sparked that brief flash of anger. It had frightened her, which was further proof that she must overcome this foolish absorption with the viscount.

Not only had his anger frightened her, but he had also hurt her by ignoring her after their return to the ball. She had waited several minutes after he disappeared into the shadows before returning to the ballroom, allowing her body a chance to recover from his kisses and the blush that she had felt heating her cheeks, to fade. He had already come inside and stood talking in a far corner to both of his brothers-in-law, Lord Ashton and Mr. Drake. He did not look her way.

Though she had understood his desire to forestall gossip after their time together in the garden, she had longed to look into his eyes and see if he had been as affected by their kisses as she. Nothing could come of it, but she did not want to believe the overwhelming feelings had all been on her side.

She had wanted, no, needed, his reassurance that her forward behavior had not given him a complete disgust of her.

She watered a *Slater's Crimson China*, reaching out to touch one red petal. The small bush lent itself to pot growth in the conservatory beautifully, so she had several. She *liked* their lack of hardiness in the cold climate, feeling a kinship with the beautiful flowers that would not survive without her constant care. She and they were both lovely to look at, but inherently weak.

She stared at the rich petals, her eyes blinded by images from the previous evening. Images that both enthralled and shamed her.

Ladies did not ask gentlemen to dance. Ladies did not sneak off to dark garden walks and allow gentlemen liberties. Ladies did not allow men they had just met to teach them to kiss. Ladies did not allow that kissing to turn carnal, but she had. She had done it all. The Angel, who was no angel at all, had kissed a man in the most carnal way possible . . . with her tongue.

And the memory had the power to elicit more feeling than she had experienced in six long years. It was as if her body and heart, shriveled after a long drought, now thirsted for the excitations his touch caused. It was insidious, this need his kiss had born in her, and she could not succumb to it.

Not that she was likely to have the chance, she thought as she put down her watering can and once again picked up the pruning shears.

He had said he would come to call, but after the way he'd ignored her completely for the last half of the ball, she did not believe he would follow through. He undoubtedly regretted their intimacy in the garden. The thought depressed her, so she pushed it away as she cut several crimson blooms. Their deeply colored petals would make pretty candy for the vicar's children.

"Your grace, the Viscount of Ravenswood requests the pleasure of your company in the drawing room."

Calantha turned her head at the precise tones of her aging butler. Thomas stood awaiting her response, just as if there were some chance she would tell him to inform the viscount that she was *not at home*. She should. For so many reasons . . . to spare her pride, to protect her heart from feeling again, to prevent him from coming to know her better, to avoid the risk of her fascination with him.

"Please have tea brought to the drawing room, Thomas," she said as she handed him her basket and stepped toward the conservatory door that led to the house.

"Yes, your grace."

Thomas was one of the few servants that had accompanied her on her move from Clairborne Park. The current duke, her dead husband's younger brother, had planned to retire the dignified servant to a small cottage on a parsimonious stipend. Knowing that Thomas supported his granddaughter and her three children on his domestic wages, Calantha had hired him as her own butler. The granddaughter lived in a nearby cottage, and her rambunctious children came to call on their grandfather at least once a week. Much to the older man's dismay, who found their frolicking a sore trial to his dignity.

Evidently, you could take a butler out of a duke's household, but you could not take the pomp and propriety of such a household out of the servant.

The sound of his very gently cleared throat stopped Calantha's progress to the door. "Yes, Thomas?"

"If I may assist you in returning your apron to your maid, your grace?"

Her gaze flew down to the India cotton that covered the pale blue muslin of her gown. Oh dear, she still had on her gardening gloves as well. She hadn't even seen Jared yet and she was already a mess.

She quickly removed the apron and gloves. "Am I all that is presentable now?"

Thomas did not smile. "Your grace is always perfectly presentable."

"Thank you, Thomas."

He left to dispose of her apron and gloves, and she made her way to the drawing room and the man waiting for her.

* * *

SHE STOOD IN THE DOORWAY AND WATCHED JARED PACE from one end of her small parlor to the other. Thomas insisted on referring to the chamber as the drawing room, but it was too small for so grand a title. Jared dominated the uncluttered room with his restless walking, making it appear even more miniscule than it was. The easy grace of his movements once again transfixed her, and she did not make her arrival known until he pivoted and once again faced the doorway.

She forced herself to walk sedately toward him.

She stopped and gave him a half-curtsy, setting her face in what she hoped was a mask of polite immobility. "Good afternoon, my lord."

He surprised her by bowing slightly in return. Their short acquaintance had not led her to expect the customary civilities from him. "Calantha."

She indicated the rose brocade sofa near the fireplace with her hand, as she seated herself on one of the matching chairs facing it. "Won't you take a seat? I've asked Thomas to bring tea."

Could he hear her heart beating its rapid tattoo in her bosom? Her hands fluttered against the pale blue skirt of her gown before she realized it and clasped them together to stop the telltale action. How unusual. In the normal course of events, she had to stir herself to movement—particularly when she was around gentlemen.

His brows raised in silent mockery. "You don't need to be nervous, *mon ange*. I am not going to ravish you, regardless of what you may think after my actions last night."

It was not his actions that worried her. "I did not believe you would. You are far too much the gentleman, Jared."

A bark of laughter erupted from his throat. "How can you say I am such a bloody gentleman after the way I accosted you last night?"

She was too honest a woman to allow him to take the blame for the previous evening's events, regardless of her own shame in admitting her part in them. "You did nothing against my will."

He stared at her as if trying to weigh the sincerity of her words. Then memories of the stolen moments in the garden flowed between them, and his eyes grew almost black with some unnamed emotion. She felt her own lips soften, almost as if they were preparing for a repetition of the wanton caresses.

She sucked in air, trying to calm the sensations pouring through her, but it did no good. Not in the face of Jared's silent perusal and blatant male hunger. It beat against her like the wind on the moors. Only rather than chill her, it caused a fire to ignite deep in her belly. The strangest sensation occurred in her bosom and her nipples tightened against the silk of her chemise.

His gaze lowered from her mouth to the skin exposed by the square neckline of her morning gown as if he could somehow sense the effect his presence had on her body. How could he have known, when *she* was so shocked by it? His face tightened in feral lines, looking almost cruel with desire, the emotion she had not been able to place swirling in the dark orbs of his gaze. It was an emotion with which she had no experience, but now recognized.

She waited for him to speak or to act, unsure what she would do if he opted for the latter.

Luckily, the tea tray arrived along with an obviously curious maid, breaking the erotic spell that had once again been in danger of overcoming her sense.

She served the tea, concentrating on performing the task with utmost care.

"You move like a duchess," he said.

She stirred one lump of sugar into her tea with precise movements. "I am a duchess, or was one, anyway."

"You said last night that your father was a vicar?"

It was something she had shared in common with her one true friend. Mary had also been the daughter of a vicar. Only her benefactor had been a local viscount, and he had paid for her education, not asked for her hand in marriage. Calantha had often thought her friend would have preferred the latter, but the idea of a viscount marrying a mere vicar's daughter was anathema amidst the *ton*.

Jared was no doubt even more surprised that this vicar's daughter had managed to snag herself a duke. "Yes."

"Did your family have connections to the Clairbornes?"

"No." Her family had very few connections at all. Her Season had been the gift of her godmother, and fate had intervened to see that she came to the duke's notice.

"You're doing it again."

"What?" She made a quick assessment of her actions serving the tea, looking for mistakes. It was a reaction born of habit, and one she had tried to stop.

"Forgetting to talk like a woman. My sisters would be very disappointed in you." His voice held a teasing note.

She did not smile in response. "I think you are right. Lady Ashton is kind, but I fear she finds my company dull."

He frowned at her. "Irisa told me just this morning that she likes you."

She felt heat steal into her cheeks in pleasure at the other woman's words. "As I said, your sister is kind."

He shrugged, as if her opinion of Lady Ashton was merely confirmation of fact. "How did you meet the duke?"

Blunt. He was so very blunt.

She felt the heat drain away from her cheeks, and she set down her teacup. "He asked for an introduction at a ball."

He looked at her assessingly. "He must have been very taken with your beauty."

"Yes." Then, she forced herself to elaborate. "He liked the idea of his duchess being an angel."

"You said last night that you aren't an angel."

She inclined her head in agreement. "I'm not. It was a source of trial for both the duke and myself that I was unable to live up to his standards of perfection."

Why had she said that? Did she want Jared to realize how far short of the ideal she fell? And, yet, after her wanton behavior last evening, he must have some idea.

"Were you happy in your marriage?"

Where had that question come from? Perhaps Jared thought it strange he had been required to teach her to kiss, and sought to know the reason for it. She didn't answer him immediately, but poured more tea into his cup. Finally, she decided that she had shared enough of her soul.

"How could I have been unhappy?" she asked by way of avoiding a direct answer. "I was the wife of a duke. It was a life well above my expectations as the daughter of a poor country vicar."

His eyes narrowed, and his mouth took on an ominous cast, as if she disappointed him. She wanted to call the words back, tell him the full truth. That she would have given every beautiful silk gown, every single jewel, her place in society, all of it, for one day of happiness in her marriage. One day that she did not have to live up to the exacting standards of her title.

She thought he would make some cutting comment about her shallowness, but instead he asked, "What happened to your parents?"

"They died in a flu epidemic early in my marriage." She did not believe the pain of that loss would ever completely fade, but she forced her voice into unemotional tones.

He surprised her and said, "I'm sorry."

She found herself admitting, "I wanted to nurse them, but Clairborne thought it a poor idea. He said he was concerned for my health."

"It hurt you not to be able to go to them, didn't it?" Jared asked with unexpected insight.

She could not deny it. "Yes. I asked Clairborne to at least allow me to send a servant with ginger-rose tea to help with their stomach upset and fever."

"Did he?"

"No."

"Why not?" His exasperated tones reminded her how little he liked her one-word responses.

"He said that my mother was quite capable of instructing her servants in mixing the tea, since she had taught me the recipe to begin with." Calantha met Jared's gaze squarely. "I obeyed my husband, and my parents died."

The bleak words hung in the air between them.

"They died of the flu, Calantha. Not by your hand."

"Yes, of course." She offered him the plate of tea cakes.

He could not possibly understand. He would never allow someone else to dictate his actions as she had done. She knew that even if she had gone to her parents, they probably still would have died, but at least she could have said good-bye. At least they would have known she cared.

"Try the lemon sponge torte. It's Cook's masterpiece."

He accepted the cake. "It has a slight flavor of roses," he said, after taking a bite.

Pleased that he had noticed, she said, "I distill rose water, and Cook uses it in several dishes."

"I would like to see your conservatory."

"If you are finished with your tea, I could show it to you now," she said with shy enthusiasm. Had he meant it? The idea of sharing her sanctuary with Jared seemed right.

He set down the tiny china plate and stood.

She took that as an affirmative answer.

CALANTHA LED JARED INTO HER CONSERVATORY, AND HE felt as if he had entered another world. The glassed-in room was large, twice as big as the parlor she had served him tea in, and it was filled with blooming plants. Dozens of large pots with rosebushes ranging in size from two to four feet high lined the walls, while baskets of other colorful flowers and fragrant herbs hung from the ceiling. A long table took up much of the center of the room.

He reached out to touch the soft pink petals on one of her roses. "This reminds me of my *Celeste*, though the bush is much smaller."

She didn't immediately reply, and he turned to find her watching him with a dazed expression.

She inhaled and then seemed to gather herself. "It's one of my favorites. Mama brought the bush from her garden at the vicarage."

"Your parents lived here?" That surprised him, but perhaps it explained why she lived in a house that amounted to little more than a cottage, rather than the more sumptuous surroundings expected of a duchess.

Although she had tried to hide it, he had seen the residual ache left by her parents' deaths in her expression when she spoke of it earlier.

"Yes," she said and then in an obvious effort to talk in paragraphs, added, "Clairborne bought this house for them right after our marriage, so my father could retire from parish work and spend more time on his studies."

"Is that why you choose to live here, rather than at the dowager house at Clairborne Park?"

"I am not the dowager duchess, since the current duke is my brother-in-law, not my son. However, when I informed him I would not be making my home with him and his wife at Clairborne Park as his mother does, he did offer the use of the dowager house. I chose to live here because this house belongs to me."

He tried to understand the cool challenge in her tone. "Didn't Clairborne leave you any other estates?"

Not all of a duke's property was necessarily entailed, only that granted by the Crown as part of the title.

"No." She reached out absently to pick a yellowed leaf

off of a stem. "Do you cultivate your roses for the hips and petals?"

He stared at her for several seconds, wondering why Clairborne had not left his wife better provided for. But she had gone cold and pale; as she had each time he had asked a question directly related to her dead husband, and he decided not to push her further on the subject.

"Yes, for both medicines and food." He didn't add that he grew the flowers primarily for the satisfaction their beauty gave him.

She nodded, her attention focused on a bush with small yellow blooms while the sun turned her honey-colored hair into liquid gold. "Did you know that the fossilization record of roses goes back thousands of years?"

"No." He knew that the study of such things had become very popular among the *ton*, but was taken aback that such a lovely creature would be interested in natural history. "My reading is limited to estate management."

And essays on the cultivation of roses, he added silently.

She lifted her gaze from the flowers, her blue eyes serious and intent. "I find fossil records quite fascinating. If I were a bit braver, I would do my own digging, but I content myself with reading the results of the exploits of others."

"Many members of the *ton* would say that you are more courageous than wise."

Her eyes widened. "Why?"

He stepped closer to her until only a handwidth separated them. "You are not afraid to be alone with Lord Beast."

She didn't step back, but reached out to touch him as if she could not prevent herself from doing so. The feel of her small hand against his waistcoat paralyzed him. She stood there, staring at her hand against him as if she could not believe she was actually touching him.

Then she lifted her face so their gazes met. "I would fear a beast, but I do not fear you, Jared."

Bloody hell, he wanted to kiss her again, and so much

more. He wanted to feel those tiny hands against his skin without the barrier of his clothes between them. She was so damn innocent. Kissing her had been like kissing a bloody virgin, and it was that knowledge that stopped him from lowering his mouth and ravaging her own like he desperately wanted.

"I did not expect you today," she said.

"I told you I would come." He'd had no choice.

His honor demanded he keep his promise to Mary; his concern for Hannah demanded he make sure of Calantha before doing so. The little girl would meet the Angel only if he were certain Calantha would do nothing to add to Hannah's grief.

"But you ignored me." She sounded hurt by the admission. "Afterward, in the ballroom."

Because he had wanted to protect her from having her name linked with his. He stepped back, and she dropped her hand from his chest, her face for once mirroring her emotions openly. Disappointment, confusion, and desire all played for prominence in her expression.

"I was trying to protect your reputation," he explained. "We had already danced twice."

And they had disappeared into the garden together, not to mention the fact that Beatrice had overheard the Angel ask him to dance. Her standing among the *ton* would take a beating as it was. He had refused to add to it by giving further cause for speculation by dominating her company for the rest of the ball like he had wanted to.

She lowered her gaze to his cravat. "I thought my wanton manners had given you a disgust of me."

The words came out in a low whisper, and he almost missed them.

How could she have thought that when she was the innocent one? "No."

"I cannot kiss you again," she blurted out, without a bit of her usual aplomb, once again looking into his eyes.

In her distress, hers had turned the color of the elusive blue rose.

She was right. Curse it. "It would be for the best."

A brief flicker of disappointment showed in her eyes before she once again took on the appearance of a marble statue. "Yes."

He took a deep breath and let it out. "Do you want me to apologize?"

"For ignoring me?"

"For kissing you," he said with some exasperation.

For just a moment, she lost her mask, and pain glittered in her eyes, before she stepped farther away from him. "Are you sorry?"

"No, but I should be."

"Please. Don't apologize."

"All right." It would be a lie anyway, and he hated deceit of any kind.

He was not sorry he had kissed her. His only regret was that he could not do so again. He could not allow his desire to cloud his thinking where she was concerned. Hannah's happiness was too important.

She picked up shears from a bench and proceeded to concentrate on cutting several blossoms. She took great care choosing the blooms and did not speak as she did so.

He had watched the delicate move of her hands for a long time as she completed her task, before he reminded himself that he had a purpose to his visit, and it wasn't soaking in her beauty. "You and Clairborne had no children?"

Her hands convulsed, and she lost her grip on the shears. They clattered to the ground, narrowly missing her toes.

He swore, but she paid him no heed. "No."

She was back to those annoying monosyllables. They told him nothing. Then he saw the drops of red staining her light muslin gown.

"Bloody hell." He grabbed her wrist, lifting her hand to better inspect the source of the blood. "You're bleeding."

She looked down at her hand as if she had not realized she had injured herself. "It is only a prick. Do not concern yourself." She tried to pull her hand from his grasp.

He didn't let go, but lifted the finger to his lips and sucked at the small wound. The salty taste of her blood mixed with the sweetness of her skin, and he longed to suck her entire finger into his mouth. She gasped softly, and she stopped trying to pull away.

With a great effort of will, he kept her finger pressed to his mouth and did not give in to his urge. He looked into her eyes. She stood motionless, just as she had sat in perfect stillness earlier in the parlor. As if she waited for him.

Regardless of what she said, she wanted him to kiss her as much as he wanted to taste her sweet, hot mouth.

The sound of approaching footsteps stopped him. He released her hand. It had stopped bleeding.

The proper butler he had met upon arriving, entered the conservatory. "Your grace, Mrs. Abercrombie requests the pleasure of your company in the drawing room."

He made it clear with his look that he thought Jared had overstayed the time allowed for a gentleman to call upon a lady—even a widow.

Calantha picked up the roses she had cut, wrapped them in a tea towel from the table, and handed them to him. "Please take these to Lady Ashton, with my regards."

She was dismissing him. He briefly considered staying and intruding on her visit with the vicar's wife, but decided against it. He had thinking to do, away from this sharp desire that plagued him whenever she was near.

THE FLOWERS TOUCHED IRISA, AND SHE WENT SO FAR AS to remind Jared that she had said Calantha was kind. He didn't make the mistake of agreeing or disagreeing. If he agreed, his sister would take that as further evidence of his serious intentions toward the duchess. If he disagreed, his pregnant sister was likely to get testy.

Personally, he found the duchess a mass of contradictions.

She had implied that the status of her title had made up for any problems in her marriage, but she did not live like a duchess now. She said she didn't want to kiss him again and then froze into immobility at his slightest touch, her feminine desire lapping at him like the waves against the shore.

And she had impaled herself on a thorn when he mentioned children, her complexion turning the color of the *White Rose of York*. That worried him. Why had the comment upset her so much?

Many ladies of the *ton* did not conceive immediately, and her marriage had lasted only two short years. Would she be jealous of Hannah's existence? Would she resent the little girl he loved like a daughter? He hated the idea that Calantha could be capable of cruelty inspired by such a petty emotion, but there was still a great deal he did not know or understand about her.

She hid too much of herself behind the emotionless mask of her beauty. Except when they had kissed.

She hadn't been able to hide her response or her innocence from him then. He knew some men reserved passion for their mistresses and coupled with their wives only long enough to ensure their seed taking root. Clairborne must have been just such an idiot, because Calantha had been too untutored in the art of kissing and the pleasure it brought to have received that kind of affection from her husband.

She hadn't been able to mask her reaction to him today, either. She wanted him. Maybe as much as he wanted her.

How would the *ton* react if the Angel had an affair with Lord Beast?

Four

"JARED CAME TO CALL ON YOU TODAY."
The sound of Lady Ashton's cheerful tones lowered in obvious inquiry forced Calantha's attention away from her surreptitious study of Jared. He was in fine form tonight, his black evening clothes fitting his muscular body like a second skin. The scar on his face lent an air of danger to him, and Calantha knew that danger to be real. Very real.

Had she not intended to stay home tonight? Yet, she had found herself dressing for the musicale under a strange compulsion she had been unable to resist, a compulsion to see Jared just one more time.

She turned her gaze to Lady Ashton. "Yes."

"I'm glad."

Calantha did not know how to respond to that, so she remained silent.

"He isn't very social. In fact, I was shocked when he agreed to come to my house party." Lady Ashton's gaze took on a considering quality. "Actually, now that I think about it, he didn't say he was coming until I mentioned you were my neighbor and had planned to attend some of the entertainments."

Calantha dismissed the possibility that Jared had come

to the house party solely to see her. They had never met before, and to her knowledge, she had never even seen him in Town during the Season. "I'm sure the prospect of seeing his family was sufficient inducement."

If she didn't know better, Calantha would have thought the other woman snorted.

Lady Ashton's warm brown eyes were definitely filled with humor when she spoke. "Don't you believe it. Jared hates socializing, and he wouldn't be here unless he had a good reason for it. At first, I thought he wanted help with Hannah, but that was a silly idea. My brother is nothing if not self-confident. He probably thinks he has all the answers to raising a little girl alone."

Calantha made a noncommittal sound, while her mind tried to make sense of what the other woman was saying. Jared had a child?

"He certainly hasn't asked Thea for a bit of advice. Unlike me." Lady Ashton gave a rueful laugh. "I'm a nervous wreck about having my first child. Thea and Lucas insist I'll be a wonderful mother, but they love me."

Calantha felt the familiar, but muted, sense of loss whenever the subject of children arose. She would never be a mother, had never had the opportunity to be one. After all, there had only been one virgin birth in history, and it had been to a woman much more worthy than she.

"I'm certain they are right," she said in an attempt to soothe Lady Ashton. "Mama once told me that she feared motherhood right up until she gave birth. She said that the moment she saw me, she knew everything would be all right."

Soft brown eyes filled with gratitude. "Oh, do you think it will be like that for me, too?"

Calantha found herself nodding. "I'm sure of it."

It had become more and more difficult to maintain an air of polite distance with others since meeting Jared. It was as if the effect he had on her senses touched her relationships with others as well.

"Thank you. Thea can't really understand. I don't think she's ever been frightened of anything in her whole life. She's just so efficient. I think she knew just what kind of mother she would be from the moment she realized she had conceived." Suddenly Lady Ashton's face turned pink with embarrassment. "I can't imagine what I think I'm doing discussing something of such an intimate nature with you. You must not take offense. Lucas says that I have a terrible tendency to speak without thinking, now that I'm not trying so very hard to be the perfect paragon. I can't even imagine how I got started on this subject, anyway."

Calantha knew. The other woman's earlier words were still burning a path through her brain. "I believe you were mentioning that your brother had not asked for advice regarding the raising of his daughter alone."

"Oh, Hannah isn't Jared's daughter." Lady Ashton flipped open her fan and waved it industriously in front of her face. "It's a bit warm in here, isn't it?"

Calantha hadn't found it so, but then she was so rarely warm. "Perhaps your condition has made you more sensitive," she said in an attempt to allay the other woman's fears of speaking about such a subject.

Clairborne would have been outraged, but she no longer had to worry about his reactions, and that truth was just beginning to make itself felt inside of her.

Lady Ashton smiled. "I'm sure you are right. What was I saying? Oh, yes. Hannah belonged to his housekeeper, but Mary died of a fever a few months ago, and she didn't have a husband. Jared has taken on the responsibility of raising her daughter. He's adored the little girl since her birth. You should see them together. It's really very sweet."

Calantha felt as if an iron fist squeezed her heart. Jared had a daughter. His sister denied it naturally, but why else would he take such a personal interest in the child of one of his servants? She didn't know why, but the knowledge hurt her. She felt a rush of envy that took her breath away. What she would not give to have been in the housekeeper's place and given birth to Jared's child.

She nearly fainted from the outrageous direction of her thoughts, and almost missed his sister's next words.

"Now that I've seen him with you, I understand."

As had happened many times in the past when speaking with Lady Ashton, Calantha found herself confused. "Excuse me?"

"I understand why he's come to my house party," she said, and laid her hand on Calantha's arm. "I really am glad."

Calantha did not know what she would have said to Lady Ashton if Jared had not arrived at that moment. "Irisa, your butler is looking for you. Something about the buffet."

Lady Ashton gave them both a serene smile, winked at her brother, and went to find the butler.

Calantha watched the other woman's progress across the room. She stopped to smile and chat with several people, reminding Calantha of a rather friendly butterfly.

"Your sister is a very kind woman."

"She says the same about you."

"She thinks you came to her house party in order to have the opportunity to meet me," she said to show that his sister's judgment wasn't always sound.

"I did."

Shock reverberated through her, and Calantha could not get enough air. "Why?" she asked starkly.

"Come riding with me tomorrow morning, and I'll explain."

How could she go with him—but then, how could she not? She could no more deny him than she had been able to deny herself the opportunity to see him tonight. "All right."

A footman came by and said the entertainment was

about to start. Jared escorted Calantha to a chair in the back of the room. "I thought you weren't coming tonight."

She clutched her fan tightly in both hands. "I changed my mind."

"I see."

Perhaps he did see . . . if he had come to the house party only to meet her. As impossible as she found it to believe, perhaps this strange compulsion that plagued her beset him as well.

"Will you have Hannah with you tomorrow?" She did not know what had prompted her to ask the question.

Of course he would not bring a child along on their ride. He wanted to discuss things of an intimate nature, but she wanted to prod him into talking about his daughter.

He stiffened beside her, and his face took on a chillingly remote expression. "What do you know about Hannah?"

"Your sister said that you are raising her."

His expression did not lighten. "That's right, but I won't have her with me tomorrow."

She drew back mentally from the coldness in his eyes. "Perhaps I will meet her another time."

He looked at her as if he were weighing her worthiness. "Maybe."

THE NEXT MORNING, JARED ARRIVED EARLY AND HELPED her mount her sweet little chestnut mare before leaping astride his own magnificent horse, a steel gray stallion of the same massive proportions as his master. Contrary to his promise of the night before that he would explain his enigmatic statement, Jared discouraged any sort of discussion by the simple method of leading her on a fast-paced, challenging ride through the fields.

Calantha used the time of silence to think. Not that she hadn't already chewed endlessly on what Jared's words had meant.

One other gentleman had made a similar claim to the one Jared had made the night before. Clairborne had told her during their courtship that he had attended the rather boring little ball thrown by his social inferiors because he knew she would be there. He had seen her in the park and wanted to meet the woman *ton* wits referred to as the Angel. She had been foolish enough to be flattered.

Did Jared see only her angelic looks as well? Worse, would he expect perfect behavior because of them, as Clairborne had?

He already knew that she was not perfect, she reminded herself. After all, she had allowed him to kiss her, had in fact invited his kiss. She had also entertained him in her home without her maid present. Was it possible that a man as strong as Jared could overlook her cowardly actions of the past as well? She could not stifle the tiny flicker of hope that ignited in her heart.

After half an hour, they came upon a small stream running through a flower-speckled meadow.

Jared reined in and dismounted. He dropped the horse's leads, and the animal immediately headed for the stream. Calantha had stopped as well, but didn't know what to do about dismounting. There was no handy stump nearby, and her voluminous riding skirts made the prospect of leaping from her mare's back daunting. Jared solved her dilemma by gripping her waist with both hands and swinging her down before she could even gasp, much less voice an objection at his forward behavior.

Not that she would have anyway, she acknowledged as she landed on her feet a few inches from his broad chest. She had no self-control when it came to Jared's touch, and she was too honest to lie to herself about it. From the very first, it had been so different from anything she had experienced with her husband.

She looked at him, drinking in his presence as thirstily as she craved his touch.

He wore a riding coat, but no waistcoat, and she could see the dark shadow of his hair under the fine lawn of his shirt. He hadn't bothered with a cravat either, and the strong column of his neck was exposed to her view. His utter masculinity, so different from the other gentlemen she had known, entranced her.

"Now we talk," he said as he stepped away.

She nodded, noting absently that her mare had left to join the stallion drinking from the brook.

Jared peeled off his coat and laid it on the soft grass. "Sit down."

She obeyed without speaking because the sight of his body clad in only the fine lawn of his shirt and tight riding breeches had left her speechless. She tucked the skirts of her peacock blue riding habit around her legs, careful not to expose so much as a hint of skin above her short riding boots. The stiffened silk rustled, but did not stifle her in the summer heat.

He sat down next to her, and she had to twist her body to see his face. What she saw there made her want to turn back around and hide her own expression of nervous anticipation. Jared looked ready to do battle, not discuss the intimacies of a man-woman relationship.

She could not help the nervous tingle that skittered up her spine.

"A little over four years ago, you had a woman named Mary working at Clairborne Park."

The words so shocked her that she tried to assimilate their meaning in the context of her meeting with Jared. Then she remembered that Lady Ashton had said his housekeeper's name had been Mary. It was such a common name; surely they were not the same woman. Besides, her Mary had been much too young to be anyone's housekeeper, and she had been a lady's companion, not a domestic servant.

"I suppose you don't remember her." Jared's voice was laced with disgust, his eyes unreadable and cold.

"Yes. I remember her, but she didn't work at the Park. She was a companion to the dowager duchess. She left unexpectedly several months before my husband died in a riding accident."

He had been riding another man's wife and died at the hands of a jealous husband, but she saw no reason to mention that fact. His brother had seen that it had all been hushed up, and the jealous husband had left for the colonies.

"She ran away because of something that happened to her."

Calantha could not misread the accusation in Jared's eyes, and guilt flayed her. It was as she had always suspected. If only she had been more aware of what was happening around her. If only she had not withdrawn into her books, she might have saved Mary from suffering some cruelty at the hands of her husband.

Jared must have read the guilt on her face because he scowled. "You were aware of your husband's depravity?"

She could not deny it. She had suffered too much at his hands to be ignorant. "Yes."

Had he beaten Mary as he'd beaten her? Is that why she had run? The very thought made Calantha sick to the depths of her soul.

"Bloody hell."

"I'm sorry." She did not know what else to say, but then something that should have been obvious fell into place. "You are Mary's viscount, the one who paid for her schooling. She ran to you when Deveril mistreated her."

"She told you about me?"

"Not your name . . . I always wished she had. I wanted to look for her. After she left. We were friends."

"And yet you allowed your husband to abuse her? That is not friendship."

She could not meet his eyes and looked away. "No. That is not friendship."

Mary had deserved so much better.

"She had a child."

She did not understand how that connected to what they were discussing, but she was more than willing to change the subject. "Hannah?"

"Yes."

"Is she yours?" She was shocked at her own blunt speech, but no less so than by his reaction to it.

He seemed to swell with fury, and his eyes filled with angry disdain. Without conscious thought, she reacted to his anger with old fear and scooted backward.

"*No*," he barked, leaning forward to close the small distance she had created between them.

"I don't understand." She pushed herself backward on her bottom until the solid trunk of a tree stopped her progress away from him.

He followed her, the look in his eyes terrifying. "She bloody well is not mine, and don't pretend you didn't know, damn it." He grabbed her arm with one large hand. "I won't tolerate your lies."

She stared at him, feeling as if a wild animal ready to shred her to pieces trapped her. His massiveness surrounded her, and it was too much. Although she was tall for a woman, she knew how puny her strength would be pitted against his.

"I'm n-not lying," she stammered, fear she thought she had conquered coming back to torment her.

Was he going to strike her? She tried to steel herself against the possibility, realizing that she could not run. His hand held her arm too firmly, though the grip was not a painful one. For once, he truly seemed the beast he had been labeled by society.

She tried to remember the gentleness he had shown her to mitigate some of the terror coursing through her body, but it did not work. His very real, very present fury overshadowed any ephemeral memory she might have.

Her breathing turned shallow. Her palms grew damp as she clutched her hands into small, useless fists. Her mouth went dry. How could she have been so foolish as to go riding alone with him? Did she not know better than anyone how risky it was to put oneself at the mercy of a man?

Bile rose in her, the acid burning against the ache in her throat. "Please. Don't hurt me," she croaked past the tightness there.

She had promised herself she would never beg again the second month of her marriage, the day her husband had stood over her with his fist raised and laughed with pleasure at the sight of her pleading, terrified form. Yet she could not hold the words back, perhaps because even in her terror, she trusted Jared to have more mercy than Clairborne.

Suddenly Jared moved. She screamed and tried to jump up, but she was too late. He grabbed her shoulders and yanked her against him, but not cruelly. The lack of pain registered at the same time as the reassuring caress against her back.

The hand she had feared would deal her a blow moved against her with soothing assurance. "I'm not going to hurt you. All is well."

He repeated the words over and over again until she stopped trembling and lay in quiet acquiescence against his chest. She listened to the steady beat of his heart, and she realized he really wasn't going to hurt her. The fear receded, and in its place came a terrible, cold anger.

She had trusted him. She had allowed him to kiss her more intimately than she had ever been kissed, had been enthralled by him, and he had used his size and anger to intimidate her. Perhaps he had not expected her fear to be so intense, but he had unleashed his anger against her, and she did not even know why. She would not put herself at the mercy of another unstable man's whim.

"Let me go." She spoke quietly, but with conviction.

He obeyed, but she sensed his reluctance. She did not care. For the first time since meeting him, she did not crave his touch.

She pushed against the tree behind her and stood up. "Perhaps you had better explain."

"First, tell me why you were so bloody terrified. I would never hurt you, Calantha. Surely you must realize that."

She did not want to discuss her unreasonable fear, but the vulnerable expression in his eyes pricked her conscience. He was used to being treated like a beast by others.

She did not want to add to the burden of his title. "I learned to fear a man's anger, and his strength. You were furious with me, and I reacted to your emotion rather than your character."

It was all she was willing to say.

It was not enough. "Who taught you that fear? Was it your husband?"

She refused to answer. "Tell me about Mary."

"Tell me about your marriage, Calantha."

"I do not discuss it. You brought me here to talk about my former friend, not my marriage." It struck her at that moment that Mary was dead.

Grief rose in her, but she tamped it down. She would show this man no more weakness. "Please say what you intended to say."

He certainly hadn't come riding with her to discuss a future together. Her naïve hope mocked her now.

"She made me promise to tell you about Hannah. On her deathbed."

Pain lanced through her, as if Mary's loss was as fresh as the day she'd gone looking for her and found she'd disappeared from Clairborne Park.

"Why?" She could not begin to understand, unless Mary hoped she would do something for her child based on their earlier friendship.

She would. She would do anything for the one true friend from her past.

"Because Clairborne was her father."

The sun-dappled meadow receded, and black shadows

blocked her vision as she swayed under the impact of the verbal blow Jared had just dealt her. Then he was there, holding her arms in a light grip that prevented her falling down.

She shook him off and tipped her head upward, looking into his dark eyes. "Mary and Clairborne had an affair?"

She could not take it in. Betrayal dealt her heart another painful blow. Mary had been her friend.

"No."

She shook her head, trying to understand. "Then how?"

"He raped her."

The words were the final shock to her system, and Calantha welcomed the feeling of numbness that overcame her just before the world went black.

THE FIRST THING SHE SAW WHEN SHE AWOKE WAS THE sun filtering through the green leaves on the branches of the tree above her head. Although she knew the sun to be warm, she felt cold all over, deep into her soul. All the warmth that Jared had brought into her life had been sapped from her, leaving her more frozen than she had ever been.

The second thing she saw was Jared's face. He leaned over her, a look of concern on his features. She dismissed it as a trick of the light. He wasn't worried for her. How could he be? It was her fault. All of it. She finally understood his anger.

She moved to sit up, but he held her back.

She did not want to remain in the vulnerable position. "I'm all right. Please let me up."

He didn't look like he believed her, but he gently lifted her into a sitting position. "I'm sorry."

Why was he apologizing? He hadn't raped Mary.

"She was so young." She'd been a year younger than Calantha.

"Yes."

"She was so sweet." She remembered Mary's laughter and ready smile, and tears burned at the back of her eyes.

"Why did you faint? You said you knew of your husband's depravity."

At first, she was confused and then appalled by the direction of his thoughts.

"Yes, but I didn't know his cruelty stretched that far. I thought she left because he had hurt her . . . I could never have suspected it would have been in that way. She was my friend. We would talk. When I was first married to Clairborne, I didn't know how to be a duchess, and I was frightened." She was babbling, but shock was still shrouding her mind. "I had more in common with her than the other titled women around me."

"Then you made friends with the others and dismissed Mary from your life?"

Calantha winced at the accusation, but her anger was gone along with any other feeling. "I didn't dismiss her."

"Don't lie to me." His rage had turned as cold as her heart, but this time it did not affect her.

"I'm not lying."

"I know the truth. She told me that you pulled away from her, stopped treating her like a friend."

Yes, but her guilt at the consequences of a behavior meant to protect wasn't something she could deal with right now. "I want to go home."

"We have to talk about Hannah."

What was there to say? Clairborne had had a daughter, but his wife had never been pregnant. He had violated a sweet, innocent girl who should have been able to trust him for her protection, but had kept his duchess pristine.

Calantha could not face that reality. "Not now. I can't talk about it now." She looked at Jared, meeting him cold look for cold look. "I won't talk anymore."

She meant it, sealing her lips shut in a firm line.

Jared opened his mouth to argue, but then snapped it

shut again. He went to fetch the horses. When he lifted her onto her mare's back, all of the glorious feelings his touch usually elicited were gone. She had withdrawn to that place of safety in her mind, the place where her emotions could not penetrate. Where even physical sensation could be ignored.

JARED LED CALANTHA BACK TO HER COTTAGE, KEEPING their horses at a more sedate pace on the return ride. He didn't want to risk her falling, not after the way she'd fainted. While the silence on the ride to the meadow had been of his making, the utter stillness between them now was of hers.

She had pulled into herself, and he knew without trying that he could not reach her. Her emotionless demeanor bothered him more than he cared to admit.

It shouldn't. She'd as good as admitted to turning a blind eye to her husband's evil, but then had said she had not known Clairborne's cruelty would stretch to rape. She'd said she thought Clairborne had hurt Mary. Like he had hurt Calantha?

He could not forget her terrified reaction when they had first started talking. She'd acted as if she thought he would beat her. Three days ago, he would have attributed that reaction to his reputation as Lord Beast, but he knew better now.

Calantha had never seen him as a beast, and he didn't like to admit that even for a brief time today that had changed. He had no doubt who was responsible for her reaction—the bastard who had married her. Why had Jared never seriously considered what sort of life Calantha must have lived at the hands of her vicious husband?

He was guilty of his own prejudice, assuming a woman in her position had had the power to stop her husband's wickedness. His own mother's life should have warned him just how much of a fallacy that sort of thinking was.

Hadn't she been forced to flee England so she could raise at least one of her children? Jared was damn certain now that, instead of being able to curb Clairborne's brutality, Calantha had been a victim of it.

She did not easily trust, nor did she open herself up to others, but that was something Jared could understand. She was a private person, holding most of her thoughts captive behind a marble-like mask.

Until she had met him. For a brief time she had allowed him to see behind her mask to the passionate woman who grew roses for their beauty, but used their healing properties to help others. He hated the fact that she'd withdrawn again.

She was not the monster he had at one time believed her to be. He would find out the full story from her, when she was ready to talk.

In the meantime, they still had to discuss Hannah. He had to know if she wanted to be part of the child's life, and in what capacity. Would she want the role of mother? Had Mary been right to believe that the Angel would do right by the by-blow daughter of her dead husband?

The prospect left Jared cold. He couldn't give Hannah up. He loved the little girl and wanted to raise her. If Calantha decided she wanted Hannah, could he ignore Mary's deathbed wish and keep the child for himself?

If he did not, he would lose his daughter. If he did, he would lose his honor.

The only solution lie in somehow connecting himself to Calantha. What if he were to marry her?

He found himself seduced by the possibility before he could dismiss it from his mind. He could fulfill Mary's desire to see Calantha raise her daughter, and he would not have to lose the little girl he held so dear. He would also have Calantha. The fire and passion she hid behind her emotionless façade would be his. Along with the right to protect her.

Lucy Monroe

He would chase the fear from her eyes and teach her that a man's anger and strength could be controlled.

Angels did not marry beasts, but she'd told him more than once that she wasn't an angel. He was beginning to think that with a certain woman, he wasn't the beast society believed him to be, either.

Five

CALANTHA WITHDREW TO HER CONSERVATORY immediately upon arriving home. She did not even take time to change her riding habit for an afternoon gown. She had been surprised by the ease with which Jared had allowed her to dismiss him, but grateful. She could not discuss anything with him right now. She had to come to terms with his revelations.

Deveril, the monster, had raped the oh-so-dear and sweet Mary, her one and only true friend during those hateful years as a duchess. Calantha sank to her knees beside a potted rosebush. Its pale pink loveliness had reminded her in the past of Mary, prompting her to pray for the gentle friend that she had lost. If only she had known just how great the loss truly had been.

She had believed Mary had gone on to another position, or back to her viscount savior . . . and she had. But the evil that had sent her running was worse than anything Calantha could have imagined. Now she had to come to terms not only with that knowledge, but also with the reality that her dear friend had given birth to her husband's child and was dead. Mary. Dead.

The busy hands forever stilled, the laughing mouth forever silenced, the rosy cheeks pale and bloodless in a coffin. No doubt, now buried in some plot reserved for sinners outside the churchyard, because her innocence had been brutally taken and along with it, her chastity.

The grief came out of nowhere, crashing through the wall of ice that surrounded Calantha's heart and bringing with it a pain so great, she thought she would shatter from it.

Silent sobs racked her body as she buried her head in her arms on the edge of the rose pot. She cried for all she had lost, not just Mary. She grieved her own stolen innocence, her hard won knowledge of the baser side of human nature, the friendships she had forced herself to relinquish, and she grieved her own cowardice, along with all it had wrought.

She had allowed her fear of her husband make her push Mary away, so the girl had not come to her when Clairborne had raped her. She would have helped Mary, even if it meant facing Clairborne's wrath—but the girl had not known that. How had she ended up Jared's housekeeper?

Giving her the position had probably been his way of coming to her rescue once again. Calantha would regret forever her inability to be there for her dear friend. She had loved Mary as much as she could have loved a sister. It had been that love that had prompted her to withdraw more tightly into the loneliness of isolation in an effort to protect Mary. A sob snaked through her as she acknowledged that her efforts had failed spectacularly.

Had Jared loved Mary?

Calantha thought of the pretty girl and her indomitable spirit, and thought he must have. Why else would he have taken on the responsibility of raising Hannah? The child that should have been Calantha's.

Oh God, she cried out silently, *how can I be so cruel and base that I would even think such a thing?*

But she had thought it, and the thought brought more pain. She, the weak one, had been unworthy of bearing a child. Unworthy of love. Clairborne had told her again and again that if she were not so common, so frigid, so foolish, so lacking in every way that counted, he would come to her.

He said she was no better than a mindless marble statue, all beauty and no substance. She made a good ornament, but nothing else. And it was because she had been so unattractive in this way to her husband that he had hurt Mary.

As the thought formed, a great well of rage erupted from her, and Calantha shot to her feet. No! No! She might be weak. She might have been a coward, but she *had not* forced her husband to such a monstrous action. He had mistresses. She ought to know, he'd thrown them in her face often enough. He did not have to resort to rape. He had been the monster, not her.

She had let Mary down because of her fear, just as she had allowed her spinelessness to stop her from helping the servant girl Clairborne had put out until it was too late. But she hadn't made her husband cruel. He'd managed that all on his own. Just as he'd managed to deposit dread so deep in her soul that she had merely existed for the past six years, not actually *lived*.

She feared her own feelings, both pain and joy. She feared attachment to others in case they were taken from her as her parents had been, and the few friends she had made during her life. She even feared meeting Hannah. What if the child carried her father's cruelty in her?

She had reacted with terror to Jared's anger, allowing her past fears and experiences to make her beg for his mercy.

But her husband was dead, had been dead for four years. What excuse did she have for continuing to live under the shadow his cruelty had cast? She shook from the enormity of the thoughts whirling through her head.

She did not have to be afraid. She had survived marriage to a monster; she could cope with meeting his daughter.

She knelt on the conservatory floor again, this time to

pray for the strength and courage to act on her newfound thoughts.

SHE WAS STILL KNEELING WHEN THOMAS CAME TO TELL her that she had a caller, the current Duke of Clairborne.

As she hurried upstairs to change her clothes and repair her appearance, Calantha wondered why her brother-in-law had seen fit to call.

The current duke and duchess did not often deign to call on her, since she refused to live in the dower house at Clairborne Park. They demanded her attendance at two important functions a year, the family Christmas celebration and the lavish ball they hosted in Town during the Season.

It was during these times that she was grateful for the location of her home. She was not forced to spend the night at either Clairborne Park or the family townhouse in London. Although it meant a great deal of travel in one day, it could be done.

When Clairborne had told her he intended to purchase a small estate for her parents in the country, she had believed he meant to buy something near their country estate, but he had found a house halfway between there and London.

He had said that would make it easier for her parents to visit often when they were living at either Clairborne Park or Town for the Season. It had worked out the opposite, of course. The house was far enough away from both the country estate and London to make travel for her elderly parents difficult, and Clairborne had made it subtly clear that they weren't welcome for overnight stays. He had always had a reason why she could not go visit them as well, but now the location of the property worked in her favor on the occasions she was forced to socialize with the Clairbornes.

The rest of the year, the current duke and duchess left her alone. She wasn't sure Henry liked it that way. She'd had the impression that he would like her to visit Clairborne Park more often, but his wife was a jealous woman. The current duchess was not jealous of Henry's numerous, but discreet, peccadilloes. No, she was jealous of her position in society, and guarded it with great zeal. She did not like having the former mistress of her home underfoot. And she made that clear in a well-bred sort of way that her husband could not find fault with. Calantha could not find it in herself to blame the other woman either.

She had learned after her marriage that everyone had expected Deveril to marry Ellen, and it had only been his fixation with tying himself to an *angel* that had stopped him. The eldest daughter of a duke herself, Ellen had been bred to her position. It would have been quite the come-down to marry the second son, when she had grown up with expectations of becoming the next Duchess of Clairborne.

Justice had been served in Deveril's death, when not only had his depraved nature finally caused him to pay the ultimate price for his sin, but the woman who had expected to become duchess had finally realized her ambition.

Quickly changing into a sky-blue afternoon gown with tiny puff sleeves and a scoop-necked bodice, Calantha went downstairs to join her brother-in-law in the parlor. He stood upon her entrance, his bow perfectly executed to her curtsy.

He had the same attractive blond looks as his brother, and the sight of him gave Calantha chills. She tried to stifle the reaction, feeling it unfair to judge the present duke by the actions of his predecessor. After all, his wife showed absolutely no indication that she suffered from the same treatment that Calantha had been subjected to.

In fact, the current duchess managed her husband admirably, and Calantha had wondered more than once if the other woman had a source of strength that was missing in her own character.

"Good afternoon, your grace. I did not expect you."

"Good afternoon, my dear. I trust my visit is not an unpleasant surprise." The way he said the words made Calantha wonder again at the reason for the unexpected call.

"Not at all. Won't you sit down?" She sat in the same chair she had used when taking tea with Jared on the previous day and watched as the duke sank onto the sofa opposite.

She could not help comparing the perfectly correct gentleman now occupying her study with the roughly aggressive Jared. The duke would not dream of taking on the responsibility for another man's by-blow, any more than he would have kissed Calantha on their first day of meeting. Feeling a prick in her heart at the thoughts, Calantha ruthlessly crushed them.

She could not afford to think of Jared, or his revelations. Not now. It took all her wits to deal with the Clairbornes. One technique she had learned early on with her husband was silence, so after ordering tea, she patiently waited for the duke to come to the reason for his visit.

He waited until the tea things had been deposited on the table between them and the servant had left before opening the subject. "I'm sorry to say this isn't strictly a social call."

"Is something the matter at Clairborne Park?"

"No. I have come because I am worried about you."

Calantha took a small, fortifying sip of tea. "Worried about me, your grace?"

His pale gray eyes filled with the semblance of concern. "Yes. I could not credit the gossip when I first heard it, but have come out of my sense of personal obligation to my brother's widow to see if there is some justification for the scandalous stories being spread in the district."

She drew herself up and regarded him with every bit of duchess-like reserve at her disposal. "*Scandal*, Henry?"

She deliberately used his first name as a reminder that she was not his social inferior. No longer merely the daughter of an aging vicar, she had paid a high price for her position as duchess, and she would not allow him to intimidate her with veiled accusations.

"Please be so kind as to explain yourself."

She could see that her aggressive tactics surprised him as much as they surprised herself, but she would not spend another interview on the defensive. She simply could not do it.

"I have it on good authority that you asked a gentleman to dance."

He made it sound as if she had propositioned a footman in the middle of the ballroom floor. "I availed myself of a partner when an obvious misunderstanding had taken place and the gentleman and myself found we were without escorts for the current dance."

"That *gentleman* is called Lord Beast by society, and ladies who desire to keep their standing amidst the *ton* stay clear of him. He's as uncouth and rough as his name implies."

The way Henry sneered the word *gentleman* and insulted Jared sent a wave of pure fury through her. She had thought after her discussion with Jared that all emotion in her was dead, but since her tears in the conservatory, she knew that was not the case.

Now, she felt a pure, cleansing anger. "He's a viscount and accepted at all levels of society. If some ladies are overset by his manners, they are of course entitled to avoid him. I, however, find him unobjectionable."

He'd scared her out of her wits that morning, but even now she was coming to realize that it had been past fear coming back to haunt her rather than an honest reaction to Jared.

The duke actually pulled out his quizzing glass and peered at her through it. She knew he meant to make her feel like a bug on a pin, but instead she wanted to laugh. The man looked ridiculous.

"It is not only his manners that one might find unacceptable."

"What do you mean?" she asked with freezing accents.

"There is talk . . . that he has a daughter. A natural child he chooses to raise in his home."

Hannah was the very last thing Calantha wished to discuss with Deveril's brother. "Yes."

"You knew?"

"Yes, but I fail to see what that has to do with you, or with me for that matter."

Henry's brows beetled. "I'm shocked at your attitude, my dear. Clearly your judgment is in question. I fear I am now inclined to believe that other rumors I've heard have some veracity to them."

"What rumors would those be?" She had learned early on never to offer information to a Clairborne.

"I have heard that not only did you dance with this *person*, but you were also seen several times conversing in his company."

"My conversation is my own affair."

"As my brother's widow, you are still a member of my family. My concern is entirely justified. Perhaps allowing you to live alone in this hovel has been a mistake. You have forgotten the exalted status of your family by marriage and your responsibility to uphold the Clairborne title. A move to the dower house at the Park may be in order."

As threats went, it should have been effective. Calantha detested Clairborne Park and all the ugly memories that resided within its vaunted walls.

However, the current duchess would not tolerate such a move without a great deal of fight. And although Henry controlled the money left Calantha in Clairborne's will, he did not control her person. She would live without the aid of servants, eating from her own garden, before she would return to Clairborne Park.

"I'm sorry you consider the house your brother saw fit to buy my parents a mere hovel, Henry."

His eyes narrowed, but he apologized. "My tongue got away with me. My brother was more than generous when he bought this property and gifted it to your family. I would think that loyalty to his memory would prevent you from desecrating his name with unacceptable behavior."

The last thing she felt toward her dead husband's name was loyalty. There *was* no honor in his name. "I consider desecration reserved to things that are holy, Henry. As exalted as the Clairborne name may be amidst the *ton*, it is not sacred."

Where had this defiance come from? She did not know herself, but it felt very good indeed.

"I do not find your flippancy in the least amusing," he said in his most pompous tones. "You do not seem to realize the delicacy of your situation, my dear."

If he called her his dear just once more, she was going to dump hot tea in his lap.

The thought stunned her, but it was so entertaining, she spent several seconds contemplating such an action before saying, "What exactly are you trying to say, Henry?"

"You will cease association with Viscount Ravenswood at once, or you will see a significant decrease in the monies available for the running of your household."

He had no right to threaten her in this manner. None at all. The marriage settlements were supposed to have protected her in the event of her husband's death, but he'd placed his brother as trustee of her funds, and no court in the land would grant her favor against a duke.

Instead of railing at him, Calantha silently considered the man seated across from her. She could bow to his dictates easily enough, she supposed. She now knew that Jared would not ever welcome her friendship or her company, but there was still the matter of Hannah.

"I cannot make such a promise, Henry. There are other circumstances that must be considered."

He glared at her, his outrage at her refusal evident. "What *other* things? You don't mean to tell me the beast has asked for your hand? You cannot consider such a thing."

She almost laughed aloud, but it would have been a hollow sound tinged with bitterness. Henry had everything backward. He thought Jared not good enough for Calantha, but she knew the opposite was true. "Do not concern yourself. The viscount is not interested in marriage, at least not to me."

A look of horror crossed Henry's face. "Do not tell me you have started an affair. Demme. If I had known you needed that sort of attention, I could have arranged a discreet visit here and there."

She was so appalled by her brother-in-law's casual suggestion of immoral behavior that she did not respond at once. Finally, she said in her most chilling tones, "I am not having an affair with him."

"Then what other circumstances are you nattering on about?"

At once she realized that if she exposed Hannah's existence to Henry, she could be putting the child's happiness at risk. She had not missed the overt censure Henry levied against Jared for having the temerity to publicly raise what the duke believed was Jared's own natural child.

Should she reveal Hannah's true parentage, Henry might very well take it into his head to demand rights to the child, if for no other reason than to see her raised as far from the eyes of the *ton* as possible. Jared was a man of power, yes . . . but not even he could stand firm against a duke of the realm when it came to a point of law. And she was not conversant enough with English law to know who had more claim to Hannah.

Calantha thought quickly. "I am friends with Lady Ashton, and the viscount is her brother."

"As to that . . . you can fob off her invitations until her uncouth brother returns to his estates."

Having had enough of being dictated to by another overbearing duke, Calantha drew herself up. "I will choose my own friends and when I will associate with them. As far as I am concerned, this matter is closed."

She'd never spoken with such temerity before and was shocked at her own boldness, but that was no comparison to Henry's reaction.

His complexion went chalk-white and then red with rage. "How dare you speak to me in such a way?"

"How dare *you* assume you can dictate my every action? You are not my husband or my father that I should be forced by law to allow you to do so."

"I control your finances."

"And if you make it too difficult for me to maintain my household, I shall spread the word from one end of the *beau monde* to the other what a pinch-purse you are." The words came out on their own volition, but she immediately appreciated the effectiveness of the threat.

The duke's countenance meant too much to him to allow her to live in total penury, no matter what threats he might make.

"You have the nerve to threaten me?"

She nodded, though she could not quite make herself repeat the warning.

"My brother dragged you out of the gutter and made something of you," Henry said with appalled outrage. "You will not taint his memory with this wrongheaded behavior!"

The slur against her family was too much to bear. "I was the daughter of an honorable and kind man, hardly a guttersnipe. Your brother, however, was a cruel monster who made my life unendurable. I rue the day I married him and hold his memory in nothing but contempt. It would be impossible for any action on my part to even come close to emulating the legacy of depravity he left behind."

After the words left her mouth, her entire body trembled with their import and fear of the retaliation the duke might choose to take. Had she not already been overwrought from her confrontation with Jared, she would never have spoken thus. Yet the freedom she experienced at finally expressing her true feelings toward her dead husband was satisfying in a way she could never have imagined it would be.

Henry jumped up and towered over her, his body vibrating with fury, his fist raised in unmistakable menace, and his face florid with his choler. "You will regret speaking of Deveril that way. I will teach you to keep your mouth shut and to accept the instruction of your betters, you ungrateful wench."

The fist came toward her and Calantha reacted without thought. She dove off her chair toward the tea table. Then she astounded herself once again when, rather than run from the room, she took a grip on the heavy tray, laden with a silver tea urn, china, and pastries, and shoved.

It slid across the polished surface of the table quite easily and rammed into the duke's legs with sufficient momentum and surprise to knock him off his feet. She kept pushing, and the whole tray went crashing down on the fallen nobleman.

He screamed as scalding tea spilled over his legs and china broke all around him.

She rushed toward the door, only to stop short when she heard running footsteps. The servants. She forced a façade of composure, one she had perfected during her tumultuous marriage, and was smoothing her dress with trembling hands when Thomas and her maid came rushing into the room.

"Is anything amiss, your grace?" Thomas asked her, just as if the duke was not writhing on the carpet, his mouth spouting obscenities.

"We appear to have had a slight accident, Thomas. Perhaps someone could help the duke find dry clothes before he returns to Clairborne Park. He must be on his way soon, or he will miss traveling in the light."

Shaking so badly, it was all she could do not to wobble like a drunken sailor, she left the room. But the victory this time had been hers. She had warned him against cutting her allowance and more importantly, she had not allowed him to hit her. A smile curved her lips, the first genuine one in too long for her to remember.

The war was not over, of that she was certain. The duke would not forget this altercation and her slights against his brother's character. Nor would he ignore her refusal to stop seeing Jared. She must be prepared for him to take devious action. He was after all, Deveril's brother, but she had won this battle, and her success felt very good indeed.

She would maintain her independent household, no matter what the duke decided to do. Not only for her own sake, but for the sake of the servants depending on her for their livelihood. If he made good his threats on cutting her allowance, she could always sell the jewels of which Clairborne had been so proud.

She didn't have the really good ones, those were entailed along with the estates, but she had the "gifts" Clairborne had bestowed upon her unworthy person throughout the two years of their marriage. He had liked to show her off, just like a well-groomed mare.

One thing was certain, she would not fail those who relied on her again. Come what may, she would continue to pay Thomas and the others their wages.

She arrived at Ashton Manor the next morning shortly after eleven. When the butler answered the door, he attempted to usher her into the drawing room, but she stayed him.

"I'm here to see Hannah."

She watched in fascination as Lady Ashton's servant

floundered for a response. He clearly wasn't certain how to tell a duchess that one did not call on occupants of the nursery.

Finally, he said, "The children are in the garden with Mr. and Mrs. Drake. If your grace will await her pleasure in the drawing room, I will ascertain their exact whereabouts and arrange for you to be taken to them."

Calantha wanted to argue. She did not wish to see anyone but the child. However, six years living up to the title of duchess came to the forefront. She acquiesced, allowing the butler to lead her to the drawing room. She needn't have worried. The room was empty. Lady Ashton must have taken her house guests on an excursion.

Filled with restless energy, Calantha paced across the room to the large window at the other end. It was open, and summer scents wafted in on a light breeze. She could smell freshly cut grass and the sweet scent of ripening fruit. Looking out the window, she saw that it overlooked an orchard.

"Your grace?"

Calantha turned around to face a young footman. "Yes?"

"If you will come with me, I will take you to Mr. and Mrs. Drake."

The footman led her outside to the entrance of a small, enclosed garden. A three-tiered fountain resided in the center of the garden, and three small children played in the base with paper boats. A puppy pranced around their feet before scampering off to chase a butterfly. Mr. and Mrs. Drake sat on a nearby bench watching the children.

As they drew near, Mrs. Drake's voice carried to Calantha's ears. "I'm concerned about him, Pierson. He's such a solitary man, and to have set his sights on the Angel. Well, it's . . ." her voice trailed off.

Calantha realized two things at once. The first was that she should make her presence known immediately. The second was that Mrs. Drake was discussing Jared and herself. The second fact overrode the first, and Calantha found herself unable to speak.

The footman had not yet been noticed.

"Did he say he plans to marry her?" Mr. Drake asked.

"Well, no. In fact, he said he's not interested in a marble statue for a wife, but I can't help worrying."

Just as his wife finished speaking, Mr. Drake became aware of the footman and Calantha standing beside him. "Yes?"

"Her grace has come to call on Miss Hannah."

Mrs. Drake's gaze settled on Calantha, and her startlingly blue eyes widened. "Oh, hello."

Calantha gave an abbreviated curtsy, calling on well-learned self-control to hide her pain at the knowledge that Jared saw her as no more than a marble statue. Just like Clairborne.

She tried to pretend the realization didn't hurt, telling herself that it didn't matter, that she knew Jared's interest in her had not been personal. It did not work, and that awful pain that had been unleashed with yesterday's tears came roaring back.

She ruthlessly tamped it down and said, "I do not mean to intrude on a family outing."

Mrs. Drake smiled. "Nonsense. The children wished to play in the garden, and Pierson and I used the excuse to duck out of the trip to a nearby abbey. There is only so much *society* I can take in one day. I'm not sure how Irisa stands it."

Calantha liked the other woman's forthright manner, and she found herself smiling. Just the corners of her lips tilted, but it was a smile, nonetheless. "I shall endeavor to be as un-society-like as possible."

Mrs. Drake chuckled. "Then you may, of course, stay."

Mr. Drake stood and gallantly offered Calantha his seat

on the bench, but she shook her head. "I would much rather walk around the garden and watch the children."

"The footman said you are here to call on Hannah?" Mrs. Drake queried.

"I would really just like to see her." Sudden timidity had her shying away from the prospect of meeting the child. Perhaps she had not broken as many bonds yesterday as she had hoped.

Mrs. Drake nodded. "She's the bigger girl in the center. The other little darlings are my son, David, and daughter, Deanna. And that scamp of a dog trailing around them is David's birthday present from Jared."

"They're beautiful children." And she meant it, but her gaze did not settle on the tiny girl or sturdy blond boy for very long.

All of her attention was riveted on the child in the middle. Hannah. She had long, dark hair, pulled into two braids that were attached at the ends with a single ribbon. Her white pinafore was mussed with several streaks of dirt, and one of her dimpled knees looked like she'd fallen on it.

She didn't look a bit like Deveril, and yet she didn't look much like Mary either, except for the bow-shaped mouth. Yet something about the child tugged at her heart and reminded Calantha of her dear friend.

"She's very sweet," Mrs. Drake said.

"Is she? Then she takes after her mother."

That seemed to startle the other woman. "You knew her?"

"Yes."

"Jared's very good with her," Mrs. Drake ventured again.

"He would be." He had all the elements of a good father, gentleness, protectiveness, concern. The puppy came trotting over and sniffed at Calantha's skirts.

Mr. Drake laughed. "The little beggar is always looking for something to eat. We have to keep him away from the kitchens, or the cook would rebel."

Calantha leaned down and scratched the dog's ears. He twisted his head and licked her wrist.

It tickled and startled a small laugh from her. "What a charming creature."

Mrs. Drake smiled, and the genuine warmth in her eyes stunned Calantha after the comments she had overheard upon entering the garden. "Yes, he's a darling. It's the only thing that saved Jared's hide when he gave a dog to my son for his birthday after I had refused to do so."

Calantha could imagine Jared doing such a thing quite easily. In his arrogance, he assumed he knew what was best for everyone around him.

She turned her gaze back to the children. "David is quite lucky to have such understanding parents."

Mrs. Drake said, "Thank you. He's a wonderful little boy, but then I am unashamedly biased."

Mr. Drake smiled at his wife with obvious fondness and said, "Yes, he and his sister have succeeded in doing what nothing else could have. They've drawn their mother's attention away from her business. There are days when her assistant despairs of getting her out of the nursery."

Looking at the precious little people playing in the fountain, Calantha could well imagine. If she had had a child, even her conservatory would have been neglected on occasion.

"Does Jared realize you've come to visit Hannah?" Mr. Drake asked the question and succeeded in drawing Calantha's attention away from the children.

"No."

"Why have you come to see her?" Mrs. Drake asked, her voice vibrating with concern for her brother rather than curiosity.

Calantha could not tell them of her husband's behavior. It shamed her. "You will have to ask Jared."

"But I'm asking you."

Calantha turned her attention back to Hannah for one last look before turning to leave. "Because I had to see her."

It was as simple and as complicated as that.

Six

LATER THAT AFTERNOON, CALANTHA SAT AT THE small round table in her parlor, papers spread around her. She'd begun a compilation of the fossilization data concerning the rose several months previously and was in the final stages of her research outline for a book she intended to write on the subject. She'd pulled her work out after returning from Ashton Manor, needing the distraction after the emotional excesses she'd experienced since meeting Jared.

Unfortunately, her mind kept wandering back to the sight of Hannah playing in the fountain, her dark hair glistening in the sunlight. Mary's baby. Deveril's baby. An innocent child. Jared's reason for seeking her out. Each disjointed thought made the prospect of losing herself in her studies more and more impossible.

She could not simply ignore Hannah's existence. Something must be done, but what? She had no legal claim to Hannah. Deveril had not left her well-off, and what money he had left her was under his brother's control.

She was under no illusions that the current duke and duchess, or anyone else in the family for that matter, would want Clairborne's illegitimate offspring recognized.

Jared certainly had more to offer the child. He wasn't afraid to claim Hannah as his responsibility.

Calantha hadn't even been able to bring herself to talk to the little girl. She'd fled Ashton Manor like a spineless jellyfish. What would Jared think when his sister told him of her visit? Would her reaction to Hannah further underscore his notion of her as a marble statue? If only she were! She had tried so hard to cut off all emotions, but they'd come rushing back in a tide of pain and suffering at the news of Mary's death. At Jared's touch.

And that small child was all that remained on this earth of Mary. Even if she had never seen her and felt the spark of recognition, Calantha would have loved the child simply because she was Mary's. Odd how easily she dismissed Deveril's legacy in Hannah, but even knowing what she did, Calantha could not help seeing Hannah as Jared's child. No doubt Mary had fervently wished that had been the case.

"Your grace, Lord Ravenswood and Miss Hannah would like to know if you are receiving visitors."

The sound of Thomas's superior accents brought her out of her reverie with a snap.

"Please show them in, Thomas, and have Cook prepare a tea tray. Tell her to put some of the candied rose petals we made the other day on it for the child."

"Very good, your grace." Thomas left.

She stood, nerves jangling, and piled her papers into three neat stacks, one for research, one for her notes, and the other her outline. She added a fourth pile, her written instructions for her servants. She had developed the habit of writing her instructions to the housekeeper when married to Deveril, because there was less chance she could be blamed for a mistake if she had a written record of her requests. Later, it had seemed the simpler way to remember to give instructions to Thomas when her mind often became sidetracked with her studies.

"Is that her? She don't have wings, Jared. How come she's an angel?" a small voice asked hesitantly.

Calantha's entire body tensed at the sound. She forced herself to turn around, knowing the time had come to meet her dead husband's daughter, but more importantly, Mary's child.

"She's called the Angel, but her name is Calantha. She doesn't have wings because she's really just a lady." Jared sounded satisfied by that fact.

Calantha could not imagine why.

"But I thought she was an angel. That's what Deanna's mama said. I wanted to meet the angel." The child's voice, so quiet at first, had risen in distress, and Calantha found herself moving forward without conscious thought.

"I am not a real angel, I'm afraid. I'm just a lady, like Jared said." She stopped in front of the man and child, giving a full curtsy. "It's a pleasure to meet you, Hannah."

The little girl returned her curtsy, her dimpled legs bending in awkward imitation, and her dark eyes fixed on Calantha with grave consideration. "You're pretty like an angel."

"Thank you. So are you."

Hannah thought that over for several seconds before saying, "I don't think angels have dark hair, but maybe they do."

Calantha nodded, maintaining her usual serious demeanor. "I'm quite sure of it."

Suddenly, Hannah's lower lip began to tremble, and she turned to hide her face against Jared's leg. Her small shoulders began to shake.

Calantha's heart squeezed in her chest. She had no experience with children. Had she done something to hurt or frighten the little girl? She turned horrified eyes to Jared, but he was not looking at her. His concerned countenance was focused entirely on the child.

He lifted her until her tiny face was at the same level as his own. "What's the matter, sweet?"

"I wanted her to talk to Mama, but she's just a lady," she said on a quiet sob.

Calantha felt like crying herself.

"I'm sorry I'm not a real angel," she said, feeling as if she had let the child down. "I wish I could talk to her, too. I miss her."

Hannah turned her head to look at Calantha. "You knew Mama?"

"She was my dearest friend. You remind me of her."

"I do?" Hannah looked doubtful.

"Yes. The shape of your mouth is the same. You must look just like her when you smile."

"Mama was pretty when she smiled."

"Yes. She was."

Hannah's eyes filled with tears again. "I miss her."

Calantha touched the child without conscious thought, rubbing her back gently. "I'm sure you do, darling. I'm sorry. Truly. I'd like to be your friend, like I was hers, if you'll let me. Maybe that will help us both miss her less."

Hannah reached out and touched Calantha's cheek.

The caress of small fingers brought tears to Calantha's eyes, and she blinked them away.

Hannah turned back to face Jared. "She's nice," she said before shyly burying her face in his neck.

"Will you stay for tea?" Calantha asked Jared.

He looked at her for several seconds, his expression indecipherable. Finally, he said, "We'd like that very much, wouldn't we, Hannah?"

The little girl nodded against Jared's neck. "I like tea with lots of sugar," she whispered without looking at Calantha.

"Then I shall make sure you have as much as you like."

With his usual impeccable timing, Thomas arrived at that moment with the tea tray. Jared seated Hannah on the sofa next to him, while Calantha took her usual seat. It took some time, but Hannah slowly warmed up to Calantha

enough to smile. She liked the rose candy, which pleased
Calantha, who discovered she very much wanted the little
girl to like her.

"How come we don't got rose candy, Jared?"

"We'll have to get Calantha's recipe, imp." He turned to
Calantha. "I've got one for rose honey we use to cure our
hams. We could trade."

The teasing light in his eyes made her breathless, and she
waited a moment to answer. He raised his brow in question,
and she said, "That sounds heavenly."

"Then it should be more than fitting for an angel."

Calantha dropped her gaze and busied herself with the
tea tray. She wasn't an angel, and she wasn't a marble statue,
but she didn't expect Jared to understand that.

After that, Calantha endeavored to spend several hours
a day in Hannah's company. She saw so much of her friend
in the small child. Mary's intelligence and sweet spirit
lived in her daughter. So did her mischievous sense of humor, though Calantha only saw glimpses of it in the girl
still grieving her mother's loss. There was nothing of Deveril's cruel nature in Hannah, but she did exhibit his arrogance on occasion.

Not that Calantha was entirely convinced she hadn't
learned that trait from the man raising her.

Although the frequent visits with Hannah meant spending time with Jared, Calantha avoided him as much as possible. She could not forget that he saw her as no more than
a marble statue.

However, just as being with Hannah brought Mary to
mind, so, too, did the little girl keep Jared at the forefront
of Calantha's thoughts. He was the center of her world, and
she talked about him constantly. In addition, his influence
could be seen strongly in her character. Her stubbornness
included, or so Lady Ashton had remarked.

Calantha was inclined to believe Jared's sister, particularly at the present moment when Hannah had refused all

invitations to join the other children on a promised excursion with the Drakes.

"I want to stay and draw," she insisted obdurately.

Calantha had given her a set of pencils and a sketchbook upon her arrival that morning. She hadn't been sure such a small child would appreciate that sort of gift, but Hannah's squeal of delight had put paid to her fear.

Apparently drawing was something she'd done with her mother. Calantha had remembered Mary's love of sketching and was delighted her daughter shared it from such a young age.

"But you must come with us," Mrs. Drake said. "The other grown-ups have all gone on a ride, and Jared is with your Uncle Lucas."

Hannah set her mouth in a mutinous line, but it was the sad vulnerability in her dark eyes that tugged at Calantha's heart.

"I will stay with her. I love to draw as well."

"Are you certain you do not mind? Irisa and her guests should be back from their ride in less than an hour."

"I will enjoy the time with Hannah, unless you think Jared would mind me watching her?"

"Why should he?" Mrs. Drake asked and then took her leave with warm thanks.

"Can I sit in your lap while we draw?" Hannah asked. "Mama used to let me."

Too choked with emotion at that reminder, Calantha merely nodded and settled Hannah on her knees. It felt indescribably good to have the little one cuddled up to her as she drew, and Calantha couldn't help fantasizing Hannah was hers.

But the fantasy was bittersweet, because each day brought her closer to the time when Jared would leave for his own estates and take Hannah with him.

Knowing Jared would return in time for lunch, Calantha

made herself leave when Lady Ashton arrived and offered
to take charge of Hannah.

JARED SWORE WHEN HE REALIZED THAT CALANTHA HAD
managed to call on Hannah while staying clear of him again.

The woman seated next to him for lunch, who had just
mentioned that the duchess had been to call, blanched.
"Really, my lord," she said in disapproving accents.

He frowned, but apologized. "Sorry."

She nodded, but turned her attention to the gentleman on
her other side. Jared shrugged. He had more important things
to worry about than offending one of his sister's guests.

He'd made the mistake of telling Calantha that Ashton
planned to show him an experimental crop planted by one
of his tenants on the far side of the estate that morning. She
had taken advantage of the opportunity to visit Hannah
once again when she knew he would be absent.

Damn it. She'd seen Hannah five times in the last five
days and him only twice. Why was she bent on avoiding
him? Was she still afraid of him? He would never forget
the look of terror that had turned her face the color of
parchment when he'd loomed over her in the meadow.

Damn. He still didn't understand everything that had
happened or why Calantha had withdrawn her friendship
from Mary. He wasn't likely to, either, when he never got a
chance to talk to her. She avoided him like some plague-
ridden rat. He bloody well wasn't going to put up with it.

"Milord?" a footman asked tentatively from behind his
shoulder.

Jared turned his scowl on the footman. "What?"

The servant jumped back and bumped a maid carrying a
water pitcher. The water sloshed, and the maid gasped, but
managed to regain her footing before dumping all the
pitcher's contents on one of Irisa's guests.

Used to small mishaps like this, Jared ignored it and fixed the footman with his gaze. "You wanted something."

"There's a p-problem, m-milord."

"What kind of problem?" Ashton's servants sure were a nervous bunch.

"In the nursery."

Jared slammed back his chair and jumped to his feet. "Is anything the matter with Hannah? What's going on, man? Spit it out."

The footman seemed to have lost the power of speech, his mouth opening and closing several times, with no words coming out.

"Calm down, Jared. You're scaring the poor man senseless," Thea chastised him in practical tones.

He thought the servant was already pretty senseless, but didn't say so. No reason to offend his sister, Irisa, on her choice of household staff, and she was bound to overhear, even if she was sitting at the other end of the table. Just look at the way she was already glaring at him.

"I'm not trying to scare him. He said something's wrong in the nursery. I'm just trying to find out what." To hell with it. He turned to leave the dining room. He'd go to the nursery himself. By the time the footman told him what the problem was, he'd be old and gray.

"She's gone, my lord."

The footman's words stopped Jared in his tracks, and he spun around to face the hapless servant. "What the bloody hell do you mean, *gone*?"

Suddenly both his sisters were crowding the footman, and his brothers by marriage were close behind. "Gone? You mean Hannah's missing?" Irisa demanded.

"Yes, milady. Gone. No one can find her. The nursery maid took Hannah and Mrs. Drake's children on a walk in the garden. She says one minute the child was there, and the next she was gone."

Jared tasted the metallic flavor of fear. "Where's the nursery maid now?"

The footman flinched. "In the library with the house-keeper, milord."

At least he managed to say it without stuttering this time.

"We'll speak to her at once," Thea said.

Jared was already on his way to the library, his family close behind. Knowing Calantha would want to know about Hannah's disappearance, he barked out the order, "Send for the duchess."

THE NURSERY MAID THREW HERSELF AT THEA WHEN they entered the library. "Oh, mistress, I don't know what's become of her. One minute she was playing peekaboo behind the trees, and the next she didn't come to my call. I thought at first she was teasing me. Despite her quiet ways, she's got an impish streak, she does, but she was gone. I'm so sorry, mistress."

The girl collapsed in sobbing hysteria against Thea's chest.

Jared turned to the footman. "The orchard has been searched?"

"Yes, milord."

"How long ago did this happen?" Ashton demanded.

"Less than an hour, milord."

"And you waited until now to tell me?" Jared could feel his rage growing.

"We searched first, but we couldn't find her."

That, at least, had already been established.

"Search the grounds again and the house. She could have wandered inside." Ashton gave the instructions like shooting bullets from a pistol.

And that is exactly what they did, to no avail. Jared was calling for his horse to expand the search when Calantha arrived riding her mare. Her usual pristine appearance was sadly askew with wisps of hair trailing down her cheeks and back. She wasn't even wearing a riding habit, and a portion of her calf showed where her morning gown had ridden up. She'd obviously come as soon as she heard the news.

"Have you found her?" she demanded as she stopped her horse in front of Jared.

"No."

Calantha flinched as if the word were a blow. "What can I do?"

"We're going to expand the search on horseback."

"I'll go."

He nodded and vaulted onto the back of his own mount, which had arrived with a stable hand. "She disappeared from the orchard," he said, taking off in that direction.

"How?" Calantha demanded of his back.

"They were playing a game of peekaboo behind the trees, and she didn't come to the nursery maid's call."

They were silent after that, their focus intent on catching any sign of the little girl's passing.

They'd ridden about fifteen minutes when Calantha shouted. "Jared! Over there!"

He looked where she was pointing, and he saw the top of a small brown head peaking behind a bush about fifty feet away.

"Hannah!" he shouted as he kneed his horse into a gallop.

Calantha's mare was right beside him.

The little head became a small body, as Hannah came out of her hiding place in the bush. He pulled his horse to an abrupt stop and jumped down. Hannah threw herself at him, and he swept her up in his arms, hugging her so tight that she squealed. He loosened his hold just enough so she could pull back and look into his face.

Her lower lip trembled. "I was scared."

He thought how far she'd wandered from the estate and said, "Me, too."

"I knew you'd find me."

Jared kissed the top of her silky head. "Calantha helped."

Hannah's head came up again, and she turned to look at the duchess. "Cali, you look funny with your hair all squiggly like that."

Cali?

Calantha grinned, and Jared just about couldn't breathe. He'd never seen her look so free and happy. "I imagine I do, not like an angel at all, hmmm?"

"You look like my Cali," Hannah responded.

She did look like a Cali, Jared decided. More of her hair had come loose from its usual coil atop her head, and her cheeks were pink with pleasure at finding Hannah. She looked delicious and wanton. It was a very good thing that he was holding Hannah, or *Cali* would find out just how tired Jared was of being avoided. And how hungry he was for her kiss.

The hunger had grown since that night in the garden. Every time he saw her, he wanted to bed her. Hell, he woke up in the middle of the night hard as a pike and wanting the same thing.

He saw the knowledge of his desire and a resultant feminine confusion in her eyes before she turned her gaze to Hannah. "How did you get so far from the house?"

"The man brung me. I didn't like him. He smelled bad."

"What man?" Jared asked, trying to keep his anger from his voice. He didn't want to scare Hannah, or make her think he was mad at her.

It occurred to him if he'd been half as careful with Calantha, she wouldn't be so bent on avoiding him.

"The one playing peekaboo in the orchard."

"She was kidnapped," Calantha whispered, her face filled with stark terror. She looked like she was going to fall right off her horse, her skin had gone so pale.

Jared shifted Hannah to one arm and used his free hand

to pull Calantha down. "Come here, sweetheart. It's going to be okay. No one hurt her, and no one is going to."

She landed against him with a thud.

"Oh, Jared." She buried her face between his chest and Hannah's small body and wrapped both arms around him, holding him almost as tightly as he had held Hannah when they found her.

They stayed that way for a long time, three people not related by blood, but irrevocably connected to each other.

SEVERAL HOURS LATER, CALANTHA SAT SILENTLY ON A settee beside Jared in the Ashton library, while he and his family discussed Hannah's misadventure.

"This is so frightening, to think some blackguard could come onto our land and kidnap a child." Lady Ashton laid a protective hand over the small protrusion of her pregnancy.

Lord Ashton's face took on a lethal cast as he laid a re-assuring hand on his wife's shoulder. "Don't worry, sweeting. We'll find whoever tried to nab Hannah."

"Damn right we will," Jared said.

He still vibrated with fury, and Calantha felt an urge to comfort him.

She curled her fingers around his forearm and squeezed. "It's not your fault," she said quietly.

He turned to meet her gaze, and she flinched at the blazing anger in his eyes. Even knowing it wasn't directed at her did not mitigate her reaction completely. But she did not move away, and that was a victory in itself.

"I bloody well feel responsible. She's mine, and some bastard thought he could take her."

Calantha wondered what it would be like to have that possessive protectiveness directed at her. Deveril had been possessive, but in a violently jealous way. It never extended to her honest protection. Certainly not from himself.

"Well, he didn't succeed, and now we need to determine

how best to handle the threat." Mr. Drake's calm voice belied the savage look in his eyes.

He'd pulled his wife into his lap upon entering the library and sat with his arms reassuringly around her. As upset as she had been that Hannah had been taken, Calantha knew that Mrs. Drake had awakened to the fear of her own children disappearing. Her husband meant to comfort, and from the calmer expression in Mrs. Drake's eyes, Calantha thought it was working.

"Hannah said the man smelled bad."

"She also said he knew her name when we questioned her later." The muscles in Jared's arm tensed under Calantha's hold.

She brushed him soothingly, but her insides were as tight as a well-strung corset. "It's almost as if he meant to take her, not just any child."

She shuddered at the thought and blinked away unfamiliar tears that seemed all too close to the surface, of late. The initial love, born of the fact that Hannah was Mary's daughter, had grown, so much that the prospect of Jared returning to his estates kept her awake nights. Not that thoughts of the often surly viscount didn't play a role in her sleeplessness as well.

"That makes no sense. Why would anyone want to kidnap her? She's just a child." Mrs. Drake's voice sounded uncertain.

"It's not as if she's heir to a great estate or something. For all anyone knows, she's Jared's by-blow, the product of a liaison with his housekeeper," Lord Ashton added.

Lady Ashton gasped. "Lucas, that's an awful thing to say. If Hannah were Jared's child, he would have married her mother."

Lord Ashton smiled at his wife. "I'm not saying I think that, sweeting. I'm saying that's what the rest of the world thinks. There's no reason for anyone to want to kidnap her, specifically."

"We don't have a lot of evidence to go on," Mr. Drake mused. "All Hannah was able to tell us was that the man had icky teeth, smelled bad, and had greasy black hair."

"She said his hair was sticky, not greasy," Mrs. Drake inserted.

Her husband shrugged. "I imagine that's what she meant."

"Are there any gypsies in the district right now?" Jared asked.

"Not that I'm aware of," Lord Ashton replied. "We can inquire in the village tomorrow."

"How did she get away?" Lady Ashton asked, looking at Jared.

It was Calantha who answered. "She said the villain stopped to relieve himself, and she ran away and hid."

Mrs. Drake scooted around in her husband's lap until she faced Calantha straight on. "There's something I don't understand in all this."

"There are a lot of things I don't understand, Thea. What in particular are you thinking of?" Lady Ashton asked.

"How the duchess fits in," Mrs. Drake replied. "Maybe I'm just being a nosy sister, but why did you send for her when Hannah turned up missing, Jared?"

"She cares about Hannah."

Mrs. Drake smiled wryly at her brother. "That's obvious, but why? How is she connected? I can't figure it out."

Calantha felt as if an entire play was going on around her and although she was on the stage, she didn't have any lines. She didn't want to expose the shame of her husband's betrayal and cruelty, and yet it seemed inevitable.

"They're going to be married, so of course she's interested in Jared's daughter." Lady Ashton sounded very certain and equally satisfied by her assertion.

"We aren't betrothed," Calantha almost shouted, in her haste to correct the mistaken impression.

Jared said nothing.

"Then why?" Mrs. Drake prodded.

There was nothing for it, Calantha realized. If she didn't tell the shameful truth, Jared's sisters were going to believe she and Jared had some sort of liaison. "My husband was Hannah's father."

There, the words were out.

But the inquisition was not over.

"Mary had an affair with the Duke of Clairborne?" Lady Ashton asked with shocked disbelief.

"No." Calantha replied.

"But then, how . . ." Lady Ashton's words trailed off, as a look of stunned horror suffused her features.

Calantha shivered from the cold that encased her heart.

"How did she end up your housekeeper, Jared?"

"She insisted on earning her keep. It was the only way I could think to keep an eye out for her."

"I don't understand," Mrs. Drake said.

"Mary was our friend when we were children, and Jared took an interest in her welfare. She was our local vicar's daughter," Irisa explained.

"You saved her," Calantha said, her focus entirely on Jared.

He frowned, his scar standing out white against his face. "I offered her a job."

"I always wondered why your housekeeper was so young," Mrs. Drake said.

"After she learned of Mary's pregnancy, my previous housekeeper did not want Mary working under her as a maid."

And Jared had opted to provide Mary a home with a well-paid job rather than allow the old biddy to have her way, Calantha surmised. He never worried about what others thought. He just did what was right. She sighed. Unlike her.

"Mary made Jared promise to tell me about Hannah

when she was dying. He kept his word, but had to make sure I was worthy of meeting her first."

Jared looked surprised, and Calantha almost smiled.

Had he not expected her to guess his reasons for seeking her out? With his sense of responsibility and honor, there would be no other option.

"So, that's why you came to my house party," Lady Ashton exclaimed. She sighed. "I had been so hoping something would come of your interest in Calantha. It's time you were married, Jared."

Calantha felt her cheeks burn as Lady Ashton's words reminded her just how unsuitable Jared found her as a potential wife.

"I agree." Jared spoke for the first time in several minutes.

Every eye in the room fixed on him.

"You agree? You mean you're going to look for a wife?" Lady Ashton demanded while Calantha's heart shriveled in her breast.

The thought of Jared married to someone else was more painful than she could ever have imagined.

"Yes. And a mother for Hannah."

Suddenly all that attention was focused on her, and Calantha valiantly tried to hold back the pain his words elicited. Not only a wife for Jared, but also a mother for the little girl she loved. She could not bear it.

Why was everyone looking at her?

The answer, of course, was that Jared was looking at her.

She stared into his eyes, her heart beating so fast she felt as if it would come right out of her chest.

"Calantha and I are going to be married."

"*Married?*" The very word sent chills down her spine. She couldn't marry again. The risk was too great. What if Jared hurt her? What if he found out about her great weakness and came to hate her? He thought she was a marble statue. It was impossible.

She jumped up from the settee. "I can't marry. *I can't.*"

Then she ran from the room, feeling as if all the demons of hell were after her. And they were . . . her own personal, private demons. Fear and cowardice.

Seven

STUNNED SILENCE REIGNED IN THE LIBRARY AF-
ter Calantha's abrupt departure.

Jared felt fury and despair well up inside, and he wanted
to smash his fist through a wall. She didn't want to marry
him. She'd run from the room like a woman terrified of being pursued by a beast.

"I could shoot her," Thea muttered, her anger reflected
in her eyes along with a concern that was a direct blow to
Jared's male ego. He didn't want his sister's pity.

Bloody hell, why had he believed Calantha was different?

"I suppose that would put her out of her misery, but it
won't help Jared," Irisa replied.

"*Her misery?* What about Jared's? How could she just
run away like that?" Thea demanded.

Irisa held Jared's gaze, her normally warm brown eyes,
penetrating and expectant. "I trust that our brother has
more sense than to allow Calantha's obvious fear to stop
him pressing his suit."

Thea jumped off her husband's lap, the dark knot of
hair tipping precariously from her abrupt movement. "He's
not a beast. She has no right to be afraid of him!"

"Of course he's not a beast," Irisa replied, her expression

much too placid in the face of Thea's wrath. "Calantha isn't afraid of him. She's afraid of marriage."

Jared felt himself tense. "What the hell do you mean?"

"You heard her. She didn't say she couldn't marry *you*, she said she couldn't get married, period." Irisa's eyes softened. "It's plain as pudding that she's enthralled by you and adores Hannah."

"She's been avoiding me for almost a week. That's not the way a woman *enthralled* acts."

So why the hell had he announced they were getting married? It had just seemed right, and maybe he was a little desperate. He didn't want to give up Hannah. He couldn't, and he wanted to take care of Calantha. He had to admit that he had tried to manipulate her by announcing their upcoming marriage in front of others, believing it would prevent her from saying no.

He'd been wrong.

Thea cupped her chin with one hand, while her other arm crossed her waist and gripped the opposite elbow. "If Irisa's right and the duchess is afraid of marriage, then of course she would avoid you. You represent a threat to her independence, precisely because she cares."

Drake stood and cupped the back of his wife's neck. "You should know, my love."

His sister's cheeks turned a delicate shade of pink. Jared had never seen Thea blush before. She was bloody self-possessed for a woman.

"Pierson is right. I was terrified of marriage, and him in particular," she admitted.

"You were afraid of Drake?" Irisa asked, sounding every bit as fascinated as Jared felt.

Thea nodded. "I had promised Mama not to marry a man like Langley."

"But Drake is nothing like Papa," Irisa exclaimed.

"I know that now, but I feared his strength. Gentlemen have a lot of power in marriage, and women have so little.

Because of Langley's cruel jealousy, Mama was forced to flee with me to the West Indies, and she died before she got to see Jared again. I was afraid of putting myself under the same type of authority."

"You were afraid to marry because of our father's base actions?" Jared asked, trying to put everything straight in his mind.

"Yes."

How much more would Calantha fear marriage after being wed to a monster like the duke? "You really think Calantha is more afraid of marriage than she is of me?"

Thea shook her head. "No. I think she's terrified of you because she's tempted. She looked devastated when Irisa started talking about you finding a wife. Now that I'm not so angry and am thinking more clearly, it's obvious to me that she's more than enthralled. I think she loves you."

Jared discounted the last as romantic fantasy on his sister's part, but he considered the rest of what she'd said. If Calantha really did fear marriage, then perhaps she did not fear him. How had she put it in the meadow when they were talking? She had learned to fear a man's strength and his anger. She had judged him by his emotion, not his character.

Bloody hell. Even he could see that implied she thought his character was sound, not something to be feared.

He assumed her husband had taught her the other fear. Would it be any surprise that he had taught her to fear marriage as well? Thea was right. Women had very little power in marriage, and even less protection when married to a monster.

"Isn't it all the same thing?" he asked. "If she doesn't trust me enough not to hurt her, then it's fear of me she's facing, not just marriage."

Thea reached out and touched him. "Perhaps it is, a little. Maybe she's afraid to trust you."

Jared looked at his sisters and considered what both his

brothers by marriage had gone through to woo them. It
sounded like Drake had had every bit as bad a time of it
as Ashton. Yet they hadn't given up, and he wouldn't either.
He had more to lose. He wanted Calantha, but he loved
Hannah like his own daughter, and his honor wouldn't allow him to keep her if Calantha insisted on raising her.

He had to keep his promise to Mary.

"YOUR GRACE, LORD RAVENSWOOD REQUESTS THE PLEA-
sure of your company in the drawing room."

Calantha didn't look up from the sweet basil she was re-
potting. Evenings were usually reserved for study, but she
could not face the empty parlor or her books. Not after
Jared's announcement that afternoon.

She didn't think twice before saying, "Please tell the
viscount that I am not at home."

She could not see him. She would have to apologize for
her bad-mannered behavior, but not now. She didn't have
the strength to face him now.

Tears burned her eyes, but she blinked them away. She'd
been a watering pot for the last hour or more, and she
couldn't stand it. She had to shore up her defenses, bring
back the wall of ice that protected her from the pain now
shredding her heart.

Thomas did not reply, but she could sense that he had
not left either. "Your grace?"

"Yes, Thomas?"

"Are you certain you wish me to send the viscount
away?"

No, her heart screamed. *Yes*, her mind demanded.

"I am quite certain," she replied.

"But, your grace . . ."

Calantha finally looked up from her efforts and beheld
her perfectly correct butler dithering. His eyes were filled
with concern, and he clearly did not want to tell Jared she

was not at home. He had been there when she tore from the house, demanding her mount after news of Hannah's disappearance reached her.

Thomas had also been there when she returned, her eyes awash with tears he had never seen her shed.

"Please, Thomas. I am not up to company this evening."

"But your grace, perhaps the viscount . . ." he let his voice trail off, obviously not certain how to proceed and maintain his dignity as a butler of the household. Proper servants did not meddle in the affairs of their employers.

"Thank you for your concern, but I must insist that you send the viscount on his way."

Thomas finally nodded and turned to go.

She almost called him back, but she bit down on the impulse with ruthless effort.

She turned back to the sweet basil, trying to focus on its aromatic scent and the cool dirt beneath her fingers. She did not want to think of Jared, or the prospect of him marrying. She knew what had prompted him this afternoon. Pity. He knew she'd come to love Hannah and in his typical heroic fashion, he'd offered her the chance to raise the little girl. She couldn't take it. Her fear of marriage was too great.

Besides, Jared deserved a wife worthy of him, a wife who did not have her black past, her terrible flaws. He would find one, too. He wanted a mother for Hannah, and he had a duty to his line to produce heirs. *Heirs.* Another woman bearing his child, his children. Calantha's hands clenched, and before she'd realized what she'd done, she had crushed several healthy leaves on the basil plant.

"Much more treatment like that, and your plant's going to start avoiding you."

She whirled around to face him. *"Jared."*

"Were you expecting someone else?"

"No, but I told Thomas to tell you that I was not at home." Why she had expected Jared to tamely accept the socially acceptable dismissal, she could not fathom. He did what he wanted, and right now, he clearly wanted to see her.

"Yes. I know, but puttering in your conservatory hardly constitutes being away from home."

She frowned at him. He knew what the phrase meant. "I am not up to company this evening, Jared."

Particularly not his.

"Not even if it's the man you're going to marry?"

"I'm not going to marry you," she blurted out with no more finesse than she had used earlier.

"On the contrary, Cali, you are going to be my wife and the mother of my children."

He could have no idea how appealing both roles were to her, but not appealing enough to compensate for her fear.

"Don't call me Cali," she said, because it was a simpler problem to address than his insistence that they would marry.

"Hannah does."

"Hannah is a child."

"And I'm a man."

"Yes." An incredible man. Even now, as upset as she was, she longed to throw herself against him, to experience the wonder of his lips once again.

He came closer, and she could see the brown depths of his eyes. Their warmth seared her. "You want to be Hannah's mother."

"Yes." There was no use denying it, and besides, she'd promised never to lie to him.

"Then the only problem remaining is that of you being my wife."

"Yes."

"Am I really so horrible a prospect that you can't stand the thought of being married to me, Cali?"

He'd been steadily coming closer and now stood less than a foot away. His body's heat reached out to wrap around her, touching her feminine desire and heart all at once.

"No." The word came out a whisper, but he heard it.

"Then why won't you marry me?"

She tried to rally her defenses, but his nearness overwhelmed her. Finally, in desperation, she said, "You think I'm a marble statue."

He shook his head and reached out to grab both her arms. He wore no gloves, and she felt the warm strength of his fingers against the bare skin of her upper arms. She almost stopped breathing at the pleasure of it. Such a simple touch, and yet for her, who had been touched more by Jared in the preceding days than by everyone in her life combined for the preceding six years, the sensation was almost unbearable.

"You're wrong."

His words filtered through the sensual haze beginning to surround her. "Please, don't lie to me. I know. I heard your sister talking about it with her husband. You told her you didn't want to marry a marble statue."

"I don't. I want to marry you."

She stood completely still in his grasp and knew she had to tell him everything. If she didn't, he would not give up this unthinkable idea of marriage.

"Clairborne called me a marble statue. He said I was empty and useless, that my beauty was all I had to redeem me, but it wasn't enough."

Jared's eyes narrowed in anger. "The man was a fool."

She shook her head. "He was cruel, but he was right. I am empty. I'm not strong like you, Jared. I let cowardice prompt me to push Mary away. When she needed me, she did not come to me because she'd learned the truth, too. I failed her."

"She loved Hannah with all her heart."

Calantha did not doubt the truth of that statement. "Yes."

"She wanted you to raise her daughter. She wanted me to promise to bring Hannah to you. Does that sound like a woman who thought you were empty or worthless?"

A small spark of warmth unfurled deep inside of her. "I thought she wanted you to tell me about Hannah."

"That's all I would promise to do, but she wanted me to bring Hannah to you. She believed you were worthy to raise her daughter."

Calantha felt a heady sense of pleasure at the knowledge, but it could not make up for the rest. "I'm glad, but she didn't know everything. If she had, she would not have made such a generous gesture toward me."

She pulled away from Jared's grip, and he let her go. She turned and fingered a small yellow rosebud. She did not want to see Jared's expression change to one of disgust as he learned her secret. "My cowardice caused the death of a young maid."

Taking a deep, fortifying breath, she went on. "It was winter, almost Christmas. Clairborne had insisted on throwing a lavish house party, even though my parents had been dead for less than a year. We'd invited several important members of the *ton* and, of course, family. We had an upstairs maid, a sweet girl named Amy. One night we threw a ball, and Amy was up very late helping ladies prepare for bed after the ball. She was summoned early the next morning by an elderly marchioness, a dragon of a woman. I'm not certain exactly what happened, but the end result was that Amy tore one of the marchioness's silk petticoats."

She wrapped her arms around her waist, trying to hold back the cold. "It was hardly important. A woman of that position has dozens of such things, but the marchioness was angry, and she told me. I apologized and offered to replace the garment. The dragon wasn't happy, but I thought that was the end of it. I was wrong. She told Deveril what had happened, and he instructed the housekeeper to dismiss the maid. He turned her out in the freezing cold. He wouldn't even allow her a ride to the village."

Lost in the horrifying memories, she didn't hear Jared's

approach, but suddenly his hands were there on her shoulders.

He pressed his thumbs against her neck. "Shh, it's over."

"But it's not. Not in my mind. I can still see her pale cheeks. It was awful. I was afraid to argue with Deveril in front of the servants. I knew he would become furious if I did, and I feared my own punishment. I was such a coward. I did not approach him until later, but he would not listen. God forgive me, but I waited until my duties as hostess gave me an opportunity, and then I took the carriage out. We found Amy a mile from the house, nearly frozen. I tried to save her, but I couldn't. I nursed her through the night, but she died."

The cold came, but Jared's hands on her shoulders stopped it from drowning her. "It wasn't your fault, Cali."

"I didn't even have as much power as the housekeeper in my own home, Jared. I let my fear of Deveril stop me from going after Amy in time to do any good. I killed her with my cowardice."

Jared spun her around to face him, and he shook her. "You aren't responsible. You tried to protect the maid, but that damn marchioness and your devil of a husband wouldn't let you."

He didn't understand. "I should have gone after her sooner."

"And then what? Faced your husband's wrath and had him put her out again?"

She hadn't considered that. "I could have hidden her."

"Were your other servants as afraid of him as you were?"

"Yes."

"Then they would have told. Face it, Cali, you did what you could."

"It wasn't enough."

"Sometimes it's not. You have to accept that. I tried to save Mary, but she just got more and more sick."

"But it wasn't your fault she was sick in the first place."

He shrugged. "I still felt responsible."

He would. "You're so strong, Jared. Can't you understand? I'd make you a terrible wife. I'm too weak."

"If you don't marry me, I lose Hannah."

"No." He couldn't let the little girl go. She was just like his own daughter. It would be too cruel.

"I have no choice. It's what Mary wanted."

"But she was wrong."

"No, she wasn't, Cali. You'll make a fine mother."

Calantha could not stand the look of vulnerability on Jared's face. She would not take his child away from him. "I won't do it. I refuse."

"You can't. You're as bound by your honor as I am by mine."

It wasn't fair. It wasn't right, but he spoke the truth. She would not deny Mary's last request, any more than Jared would. Was there no way out of this tangle?

"I *can't* marry again, Jared. The risk is too great."

"You think I would treat you like he did?"

"No. I don't *believe* it, but I'm afraid," she admitted.

"Then he wins again. He's made you afraid of marriage, and I lose Hannah because of it."

"No," she whispered, but she knew Jared spoke the truth.

If she refused to marry him, he would insist on following through on Mary's last wishes and leave Hannah with Calantha. And Hannah would lose the only father she'd ever known—a man superior in every way to the one who had sired her. Calantha would not let her cowardice result in another grave sin. She could not. No matter what her personal risk, she wasn't going to live under the shadow of fear and continue to hurt those she cared about. Not Hannah. Not Jared.

"I'll marry you, if you're sure you want me."

"Oh, I want you all right, Cali."

He was talking about the marriage bed. She'd have to tell him the truth about that, too, and when she did, would he change his mind?

"Deveril said I didn't know how to be a duchess, and he was right. I learned, though. He made sure of it. But I don't know how to be a woman. He couldn't teach me that, Jared. I'm not sure anyone can."

She admitted her greatest fear, that she had lost her humanity married to a monster, but Jared only smiled. "You're all the woman I need."

If only she could believe that, but Clairborne had made sure she knew how very lacking she truly was. "I'm not responsive, Jared. Deveril said I was frigid."

"You were so bloody responsive when I kissed you in the garden that I almost stripped you naked and took you right there. I want you, Cali, and I can make you want me."

She didn't doubt it. She wanted him right now, but it was the doing that frightened her. "What if I can't satisfy you?"

"It's my job to make sure you do, and I will, Cali, I will."

She shivered, and he felt it since his hands still held her by the arms.

He smiled, his eyes glinting with a wicked gleam. "Come here, *mon enfant ange*."

Then she was flat against his chest, his mouth soft and hard against hers at the same time. It felt so good. So overwhelming. Did he have any idea of the power he wielded with his lips? She wanted to stay that way for the rest of her life, with her mouth being hotly devoured by his.

She moaned as her legs lost their ability to hold her up, and she sagged against him.

He released her arms to clasp her waist and lifted her until her slipper-shod feet dangled several inches above the floor. He moved his hand to a most intimate hold on her bottom, molding her body against his in a scandalous fashion.

She should protest. They were not married. Not yet, but it was so delicious, this feeling of her softness pressed against the muscular ridges of his flesh.

She buried her hands in his hair, thrilled that she had left her gloves off to plant the basil. She could feel the silky texture of his hair and the warmth of his head. She let her hungry fingers explore the feel of him. His head was big, like the rest of him, his forehead hard. She brushed his eyebrows over and over, loving the contrast of his hair against smooth skin. Then she moved to his cheeks. He stilled, pulling his mouth away as her hand contacted the jagged lines on one side of his face. She delicately followed each line evidencing the old wound and his bravery on his sister's behalf.

"You're beautiful," she couldn't help whispering.

His eyes closed, and he swallowed.

Unable to stop herself, she leaned her head forward and traced the paths of raised flesh first with her lips, and then when he did not rebuke her, with the very tip of her tongue.

He shuddered, and she gently kissed his jaw just below the scars. "You are so good, Jared. Every time I see these marks, I want to touch you to see if you are real, if a man like you truly exists."

"I'm real, all right." He shifted their positions and rubbed the juncture of her thighs intimately against his hardened ridge.

She gasped. "Please, do that again."

He groaned and did as she asked, this time thrusting his hips against her while slamming his mouth onto hers with so much power she felt bruised and elated at the same time. He wanted her. He truly wanted her.

When he pressed against the seam of her lips with his tongue, she opened them without thought. Oh, yes. It felt so good. She sucked on his tongue, like he'd taught her, and he swayed. He lowered them to the conservatory floor without breaking the connection of their mouths, lying on his back, her body on top of his.

She had no idea it could be like this, that a man would allow a woman to lie on top of him while they kissed. She liked it, a great deal. It made her feel bold, and she lowered her hands from his head to his chest, madly attacking the buttons of his waistcoat. She wanted to feel the heat of his skin, to touch the rippling muscles of his chest.

She got the first two buttons undone, and then he did something with his hand below the curve of her bottom and she arched toward him. Her femininity pressed against his masculine hardness, and pleasure shot through her. She moved just the tiniest bit and felt the pleasure again.

"Easy, Cali, or we're going to have our wedding night before our wedding."

She stilled at the harsh tone in his voice, hearing it more than the words he'd uttered. Had she done something wrong? "I'm sorry."

"Bloody hell. Don't apologize. You make me feel like a randy buck getting his first taste of a woman, but I don't want to take you for the first time on your conservatory floor."

Was that all? Did he think she cared where they made love as long as they actually did it? "It doesn't matter."

His hand brushed along her backside and down her thighs. "It matters, all right, but I'm having a bloody difficult time trying to remember why."

She undid another button on his waistcoat and kissed the underside of his chin. "Then don't."

She'd never felt like this before, and she was terrified if they stopped, she never would again. She released the last button and pushed aside the brocade before laying her hands against the heat of his chest. Two small, hard nubs pressed against her fingers, and she circled them.

He groaned, and his hips lurched up toward her body, hitting that pleasure-intense spot once again. Incredible sensation coiled tight in her belly, and she pressed down-ward, wiggling just a bit to maximize the contact. She had left off her petticoats due to the heat, and only one thin layer of muslin and lawn separated her tender flesh from the hard-ness pressing against it through his breeches. She wanted to kiss him again, but she also wanted to taste his skin. Decid-ing on the latter, she tore open his shirt, hearing buttons pop as she did so.

He laughed, the sound guttural and tight.

She didn't care.

She lowered her mouth to his chest and kissed him. It wasn't enough. She licked him and tasted salty manliness. She spied the dark nub she'd been touching a moment ago and closed her lips around it. Suddenly Jared was thrusting up against her in a steady motion, his hand pressed hard on her bottom. Each heavy thrust brought incredible sensation to her most feminine place, and she never, ever wanted it to end.

Then his free hand cupped her breast. She arched her lower body against his while thrusting her breast more fully against his hand. He tugged down the bodice of her gown and exposed her curved flesh. Taking her nipple between his thumb and forefinger, he rolled gently then tugged. She screamed against his chest, and the coiling tension in her lower body exploded like gunpowder lit with a match.

Her cries were drowned out by his mighty roar as he held her almost painfully tight against him.

She collapsed against him, her body feeling boneless with pleasure. So this was what it meant to be a woman. "I thought it required being naked," she murmured against his hair-roughened chest.

His laughter made her feel as if she were lying on a rumbling mountain. "It's better naked."

"If it is, I don't think I'll survive the experience."

"I'm not certain I will either. I've never climaxed in my

breeches before. I should be embarrassed, but you're so bloody hot, *mon ange*, that I'm blaming it all on you."

She felt her cheeks warm and was grateful for the shadowed light in the conservatory that hid the evidence of her embarrassment from him. He acted so casually about something she found cataclysmic.

Then he went still. "Cali?"

"Yes?"

"You said you *thought* you had to be naked."

"Yes."

"Does that mean you don't know?"

She buried her face against his chest and nodded in shame.

"You mean he never touched you?"

"He touched me . . . a few times, but we never . . . He wouldn't . . . He said I was too frigid," she confessed, humiliation making her voice low.

"He hurt you, didn't he?"

"Yes, but the words left deeper scars than his fists."

"Damn him to hell." It sounded like he meant the curse in its most literal interpretation.

"I felt like such a failure."

Jared sat up, adjusting her on his lap, his expression grim. "By making you feel lacking, Clairborne felt bigger than the sorry bastard that he was. It was part and parcel of the abuse he used to control you and keep you feeling inferior. He was a sadistic blackguard who got a thrill out of marrying the most beautiful woman he'd ever seen and then convincing her she had no feminine value, when in reality, he was the one incapable of being a man."

"He had mistresses. He wasn't incapable."

"I didn't say incapable of sex. I said incapable of being a man. He was nothing short of a monster. Pity the women he took to his bed and be grateful the sickness in his mind kept him from taking you. I know that I thank God for it."

"You're not worried I'll be too cold for you?"

He laughed long and loudly. "*Mon ange*, after what we just did, there's no bloody way you're too cold. Clairborne was a fool and a bastard, but I can't say I'm sorry for it. You're mine."

Eight

THE FIRST READING OF THE BANNS, TWO DAYS
after Calantha agreed to marry Jared, had coin-
cided with the end of Lady Ashton's house party and her
guests' departure. That undoubtedly accounted for the fact
that the plans for the wedding between Lord Beast and the
Angel did not spread in the district until after the second
reading of the banns, a week later.

Which had given her a few days' reprieve before dealing
with the Clairbornes, Calantha thought as Thomas informed
her early Monday afternoon that the duke and duchess
awaited her pleasure in the drawing room.

"Thank you, Thomas. I must go to my room and tidy myself. Tell them I will be with them shortly." She had been
preparing her plants for transfer to Raven Hall, and although
she had worn an apron, her dress's hem was marred with dirt.
She would have to change, as well as put her hair to rights.

Entering her bedchamber a few minutes later, she stifled
the dread snaking through her. Remembering the ungovern-
able rage in Henry's eyes on his last visit was bad enough,
but the prospect of listening to a tirade on family responsibility from her sister-in-law was even more daunting.

Thomas, with his usual efficiency, had summoned her

maid before informing her of the Clairbornes' arrival, and
a new gown had already been laid out.

Jenny stepped forward and began undoing the tapes on
the back of Calantha's bodice. "The packing's coming along
nicely, your grace."

"Yes." Calantha stepped out of her gown, her attention
split between the upcoming interview with her in-laws and
Jenny's comment. The packing was coming along surprisingly well, but then it seemed when Jared decided a thing
was to be done, it got done quickly. "You won't mind moving to Raven Hall will you, Jenny?"

"No, your grace. I'm pleased to see another part of
England."

Calantha allowed Jenny to drop a gown of sky-blue
muslin over her head. The three-quarter-length sleeves, simple straight skirt, and square neckline gave it an almost me-
dieval look. "Thomas appears happy with the arrangements
as well."

"Yes, your grace. I do believe so, but he's a dignified
one, he is. His granddaughter is happy as can be to move
in, and not ashamed to show it. She and her three kiddies
were growing out of her little cottage, they were."

Thomas would stay on as butler-caretaker, while his
granddaughter would move in with him to act as housekeeper and cook on the occasions when Jared and Calantha
came to visit Jared's sister at Ashton Manor. Cook had
asked to retire, wanting to move to Kent to be with her son
and his family. Jenny, the housemaid, and the lone stable
boy would be coming with Calantha to Raven Hall. The
groundskeeper, a man even older than Thomas with no
family, would stay on to care for the gardens.

And so her upcoming marriage would ensure the well-
being of those who depended on her.

Jenny pulled the pins out from Calantha's hair and gave
it a swift, expert brushing, making the blond strands glis-
ten in the early afternoon light. The maid then braided it,

wrapping it around Calantha's head like a coronet. It wasn't the usual fashion, but it complemented Calantha's face.

When dealing with the Clairbornes, the only advantage she had was her angelic looks, and Calantha was grateful to Jenny for making the most of them. "Thank you."

Jenny surprised her by reaching out and patting her arm. "It will be all right, your grace. He'll be'ave with his wife around. You'll have no need for tea trays and the like today."

Unsure how to handle the reassurance and obvious concern of her maid, Calantha merely nodded.

If only Jared were here.

Not that he was likely to be. After she had agreed to marry him and they had shared that amazing experience in her conservatory, she had seen very little of him. He had given more instructions to her servants than she had in the past week.

He, Lord Ashton, and Mr. Drake devoted every spare minute to tracking down the blackguard who had tried to kidnap Hannah. Thus far, they had met with no luck.

Hannah's description had been that of a frightened four-year-old and not very precise. Although, she had remembered that the man had a *picture* of a dragon on his forearm. As identifying marks went, a tattoo wasn't all that helpful, because it would be too easy for a man to pull his shirt-sleeves down to hide it, but it was something.

Calantha understood Jared's preoccupation with the search, but grew increasingly nervous about her upcoming nuptials when he made no effort to be in her company at all. She wasn't a fool. She realized he did not love her. He was marrying her so he could honorably keep Hannah.

After the incident on the floor in her conservatory, however, she had believed he at least desired her. Yet there had been no indication of it in the days since, and she had begun to wonder if she'd imagined Jared's incredible reaction to her touch. She could not stomach the prospect that Jared might find her cold as a marble statue after all.

It seemed unlikely after the intimacy they had shared, but she readily admitted she had too little knowledge of gentlemen to know how important what they had experienced together would be to Jared.

Perhaps, now that he'd had a chance to consider the matter, he resented his need to marry her. She had tried without success to think of a solution to their dilemma that did not include a forced marriage between the two of them. Jared had made it clear that, in his mind at least, marriage to her was the only honorable way for him to keep Hannah.

She had been unwilling to allow her fear of the married state to rob him of his daughter, and she would not allow her fear of him coming to despise her do it either. She had lived six years under the shadow of fear.

She would not live that way any longer.

"AH, SO, YOU HAVE FINALLY DEIGNED TO HONOR US WITH your company," Ellen remarked as Calantha entered the parlor a few minutes later.

Her first reaction to her sister-in-law's unsubtle criticism was to apologize for keeping her and the duke waiting, but Calantha bit back the words. When dealing with a Clairborne, one must think before speaking, she reminded herself. An apology would imply she had done something wrong and give Ellen an edge in the upcoming interview.

Calantha curtsied without lowering her gaze from Ellen's. "If you had sent word of your impending arrival, I would have made certain I was ready to receive you."

Henry, who had risen from the brocade chair upon her arrival, bowed. Ellen did not rise, but she inclined her head in an arrogant gesture of greeting. She was a good three inches shorter than Calantha, but she held herself with such noble bearing, the disparity in their sizes went unnoticed.

"We did not have time to send word ahead. Indeed,

gossip concerning you reached us late yesterday evening, and Henry and I rushed down here out of our deep concern for a sister."

Remembering the last *concerned* visit from her brother-in-law, Calantha remained mute, but she shot Henry a considering look.

He remained standing, waiting for her to take her seat and looking for all the world as if nothing untoward had ever occurred between them. "We've heard the most preposterous tale, and I tried to assure my wife that it is patently false, but she's overset and insisted on coming straight down to assure herself of the truth in the matter."

A duchess did not become overset. She might privately grieve or worry, but she did not express those emotions openly, not even before family. Did Henry not realize that pertinent fact? Calantha knew Ellen did. Her sister-in-law did not look in the least discomposed, her patrician features set in their usual dignified lines.

Taking a seat on the settee opposite her in-laws, Calantha asked, "What matter might that be?"

"The matter of your so-called marriage to Lord Beast. I told Ellen you had already set my mind at rest on the matter, but she's worried about how such a scandalous bit of gossip could have gotten started in the first place."

Again Calantha saw no sign of worry in the other woman's expression or mannerisms, however, Henry sounded angry. Very, very angry.

Calantha found her response to that anger to be defiance, rather than her former instinct to placate. "I imagine it got started when the banns were read this last Sunday and the one before." She watched with interest as both the duke and the duchess grappled with her words.

"The banns have already been read?" Ellen asked faintly, her perfect composure cracking slightly for the first time in their acquaintance.

Calantha nodded.

"Twice?" Henry confirmed, sounding none too steady himself.

"Yes."

"Have you set a date for the wedding?" Ellen asked, her tone a bit stronger.

"We are to be wed a week from today." Calantha still found that fact somewhat overwhelming and made no attempt to soften the truth for her family by marriage.

"That's impossible," exclaimed Ellen.

"Not at all. The third reading of the banns is scheduled for this upcoming Sunday."

"But there is no way a proper wedding for a duchess can be arranged in such a short time." Ellen sounded truly shocked, and Calantha almost pitied her.

"But I will no longer be a duchess. As of a week from today, I will be a mere viscountess." That should please her successor to the title of Duchess of Clairborne, almost as much as Calantha herself was pleased by the prospect. The fact that she would never again have to respond to the hated title of duchess or your grace filled her with delight. "I am content with the arrangements."

"Even a viscountess marries with more ceremony than a hurried affair that gives the impression haste is *necessary*."

Of course. Ellen's first concern would be with the appearance of the wedding. After all, Calantha was still a Clairborne. The prospect of gossip of the sort she was implying would distress the current Duchess of Clairborne excessively. However, Calantha found the concept that she would be the subject of speculation that she had to marry due to her virtue being compromised almost humorous.

She'd been married two years, and the closest she had come to any sort of intimacy had been with Jared . . . fully clothed and nowhere near a bedroom.

"This is intolerable. As the primary trustee of your funds since my brother's death, surely I would have been notified when marriage settlements were drawn up." Henry's face had turned a dangerous shade of red.

Calantha hoped Jenny was right that his wife's presence would prevent the loss of his temper. She instinctively moved to the edge of the sofa, from which she could stand quickly.

"We haven't drawn up any settlements. I'm not sure Jared plans to do so."

Shocked, she realized she hadn't even considered it. She should have been worried about retaining ownership of her home to guarantee a certain level of independence, but the thought hadn't even entered her mind. She trusted Jared's integrity. Hadn't he agreed to marry a woman he did not love in order to fulfill his obligation to a dead woman? He would surely keep his promises to her.

Besides, her marriage settlements had hardly protected her in Deveril's death. Henry still controlled her money and in turn, tried to use it to control her.

"A lady does not enter a marriage without first insuring her future and that of her potential offspring," Ellen said.

"As my future was insured by my settlements with Deveril?" Calantha asked with dry sarcasm.

"Exactly," Henry answered for his wife, missing Calantha's sarcasm entirely.

"I am content to go without that kind of insurance."

"Then you are a fool." Henry's voice had risen, and Ellen gave him a sharp look. He brought himself under control with obvious effort. "You cannot possibly trust Lord Beast. As soon as you marry, your funds become his. I will have no authority to protect your assets any longer."

Calantha stood and glared down at her brother-in-law. She had no doubt that the only true concern Henry had was over the fact that he would no longer be able to threaten her with a decrease in her allowance to force her to his will.

She didn't tax him with that truth, however, instead focusing on something far more important to her. "You will cease using that awful term to refer to my fiancé, or you will leave my home at once."

The tenuous control Henry had on his temper slipped. "How dare you threaten us? You were nothing but the penniless daughter of an unknown clergyman before you met Deveril. You dare to take on airs of importance when you are nothing more than what my brother made you!"

"He made me a duchess," she acknowledged, "but I would rather have married a stable boy than suffer the ugliness of two years as the Duke of Clairborne's wife."

Henry shot to his feet, his rage palpable, and opened his mouth to blast her, but he didn't get the chance.

"Clairborne." Ellen's voice cracked like a whip, though she spoke in the well-modulated tones of a perfect duchess. "Remember your position."

Calantha could not make herself back up even an inch, and her eyes fixed on Henry with her fury, although she sensed her own position was a precarious one.

"Sit down, Duke. You will give Calantha's servants fodder for gossip of the basest nature."

Surprisingly, Henry listened to his wife and sat. This woman truly would have made a better wife to Deveril.

Ellen spoke to Calantha, her attention firmly fixed on her spouse. "The duke and I are aware that your marriage was not as happy as it could have been, but you must understand that Henry cared deeply for his brother. Please excuse his emotional comments."

Henry nodded, visibly swallowing his anger. "I didn't mean to offend you, my dear."

Calantha refused to give in so easily. "I will have your word that you will not refer to my fiancé in an insulting fashion again," she spoke directly to her brother-in-law, ignoring Ellen's apology.

"You have it."

"I am quite shocked," Ellen said. "You have not shown the least desire to wed again in the last four years."

"I did not have the desire to remarry until I met Jared," Calantha responded in all honesty. She didn't have the desire now, but she had even less desire to hurt Jared or Hannah.

"Surely you realize that had I known you were thinking along those lines, I would have done all I could to help you find a suitable husband."

What would Ellen's reaction be if she learned her husband had made a similar offer regarding finding Calantha a paramour? She did not believe that Ellen would find his offer to warm Calantha's bed nearly as acceptable.

"I know that you do not mean to imply that the viscount is unsuitable in any way. He is, after all, heir to an earldom, and that is quite an advantageous match for the *penniless daughter of an unknown clergyman*. However, let me assure you, even as Calantha, Duchess of Clairborne, he is the only gentleman I would ever consider marrying." That also was the truth.

She did not learn what Ellen's response to her words would have been, because at that moment, Thomas announced Jared and Hannah.

Calantha turned to greet them. Jared's massive body filled the doorway, his shoulders almost touching either side of the jamb. His face wore an arrested expression, and he had not moved forward into the room. Hannah squirmed in his arms, and he let her down, his gaze fixed on Calantha.

What had put that look of intensity in his eyes?

She did not get time to ponder it as Hannah rushed across the room and threw herself at Calantha's legs, hugging with all her might. "Cali! Jared brung me to visit. Can we have tea?"

Calantha bent down to press the little girl close before releasing her. "What a lovely surprise to see you, sweeting. Of course we shall have tea."

She straightened, and her gaze collided with Jared's.

He had come near and now leaned down to kiss her

cheek. "Good afternoon, *mon ange*. I trust I am not inter-rupting."

Shocked at his casually possessive greeting, she almost reached up to press her fingers against her cheek where he had kissed her, but stopped herself from the telltale action.

"The duke and duchess are eager to meet you, Jared."

Jared smiled, and the wicked gleam of laughter in his eyes told her he didn't believe her. She found herself smiling in return, and he went still.

He reached out and brushed her bottom lip with his forefinger. "You have a very sweet smile, *mon ange*."

And it was her turn to go still, even the breath in her chest momentarily arrested.

She heard Henry's disapproving snort and felt Hannah's small fingers clutching her own, but she could not make herself look away from the warmth in Jared's eyes. She forced her lungs to take in air once again. "Thank you."

He broke eye contact to face her guests, keeping one possessive hand on her arm. "Introduce us."

"Jared, may I present the Duke and Duchess of Clair-borne?"

Jared bowed, but it was more a movement of his shoul-ders and head than his upper body. Henry was bound to be offended, just as he would be offended that she began the introductions with her fiancé rather than following propri-ety and presenting the viscount to the duke.

"This is the man I intend to wed, Lord Ravenswood." She pulled Hannah forward. "And this is Hannah."

Jared tensed. Was he thinking of what Deveril had done in siring a daughter?

Funny, but she could not even see the duke and duchess as Hannah's family. Deveril's cruelty had died with him, and Calantha would not allow the past to creep into the present to taint Hannah's life. She would not cede that power to the monster.

She turned to Hannah. "Curtsy to the duke and duchess, sweeting."

Hannah did as instructed, dipping down and raising her skirts enough to reveal her little dimpled knees. Then she straightened and turned her face up to Calantha. "Did I do it right?" she asked in a loud whisper.

"Just right, darling," Calantha assured her before leading Hannah and Jared to the sofa.

She meant to get another chair from the table in the corner for her own seat, but Jared's hand snaked out and grabbed her arm, halting her. He shifted Hannah from the sofa to his lap and pulled Calantha down beside him, pressing her close to his hard thigh because there was so little room.

Ellen's lip curled in a well-bred sneer, but she said nothing. Neither Clairborne acknowledged Hannah in any way.

"Can we have tea now?" Hannah asked.

Calantha nodded. "I'll call for the tea tray immediately."

When the tea tray arrived, Jared arranged Hannah on a cloth-covered footstool. She drank her tea, happily devouring several sugar-coated rose petals.

Ellen gave Jared a socially polite smile that did not quite reach her eyes. "My lord, we've just now learned that you intend to marry, and in only a week's time." Ellen's tone left no doubt what she thought of that plan.

"I'm sure you want to wish us happy," Jared replied, his voice steely.

Henry, who had been eyeing Jared with a certain wary caution since his arrival, immediately agreed. "Of course."

A reputation for being a beast could be a useful thing.

Ellen was not so easily cowed. "The hasty nature of the wedding will give rise to a certain amount of unpleasant gossip. Such a situation is hardly fair to our dear Calantha."

Jared turned to Calantha, his gaze probing. "Are you concerned about the gossip?"

She shook her head. "I am content with our plans as they stand."

He smiled and winked, his approval warming her.

She hardly ever felt cold anymore.

Turning back to Ellen, he said, "It will be a nine days wonder, if it is anything at all."

Ellen pinched her lips. "If you would but wait and give us sufficient time, I would be pleased to help our dear Calantha plan a wedding suitable for a duchess. She can be wed at Clairborne Park and the most notable members of the *ton* invited to the festivities."

"There would be time to draw up proper marriage settlements as well," the duke added.

"The settlements are being drawn up already. I've contacted my solicitor, and he will have the papers ready for our signature on Friday."

The news should have surprised Calantha, but it didn't. In his typical protective fashion, Jared had taken care of the matter.

"As the head of Calantha's family, I will go over the documents with my solicitor. We cannot possibly do so before Monday morning." Henry's wariness dissipated in the face of his arrogant assumption of authority over her life.

Calantha set her teacup down and clasped her hands together in her lap. "That will not be necessary."

"Don't be ridiculous, gel. It is my duty to watch out for your best interests."

Jared tensed like a predator ready to strike. "Calantha belongs to me now, and I will look out for her."

Henry's eyes narrowed with a crafty gleam. "I wouldn't want you to be deceived, Ravenswood. Calantha can bring very little to your marriage. She brought nothing to Deveril, and in his generosity he left her provided for, although she didn't give him an heir. But she's no heiress."

Calantha felt the blood rush from her face. Henry made

it sound as if her lack of a child were her fault, as if she had somehow failed Deveril.

Jared put his arm around her and squeezed her shoulders. It was totally improper behavior for a lord of the realm toward his lady, but she didn't care. She felt comforted and inched infinitesimally closer to him.

"I don't want an heiress."

But did he want her?

Jared fixed Ellen with his penetrating stare, "I need to return to my estates soon, and I have no intention of leaving Cali behind. The gossip is bound to be less severe in the event of our marriage than if I were to take her to my estates before we are wed."

Ellen's mouth dropped open, and a breath of angry air hissed from Henry, but he said nothing. It was all Calantha could do not to laugh out loud. Jared's outrageous comment had routed her in-laws quite thoroughly, and they took their leave ten minutes later.

Calantha turned to Jared after they had gone. "You have a singularly pleasing effect on the duke."

Jared's brow arched. "He didn't say much."

"Exactly." She couldn't keep the profound satisfaction over that fact out of her voice.

Jared threw his head back and laughed, the deep sound reverberating through her. She smiled in response, and he stopped laughing. "Bloody hell, I like it when you do that."

"What?"

"Smile. You don't do it enough. You're such a serious little thing."

"Hardly little." She was taller than most of the other women of her acquaintance.

He reached out and touched her cheek. "You seem tiny to me, and so bloody fragile I'm afraid to touch you sometimes."

Feeling breathless for no particular reason, she was glad Hannah had gone off to tell herself a story on the other side of the parlor and wasn't nearby to ask the reason for Calantha's sudden blush.

His hand cupped her chin. "You're so sweet."

She didn't say anything. She couldn't. She wanted him to kiss her too badly and was afraid if she opened her mouth, she'd beg him to do it.

"Don't look at me like that." He sounded angry.

She blinked and ignored the impulse to pull away from him. He didn't look angry. He looked like he wanted to kiss her, too. "How am I looking at you?"

"Like you're mine for the taking."

She was. Didn't he realize that? She closed her eyes.

"Why did you do that?"

His voice sounded very close to her ear.

"So I wouldn't look at you that way."

He swore. "You don't know what you do to me."

Then his lips were exactly where she wanted them to be . . . on hers.

Nine

CALI MELTED AGAINST HIM WITH THE FIRST touch of his lips, and Jared gave in to the urge to pull her onto his lap, which he'd been fighting since they sat down. The feel of her lithe body nestled against his hardening male flesh was almost enough to make him forget where they were and take her on the carpet.

Only the sound of Hannah's little girl jabber kept his raging desire under control.

Bloody hell, Cali felt good.

She locked her hands on his shoulders, her fingers digging into the fabric of his coat, and her mouth softened under his. He ate at her lips, feeling like a man who had been given his first taste of food after a forty-day fast.

She affected him like no other woman ever had. There was no way he could wait for her to plan a big society wedding. He'd have her in his bed soon, or go mad.

Desperate to feel her, he pulled off his gloves and cupped her neck, rubbing his thumbs across her collarbones, the only exposed flesh he could reach without scandalizing the servants and Hannah.

Squirming against him so that her breasts pressed against his chest, Cali moaned.

"Is Mama all right? She's making funny sounds." Hannah spoke from near Jared's elbow.

He stilled the movements of his hands and ripped his mouth away from Cali's. She made a sound of protest and tried to recapture his lips.

He held her in place with his hands. "Hannah wants to know if her mama is all right."

"What? Hannah?" Her gaze was as unfocused as her thoughts, and he smiled in blatant male satisfaction.

Cali wouldn't find it any easier to wait to come to his bed than he would in getting her there.

Cali's gaze sharpened and then turned misty. *"Mama?"*

"Papa said you are going to be my mama, and he is my papa. I want a mama again, but I still love my first mama. Papa said that was all right."

"Of course it is. I still love your mama, too. I always will."

He'd made the right choice bringing Cali into Hannah's life on a permanent basis. She seemed to instinctively know the right thing to say and do to comfort their daughter.

"Mama?" Hannah tugged on Cali's arm. "Are you sick? You're on Papa's lap. Sometimes I sit on his lap when I don't feel good. Are you gonna throw up?"

Jared grinned as Cali seemed to realize where she was. Her cheeks turned the color of her *Slater's Crimson* in full bloom, and she jumped off his lap. "I'm fine, sweeting. Your papa and I were just talking."

"I thought you were kissin'."

Cali's blush deepened and spread to the skin of her bosom. "Yes, well. That, too."

Hannah looked very serious. "I like kisses. May I have one, too?"

"Of course, poppet." Cali leaned down and kissed Hannah's cheek gently, turning her face to receive the child's affectionate gesture in return.

Then Hannah came over to Jared and demanded he kiss

her as well. Afterward, she lost interest in the adults and began playing with the tea things.

Cali did not return to her seat next to him on the sofa, but went to stand by the window. He got up and followed her, stopping when he stood just behind her left shoulder.

"Will you be ready to leave for Raven Hall after the wedding?"

She spun around to face him. "So soon? I had thought you would stay in the district for a while longer. You still have to find the man that tried to kidnap Hannah."

Familiar anger filled him when he thought of the bastard that had tried to take his daughter.

"I've still got a week." He found it hard to believe the man was still in the district and had eluded them this long. "I'm needed on my estate. We'll have to take a tour of my father's properties in a month or so, and I'll want to make sure everything is in order on my own estate before going."

"Why do you have to tour your father's estates?"

"He and my stepmother are on an extended stay on the Continent." He didn't add that the coward had left England rather than face the consequences of his dishonorable conduct. "And I'm not the only one who will be touring his estates. I plan to take you and Hannah with me."

Cali was his woman, and Hannah, his daughter. They would stay with him. It wasn't the way the *ton* operated, but Jared didn't concern himself with society's dictates. Those same dictates had made it possible for his mother to be treated like a pariah and his father to hide behind a mask of propriety, when his character was as flawed as broken glass.

"My packing is coming along well, but I don't see how I can be ready to move my household to Raven Hall in only one more week."

"You aren't moving your household, you're moving you."

Her usual composure cracked, and irritation showed through in the frown she leveled at him. "I've lived on my own for four years, Jared. I've got an entire way of life to pack up and transport, not least of which are the plants in my conservatory, my books, and my papers."

"Leave your plants—" He'd meant to say he would send servants to transport them to Raven Hall, but she interrupted in a very un-Calantha-like way.

"I'm not leaving my roses and herbs behind."

"Calm down, Cali. That's not what I meant. It will take a while to ready the conservatory, since it hasn't been used in several years. I'll send servants for your plants once we've arrived at Raven Hall."

She didn't look placated. Her eyes were frantic, and she bit on her bottom lip in agitation. "Who will care for them after I've gone? Who will ensure they are properly packed for the journey?" She spun on her heel and paced to the table. "You'll have to leave me behind, Jared. It's the only workable solution. I'll come along once I've finished preparing them for travel and have made the arrangements to get them to Raven Hall without injury."

"Are you suggesting we postpone our wedding?"

Her eyes widened. "Of course not."

"Your sister-in-law was right. It's not exactly the type of wedding worthy of a duchess."

"But I won't be a duchess. I'll be plain Lady Ravenswood." She sounded quite satisfied by that fact.

"You'll be my lady," he affirmed.

"Yes."

"So, you don't want to put off the wedding in order to plan something more elaborate?" he pressed.

"Don't be ridiculous. The plans are already in motion. Your sisters and the Ashton servants have already put forth tremendous effort on the wedding."

And Cali wouldn't dream of putting his sisters out. "But you want me to leave my new wife behind while I travel to my estate so that she can watch over her bloody plants?"

Try as he might, he couldn't keep the anger out of his

voice, and he prepared himself for the look of fear he was sure would fill her eyes. Every time she looked at him that way it was like being kicked in the testicles by an untamed horse.

She surprised him by glaring instead. "They aren't *bloody* plants. They're *mine*."

He reached out and gently pulled her close. "And you are mine. There is no way I'm going to leave you behind."

The look of fear came, but she didn't try to pull away, and he counted that as a victory in itself. One day she would trust him completely.

"I'm just trying to be practical."

"You're being bloody ridiculous."

She gasped and glared at him, all fear receding from her eyes. "It is not ridiculous to want to care for the living things that depend on me. They need me."

He stopped trying to glare sense into her and considered what she'd just said. She talked as if her plants were her only friends in the world and with sudden, blinding clarity, he realized they were. "You said once you were Mary's friend."

Her gaze turned wary, but not fearful. "Yes."

"You implied that when she left, you were no longer friends."

"Yes."

"What happened?" He'd assumed she pulled back from friendship with a servant because she had made other friends among the titled women of her acquaintance. Now that he knew her better, he doubted that assumption.

"Clairborne was not pleased with my imperfection."

"You said he punished you."

"Yes."

He waited, not willing to accept her monosyllabic response.

"He learned that it was even more effective to hurt those I cared about when trying to bend me to his will."

"Did you defy him often?"

"No. It wasn't that." She laughed, and it was a dry, humorless sound. "In fact, I tried to be as perfect as he believed an angel should be, but I failed. Often. When I failed, he hurt me, or he hurt those I cared about."

"So you pushed away anyone who was close to you in order to protect them?" He knew it was the truth the moment he spoke, from the look on her face.

"Yes."

"You didn't allow yourself to care for anyone or anything but your plants, is that it?"

Cali's expression did not reveal anything. "Yes."

"Oh, *mon enfant ange.*" He pulled her close and rubbed her back in a soothing motion, pressing her face against his chest.

She stood stiff in his embrace for a full thirty seconds, but then she relaxed against him. Her fingers curled into his waistcoat with surprising fierceness.

She was wrong. She'd cared for others, or she wouldn't have been so upset over the death of her maid. She'd tried to protect those who her husband threatened, but she didn't allow them to care for her, and she had somehow convinced herself that no one or nothing but the beautiful roses she tended in her conservatory needed her. He was surprised Clairborne had not realized how important her plants had become to her and used that to punish her, too, but then Cali had learned to hide her emotions very well.

"Your roses aren't the only things that need you now."

"What do you mean?" she asked, the sound of her voice muffled against the brocade of his waistcoat.

"Hannah needs you. You're her mother now, and she'll be upset if you stay behind."

"She can stay with me. We'll travel together. That will leave you free to take care of your estate's needs without worrying about us." She sounded bloody pleased with herself.

"Damn it, I need you, too, *mon ange*. I'll help you prepare your roses for transport, but you will travel with me when I go back to Raven Hall."

She pulled her head back, so that she could look into his face. Her eyes held wonder. "You need me?"

Hadn't she guessed? "Yes. I'm so hungry to have you in my bed that I lie awake at night shaking with the need."

"You want to bed me?"

How in the world could she sound so surprised? She'd been with him when he climaxed in his breeches on her conservatory floor. Maybe that had offended her. Maybe she didn't want to be needed in such a basic way, but he couldn't dress it up in ribbons and fancy words. His need for her was too elemental, too primitive. "Yes."

Rather than looking offended, the expression of wonder was back. "I'm glad."

He stared at her and felt the same disbelief that he'd experienced earlier upon hearing her tell the duke and duchess he was the only man she would consider marrying. The angel wanted the beast. He knew he could make her body respond, but her open admission of that desire stunned him.

Jared understood her obvious fear of marriage. After her experiences with Clairborne, it would surprise him if she *weren't* concerned about marrying again. What he could not comprehend was the fact that she would set aside that fear for him. He'd manipulated her with the knowledge that he would have to give up Hannah if Cali didn't marry him. Her deep sense of honor would not allow him to lose his daughter because of her fear, but she *wanted* him, too. It was more than he deserved.

With her beauty and position, she could have any gentleman in the *ton*.

She could marry a man as comely as she, not a scarred giant who found the gentility of society a trial and a bore. "Why haven't you remarried?"

Her eyes went blank, hiding her emotions from him. "You know why."

"Because you were afraid."

She nodded, but said nothing.

"You're going to marry me." He wanted to hear her say she wasn't afraid of him, that she knew he wouldn't hurt her.

"Yes."

"Why?"

"So you won't lose Hannah."

Inexplicable tension gripped him. He knew that was why she was marrying him, but he wanted there to be more. He wanted her to trust him. "I won't hurt you the way he did."

"I know."

That, at least, was something. "I'll take care of you. I'm having the marriage settlements drawn up to protect what you now have. You'll control your own funds."

She wrinkled her nose. "That's not necessary."

He cupped the nape of her neck. "Don't tell me you like having the duke in charge of your finances."

"No, but you aren't the duke. You won't try to control me with my allowance, or lack thereof, and I'm far more interested in my studies than money."

She did trust him. She had to, or she would jump at the chance to maintain her independence in their marriage. "I'll take care of your investments for you, if you like."

She smiled again and he felt his chest expand with pleasure at the sight. "I'd like that. Thank you."

"I've got to get back to Ashton Manor." He didn't want to leave her, but he, Ashton, and Drake planned to continue their search for Hannah's would-be kidnapper by visiting the outlying farms on Ashton's estates.

He and his brothers by marriage had already questioned the villagers and the nearby tenants, to no avail. Their plans had been to leave earlier, but then Cali's stable boy had arrived with the news that the duke and duchess had come to call.

"Thank you for bringing Hannah for a visit."

"I didn't want to leave her with the nursemaid when the message from your butler reached me." And Hannah was always thrilled to see Cali. Perhaps he should leave the child with her while he conducted his investigations this afternoon.

She stiffened. "Thomas sent you a message? Why?"

"Apparently, he doesn't trust the duke any more than I do. When he and the duchess arrived unexpectedly, Thomas sent the stable boy to let me know." He didn't add that the message had asked him to come as well.

It hadn't been necessary. The knowledge that the duke was visiting Cali was all he'd needed to hear before calling for his carriage.

An odd look passed over her face before she masked it with the blank expression that irritated the hell out of him. "Yes, of course."

"Why of course?" What had the butler seen that might lead him to believe Cali wasn't safe with the duke?

"The last time he called, Henry's temper got away with him."

"Did he strike you?" He'd kill him. He couldn't do anything to the dead Clairborne, but the live one would pay a high price for hurting Cali.

"No. I didn't let him. I used the tea tray to my advantage." She sounded both surprised and pleased with herself.

"He tried."

The deadly intent he felt must have shown on his face, because she laid a placating hand on his arm. "I don't know if he would have or not. I struck out at him first. Please, don't concern yourself. It's over."

It wasn't over. Not by a bloody mile. The duke had reinforced Cali's fear of a man's anger, and Jared would make him pay for that stupidity.

* * *

THURSDAY MORNING FOUND CALANTHA IN HER CONSER-
vatory, supervising the final packing of her precious flowers. True to his word, Jared had helped her prepare her
plants for shipment and hired flatbed wagons to transport
the luscious roses and fragrant herbs to her new home. He
had hired an experienced gardener specifically to tend them
on the journey, and she'd spent several hours with the man,
telling him how to care for the delicate China roses and
hardier herbs.

"I knew I'd find you here."

She spun around at the sound of Jared's voice. "Good
morning, Jared. Are you sure the packing crates will hold
these heavy pots? It would be terrible if one should break."

He'd devised a plan by which each pot was placed in a
packing crate with hay crammed tightly around it to hold
it in place. The crates would be tied together and attached
to the sides of the wagon, protecting them from jostling
during transit. When she had expressed concern over the
elements, in case of an unexpected summer storm, he had
arranged for coverings for the wagons.

He frowned. "They'll be fine, damn it. I told you, we've
done all we can for your precious plants."

Jared's mood had deteriorated over the past week, as no
additional information had surfaced about Hannah's would-
be kidnapper. Ashton was convinced the man had left the
district. Jared had been forced to agree, but he'd made it clear
he didn't like it any more than he had liked admitting that
Calantha needed a few more days to prepare for the journey.

He'd grudgingly told her they could wait to leave for his
estate until Wednesday, two days after the wedding. She
knew they would be leaving that morning if it meant leaving her clothes behind.

Rather than desiring to withdraw in the face of Jared's
irritation, Calantha found herself wanting to comfort him.

She stepped forward and brushed his cheek with her hand. "I'm sorry. I know I'm behaving like an old woman about this."

He caught her hand with his own, pressing it against the warm skin of his face. "It isn't you. It's this bloody investigation. We can't find the man who tried to steal Hannah, and I feel like I've failed her."

"You haven't failed anyone, Jared." She willed him to believe her. "Because of your persistent efforts, parents in the district will be on the lookout for him and more protective of their own children."

"But I didn't catch him, damn it."

"Didn't your mother ever tell you a gentleman does not swear in front of a lady?" she asked whimsically.

She was trying to take his mind off his unsuccessful efforts, but was unprepared for his response.

He tensed and pulled away from her. "No. She didn't. I never met my mother."

"She died giving birth?" It was common enough, but the thought of Jared living with that tragedy tore at her heart.

"No. My father took me away."

She sensed there was more to the story and remained silent, waiting for him to share it. If he wanted to.

"He thought she had been unfaithful during her pregnancy. He was wrong, but that didn't matter to him. He treated her shamefully, and she ran away." Jared's great shoulders were stiff, and his head averted.

"She abandoned you?" Calantha could not fathom such a thing.

"Thea was born half an hour after my father tore me from her arms and took me from the house. He vowed she would never see me again. My mother, Anna, kept Thea a secret and tried to see me with the help of my great aunt, but Langley found out about the visits. He threatened her, and she fled England, afraid he would discover my sister's existence and take her away, too."

"She never came back to see you?" A woman with that sort of fortitude would surely have found a way to see her son.

"She came down with a fever before she could make the journey. The disease eventually killed her."

"How did you learn about Thea?"

"She returned to England five years ago."

"But Lady Ashton—"

"Is the daughter of Langley's second wife."

"I see."

Jared whirled around to face her. "What do you see, Cali?"

"I see why you are so intent on doing the honorable thing. You do not wish to be like your father. I see that I can trust you with my life, because you would never treat me with the same cruelty your father did your mother."

Jared reached her in two great strides, standing so close they were almost touching. She had to tilt her head back to see his face, that beautiful scarred face.

"How can you be sure?"

She touched the raised flesh on his right cheek, once again grateful she had left off her gloves to handle the tender plants. "Because of this."

"What the hel—what do you mean?"

She smiled at how he broke off mid-curse. "A man who would risk his life to save his sister would not treat a wife the way Langley treated your mother. Every time I see this, it reminds me how blessed I am to have you."

His dark eyes went almost black with some strong emotion. "You are amazing, *mon ange*. The rest of the *ton* sees me as a beast, but you look at my disfigured face and find honor."

"I was married to a beast that society called an angel. His face was perfection, but his heart was black. You aren't like him at all. You are no beast."

"You're so sure." He sounded awed by her certainty.

"I wouldn't marry you otherwise, not even for Hannah."

He lowered his head and sealed those words with his kiss.

When he pulled back, she held on to his arms to keep her balance. If his kiss had such a profound effect on her, how would she stand her wedding night? She was likely to faint during the most interesting part.

"Where's Hannah?" She had just realized the little girl hadn't accompanied Jared into the room.

"She wanted to visit Cook. I think she was angling for some candied rose petals."

Calantha laughed softly. "I'll make sure to keep a supply at Raven Hall."

"And will you keep me supplied with the sweetness I crave?" His expression was both feral and teasing, and she shivered.

Could she keep him satisfied with her sweetness? She had to. She could not stand the idea of Jared seeking out mistresses the way Deveril had.

"I'll try," she whispered.

He shook his head. "You don't understand yet, do you?"

"What?"

"How much I want you."

But what if that ended on their wedding night, like it had for Deveril? "Will it be like it was the other night?"

He didn't ask her to explain what she meant, and for that she was grateful. "No."

She felt her heart plummet.

"It will be better."

"Oh."

"You said you trusted me with your life, Cali."

"I do."

"Then trust me with your body. I'll teach you all the pleasure it can experience."

Something happened low in her belly, as the intimate tone of his voice and the meaning of his words soaked into her. Her lips parted, and her breath came in short gasps. "I'd like that."

He smiled, his expression primitive and promising all at once. "Yes, you will."

She waited, hoping he would kiss her again, but he did nothing. He just stood there, waiting for she knew not what.

"Jared?"

"Hmmm?"

"Will you . . . Will you kiss me?"

He shook his head.

Heat suffused her cheeks, and she wanted to turn away to hide her embarrassment, but she couldn't make her body move away from him.

"Cali?"

"Yes?"

"Will *you* kiss *me*?"

Her heart stopped for one heartbeat and then started again at a gallop. Yes. She *wanted* to kiss him. Putting her hands on either side of his face, she pulled his head down the few inches that separated them. He came easily, and she smiled just before placing her lips against his.

Ten

SHE KISSED HIM WITH EVERYTHING HE'D taught her in the garden the first night they'd met, and since then. Within seconds, Jared was ready to tear her dress and apron off and touch the soft, naked flesh underneath. He wanted to bury himself inside of her, putting his claim on her in the most fundamental way a man could possess a woman.

Would he be able to wait four more days?

He yanked her against him, crushing her soft womanly curves against his hardened flesh. She moaned, and he stilled. Had he hurt her?

Her tongue plunged inside of his mouth, and she rocked her lower body against his, making an impatient sound of frustration when the disparity in their size prevented her from matching her femininity to his masculine hardness. He would have laughed if his mouth weren't already busy fighting a sensual duel with hers. His little marble angel was hot, and she wanted satisfaction.

He briefly contemplated picking her up and finding a place where he could give it to her in privacy, but the final remnants of his self-control stayed him. He gently nipped at her lips, withdrawing his mouth from hers. "You're killing me, angel."

"No, Jared, please don't stop." She blindly sought his lips again, her eyes closed and her face suffused with passionate color.

When he kept his face averted by a monumental effort of will, she sought the curve of his throat with her lips.

Bloody hell. He knew better. He had known where the kissing would lead, even if she didn't. They were like tinder and gunpowder. Whenever they touched, passion exploded between them. Despite their previous encounters, his angel was still very innocent. She didn't know how to control her ardor, and he had deliberately urged her to show him how much she wanted him in order to feed his male ego. Now, she clung to him, ready to be taken on the conservatory floor.

While part of him found fierce pleasure in her obvious desire for him, he felt guilty as hell for bringing her to such a place and having to leave her unsatisfied.

She arched against him again, making a needy sound deep in her throat, and tried to undo the buttons of his waistcoat, but her fingers fumbled.

The hell with it. He swung her up in his arms and strode outside. He'd find someplace private enough to do what needed to be done. Remembering a small outbuilding he had seen when he'd taken her riding, he carried her in that direction.

"Jared?" She sounded disoriented, her hands still gripping his waistcoat.

"What?"

"Where are you taking me?"

"Someplace to finish what I've started."

She went silent and then said, "Oh," renewing her attack on his waistcoat, this time getting all the buttons undone by the time he reached the shed.

He bent down with her in his arms. "Open the door."

His voice sounded harsh to his own ears, but she didn't seem to notice. At least she did not tense against him. She obeyed and pushed the door inward. He carried her inside, surprised by the cleanliness of what he now realized was a potting shed. The dim light from the single window did not reveal a single pot or tool out of place.

"Do you keep all your outbuildings this clean?"

Her hot little hands were all over his chest. "Of course," she mumbled against him, sounding surprised by the question.

He smiled, thinking of his own cluttered potting shed. He wondered what she would say when she saw it. He gently let her legs down until her feet touched the floor.

She took a step back and slipped off her apron, tossing it in an untidy pile on top of a table near the window, and then stared up at him. "Should I take off my dress?"

Not if he was going to keep any kind of control. "No."

Her eyes narrowed. "I don't understand."

"Don't worry, *mon ange*, I'll take care of everything."

Suiting action to words, he sat down on the potter's bench and pulled her onto his lap. She gasped as she landed against his chest with a thud, her thighs sliding apart to clasp his waist. Then he put his hand on the side of her cheek and held her still for his kiss. Her instant response went straight to his groin, which had already been hard and now ached with unfulfilled desire.

He let his hand trail down her neck and curve around to cup her breast. One small nipple tightened under his palm, its hard point pressing against the thin muslin of her gown. He tugged her sleeve down, bringing the bodice with it, until her sweetly curved flesh was exposed to his probing fingers. She was so perfect. He had to taste her. Bending his head, he circled her nipple with his tongue.

She cried out, and he did it again. He had never touched a woman who responded to him the way she did. He knew how to give a woman pleasure, but Cali made him feel like she needed *him*, not just what his touch could do for her. Her response touched deep down inside him.

She squirmed on his lap, and he knew what she craved, even if she didn't. He pulled her skirts up until his hand rested against bare thigh. He made a circular motion with his thumb, and she went absolutely still. Raising his head from her breast, he caught her gaze. Her pretty blue eyes were darkened with passion, and her usually creamy white skin was tinted with a warm blush.

"Don't be afraid, *mon ange*. I'm going to touch you."

"Yes." The word came out a breathless sigh as his hand inched up closer to her feminine core.

She jumped as his fingertips brushed the moist patch of curls between her legs. He used his other hand to stroke her neck in a gentling motion. "It's all right. Do you trust me?"

Mute, she nodded.

He let one finger slip inside the soft feminine folds and shuddered at the slick wetness he found there. Using the tip of his finger, he spread the wetness until her hardened little nub was as slick as the rest of her.

She cried out again and pressed her body against his hand. Carefully replacing his fingertip with his thumb, he drew erotic circles around the sweet spot and felt her thighs tighten against his hand. He gave her an open-mouthed kiss, voraciously eating her lips until she was mindless with her need. Then, he lowered his head and took her tight, pink nipple into his mouth and sucked. Hard.

She screamed and came apart in his arms, sobbing out her pleasure as he rubbed the sweet spot between her legs and teased her velvet nipple with his teeth and tongue.

CALANTHA WAS STILL REELING FROM THE PLEASURE SHE had found in Jared's arms two days later as she packed her books for transport to Raven Hall. She had thought he meant to make love to her, not understanding, even after their experience on the conservatory floor, that he could finish what they had started without the final act of joining. She'd learned, however, that her fiancé had startlingly talented hands. She still blushed when she remembered the way she had screamed and sobbed her pleasure aloud.

Afterward, she had expected him to seek some sort of satisfaction as well. The evidence of his desire had been so hard against her, and yet, he had refused, saying he would bloody well wait until they were married. She had been too dazed from pleasure to argue with him, but she looked forward to her wedding night with less and less trepidation. Jared wanted her, and she told herself that wouldn't change just because they got married, not like it had with Deveril.

She thought Jared must have been right. Deveril had failed to consummate their marriage not because she was undesirable, but because it had been one more way of hurting her and making her feel inferior. It seemed to her that there had to be some insanity in that, but it no longer mattered. Deveril was dead, and soon she would no longer even be a Clairborne in name.

Kneeling on the floor, she placed a book on eastern archaeological digs into the packing crate with renewed purpose. The last plant had been removed from her conservatory yesterday evening, and the wagons carrying her precious cargo had already begun their slow journey to Raven Hall.

She had left behind the "babies" from her current bushes and herbs for the groundskeeper to maintain. She had also left written instructions for Thomas's granddaughter to continue Calantha's practice of providing candied rose petals to the vicar's children and certain teas and recipes to the local people for their various ills once the "babies" had grown large enough to harvest. She liked the idea of having a few plants to tend on the occasions she, Jared, and Hannah came to visit the Ashtons as well.

Although her life was irrevocably changing, that bit of continuity gave her peace. Soon, she would take up residence as the Viscountess of Ravenswood. A mere lady, no longer a duchess. Jared would not expect perfection. He did not consider her a marble statue. He could not possibly, after the passion they had shared.

"Really, my dear, that is hardly appropriate behavior for a duchess. Surely your servants could have seen to the packing of your books."

Calantha shot to her feet at the sound of Henry's voice. Why had he returned? He must realize she had no intention of changing her mind about the marriage. The settlements had been signed yesterday, and Jared had proven to be extremely generous. He had protected her future just as he had promised to do.

The duke wore riding breeches and coat. "Henry, I did not expect to see you today. Has Ellen come with you?"

And where was Thomas? Why hadn't he announced the duke?

"My wife chose to remain at Clairborne Park."

"I see." But she didn't.

She could not fathom the reason for the duke's visit, nor why he had elected not to bring his wife.

Henry turned and closed the door to the parlor, making the room feel even smaller than usual.

She took an involuntary step backward. "Why did you do that? It is hardly proper for me to entertain a gentleman with the door shut."

Even a widow had certain restrictions on her behavior, and a young widow more than most. She did not observe them with Jared, but found protection in them when dealing with Henry.

"I'm afraid I have things to say to you of a very delicate nature. I would not want the servants to overhear."

"I cannot imagine what you have to say to me that you fear my servants overhearing, but I must insist you open the door at once." She edged around the table, making her own way toward the door.

"Do not be so obstinate. Of the many flaws Deveril complained you had, stubbornness was not among them. I cannot imagine what has happened to you."

She had learned to live without fear. "Say what you have to say and then leave. My fiancé would be very displeased to find you here alone with me."

As she hoped it would, the mention of Jared brought a wary expression to the duke's face. "Very well. I must say that you have lost a certain amount of the polish Deveril tried so hard to instill in you."

She shivered when she thought of the way her dead husband had gone about "polishing" her, but refused to be goaded into an answer.

"I have investigated the viscount's background, since you seemed intent on rushing headlong into marriage without doing so."

"There was no need. I know all that is necessary to know about my future husband. He is a man of honor." And Jared was gentle rather than cruel toward those weaker than himself.

"I think you will change your mind when you hear what I have to say."

Nothing would make her change her mind about Jared. "You are wrong."

Henry frowned, but he didn't take issue with her impudence. "The viscount comes from a family rife with scandal."

She raised her brows in mocking disdain. "I'm very fond of his sisters and their families. I cannot imagine to what you refer."

Henry's frown deepened when her response was not what he had clearly expected. "His mother ran off to the West Indies rather than face the just wrath of her husband after she was caught in a compromising position with another gentleman."

"If the man compromised a married woman, he can hardly claim the title of gentleman, no matter the nobility of his birth."

"Do not be ridiculous. A lady must at all times take precautions to guard her reputation."

"And the *gentlemen* around her, are they not similarly bound?" she asked with a pointed look at the closed door.

The duke's hands curled into fists at his side, but he made no move toward her. "His sister married the baseborn son of a nobleman. Drake is only accepted by the *ton* because his grandfather is an eccentric duke and insists on it."

"Mr. and Mrs. Drake are all that is charming, Henry. I cannot believe that you hold his father's ignoble actions against him, but I can assure you that I do not."

Her brother-in-law's eyes narrowed. "It is a clear matter of propriety, but I see that you have forgotten all that Deveril tried to teach you on that subject."

"My parents may not have been high-ranking members of the *ton*, but they were gentry all the same, and my mother did an excellent job teaching me the rules of proper behavior." She was tired of hearing about her husband's tutelage.

"Then you should realize that a man whose father would wed one woman while still married to another is completely unsuitable as a prospective husband for a duchess." Henry stood several feet away, his entire being radiating complacent victory after making that statement.

So, Anna had still been living when Langley married his next countess. Calantha shrugged, refusing to even acknowledge the ugly slur with a word of denial.

"Didn't you hear what I just said? Lady Ashton is the earl's by-blow, not his legitimate daughter. And your fiancé," he said the word sneeringly, "is no better, the way he flaunts convention to acknowledge his own by-blow. Ellen informed me the child is rumored to be that of one of his servants. Bad blood runs in that family like the watery punch at Almack's. You cannot possibly consider linking your name with theirs. You are Calantha, Duchess of Clairborne, and owe certain duties to that title."

Deep, cleansing rage filled her. How dare this pompous idiot pass judgment on Jared's family? "You pretentious, puling cur! I will not tolerate one more second of this defaming of my fiancé and his family. He is more gentleman than Deveril ever hoped to be, or you for that matter. Jared would never raise his fist to strike a woman, but you and your brother both have that weakness in your character. If Jared had something to say to you, he would say it to your face, not hide behind false protestations of concern to drip venom in Ellen's ear. The only bad blood that concerns me is that which I allowed to taint me as the wife of that beast you called brother."

Too late, her common sense reasserted itself, reminding her how violently Henry reacted to words spoken against his dead brother. She sidestepped to the fireplace, and satisfaction gleamed in Henry's eyes at the indication of her fear. The satisfaction turned to fury as she picked up the fireplace poker and brandished it before her, clutching it tightly with both hands.

"Have you taken to brawling, my dear?" he asked as he took a step toward her, his expression dangerously angry.

"I won't let you hurt me."

"Do you really think you can stop me?" He sounded amused.

She drew herself up, holding the poker even more tightly. "Perhaps not, but I will inflict my own damage, and once Jared learns of it, he will kill you."

The duke stopped in his tracks, and his face tightened.

"It's true, and you know it. You fear him, and with good reason."

"A viscount would not dare threaten a duke."

Henry didn't sound at all certain of that statement, and she rushed to bolster his uncertainty. "Jared is no common viscount. He fears nothing, and he protects his own."

"You deserve to be slapped for slinging such insults at my brother."

"Do you want to die so young, then?" she asked, not at all sure if the argument would work.

Once Deveril had been in a rage, even the prospect of leaving bruises that would show had not stopped him from meting out his fury with his fists.

"I will not waste my time with you, but know this. If you marry the viscount, no Clairborne will acknowledge you in any way. If he is counting on our countenance and a connection to it through you, he will be sorely disappointed." The venom in Henry's voice made her shiver, but she kept it inside.

"Jared and I will both be content to sever any connection to your title." She did not relax her position of vigilance with the poker until Henry had left.

Lady Ashton and Mrs. Drake arrived to help Calantha prepare for her wedding two mornings later.

"It is very kind of you to take time to be with me this morning, Lady Ashton. I'm sure you have things you could be doing at the manor." Only a small party of local gentry had been invited to the wedding breakfast, but Calantha knew what it was like to arrange entertainments of that sort.

"You must call me Irisa now," the blond woman said with a warm smile. "We are to be sisters."

An only child, the prospect of having sisters delighted Calantha to the tips of her gold satin wedding slippers. "Thank you. You may call me Calantha."

"I like Cali better," Thea announced from the other side of her.

"Please call me whatever you like, Thea."

Jenny stepped forward to slip the virginal white gown over Calantha's head. Her hair had not yet been dressed.

As the satin folds settled around Cali, Irisa applauded.

"It's lovely, Cali. I don't think I've ever seen you in anything but blue."

Calantha looked at the formal white gown with a critical eye. The bodice was cut lower than her usual modest style and exposed the top swell of her small breasts. They did not look quite so small with the corset pushing her curves upward and the gathered bosom of the gown giving her added dimension. The skirt fell in several elegant tucks, accentuated with gold rosettes and streamers, which revealed the gold shot white satin underskirt below.

"As soon as I finished the traditional black of mourning, I had an entire wardrobe made up in as many shades of blue as I could find."

"It's a very good color on you," Thea remarked diplomatically.

"My first husband did not think so. He said that it was too common for a woman with blue eyes to wear the color, and during the entire two years of my marriage, I never so much as had a blue handkerchief."

"I can attest to that," Jenny said, breaking the silence that had gripped her since Jared's sisters invaded Calantha's bedchamber.

"Jared won't care what color you wear," Irisa predicted.

Calantha smiled at her reflection in the mirror, for once finding pleasure in the beauty reflected back at her. She wanted to be beautiful for Jared. She agreed with his sister's assessment. He wouldn't care what color she wore, or if her gown was the latest fashion. Those sorts of things didn't matter to the man she was going to marry.

"I think that married to your brother, I shall wear a rainbow of colors." Only then would her happiness at finding such a man be reflected accurately.

His sisters seemed to understand because they gave her matching smiles of approval. Jenny pulled the mass of golden hair that hung to Calantha's waist into several intricate curls and tucks on top her head. When she was finished, she placed a small ringlet of pearls Calantha's mother had given her on her comeout around her neck.

"You look like the angel the *ton* claims you to be." Irisa's words did not elicit even a twinge of pain, as they once might have done.

Jared called her *his* angel and that had made all the difference.

"She looks like a woman fit to be our brother's wife," Thea replied, "but I'll wager he's going to have a fit about that neckline on Calantha's gown. Pierson would, but I'd wear it anyway."

Calantha stared at her sister-in-law-to-be, and then burst out laughing. "And *I* wager you would. Do you think Jared will be angry?" Perhaps she should tuck a bit of lace into the bosom to make the neckline more modest.

"No. He'll be overcome with desire and blame it on you, but I've found that state of affairs very pleasant. Do not let it worry you." Thea's practical advice settled Calantha's nerves, and she hoped the other woman was right.

The idea of Jared overcome with passion was very pleasant indeed.

Irisa gave Calantha an impulsive hug, which she returned, only to be embraced warmly by Thea as well.

LATER, AS SHE FACED JARED IN FRONT OF THE CONGRE-gation gathered to witness their wedding in the village church, she knew his sister was right. He had watched her progression up the aisle of the old church with such a heated look, she felt singed. As she took her place to his left, facing the priest, she permitted herself a small smile.

"Dearly beloved . . ."

The priest began his introduction to the marriage vows, and Calantha tried to listen, but her mind was occupied with the giant standing next to her. From this day forward, she would be his wife and he would be her husband. As the priest asked if there were any who knew why she and Jared should not be bound by the laws of matrimony, she almost turned to see if the duke had come to her wedding after all. She kept her focus forward with an act of will, but could not completely suppress a sigh of relief when no objection was found.

Facing Jared, the young priest asked, "Jared Selwyn, Viscount Ravenswood, wilt thou have this Woman to thy wedded Wife, to live together after God's ordinance in the holy estate of Matrimony? Wilt thou love her, comfort her, honor, and keep her in sickness and in health; and, forsaking all other, keep thee only unto her, so long as ye both shall live?"

Jared's voice came out sure and strong. "I will."

Turning his gaze to her, the priest asked, "Calantha Clairborne, Dowager Duchess, wilt thou have this Man to thy wedded Husband, to live together after God's ordinance in the holy estate of Matrimony? Wilt thou obey him, and serve him, love, honor, and keep him in sickness and in health; and, forsaking all other, keep thee only unto him, so long as ye both shall live?"

The words of her vows washed over her, and she said, "I will," acknowledging before God and man her absolute faith in the man she accepted as husband.

"Who giveth this woman to be married to this man?"

Lord Ashton said, "I do," and placed her right hand into Jared's right hand, in the manner of the centuries-old wedding ritual.

For Calantha, though she'd been married once before, it felt new and binding in a wholly different way. She had never truly belonged to Deveril, for he had not wanted the real woman, but she would belong to Jared until death.

Following the priest's instructions, Jared said, "I, Jared, take thee, Calantha, to my wedded Wife, to have and to hold from this day forward, for better for worse, for richer for poorer, in sickness and in health, to love and to cherish, till death us do part, according to God's holy ordinance; and thereto I plight thee my troth." He met her gaze, his intense and direct, and made the promises with his eyes as well as his mouth.

He let go of her hand, and she reversed the hold, taking his right hand in her own. She repeated the vows as spoken by the priest. "I, Calantha, take thee, Jared, to my wedded Husband, to have and to hold from this day forward, for better for worse, for richer for poorer, in sickness and in health, to love, cherish, and to obey, till death us do part, according to God's holy ordinance; and thereto I give thee my troth." Her voice shook as she said the words, not because she feared them, but because she realized with blinding clarity that she meant them.

All of them.

She loved Jared. How could she not? His protective nature astounded her and made her feel safe all at once, and her heart, which had been frozen when they met, had melted at his feet.

She gave it to him freely, saying with her eyes what she knew she did not have the courage to speak with her mouth as she voiced her wedding vows.

Upon the priest's instructions, she let Jared's hand go, but could not help that her fingers trailed over his as she did so. His eyes filled with dark promise before he turned to face the priest, laying a ring of blue sapphire on the prayer book. The priest picked up the ring, blessed it, and handed it back to Jared. He took her left hand and slid the ring on her fourth finger, keeping hold of her hand with both of his as he repeated the words the priest instructed.

"With this Ring I thee wed, with my Body I thee worship, and with all my worldly Goods I thee endow: In the Name of the Father, and of the Son, and of the Holy Ghost. Amen."

Then Jared helped her kneel before the priest as he prayed over them. She heard the prayers and the Psalm that followed, but her mind still grappled with the knowledge that she loved the man beside her. She had thought she had lost the ability to love, but she had been wrong. She loved Hannah. She cared for Jared's sisters and their families. She cared for her own servants and those who relied on her for help with her herbal remedies. But she loved Jared so deeply, so completely, that she knew if she lost him, it would destroy her in a way that Deveril's cruelty had been powerless to do.

The congregation joined the minister in the responsive reading, while she and Jared knelt before the altar. As she shared in the Holy Eucharist with her new husband fifteen minutes later, she felt connected to him and all those present in a way that almost splintered her with the joy of it.

The priest blessed them and introduced them to the congregation as Lord and Lady Ravenswood. Finally, the title of duchess that had brought her so much grief was lifted from her and replaced with one claiming her as Jared's lady.

Laughter burst out of her as Hannah squirmed from Irisa's arms to rush forward and throw herself at Calantha's legs. "Now you really are my mama."

Eleven

"ARE YOU SURE HANNAH WILL BE ALL RIGHT with your sisters?" Cali asked as Jared set the horses in motion, taking his wife and him away from Ashton Manor after the wedding breakfast.

His *wife*. He had known he must marry sometime, but had never envisioned taking such a beautiful, passionate woman to wed. Cali was legally his, and soon he would put the bond of flesh on her that would make her completely *his* woman.

"It will only be for one night." His sister had insisted on keeping Hannah at Ashton Manor for the wedding night. "Irisa promised not to leave Hannah alone for so much as a minute."

Cali turned back from looking over her shoulder and waving as the carriage rolled away and sighed. "I'm sure your sister will take very good care of our daughter, but Hannah has not been away from you, and she might worry."

Remembering the little pixie's casual reaction to the news that he and Cali were leaving for the night and would be back the next day, he doubted it. She'd come a long way in dealing with the loss of Mary since meeting Calantha. "She'll be fine. Stop worrying, Cali. You have other things to think about right now."

"What other things?" she asked with a fair imitation of the teasing tone he'd heard Irisa and Thea use with their husbands.

"Satisfying my craving for angels."

Cali went silent at that, and Jared wondered what she was thinking. "Are you scared, *mon ange*?"

"Jared, do you remember you said once that it was your responsibility to make sure I satisfied you?" she asked, not giving him a direct answer.

"Yes."

"What happens if I can't?"

Damn it. She *was* worried. "You will."

"But if I don't?"

"Cali, just touching you makes me so hot I feel like I could melt iron. When I get inside of you, I'm going to be so damn satisfied, I just might die of it."

In a very un-Cali-like way, she twisted her hands together in her lap. "Jared?"

"What?" Was she still worried?

"Do we have to wait until night?"

He didn't remember much of the carriage drive from that point on. His focus was entirely on the woman sitting next to him. When they reached Rose Cottage, he tossed the reins to her stable boy, picked up Cali, and jumped down from the carriage. Thomas and her other servants had gathered to wish them happy and to welcome him as new master of the house. He tossed his thanks to them over his shoulder as he carried Cali up the stairs. Her face was buried in his waistcoat. When he reached the bedchamber they were to share, he stepped inside and kicked the door shut with his heel.

The bed looked too small, and he would have to see that another one replaced it before their next visit, but the thought couldn't remain in his head for long. Not with Cali's soft body held tightly against his. He let her legs down gently, until she stood in the circle of his arms.

She still hadn't looked up to meet his gaze.

"Cali?"

"Yes, Jared?" she answered his waistcoat.

"We don't have to wait for night."

Her head bobbed up then, and her uncertain gaze caught his. "I'm a little nervous."

She was white as a sheet.

"It's going to be all right."

"Will it?"

He lifted one hand from her waist to cup her cheek. "Yes. Do you trust me?"

She'd said she did, but he needed to hear the words again.

"Yes."

"Say it."

"I trust you, husband."

Bloody hell. His knees nearly buckled when she said the word *husband*. "Right now, it's just us. There's no room in our bed for bad memories. I'm the only man you're going to be with today and for the rest of our lives. Do you understand me, angel?"

As Jared's words registered, Calantha felt a deep calm settle over her. No room for bad memories. Their bed. Not her bed any longer, but *theirs*. She wondered if they would share a room at Raven Hall. It was quite unusual among the *ton*, but not unheard of.

She smiled up at him, feeling light-headed with anticipation. "You're the only man I want."

He bent down and brushed her lips with his. Then, he took both of her hands and pressed them against his waistcoat. "Undress me. I want to feel your hands on me."

She wanted that, too. She wanted to undress him, to have the power to reveal his body to her gaze. She reached up behind his head, gently tugging on the black ribbon that tied his dark hair back. He rarely made such a concession and must have done so in honor of their wedding. As she pulled the ribbon away, his heavy black hair swung forward to frame his face, and he looked almost wild. She smiled. She liked the untamed parts of him.

"You look pleased with yourself, angel, and all you've done is release my hair."

She shook her head. "I'm pleased with you, Jared."

His eyes darkened, but he remained passive as she helped him shrug out of his coat. She laid it neatly over the back of a chair and turned back to him. Unbuttoning his waistcoat, one slow button at a time, she said, "I believe I have the makings of a proficient valet."

"My man is faster," he growled.

She just smiled. "I am in charge, am I not?"

"*Yes.*" He bit the word out, but she wasn't worried. She'd learned to tell the difference between anger and desire with this man.

"Then you will be patient as I take my time unwrapping my fabulous gift."

"Is that how you see me?" Jared demanded, awed that Cali would perceive him as some sort of present.

Her eyes were warm and very serious when she nodded.

Then she pushed his waistcoat over his shoulders, and her eyes flared. She gently circled each of his male nipples, and it took every ounce of self-control he had not to toss her on the bed, ruck up her skirts, and bury himself inside of her.

He groaned. "Maybe this wasn't such a good idea."

She laughed softly. "Relax, Jared. There's nothing to be worried about."

He closed his eyes and mentally counted the ewes in his largest flock of sheep. It helped . . . barely.

He felt her tug on the ends of his cravat, and then it came free, slipping from around his neck in a gentle caress. As her fingers moved to the fastening of his shirt, he thought of the scars left behind by the wolf that the rest of the *ton* had never seen. Parts of his chest and back were marred with the same savage lines that ruined his face.

He wanted to resist taking his shirt off, but she would have to get used to seeing the marks sometime. He heard a sharply indrawn breath as his shirt fell away and his torso was revealed to his wife's curious gaze in the afternoon light. Perhaps they should have waited until after dark. At least the shock would not have been so glaring by candlelight.

Then he felt her fingers tracing the paths left behind by the sharp animal claws, just as she had done on his face. "I didn't know, but I should have realized. You cannot fight with a wolf and end up with only the paltry marks on your face."

His eyes flew open, expecting at least some disgust; he was totally unprepared for the tears that washed her eyes. As two spilled over and rolled down her cheeks, he reached out and wiped them away with his thumbs. "Don't cry."

"I can't help it. You were wounded."

"It happened a long time ago. They don't hurt." Especially when she touched him with those feather-light caresses. Far from pain, his body was suffused with desire.

She shook her head, but didn't say anything. Instead, she leaned forward and treated the scars on his chest with the same teasing kisses she had given his face that night in the conservatory. His manhood, already rock hard, felt like it would burst out of the black satin breeches he'd worn for his wedding. He reached out and grabbed her waist, pulling her body flush with his.

She rubbed his chest with her hands while continuing the gentling touch with her lips. She didn't limit herself to kissing the marks left behind by the wolf, but kissed both of his nipples in turn. If she didn't get to his breeches soon, he was going to die.

Reaching behind her, he undid the tapes of her gown, glad that he didn't rip it in his haste. He didn't want to scare her, but he didn't have much control left. She didn't seem to notice when he tugged the dress over her arms and down her body so that it hung on her hips. She was too busy tasting the skin she had bared and driving him insane with the teasing touch of her tongue and teeth.

He pushed her dress off, and it foamed around their feet in a pile of white and gold satin. Her chemise was made of the thinnest silk and did nothing to hide her rosy pink nipples from his hungry gaze. Taking another firm grip on her waist, he lifted her up until her perfect breasts were in line with his mouth. Then he closed his lips over one sweet, hard little berry and tasted her through the diaphanous silk.

She cried out, her hands clenched in his hair. He opened his mouth a little wider and bit gently.

She screamed his name. *"Jared."*

CALANTHA FELT AS IF SHE WERE COMING APART. JARED'S mouth on her breast was driving her wild with need and desire. An ache, which had started deep in her belly when he had first kissed her, now throbbed between her legs in her most feminine place. She wanted to feel him there, just as she had in the potting shed. "Please, Jared, please! Do something!"

He let go of her nipple with his mouth, and she almost screamed. "What do you want me to do, *mon ange*? This?" He kissed her other nipple through the silk, using his teeth and tongue, and she moaned.

"Yes. Yes. That and . . ." something more, but she didn't have the words.

"Or this?" He used his teeth to tear her chemise away from her bosom, which had grown tight and full with desire. Then his mouth was on her flesh, licking the underside of one breast, kissing her nipple, nipping the other one with his teeth, licking her again, kissing the small valley between her feminine curves, licking where his lips had just been . . . tormenting her beyond her bearing.

She writhed against him, bringing her legs up to wrap

around his torso. The silk of her chemise fell away, and his hair-roughened chest rubbed between her thighs. She spread her legs wider, trying to increase the friction, and shuddered with relief when it worked. It felt so good. She rocked against him with her hips just as his mouth closed over her nipple, and he began sucking like he had in the potting shed.

She grabbed his head with both hands and held it in place with all her strength. She felt his gentle laughter against her breast, but didn't care. Not as long as he went back to that delicious torment with his mouth, and he did, suckling at her nipple with almost painful pleasure. Tightening her thighs on his torso, she rubbed against him, searching for release from the agonizing delight her body could not seem to get enough of.

Then it came, in a shocking, blinding rush, and she screamed his name over and over again, begging him not to stop, rubbing herself against him like a feline in heat.

When it was over, her body went limp, her legs falling away to dangle above the floor. Jared kissed her breast softly, so tenderly that she almost cried. Or was she already crying?

He swung her up in his arms and carried her to the bed without saying a word. He pulled back the coverlet and laid her down. She did not have the energy to pull the blankets over herself and watched with sleepy eyes as he finished removing his clothes. She was grateful for her exhaustion when his male flesh sprang free of his smalls. Like the rest of him, it was huge, and she wondered how in the world he was supposed to mate with her, but she trusted him. So she didn't give into the urge to drag her spent body from the bed and run from the room.

JARED SAW CALI'S EYES, WHICH HAD BEEN HEAVY LIDDED from spent passion, flare wide at the sight of him completely naked. Her gaze fixed on his manhood, and she swallowed.

He sat down beside her on the bed, his body shaking from the need not yet satisfied. "It's going to be all right."

He wanted to assure her. He didn't want her to be afraid of him or what was going to happen. He only hoped the words were enough, because after the way she had gone wild in his arms, he didn't have the control for another gentle wooing.

She shifted her look to his face, her eyes deep blue with residual desire. "I trust you."

He didn't reply. He couldn't. His throat was blocked by some unnamed emotion. This fragile woman had put herself completely in his keeping. "I don't want to hurt you."

"I think it is inevitable the first time."

His hands trembled as he pulled the torn chemise from her body and then undid the laces of her corset. As he took it off her, he was glad to see that she didn't wear it tight enough to leave the angry red marks he'd seen on other women's flesh. She was finally completely naked and so enticing, it hurt to look at her. He pressed her legs apart in silent demand for her to open herself to him, and she obeyed.

"You're beautiful." The words were a bare whisper as Jared gazed intently at her most intimate flesh.

Calantha wanted to press her legs together again, but the look of desperate need in his eyes stayed her. She couldn't stop the blush that heated her skin, however, as the renewed desire flickered to life within her.

"I want to taste you."

Her whole body tensed, and she tried to close her thighs as the import of his words sank in, but she was too late. He had already settled between them, his face so close to her feminine flesh that she felt his breath there. He turned and kissed the inside of one thigh and then licked her.

Oh, Heavens, he was licking a path to . . . to . . . Yes! There. Surely this was too scandalous, but it felt better than anything she'd ever known. His mouth was hot and wet, and his tongue touched her intimately until she felt the shattering tension begin to coil within her.

She felt one finger slide inside her wet heat and groaned from the pleasure of it. She could not stop herself from moving against that finger anymore than she could have held her breath. It felt too good. He felt too good. His teeth nibbled that spot that brought her so much pleasure, and the coiling tension inside her threatened to consume her.

"Jared, please, oh please, oh please."

He pulled his finger out of her femininity, and she wanted to cry. "No. Please . . ."

But then his hand was back, this time pressing two big fingers inside of her. It hurt. It felt wonderful. It stretched almost unbearably, but she didn't want him to stop, and he didn't. He kept up the intimate caress with his fingers and mouth until she was writhing and her body was slick with sweat.

She could feel the ultimate pleasure begin to overtake her, and her body tightened in anticipation.

Jared felt it, too, because he stopped and said, "This time I'm going to be in you."

He swarmed up her, keeping her legs wide-open, until his hardened male flesh was positioned at the entrance to her body. Then he pressed inside her with inexorable force. Her flesh stretched to accommodate his hardened maleness, and just as with his fingers there was both pain and indescribable pleasure. Until he hit the barrier that proclaimed her untouched. It hurt. Tears seeped out of her eyes as she tried not to give in to the urge to push him away.

He stopped. "I don't want to hurt you, but it will only last a little while."

She nodded, beyond speech.

With one great thrust, he broke past her body's barrier and was deep inside her. She cried out at the pain of it, and he stilled. She tried to move under the massive weight of his body, to ease the discomfort. He groaned.

"Please, *mon ange*, don't move."

She couldn't help it. "I have to." And she did. Only this time when she shifted her hips, she felt unexpected pleasure zing through her body. *"Oh."*

Jared heard the small exclamation and bit back a shout of thanks. Her little movements were driving him over the brink, and he couldn't stay still another second. He pulled back and thrust into her as gently as he could, but when he felt her flesh mold to the shape of his shaft and her thighs tighten around him, he was lost.

He drove into her again and again, rolling his hips on each deep thrust, hoping the sounds she was making were of pleasure and not discomfort. Then she convulsed around him, sobbing out his name, and he spilled his seed into her with a roar that probably deafened her.

He collapsed on top of her, their bodies slick with sweat. He had never experienced anything like this in his life.

His angel was so responsive, he was still reeling from the way she'd found completion against his body while he sucked her nipples. Once again he thanked God for Clairborne's stupidity. Realizing that he was much too big to use his wife as a mattress, he rolled to the side and pulled her against his body.

She snuggled into his side. "That was wonderful. Thank you, Jared."

He almost laughed aloud that she would thank him. "The pleasure was all mine, Cali."

She laughed sleepily, and he rejoiced in the sound. He wanted to hear his too-serious wife laugh more often.

"I'd say the pleasure was definitely mutual, my lord husband."

CALANTHA WOKE THE NEXT MORNING PINNED TO THE bed by a heavy arm and even heavier thigh. She inhaled Jared's masculine scent and snuggled against him. She had had no idea that marriage could be like this. The special intimacy of not only making love, but sleeping in one another's arms, wrapped around her like a cloak of contentment.

Everything had changed, and she never wanted to go back to the lonely, frozen existence she had known when she met Jared. She now had a passionate husband, who might not love her, but clearly wanted her. She'd never known the kind of desire he showed for her, and yet he tempered it with self-control and brought her body pleasure while conquering her heart in the process.

She had a daughter, a sweet little pixie of a girl who lit Calantha's days with her smiles and warmed the last vestiges of her cold soul. It was all so wonderful that it was frightening. This kind of happiness came at a price, she was sure of it. Yet, for now, it had been given her freely for the taking. And she would take it. She would be wife and mother. Friend and sister.

Curling closer to Jared, she let memories of the previous evening wash over her. After consummating their marriage, she and Jared had fallen asleep and woken to make love again. He hadn't wanted to press her, but the evidence of his desire had been unmistakable, and she had prevailed.

The knowledge that she had the power to seduce him warmed her and brought a secret smile to her lips.

They had eaten a late dinner, dressed in nothing but nightrobes—an act as intimate as making love. Then Jared

had insisted she soak in a very hot tub. It had helped with
the soreness, and she had gone to sleep more relaxed than
she had ever been. She contemplated waking Jared with a
kiss, but the residual soreness between her legs decided her
against it.

He had said she should take another bath this morning
and wait to make love again until her inner flesh had an opportunity to heal.

She had every intention of being *healed* by that night,
but she would forego intimate tussling with Jared this morning. After all, there was still a lot of packing to do, and he
insisted they leave the next day. Besides, the poor man
looked exhausted.

Careful not to wake him, she slid from the bed and went
to the adjoining chamber to dress.

When Jared came downstairs an hour and a half later,
she had already sorted several drawers of her papers. He
walked over to where she sat at the dining table surrounded
by piles of her parents' notes and her own, and placed a
soft kiss on her temple. "Good morning, wife."

She smiled at him, feeling an effervescent bubble of happiness light her eyes. "Good morning, husband."

The expression of arrested wonder on his face mesmer-
ized her, and she did not turn her attention to Thomas until
the butler had repeated himself twice.

"My lord and lady, you have visitors in the parlor. Lord
Ashton and Mr. Drake."

So, now that she was no longer a duchess, her parlor was
no longer a drawing room. She smiled at the elderly servant. "Thank you, Thomas. We will be in directly."

Jared nodded his agreement, and Thomas left.

"I wonder what your brothers want," Calantha mused as
she followed Jared into the other room.

"I don't know, but they're bloody lucky not to catch us
in bed."

She felt the heat of a blush stain her cheeks. "It's mid-morning, of course we would be up."

"We wouldn't be if you hadn't snuck out of our bed before I woke up." The sensual promise in his voice sent shivers down the back of her legs.

But she could not speak. She was not used to this game of amorous bantering yet.

Jared let out a low, rich chuckle. "Don't tell me you are embarrassed after last night."

How could she not be after what she . . . they had done? "Perhaps a little," she admitted, infusing her voice with the *duchess* tone.

He turned and smiled down at her, his eyes full of wicked humor. "Maybe after tonight it will be more than a little."

What could be more embarrassing than what they had done last night?

"There is still a great deal I have to teach you about satisfying your husband, *mon ange*," he said, reading her mind.

She tried to frown at his arrogance, but could not suppress a smile. The thought of Jared teaching her more of what she had experienced in his arms last night filled her with anticipation.

"I am a very eager pupil," she said and then blushed even hotter at her own impudence.

He was laughing when they entered the parlor.

Ashton and Drake stood near the fireplace, their looks of serious regard drying up Jared's laughter.

"What?" Jared asked. "Has something happened to Hannah?"

"No," Ashton replied. "She's fine."

"Then why in the bloody hell do you both look like Langley's just returned from his trip to the Continent and threatened to take up residence in your homes?"

Drake's mouth tipped in an almost smile before returning to its earlier serious lines. "The would-be kidnapper has been caught."

Jared's entire body vibrated with sudden purpose. "That's bloody good news. How did it happen?"

"He was spotted in the village and apprehended by the local magistrate. He's in gaol now," Drake replied.

"Then let's go question him." Jared looked fully prepared to leave the house that very moment.

Calantha's heart filled with hope. She hated the idea that some unnamed monster had been running free that might kidnap another child. She wanted answers, too. Why had the man known Hannah's name, and what had he been doing on Ashton property?

"We've already questioned him. The magistrate came to me with the news that he had been caught early yesterday evening."

Jared glared at his brother-in-law. "Why didn't you come and get me? It was my daughter the bastard tried to take."

"It was also your wedding night," Drake remarked somewhat dryly.

Jared's frown didn't lighten. "You should have come to get me."

Calantha wasn't in the least offended that Jared would have gone on their wedding night. Hannah's safety was more important than making love. She could have waited. At least she thought so, she acknowledged honestly. There were times the evening before that she hadn't had even a shred of her usual self-control.

"We're here now," Ashton said.

Jared made a visible effort to rein in his impatience. "So, what did you learn?"

"He told us who hired him to kidnap Hannah." Ashton didn't sound pleased by that fact.

"Who was it?" Jared demanded.

Someone had hired the blackguard? Calantha could not imagine who would wish to do the child harm. She waited in silence for her new brother-in-law to answer.

Drake looked at Calantha with something like sorrow in his eyes. "The Angel."

Twelve

"THE HELL SHE DID." JARED'S ROAR ECHOED off the ceiling of the small room. He rammed his large fist into his other hand. "I'll talk to him and find out just what the bloody hell he thinks he's doing, accusing my wife."

Calantha stood perfectly still. Jared's disbelief and threats only registered in part of her mind. The other part was trying to deal with the terror of being accused of the heinous crime. How many times had she faced unjust accusations, powerless to defend herself against her husband's anger because of them?

"I already talked to him. He believes the Angel hired him." Ashton spoke with frightening certainty.

What if Jared believed him?

"He'll change his tune and start singing the truth when I get hold of him."

Jared's continued defense loosened something inside of Calantha. He didn't believe she was guilty. He would listen to her. This was not Clairborne Park. She did not need to fear speaking in her own defense.

Shame at the fact that she'd stood silent, allowing Ashton to make his accusations gnawed at her. "I didn't do it."

As impassioned defenses went, it wasn't much, but for a woman who had stood in mute dread time and again while her husband passed judgment, the words represented inner strength she had not possessed at one time.

Drake's gaze raked her. "He says you came to him wearing a black gown, long black gloves, and a veil that obscured your face, but he could tell you had blond hair and an angel's beauty. He said you smelled like roses."

She shook her head and then forced herself to speak again. "I have not worn black since the one-year anniversary of Deveril's death."

She did smell like roses. She couldn't deny it. She bathed regularly in water scented from her conservatory flowers.

Ashton turned to her. "Do you still have your widow's weeds from after Clairborne's death?"

The sound of his voice was like a trap closing around her. She could feel it and yet was powerless to lie to protect herself. She reminded herself that the truth could not hurt her; only the ugly lies of a madman threatened her. "Yes."

"Where are they?" Ashton asked, his voice almost gentle.

She forced her lungs to take air and expel it before answering. "In the attic."

"Do you own such an outfit as the one Drake described?"

Why was he asking all these questions? Did he hope to prove her guilt? *Why?* "Yes."

Jared put his hands on her shoulders. "That doesn't prove a bloody thing. Most women of the *ton* have a black dress and veil for mourning."

The band constricting her chest loosened, and she stepped backward, seeking the warmth of her huge husband's body. She needed it very badly right now. As her back touched Jared's hard body, she felt some of the tension drain from her. He would protect her from that blackguard's insinuations.

* * *

JARED COULD FEEL CALANTHA'S TERROR AND IT CON-
fused him. Surely she knew he wouldn't let the bastard
kidnapper get away with trying to accuse her of the crime.
He and his brothers-in-law would get to the bottom of
this.

He caressed her neck in a soothing motion. He knew
she wasn't going to like what he was about to suggest. Hell,
he didn't like it, but it was the only way to establish the
truth. "We'll take Cali to the bastard, and he'll have to admit he's never met her."

Then they could start looking for the real culprit.

CALANTHA'S BODY STIFFENED. GO TO THE GAOL TO MEET
with the blackguard? She couldn't do it. What if he accused her to Jared's face? What if Jared believed him?
"No."

Jared's hands tightened on her shoulders. "It's the only
way, Cali."

"If you're innocent, meeting the man should not
frighten you," Ashton added.

How could she explain her fear to them?

She'd had too many experiences being punished for
supposed crimes when she was innocent. After the first
month of marriage, her husband had conceived a mad
jealousy of any gentleman who spoke to her longer than a
few seconds. He said her sluttish ways were one more reason he would not come to her bed, that and her emptiness.
*Just a marble statue, with nothing but her beauty to sus-
tain her.*

She was *not* a marble statue. She had a mind and a
heart. Jared had helped her realize the last. She had to trust
him. He had helped her reclaim her humanity.

"If you believe it is best, Jared, then I will go."

Ashton's eyes flared in surprise, and Drake looked strangely satisfied.

THE GAOL WAS NOTHING MORE THAN A MEAN LITTLE building with bars over its single window. It looked much like her own potting shed from the outside and was located on the magistrate's estate at the other end of the village from Ashton Manor and Rose Cottage.

Jared held her arm protectively as the magistrate led them into the dimly lit interior. Calantha lifted her skirts to avoid the thick layer of dust on the floor.

A man sat on the lone bench, his leg secured in an iron attached to the floor. In the carriage on the way over, Ashton had said his name was Willem. He wore a dirty coat and even filthier shirt, and his breeches were stained in several places. Hannah had been right. The man was rank. Calantha could smell him as soon as she walked in the door. Trying not to take deep breaths in case she became nauseous from the odor, she hesitated, but Jared's hold propelled her forward.

"So, you've come to visit me, 'ave you, luv?"

She shivered as the man spoke to her as if he knew her.

Jared released her arm and took a threatening step toward the kidnapper. Willem cringed at the look of blatant hostility in Jared's face.

"You told the magistrate that the Angel hired you." Jared made the words sound like an accusation.

Willem rallied to belligerence. "Aye, that she did."

"I do not know this person." Out of habit developed to hide her nervousness, she spoke in the tones of the duchess she used to be.

"Just like the quality. 'ire a man to do a bit 'o work for ye, but throw 'im to the wolves when it goes sour."

Jared grabbed Willem by the lapels of his grimy jacket and lifted him as far as the leg iron would permit. "My wife says she does not know you."

"Well, there's knowin' and there's knowin'. Wouldn't talk to me in the street, she wouldn't, but she 'ired me all right. Paid me good blunt to nab that little knicker. Weren't my fault I couldn't deliver. The kiddie was smart like."

Jared shook him, and spittle flew from the rough man's mouth. "Tell us the truth, damn you."

"Put him down," Ashton barked.

Jared ignored him. "I want the truth."

"I'm tellin' you the truth," Willem whined. "That duchess lady is what hired me. Told me to take the little knicker to the shed in the trees be'ind 'er 'ouse, but the kiddie got away, and I didn't get paid."

Jared tossed the man back onto the bench, his body shaking with rage. Calantha was shaking, too, but not with anger. If she didn't know that she hadn't done it, she would believe the awful little man. He was too terrified to lie convincingly.

She stepped forward, until she was close enough for him to get a good look. "I've never met you, how can you say I hired you to kidnap my daughter?"

"She waren't your daughter then, was she? You said she was a little blight that would embarrass you, you did."

Calantha thought she would retch at the cruel words. She started shaking and backed up until she ran into Ashton's unmoving form.

"Is this the woman that hired you?" he asked the other man.

"Yes. I said it, didn't I? Face like an angel, she 'as, but her 'eart's not so pure." He cackled as if he'd made a wondrously funny joke.

Jared spun around and grabbing her arm, pulled her away from Ashton and out of the building. The sunlight blinded her eyes as they emerged outside, and she blinked several times to try to adjust. He lifted her into the carriage and jumped up to join her. Ashton and Drake followed after a few words with the magistrate.

Jared's silence grated against her taut nerves.

"He's mistaken," she said, not holding out much hope that her husband or his brothers by marriage would believe her.

The evidence was strongly against her.

Jared glared at Ashton. "I think you're right. The man's telling the truth. He thinks Cali hired him."

Calantha could not believe that Jared had spoken the words. It was her worst nightmare come to life. He believed that awful little man over her. The awful distrust and accusations were all beginning again, and she couldn't stop it.

"So, who do you think hired him?" Drake asked.

She stared at him in confusion. Hadn't Jared just said he believed she had hired Willem?

"I don't know, but when I find out, there's going to be hell to pay."

"I don't understand," she whispered, but Jared heard her.

"Someone posed as you and hired that bastard to kidnap Hannah." He turned to Ashton. "Where did he say he met her?"

"At the Blue Goose, a tavern in a village a few miles north of here. It was late at night."

Drake added, "He'd been known to frequent the tavern and take on less than honest jobs if the pay was right."

Jared nodded once. "We'll need to question the tavern keeper and the locals. Maybe they saw her carriage, or horse. That would be more helpful than trying to identify a woman dressed in black, her face covered by a veil."

Calantha slipped her hand into Jared's. Unbelievable as it might seem, he trusted her. Her gratitude brought the sting of tears to her eyes, but she blinked them away.

From the look of doubt on Ashton's face, he wasn't so certain of her innocence. "When I worked in espionage, I found that the simplest solution was usually the right one. Before you develop some complicated conspiracy theory, why don't you make sure your wife is innocent?"

Jared's fury still made her nervous, but she didn't pull her hand from his.

Her husband believed her, and his anger was directed at Ashton. "I already know she's innocent. You've seen her with Hannah. She'd never hurt her."

"Although Willem did not act until later, he was hired before your wife *met* Hannah, before she grew close to the child." Ashton focused his attention on her. "Did you resent Hannah at first? Did it make you angry that another woman had given birth to your husband's child?"

Shame at the memory of her thoughts upon discovering Hannah's existence stained her cheeks. She had resented Mary's giving birth, but not for the reasons Ashton supposed. "Yes."

Jared withdrew his hand and stared down at her. "What the hell do you mean?"

"Don't swear at me." Somehow, on top of everything else, that was too much.

"Excuse me, duchess. I forgot your regal background."

She felt bile rise in her throat and swallowed it down, forcing herself to answer Jared's question. "I resented that I never had the chance to be a mother."

Jared now knew for certain that she had never had the opportunity to become pregnant, that Deveril had been unable to work up sufficient enthusiasm to touch her. After last night, there could be no doubt.

"You wanted that monster's baby?" Jared's enraged question sounded like an accusation.

And it made her angry. She glared at him, surprised at her own daring in doing so. "No. I wanted a baby, period." Her anger drained away as she admitted the truth about her marriage, "Once I knew . . . Once I realized what life with Deveril would be like, I was grateful not to bring a child into it, but part of me always grieved the loss of motherhood. I thought I would never marry again."

Please let him understand, she prayed silently.

Jared turned away from her, his silence testifying to the fact that her prayer had gone unanswered.

"I didn't hire that man." Her almost whispered words went unanswered by the other occupants of the carriage.

They reached her home a few minutes later. The oppressive silence continued as they made their way into the parlor.

JARED DIDN'T NOTICE HIS SISTER WHEN HE FIRST ENtered the parlor. His mind was still grappling with the ramifications of Cali's confession. She claimed she hadn't hired Willem to kidnap their daughter, but she admitted she had resented Hannah.

Bloody hell, what a mess.

"How could you do it?" Thea demanded in a near shrieking tone, bringing Jared's whirling thoughts to a halt.

He had never seen his sister lose her composure like this. She was glaring at Cali as if she wanted to kill her with her bare hands. Jared couldn't believe she was that upset over the would-be kidnapping. He also wondered at the fact that Thea believed his wife to be guilty.

Even with the evidence and her own confession of bitterness, he was hard-pressed to believe his sweet wife capable of such an act.

Drake took three large steps and reached Thea. Placing his hands on her shoulders, he asked, "What happened?"

Thea shook him off and pointed an accusing finger at Cali. "That monstrous woman almost killed our children."

"Darling, you aren't making any sense. Tell me what happened." Drake's voice was calm, but commanding.

Jared envied him his control.

"The puppy. It's dead." Thea started to cry. "David found him. It was awful. And it could have been my babies."

Cali stood frozen by the door, her expression blank except her eyes, which were almost white with terror. Damn it. What had she done?

Drake pulled his wife into his arms and spoke to her in a low, comforting tone until she calmed down. "How did it happen?"

"He ate the candied rose petals Cali sent for Hannah on Saturday. I had nurse put them away because Hannah had already had cake that day, and the children don't sleep well when they have too many sweets. With plans for the wedding, we all forgot about them. But the puppy found them. You know how he could nose out food if it was wrapped in ten layers of cheesecloth." Thea started to cry again. "He ate them and then died. He threw up all over the floor, first, though. Drake, it was terrible. Our children and Hannah could have eaten them. *They could all be dead.*"

Drake pulled Thea against him again, wrapping his arms tightly around her. He looked at Cali over his wife's shoulder, and the look he gave her was lethal.

Cali flinched and backed toward the door.

Jared stormed toward her, not wanting to believe what he was hearing. The passionate and gentle woman he had taken to his bed last night could not try to kill a child. He grabbed Cali's arm and halted her retreat. She was shaking.

Part of him wanted to comfort her and tell her everything was going to be fine, that he wouldn't let anyone hurt her. But a bigger part needed the truth . . . now.

"Did you send the candy to Hannah?"

"No."

"Who did?"

Cali's mouth opened, but no sound came out.

Jared turned to his sister, keeping a firm grip on Cali's arm. "How was the candy delivered?"

"Her stable boy." Thea hadn't raised her head from Drake's chest, but Jared heard her answer without problem.

"Bloody hell." Ashton's voice held disgust and disappointment.

Cali's head was shaking from side to side. "I didn't do it. C-call the stable boy. There must be a mistake."

Jared bellowed Thomas's name, and the butler came rushing into the parlor, his usual dignity conspicuously absent.

"Yes, milord?"

"Get the stable boy."

"Yes, milord."

Thomas left. No one spoke while they waited for the young servant to arrive.

When the boy entered the room, he looked nervous, and Jared decided to let Ashton deal with him. In his present mood, he'd probably terrorize the lad beyond speech. He nodded toward his brother-in-law, and Ashton nodded back.

He motioned the stable boy closer. "You delivered a package for your mistress on Saturday. Do you remember?"

"Yes, milord."

"Do you know what was in it?"

"Candy for the little tyke," the boy said.

Ashton turned to Thomas. "Who instructed you to have the candied rose petals delivered to Hannah?"

"Her ladyship." Thomas turned toward Cali, his expression showing concern. "Is anything amiss?"

Cali's voice came out in a dry whisper. "Thomas, I didn't give you any package to deliver to Hannah."

"You left it with my usual list of instructions, your ladyship, don't you remember?"

"No. Please, Thomas. I didn't leave it."

"But the last item on your list was to have it delivered."

"What list?" Jared demanded.

"Her ladyship leaves a list of instructions for me weekly, your lordship."

"And the package was with this list of instructions?"

"Yes, your lordship."

"Bring me this list."

Thomas's face registered worry. "I will try, your lordship, but the house has been turned upside down with the packing. I am afraid it may have been lost."

Jared swore.

Cali flinched and pulled on her arm. "Please, let me go."

Jared released her, moved in spite of himself by the plea in her voice. She looked ready to faint from fear, and no matter what she had done, he couldn't stand to see that expression on her face.

"I need to get back to my children," Thea said from the circle of Drake's arms.

Jared nodded. "Ashton, you will want to check on Irisa. She's bound to be upset by this turn of events."

He wasn't surprised Thea had been the one to come to confront Cali. She had acted in her anger, so like his own, and then come to regret the impulse to leave her children with Irisa once she'd had time to think.

Ashton looked at Cali and then shrugged. "There's nothing more to do here for the moment."

"Jared, you had better come and comfort Hannah. She was terribly upset by the puppy's death. None of the children realize yet that he was poisoned," Thea said.

Jared looked at Cali before nodding his agreement. Her look of frozen fragility reached out to him, but he had to take care of Hannah. He also needed to think, away from the influence of his wife's tormented blue eyes.

"I'll ride over on Caesar."

"May I come with you? I should like to see Hannah." Cali's voice held none of its usual assurance, and Jared hated to deny her the request.

Thea saved him the task. "I'm sorry, Cali, but until this is all sorted out, I wouldn't be comfortable having you around my children."

He could hear the regret in his sister's voice and wondered if Cali did as well. Now that Thea had calmed down, she doubted Cali's guilt, just like he did. If only Thomas could find the list of instructions from Cali. There were ways of determining if the last item were written in her handwriting. Perhaps the ink would be a slightly different pigment. Something would surely indicate her innocence in the matter.

Cali retreated another step, widening the gap between her and the rest of his family. "Yes, of course. I'll stay here. Did you want to assign a servant to watch me?" she asked Jared, her voice flat and lifeless.

He wanted to say no, to tell her that he trusted her and they would get to the bottom of this mess soon. He couldn't, though. Not and keep his commitment to protecting Hannah.

Cali's feelings would be hurt, but she would get past that once her name had been cleared. She would understand his need to find the truth for Hannah's sake. Cali herself would undoubtedly respond just as he was, in a similar set of circumstances. After all, the safety of a child must come before an adult's feelings.

Besides, in her current dazed state, it would be best to have someone watch over her. "Jenny can keep you company while I am gone."

Something flickered in Cali's eyes, but she said nothing.

LATER, AT ASHTON MANOR, JARED REFLECTED ON THE fact that his wife had not broken her silence even after his sister and the men had left. She had gone quietly to her room, in Jenny's company, avoiding Jared's gaze all the while.

Unlike his sister, Irisa.

She had disappeared while he checked on Hannah, only to reappear later in the library with the rest of his family once the children had been seen to, her expression murderous. She'd opened her mouth to harangue them all and hadn't closed it since.

"I can't believe you accused Calantha of trying to murder her daughter," she glared at Thea. "You've seen her with Hannah. She loves her. Even if she didn't, Calantha is not capable of that sort of base behavior."

"But she left the note, Irisa. I know she's your friend, and it's difficult for all of us to believe she's responsible, but someone tried to poison Hannah, and all the evidence points to Calantha."

"What difference does that make?" Irisa demanded, her eyes shooting brown fire. "If I caught you standing over a dead body with a bloody knife in your hand, I wouldn't believe you capable of the crime."

Thea was momentarily silenced by that, and Irisa turned her ire on Ashton. "I still cannot fathom what made you believe that nasty little man when he said that Calantha hired him. He's obviously lying. She would never stoop to kidnapping a child."

"He identified her when we took her to meet him—" Ashton started to say, only to be interrupted by his irate wife.

"What were you thinking taking Calantha to see a man like that? What if he had hurt her? Would you have taken me to see him? I suppose you would, if you thought the evidence was strong enough."

Ashton flinched under Irisa's scathing tone, and Jared felt compelled to defend him. "It was my decision to take my wife to see him. I thought we could get to the truth that way."

"Instead you allowed him to defame her in your presence. If your wife forgives you before you're old enough to be a grandfather, you'll be a lucky man, Jared Selwyn!"

Ashton laid a hand on his wife's shoulder. "Calm down, sweeting. This kind of excitement isn't good for the baby."

"I get excited when we make love, too. I suppose you're going to say you want to give that up for the rest of my confinement," Irisa stormed.

Ashton's face actually lost a little color at that comment, and Jared was hard-pressed not to laugh, regardless of how bad his mood from the current situation.

"Irrational behavior seems to go hand in hand with

pregnancy," Drake said in an obvious attempt to comfort his brother-in-law.

Thea glared at him. "What is *that* supposed to mean?"

Irisa gave everyone in the room the meanest look he'd ever seen on his sweet sister's face. "I'm not the irrational one around here. I haven't accused a compassionate and kind woman of kidnapping her own child and then trying to kill her."

"She didn't even know Hannah when Willem was approached," Ashton said in exasperation.

"Are you saying that just because she didn't know her, Calantha would have plotted to do her harm? Are you forgetting how diligently she cares for the ailments of the local village children, or the way she's so gentle with them? You've lived in this district longer than I have. Even when she was married to the duke, she didn't have a reputation for snobbery or cruelty."

"Then who's behind the attacks on Hannah?"

"I don't know. What about the new duke? I've never liked him. His brother is Hannah's real father. Maybe he's trying to get rid of a potential embarrassment."

"He doesn't know about Hannah being Deveril's child," Jared felt the need to point out.

His sister snorted. "And you know this how? You're omniscient? And here I believed that particular trait was reserved for the Almighty. For all you know, his brother told him about Mary. The monster probably bragged about raping her."

Jared hadn't considered that possibility.

"The person who hired the blackmailer was a woman, and if she wasn't Calantha, she bore a striking resemblance to her," Drake had the courage to point out.

Irisa wasn't swayed in the least. "So, he hired someone to do it. Maybe his current paramour. His infidelities are legendary in the district, even if he does try to be discreet."

Maybe there was someone besides Cali that had a reason for wanting to do Hannah harm. Cali had admitted to an initial bitterness. There had been no evidence of it remaining.

The pain in Jared's chest lessened a little at the thought.

Thirteen

CALANTHA COULDN'T THINK. SOMEONE WAS trying to hurt, maybe even kill, Hannah, and they wanted her to be blamed for it. And Jared did blame her.

She looked over at Jenny, industriously packing her clothes while Calantha paced the room. She wanted to tell the maid to stop, but she couldn't make herself speak. Not even to Jenny.

Jared had refused to let her see Hannah. Thea thought she was a threat to her children. None of Clairborne's punishments had come close to hurting like this.

Who was behind it? *Who?* And why would anyone want to hurt the child?

She paced back over to the window.

She couldn't think. She just didn't know. Her mind kept dwelling on the look of infuriated shock in Jared's eyes when Thea told him about the puppy. That sweet little animal, dead. It was too horrible to contemplate. Jared had started off believing her. She had been surprised and then so relieved, she'd almost cried when she realized he wanted to believe her.

Yet as the evidence mounted, his trust dried up like a potted rose that had not been watered.

She knew she should not blame him, but she couldn't help feeling betrayed. If the situation were reversed, she would have believed in his innocence. She would have believed in him. Because she loved him.

But Jared didn't love her. He'd married her to keep Hannah. He wanted her, but clearly that was no more than physical lust. Any tender feelings he had toward her were as shallow as a puddle after a spring rain.

The pain of his distrust would destroy her, if she let it. She could not let it. She had survived so much worse, she told herself, but deep in her heart she wasn't sure that was true.

Just like the first time, her marriage was over before it had begun. She had had one day and one night of contentment, of happiness. That was more than she had experienced in six long years, but was it worth the pain that now lacerated her soul?

Even if she convinced Jared of her innocence, she would never have that kind of happiness again. She had finally learned the lesson Deveril had tried so hard to teach her.

She was not worthy of love.

What would Jared do? Would he turn her over to the magistrate?

She knew he would not beat her. He might hate her, but Jared would not use his fists to vent his fury.

She thought of the duke's words on that fateful Saturday, his accusations against Jared and his family. She had believed in Jared, even in the face of the scandalous facts. *Because she loved him.* He was furious right now. So angry, his feelings had vibrated in the parlor, and yet she trusted him not to physically hurt her. *Because she loved him.*

But he did not love her. He did not trust her.

It hurt.

She didn't want it to hurt. She didn't want to feel, but she couldn't help it. She loved, and she hurt.

She loved Jared so much that she could not bring back

the ice to protect her heart from the pain it now suffered. And he despised her. He believed she was capable of trying to murder their daughter. How could he believe her capable of such base cruelty? She had been a coward, but never cruel.

Her hands clenched at her sides until her short nails dug into her palms.

Jared could not know her at all if he believed her capable of such ugliness. Once again, she found herself married to a man who saw only the surface. Jared did not expect perfection, but he didn't believe in her basic integrity either. Only a monster would try to kill an innocent child.

She was no monster.

She *loved* Hannah. Someone was trying to kill her daughter, and Calantha would rather die than let that happen. The thought of losing the child she had grown to love so deeply tore at her insides. Hannah, of the sweet smiles and dimpled knees. The more she got to know the child, the more the sweetness of her mother, Mary, shown through. A woman Jared had obviously believed worthy of love.

The only thing she didn't understand was why they had never married. But then, she only had to look at her own past to find the answer. She had never wanted to marry again after suffering Deveril's cruelty, how much more would Mary balk at the prospect, after being raped by him? Even those thoughts could not hold her attention now.

Hannah adored *her* rose candy, and someone had used that knowledge to try to harm the little girl. As Thea had said, all of the children could have been harmed. The only person she had ever known in her life who could be that vicious was dead. How much of that evil lived in his brother?

No matter what it took, Hannah must be protected.

That meant Calantha had to prove her innocence, or Jared would believe he had the culprit and relax his vigilance on Hannah's behalf. He must not do so. Not while the true villain still remained in the shadows ready to strike again.

Calling on two years of dealing with brutality and pain, she withdrew into herself, to that place of safety she thought she would never have to use again. As she clamped down on her emotions, her fear receded and her mind began to function once again.

She let her mind drift back over the past three weeks, trying to piece together a clear picture of the order of events. Henry came to call. He adamantly opposed her relationship with Jared. She went to see Hannah. She left without meeting the child, once again giving in to her weak-kneed fear.

Jared brought Hannah to see her. She fell in love with the little girl and her adopted father. Henry came to call again, this time with Ellen. Neither were pleased with her association with Jared, or her upcoming wedding. Were the reasons they had given sufficient for the level of their distaste? She had to admit that in the eyes of a Clairborne, they would be.

Calantha had then learned her body's response at Jared's hand. She could not afford to remember that now, so she pushed the thought away. Henry came to call again, to try to talk her out of the marriage. He had come on Saturday. The candy had shown up on Saturday.

Every path led back to the duke.

But she could not fathom a reason. He believed Hannah was Jared's—or did he? The Clairbornes did not even have a passing acquaintance with honesty. Had Deveril boasted of his "conquest" of Mary? Had the duke known the truth of Hannah's paternity? If he did, would he go to such lengths to prevent scandal? If he was as wicked as Deveril, he would not see the death of a child too high a price to pay for his countenance.

But how was she going to prove to Jared that she wasn't the one who had planned the attacks against Hannah?

SHE WAS WAITING FOR JARED IN HER ROOM WHEN HE got home later that night. He dismissed Jenny and turned to

Calantha. His expression was grim, and he looked haggard with tiredness. She almost reached out to sooth him, but stopped herself. He might not love her, but she loved him, and she was likely to disgrace herself if she allowed herself to touch him.

"The duke was here on Saturday."

Jared's expression said he didn't understand the significance of that statement.

"He came to call the day the poisoned candy showed up."

A soft knock sounded at the door.

Jared walked over and opened it. Thomas stood on the other side.

"Jenny told me her ladyship asked to see me."

She had instructed Jenny to send Thomas up once Jared arrived. "Come in for a moment, Thomas."

Jared stepped back in order to allow Thomas to enter.

"I was just telling my husband that the duke came to call again on Saturday."

Thomas's expression turned blank, but not before she saw his startled surprise at her words.

Jared noticed it as well. "Did you admit his grace to the house on Saturday, Thomas?"

"I'm not sure, milord. Things have been so confusing with the wedding and preparing her ladyship to move." He was not a convincing liar.

"Tell me the bloody truth," Jared roared.

Thomas jumped, but remained silent.

Calantha turned to Jared. "Do not yell at him, my lord. He is only trying to protect me."

Her loyal servant did not want her caught in a lie, but she wasn't lying, and she would find a way to prove it without compromising the older man's honor. He looked as if he would continue to refuse to answer, and Calantha stepped toward him.

She laid her hand on his arm. "It is all right, Thomas. You may tell his lordship the truth. Just because you did not see his grace does not mean he wasn't here."

"But I *didn't* see him, your ladyship. If I had, I would have called for your husband."

She nodded and released his arm. That is what she had thought at the time. "He must have snuck in. I wondered why you did not announce him."

Jared made an impatient sound, but she ignored him.

"That will be all, Thomas. Except, would you please ask the other servants if any of them saw his grace on Saturday?"

"Yes, milady."

Thomas left, a look of concern on his face. Her servants would have no idea why Jared had asked Jenny to stay with her while he was gone, or why things had become so strained between their master and mistress.

She turned to her husband, her face and tone as expressionless as she could make them. "How was Hannah? I'm assuming you did not bring her home with you."

Jared rubbed his eyes with his thumb and forefinger. "No. She was distraught about the puppy, but is better. She was sleeping when I left."

The silence stretched in the room, but she did not mind. At least when it was silent, she was relatively safe. Words had destroyed her newfound happiness, not silence.

"She wanted to stay with her cousins, and I thought, under the circumstances, that would be best."

Calantha didn't respond. If he expected her to agree with him, he would wait a long while.

"Damn it, Cali. I don't like this situation any more than you do."

"I'm sure you don't." The prospect of being married to a would-be murderess must be very upsetting.

"Did you eat dinner?" he asked.

"No."

"Why the hell not?"

She shrugged and turned away from him. "I wasn't hungry."

Jared made another explosive sound, but she ignored it. She walked to her wardrobe and pulled out a night rail and sleeping robe. "I'm rather tired, Jared. I think I'll go to bed."

"I have to talk to the servants, and then I'll join you."

He was probably going to question them about her activities. He wouldn't trust Thomas to question the other servants about whether or not they had seen the duke on Saturday either. She kept her gaze averted, saying nothing, and waited for him to leave.

With another muttered curse, he did.

She had changed into her nightclothes and braided her hair ten minutes later when the door opened to reveal Jenny carrying a tray. "His lordship said to bring you some food, milady."

Calantha stared at the tray and then at Jenny. "I am not hungry."

Jenny nodded. "I told him you were feeling a little peaked tonight, milady, but he said I wasn't to leave until you'd eaten."

Calantha wanted to be alone, but the look of nervous determination on her maid's face told her that wouldn't happen until she bowed to Jared's dictates. More importantly, if she was going to set about proving her own innocence in the face of her new family's mistrust, she would need her strength.

She could not afford to starve herself, no matter how little she relished the thought of eating. "Set the tray on the table by the window."

She followed the maid and sat down to eat. Thankfully, it was only some bread, cheese, and a small glass of wine. She did not think she could have eaten more. She consumed most of it and drank all the wine before telling Jenny to take the tray away.

Jenny surveyed the tray as if determining whether or not Jared would be satisfied. She must have decided he would, because she picked it up and left.

Calantha rose from the table, crossed the room, and opened the adjoining door. Hannah was supposed to sleep in the smaller bedchamber, but the little girl was *safe* at Ashton Manor. Safe from her. Calantha would use that bed tonight.

No doubt Jared had no more desire to sleep with her than she did with him. She had no intention of waiting to be evicted from their bedchamber.

She crawled into the narrow bed, turned on her side, and tugged the covers up to her chin. Then she let the tears, which had been blocking her throat since her brothers-in-law's arrival that morning, fall.

SINCE HE DIDN'T WANT TO WAKE CALANTHA, JARED DID not light a candle when he entered their bedchamber an hour later. He'd spoken to Thomas again, verifying the servant hadn't forgotten the duke's arrival on Saturday. Then he'd questioned Jenny, the stable boy, and the groundskeeper. Cook and the maid that came in daily from the village had already left for the night. He would have to wait until the following day to speak to them.

One of them must have seen the duke's arrival.

He needed to ask Cali if she knew whether or not the duke had known about Hannah. He stripped out of his clothes, looking forward to holding his wife. He didn't think she'd let him make love to her, not with the way she'd been avoiding him, but he needed to hold her and know that she was safe. Just as he had held Hannah earlier and confirmed that she was indeed well.

Cali needed to see Hannah. He'd go and get their daughter in the morning. He couldn't deny either of them the solace.

He slid into the too-short bed and reached for his wife,

only to encounter empty bedding. He jumped out of the bed and lit the candle he had foresworn moments before. There was no sign of his wife's whereabouts. About to shout for her maid and demand where her mistress had gone, his gaze settled on the connecting door. Hannah's room.

Cali had arranged it so that Hannah would be in the room next to them, so they could hear her if she woke in the night. Was she in there now, brooding over today's events?

He walked to the door, prepared to comfort his wife. He wasn't sure how he was going to do that, but he had to try. He couldn't stand another minute of her frozen composure. Opening it, he realized it was dark. Had he been wrong? Where was Cali? Then he heard a soft sigh from the vicinity of the bed. He squinted, trying to make out the shapes in the room in the near darkness. *She was sleeping in Hannah's bed.*

She did not want to share a bed with him.

Somehow that prospect had never occurred to him. He'd thought she would understand, but the small form in the narrow bed bespoke rejection, not understanding.

He stalked over to the bed.

"What are you doing in our daughter's bed?"

"Trying to sleep," a flat voice replied, sounding too much like the Calantha he had first met.

"I thought we agreed we would share a bed."

"I do not wish to share your bed."

"You belong to me, Cali. You sleep in my bed." He winced at the arrogance of his words, but could not take them back.

"I think not, my lord. Aren't you afraid of sleeping with a would-be murderess? Who is to prevent me from killing you in your sleep?" she asked scathingly, the false front of calm disappearing.

She was bloody furious with him, he realized.

After spending the day with two sisters bent on venting their spleens in every direction, a household in uproar, and a daughter beside herself with grief over the dead puppy, Jared's less-than-stellar reserves of patience were used up.

He tugged the covers off of his wife and leaned down to pick her up before she could voice an argument. He lifted her into his arms.

She was rigid against him. "What do you think you are doing?"

JARED CROSSED THE ROOM IN BROODING SILENCE AND then dropped Calantha gently onto their bed. He stood above her, magnificently naked and aroused. How could he be aroused at a time like this?

And how could she be responding to that knowledge? The last thing she needed to deal with right now was the betrayal of her own body.

He moved as if to get on the bed, and she glared at his arousal. "Don't even consider it, Ravenswood."

He wiped his hand over his face and shook his head. He looked so tired, so defeated. "It's been a rotten day, and all I want is to hold my wife and sleep. Is that such a great deal to ask?"

Rage at his words and fury at the treacherous compassion stealing into her heart exploded in Calantha in a way she had never known before.

She shot to her feet, standing in the middle of the bed. "How dare you complain about today's events? You aren't the one who stands accused of trying to kidnap and murder your daughter! You refused to let me see Hannah after hearing that someone had tried to poison her, allowed your sister to accuse me of heinous crimes, and dare to stand there with . . . with . . . with an *erection* and yell at me! Is it any wonder I wanted to sleep in a different bed?"

"I'm hard as a spike because that's the effect you have on me, Cali. I can't help it!"

"I suppose you think I should be flattered that you lust

after my body? Do you think that just because Deveril thought I was a useless marble statue, I should be grateful that a man who thinks I tried to kill my daughter finds me appealing?"

He seemed to swell with outraged fury, but responded to her accusation with rigid silence at first. Then taking a visible rein on his temper, he bit out, "No, damn it. Your first husband was an idiot, and I don't want your gratitude. I want you."

"Well, I don't want you," she lied and wasn't even sorry she did it.

"I'm not stupid," he gritted out. "I know you don't want to make love to me after today, but you damn well will sleep with me. Whether or not you realize it, we both need the comfort."

That truth wasn't one she needed to hear at the moment, and while he might not be stupid, he certainly was blind.

Her nipples were already hard, and it was all she could do not to throw herself at her husband and beg him to help her forget the awful day in the pleasure of his arms. If they made love, she could pretend he cared for her, and that was a weak desire, one she did not want to give in to.

"I suppose you thought I should have waited until you deigned to kick me out of our bed before I went," she said with angry mockery she'd never indulged in before.

"I'm not kicking you out of our bed," he growled sounding exasperated.

"You're saying you want to sleep with a conniving, cruel monster who would first try to kidnap and then kill a child?" she taunted.

"No. I want to sleep with my wife." His shout was loud enough to be heard in the next county.

The temper he'd been holding in had finally snapped, and instead of fearing it, she welcomed his loss of control. It matched her own.

She glared at him while considering his words.

Was he saying he didn't believe she'd done those things? Or was he just demanding she sleep with him?

There was no way he could be completely convinced of the evidence against her and still want to hold her. He must have some doubts, which meant he had to trust her a little. It wasn't much, but it was something. And he'd been right about one thing. She did not want to spend the night alone with her fears for Hannah and her tormented thoughts.

"Fine. I'll sleep with you, but that's all," she reiterated.

She hoped that was true, but she had her doubts. He might be quite capable of keeping his hands off her. However, she was not at all sure of her own self-control where he was concerned.

His gaze dropped to her breasts and then rose to her face. He'd finally noticed what the muted light from the single candle could not conceal. Her body's reaction to his presence.

"You want me." He sounded awed and extremely pleased by the fact, if somewhat confused.

"Do not concern yourself. I'll overcome my idiocy. Apparently, one's body is not at governance from one's head in these matters."

He shook his head, his black mane swaying against his shoulders. "I'm concerned, all right."

Oh no, it was that seductive voice. The one he used when they made love. She backed up a step on the bed and almost fell as the feather ticking dipped under her feet. "No."

He moved closer to the bed, until his legs were braced against the high wooden frame. "Yes. Cali, *please*. We both need this."

No. She couldn't let him make love to her, *could she*? She was furious with him. He didn't believe in her. She couldn't want him. *She shouldn't.* But, oh heavens, she did.

She warily waited for him to move, not sure what her response would be if he attempted seduction.

He climbed on the bed, his male member bobbing with

the movement. She wanted to reach out and touch it to see if it was always that resilient. She almost screamed as the thought entered her mind. How could she do this to herself?

With the speed of a striking snake, his hands shot out and grabbed her, yanking her down beside him in one fluid movement.

She did scream then, but the pressure of his lips quickly cut it off. The erotic taste of his mouth battered against her resistance, but she couldn't meekly submit.

She'd never been so angry with anyone in her entire life, but her body latched onto a truth that had eluded her mind. There was a safe outlet for that anger, even a pleasurable one.

So, she kissed him back with ferocious hunger, biting at his lips and thrusting her tongue into his mouth with more aggression than she had believed herself capable of. He let her do it and groaned his response. "That's it, angel. Kiss me like you mean it."

She meant it, certainly, but she didn't think he'd like to hear just what she did mean.

He yanked at her nightgown, and she heard the fabric rip. She didn't care. She wanted her naked skin against his. In seconds, she had her wish. She rubbed her aching nipples against the curling hair on his chest and moaned her pleasure at the sensation.

He cupped her bottom and pushed the juncture of her thighs against his throbbing flesh. She hooked her thigh over his leg, opening her feminine softness to brush against his engorged manhood.

"You make me crazy."

"Make *me* forget," she demanded.

And he did. He slid the hand that had cupped her bottom down, until his fingers were between her legs, touching and tormenting her sensitized flesh. "You're wet."

He slipped a finger inside of her, and she arched her body against his hand. "Yessss."

"You're so hot and tight. It feels good."

It did. Good enough to get lost in. She wiggled her hips, and shards of pleasure splintered through her. He pressed his thumb against the center of pleasure above her opening and thrust his finger more deeply into her.

"Jared."

He did it again, this time making a small circle with his thumb. And then he just kept doing it. His finger moved in and out of her tight channel, and his thumb made little circles or up and down movements against her swollen nub.

She moved her hips against him, maximizing the contact with his hand. She grabbed his face and kissed him again, her tongue playing sensual games with his, while he touched her with intimate abandon. Then she was on her back, and he was poised to enter her.

"Tell me you want me, Cali. Let me hear the words."

She shook her head. She'd given as much as she was going to.

"Say it, angel. I have to hear you say it."

His erection throbbed against the entrance of her body, and she tried to tilt her hips up to receive him, but he wouldn't let her complete the joining. He wanted the words.

She glared up at him, her whole body shaking with unsatisfied desire. *"You say it.* Tell me you want me, after everything that happened today."

He grabbed her wrists and yanked them above her head, his expression fierce. He leaned down and kissed her with a feral intensity, then raising his lips just a breath from hers, he growled, "I want you, now and forever."

Tears spiked her lashes, but she ignored them. "Then come inside me. I want it." She would not say she wanted him, she would not give him the satisfaction. And right now, she wasn't sure it was him she wanted. What she craved was oblivion. Apparently content with her semantics, he kissed her again and pushed slowly forward with his hips. Everything else had been so wild, she'd expected him to roughly shove himself into her, but he didn't. He took his time, waiting for her body to adjust to the width and length of him.

He rocked gently against her. "Take all of me, *mon ange*. Please, wife. All of me."

She wanted all of him. She wanted his body so melded to hers that she didn't feel alone anymore. Spreading her legs as wide as they would go, she arched her hips up, and he slid the rest of the way in. And stopped.

He kissed her again, this time his lips as soft as a butterfly's caress against hers.

Then he started to move, careful thrusts that built the pleasure in her one slow degree at a time, until she was panting and begging him to go faster.

"Harder, Jared. Please. Faster." She needed more. That incredible explosion of pleasure hung just out of reach as he rocked his body slowly against hers.

"I want this to last. I don't want it over too soon."

She knew what he meant. Right now, nothing existed for them except each other. No ugly accusations. No poisoned candy. No danger. Not even the oblivion she thought she craved. Just pleasure and oneness.

She kissed his face, his lips, his chin, his neck, soft nibbling kisses that expressed what she would not say in words, what she might never give voice to: her love, an emotion strong enough to withstand even the painful betrayal he had dealt her.

Then her mind went blank of anything but the pleasure in her body as the slow, burning thrusts built up the coiling tension inside her. She felt the warm track of tears down her temples as her body went stiff and pleasure splintered through her, overwhelming her until she cried out with it.

He let go of her wrists and hugged her tightly to him, while his thrusting went out of control, bringing an almost instant replay of the spiraling enchantment. As his warm seed filled her, she convulsed around him again, crying out his name.

He opened his eyes and met her gaze, his expression so intense it shattered her. "You are mine."

She didn't deny it. She couldn't. But she refused words of confirmation.

He rolled off of her and tucked her into his side. She lay there for several minutes letting her thoughts float in the aftermath of the loving, but eventually reality once again intruded.

"Do you think I'm guilty, Jared?"

"I think there's a lot I don't understand, but I'm going to figure it out."

She frowned in the darkness. "I could be pregnant. After yesterday and tonight."

His arms tightened around her. "Yes."

"If I am, and you aren't convinced of my innocence when the baby comes, will you take it from me like Langley took you away from your mother?"

Fourteen

"WHAT COLOR WAS THE CANDY?"

Cali's question exploded in the silent room like a firecracker on Boxing Day, although she spoke in her usual low tones. She had stood in silence at that bloody window for what felt like forever. She'd asked him to request his family come to Rose Cottage this morning, and he'd agreed.

He didn't know what her plans were, and he hadn't asked. He was still so furious over the question she'd asked him after making love the night before that he didn't trust his temper talking to her. How could she ask if he would act like Langley? He wasn't his father, and he bloody well knew it. But the worst part of it was the fact that he hadn't had an answer for her.

What could he say?

If she were guilty, she wouldn't be a fit mother, but he couldn't make his mouth form the words.

Her face now wore the expression it had on the first day he met her, its creamy smoothness revealing nothing of her thoughts. After the intensity of their lovemaking last night, having her look at him with that blank calmness both angered and frightened him.

Thea asked, "What does it matter?"

Cali met Thea's gaze, her own unflinching. "As long as you all believe I'm guilty, you will only think to protect Hannah from me. I must establish my innocence so that Hannah can be adequately protected until the true villain is caught."

Didn't she think he would watch over their daughter?

"How will knowing what color the candy was aid you in doing so?" Ashton asked, his face an impassive mask.

His wife glared at him. Jared wasn't the only one with woman problems.

"I only make candy with red roses. My *Slater's Crimsons* are my favorites for the task. You can verify that with both my cook and the vicar's wife. If the candy was a different shade of rose petal, then that will be a chink in the wall of your belief in my guilt. That chink alone may be sufficient to encourage you to keep your guard up, even if you don't stop suspecting me."

"That won't prove anything. You could have made another color deliberately, just to try to get us to believe your innocence." Thea didn't sound accusatory, more like she was hoping Cali had an answer for that eventuality.

"Oh, for Heaven's sake," Irisa exclaimed, clearly irritated with all of them.

Cali ignored her interruption and answered Thea's question. "Preparing rose candy is a very long process and certainly not something I could have hidden from my cook. If I had made any using a different color of roses, she would have known. Again, you are free to ask her. Besides, if I'm muddleheaded enough to use my own servants to deliver the poison, I'm too lack-witted to think of making the candy with a different type of rose petal."

Hope exploded in Jared. His wife was bloody smart, too intelligent to do as she'd just said and have used her own servant to deliver the poisoned candy. She was also too clever to have approached Willem, disguised only in her widow's weeds.

Thea smiled. "The candy was pink, a very pale pink."

"Thank God," Cali whispered, her clenched hands relaxing at her sides.

She hadn't known. She had been hoping, but she hadn't known.

Jared wanted to shout hosannas. He'd been unable to accept that his gentle wife was guilty of something so foul from the beginning, but the evidence against her had been strong. Too strong to dismiss out of hand, when coupled with her admission that she'd resented Hannah at first. However, using that clever little brain of hers, she'd poked holes in the case against her. She'd be a damn fine chess player.

"You said the duke came to see you on Saturday." Ashton's mask had dropped away, and he appeared as relieved as Jared felt.

Jared had told them all what Cali had said about the duke coming to call when he went to the manor to fetch them that morning.

"Yes, but I have no proof." Cali's expression had not lightened.

Didn't she realize they believed her? Jared wanted to go over and take her in his arms, but the remoteness of her expression stopped him.

"You don't need proof. We believe you," Irisa announced.

Cali turned to face her sister-in-law and smiled. It was a small smile, but genuine, and Jared would give anything to see it again. "Thank you."

"Why did he come, Cali?" Drake asked.

"He wanted to warn me off marrying into a family so rife with scandal."

"The hell you say." If the duke had been there at that moment, Jared would have flattened him.

Cali turned expressionless eyes to him. "Yes. He was particularly concerned that as the son of a dishonorable man, you would have no honor yourself."

"He told you about my father?" How had the duke learned the truth?

Jared supposed it wouldn't be that hard. Rumors had circulated since his parents left for the Continent, but no one had ever come out and made an accusation. Funny how his father fleeing had actually been the catalyst to destroying his reputation, rather than the refuge he sought.

"Yes. Apparently your mother was not dead when he remarried the current countess. Lady Ashton's birth was illegitimate?"

She asked the question of Ashton, and he was the one that answered. "That is correct."

Pink stained Irisa's cheeks, and Cali met her eyes. "Your father's actions are no reflection on you."

Irisa nodded. She knew that. They'd told her often enough, but her illegitimacy had almost cost her Ashton, and she did not dismiss it lightly.

Cali turned back to Jared. "He was angry when I refused to back out of the marriage. He threatened to refuse to acknowledge me in the future. He implied you might be counting on my connection to the Clairborne title."

Jared wasn't sure how to reply. She had married him anyway, so the duke's words must not have swayed her, but it bothered the hell out of him that someone had tried so hard to convince Cali not to marry him. "I don't care about the bloody title."

"That is what I told him."

"And you married Jared, despite what you learned about his family," Thea said, her voice warm with approval.

Cali's brow rose fractionally. "Yes."

Something was wrong, but Jared couldn't quite figure out what. Cali should be happy. The sparkle that had lit her eyes after their marriage should be returning, but she was watching them all with that bloody emotionless *duchess look.*

His sister's prediction that Calantha would not easily

forgive him his lack of trust came back to torment him. He hadn't meant to hurt her, damn it. He had only wanted to protect *both* his wife and his daughter.

"You think the duke left the poisoned candy and added instructions to your list for Thomas?" Drake asked, getting back to the subject at hand.

"I don't know. He was very angry when I refused to call off the wedding."

"Does the duke know that his brother is Hannah's father?" Ashton asked.

"He behaves as if he doesn't, harping on Jared's willingness to raise his illegitimate daughter in the public eye as proof of his unsuitability."

"That could be a clever ruse to protect himself from suspicion," Irisa said, her expression thoughtful.

Calantha nodded. "I considered that possibility. If we don't, nothing else makes sense."

Thea's brow creased. "Do you think the duke is capable of killing a child to protect himself from uncertain scandal?"

Calantha said nothing, nor did her expression give a clue to her inner thoughts, but Jared could easily imagine how offensive she would find the question, when the day before Thea had been accusing Cali of something similar.

"He's far more likely a suspect than Cali," Irisa said, her tone acidic.

"A woman hired the would-be kidnapper," Drake reminded them.

"A woman who looks, smells, and speaks like me," Cali added, her voice showing neither concern nor anger at that fact.

"The duchess?" Jared asked.

Cali's attention swung to him. "I don't think so. She is a duchess. A real duchess. She would never stoop to consorting with a man like the one I met at the gaol. She's been trained from birth to ignore the unpleasant, and I don't think she would care enough about Hannah's parentage to take action. If she knows the truth, she is much more likely to simply pretend Hannah does not exist. Besides, she has brown hair, not blond, and she scents her bathwater with an exotic French bath oil, not rose water."

It struck Jared that Cali was talking in paragraphs for the first time since he'd met her.

"I think the time has come to call on the duke," Jared said.

He was surprised when Cali shook her head. "What would be the point? If he is guilty, he isn't going to admit it. If he isn't, he'll be terribly offended."

"I don't care about his tender feelings."

"You should. He's a powerful man, and he can cause you and your family a great deal of harm, Jared. He's not above doing so if you anger him."

Jared couldn't believe she thought he couldn't protect her from Clairborne. "I won't let him hurt you."

"If he's the one who is behind all this, he already has." She didn't say it like it mattered. He knew it did. Damn it, didn't she realize that was the reason he had to talk to the duke? Not only had the man tried to hurt Hannah, but he had succeeded in hurting Cali, and for that alone, Jared might kill him.

"At any rate, I wasn't referring to myself," Cali continued. "I meant your family, Jared. Henry could make trouble for Drake's shipping company or spread the scandal about Irisa's illegitimacy in the highest echelons of the *ton*. He could drag your mother's name through the mud."

How the hell had she come to the conclusion that she wasn't his family? She was his *wife*.

Drake frowned. "None of that matters if he's responsible for trying to harm Hannah. As Thea said, whoever poisoned the candy could have killed all the children. That sort of mad evil has to be stopped."

Thea hadn't accused some unnamed person of trying to

kill her children, Calantha thought. She had accused *her.*
"I'm aware that whoever is responsible must be stopped,
but it would be prudent to seek out more information before accusing a duke of the realm of such a heinous crime."

She went to the bellpull and gently tugged on it. Thomas
had insisted on having a local handyman install it after they
took up residence at Rose Cottage. A duchess should not
have to call for her servants, he had said.

Thomas arrived moments later. His eyes were filled with
wary concern.

"Will you please have Cook come to the parlor?" Calantha asked.

Thomas did not show by so much as a flicker his surprise at having the cook called to meet with nobility in the
parlor. "Yes, milady."

"Why did you call for the cook?" Jared asked, clearly
puzzled.

She wondered at his ignorance. "To verify my statement
concerning the color of rose petals I use to make candy."

Why were the others staring at her like that? Surely they
did not think she had been bluffing. Moments later, the
rounded form of her cook appeared in the entrance to the
parlor.

"Come here, please."

The woman came forward, her mobcap slightly askew.
The house truly had been at sixes and sevens preparing for
her move to Raven Hall. Calantha was grateful that her cook
had insisted on staying until she departed with Jared for
her new home. She did not know how she would have sub-
stantiated her claim, otherwise. The vicar's wife could verify that Calantha only sent red candy to her home, but not
that she had not made another color.

The cook looked nervous, and Calantha sought to put
her at her ease. "Do not be concerned. I need to ask you a
few questions, and then you may get back to your preparations for the afternoon meal."

Cook slid Thomas, who had followed her into the parlor, a sidelong glance. The elderly butler's face remained impassive.

"It is imperative that you tell the truth. Do you understand?" Calantha asked.

The other woman nodded. "Yes, your gr—milady."

"Please tell my husband how long it takes to make rose candy."

The cook smiled, obviously relieved at the simplicity of the question. "Well, we've been known to make it in one long day, milady, but usually it takes two."

"What color of petals do I prefer for my candy?"

"Red, milady. You complained that the lighter colors turned brown, and they did," she said with an emphatic shake of her head.

"When was the last time I made candy with a different color of petal?" Calantha asked, realizing that the cook's last answer could imply she had done so recently.

"Why the first year we come to live here, milady. We used them pretty yellow roses, but they turned an awful brown."

"Have I made any rose petal candy lately?"

"About a week ago, milady. Don't you remember? You brung in them pretty red roses all blooming big, like, and said you wanted to make a batch for the vicar's kiddies. You had me save a few for the tea tray when Miss Hannah comes visiting."

Calantha nodded. "I remember. Thank you, Cook."

She turned to her husband. "Are you satisfied, or would you like to question her further?"

Jared looked furious, but she couldn't imagine why. "No. I'm satisfied," he ground out between clenched teeth.

She then faced Ashton, Drake, and his wife. "Would any of you like to ask Cook anything before she returns to the kitchen?"

She was not at all surprised when Ashton nodded.

"Do you know of anyone else locally who makes that type of candy?" he asked.

Calantha had not considered that, but it was a good question.

Cook started to shake her head and stopped. "If you mean by local, a few miles north, then there's a lady what makes candy from her roses, but it isn't half so nice as milady's, and she doesn't share it around the village like. She saves it for her titled guests. Won't catch her giving it to the vicar's children."

"Who is it?" Ashton asked.

"Squire Jensen's wife."

"When you say that she lives north, how far north do you mean?" Drake asked.

"She's about halfway from here to Clairborne Park, sir."

Calantha waited, but no one asked any further questions. She was going to dismiss the cook, when Thomas spoke.

"Milady, I hope you don't mind me speaking out of turn."

"No, Thomas. It is quite all right."

"You asked me to talk to the other servants and see if any of them saw his grace when he came to call on Saturday."

"Yes."

"Cook said she saw the duke's horse in the trees behind the house when she went out to gather in some herbs she had drying in the sun in the back garden."

Calantha turned to the servant woman. "Are you quite sure it was his grace's horse?"

"Yes, milady. It was that nasty spotted horse what bit Timmy, the stable lad, before he came to work here."

"Why didn't you tell Thomas at the time?" Jared asked, his voice barely below a roar.

"I didn't know I was supposed to," Cook gasped, her face red from embarrassment.

Calantha gave Jared a quelling glare and then turned back to her cook. "It's quite all right. You are not responsible for the comings and goings of visitors."

"Are you satisfied?" she asked the other occupants of the room, once again.

This time each one nodded, except Jared. He looked ready to throttle someone.

She turned her back to him and spoke to Ashton. "I cannot prove that I did not hire the man who tried to kidnap Hannah. My servants do not bother me at night, and I am in the habit of preparing myself for bed because I often stay up late with my studies. Therefore, my maid cannot tell you if I was in the house the night he was hired."

To her surprise, Ashton's face flushed a dull red. "Irisa told me not to believe it. She said you would no more hire someone to take Hannah than you would dance naked on our tower roof. I just had to be sure," he said by way of apology.

"Of course. You have no reason to trust me, Lord Ashton."

"On the contrary, my husband is every bit as aware of your good works in the district as I am. You have always been very kind to the village children and go out of your way to treat their ills. He should have taken that into consideration when that nasty kidnapper accused you of hiring him."

It struck Calantha that at no time had Irisa shown even the slightest doubt in her innocence. If only Jared had been as stalwart in his belief in her. "If your husband is now convinced of my innocence, I am content."

"We all are," Jared announced.

Calantha looked at Drake and Thea, waiting for them to answer her unspoken question.

"We are," Thea said, "and I'm terribly sorry for the way I behaved yesterday. My only excuse is that my protective instincts as a mother had been aroused, and it took me a while to remember what a gentle creature you are and how much you love your daughter. I let the smoke screen of evidence cloud my thinking."

Calantha did not know what to say. She had not expected an apology. "There was no reason for you to believe in my innocence. The evidence looked very convincing. Please don't trouble yourself about it further."

Thea jumped up from her seat beside Drake and rushed across the room to hug Calantha. Calantha awkwardly patted her back, not knowing how to respond. She had hoped to convince them all that they needed to be even more vigilant about Hannah; she had not hoped to convince them of her complete innocence.

"I WANT A HUG, TOO, MAMA."

The housekeeper shrugged from the doorway as if to say there had been no keeping Hannah from her new mama any longer. Jared dismissed the servant with a small inclination of his head.

Cali stiffened at the sound of Hannah's voice and whirled around, breaking away from Thea's sisterly hug. The look of joyous relief on her face crashed into Jared like a hammer. How could he have withheld Hannah from her? He had been blinded by circumstances the day before and forgotten the strong bond already forged between mother and adopted daughter. Cali could no more hurt Hannah than set fire to her conservatory filled with plants.

Her heart was too tender to deliberately hurt anyone, particularly a child she loved. He grimaced at the thought of that tender heart under the domination of a man like Clairborne. Jared hadn't done such a good job of protecting it himself, but things would be different from now on. He would not forget the passionate little heart that beat beneath the marble façade.

Going down on her knees, Cali held her arms out, and Hannah went rushing into them.

She hugged her mama's neck and announced, loudly enough for the rest of the room to hear, "I missed you."

"I missed you, too, sweeting. So much." Cali's voice

cracked, and she buried her face against the black silk of Hannah's hair.

"I wanted to see you yesterday when Puppy died, but Papa said you had to pack to come live wif us."

Cali's head lifted, and for a moment her gaze met Jared's. The accusation he read there smote him.

Bloody hell. What else was he supposed to do?

"You're with me now, my darling, and we shall spend the rest of the day together. Would you like that?"

Hannah nodded. "I want to play in the garden. Nursey wouldn't let us."

Cali gently touched Hannah's face, her hand visibly trembling. "I had truly hoped you would help me take care of the baby plants in the conservatory today. They will be so lonely when we are gone, with only Old Benjamin, the groundskeeper, to care for them."

"I like to water them."

"I know." Cali stood up, lifting the sturdy little girl in her arms and moved over to the table on the far side of the room. "I left our puzzle out so we could finish it before we left for Raven Hall. Shall we work on it now?"

Cali had brought the wooden puzzle down from her attic last week in order to entertain Hannah on a day full of summer rain showers.

"May I help?" Irisa asked.

"Yes, but I get to do the edges," Hannah announced.

"I need to get back to David and Deanna," Thea said. "Perhaps I can bring them over later to play in the conservatory, as well? David's quite jealous of Hannah's accounts of helping you pot your plants. He loves to dig in the dirt."

Cali turned and nodded, her expression slightly puzzled, as it had been when Thea apologized and hugged her. She obviously didn't realize that the terrible suspicion of the last two days was over.

"Why don't I go fetch them now?" Drake asked.

Thea turned a shrewd gaze on her husband. "Why? I thought they could take their naps first."

"They can nap here, but I'll feel more comfortable if you are all together while we are gone."

"Where are you going?" Irisa asked, while helping Hannah place a puzzle piece.

Cali tensed beside her, but did not look up from the wooden puzzle.

"There are several leads that need investigating," Jared replied for his brother-in-law, being deliberately evasive.

He didn't want Cali upset with the news that they were going to question the duke, among others.

Before the women could ask any more probing questions, he led Drake and Ashton outside to make plans.

"We need to call on Squire Jensen's wife." Ashton said without preamble once they were away from the house.

"Someone will have to talk to the tavern keeper at the Blue Goose, as well," Drake added.

"I'm going to call on that bastard, Clairborne," Jared stated.

"He looks like the most likely culprit." Ashton's voice sounded reflective.

"We don't have any other prospects right now." Jared wished they did. Not because he cared what the idiot, Clairborne, might try, but because he didn't want to upset Cali.

"Let's talk to Mrs. Jensen first, and the tavern keep. It's too far to ride to Clairborne Park and return before nightfall."

Curse it, Drake was right. The Jensen's place would be far enough to travel today and return by night. "I don't want the women alone tonight. This business is too odd and potentially dangerous."

"Exactly," Drake said before going forward and readying his carriage. The stable boy rushed up to help.

"Do you think they'll be all right if all of us leave?" Ashton asked.

Jared didn't know. "If one of us stays, that's less ground covered. On the other hand, leaving them with only servants to protect them could be a bloody idiotic move."

"If you two leave now, you'll have almost an hour's start on waiting for me. I'll go to Ashton Manor, get my children, and come back to stay with the women and children until you return."

"Your wife is going to be offended when she realizes why you didn't go with us," Ashton predicted, his mouth slanted in a teasing smile.

"Your wife is already pissed as hell at you," Jared reminded his brother by marriage.

Ashton's face lost its humor. "I know."

"Calantha didn't seem too warm toward you, either," Drake said.

Jared frowned. She had been a bloody iceberg all morning. "I don't think she understands."

"She's probably got it all twisted with her feminine logic. You should have heard the things Irisa thought while we were engaged. Women do not think like men." Ashton's pronouncement was met with silent agreement.

Cali sure as hell didn't think like him, and he didn't know how to fix the problems caused by that.

He wanted her to smile at him again, but even in the deepest moments of their lovemaking last night, he'd felt like she held part of herself away from him.

He wanted his wife back, damn it.

He'd had one day of bliss, and then everything fell apart around them.

Once he found the blackguard trying to harm his family and dealt with him, he was going to take Cali to Raven Hall and keep her there until they had everything worked out between them.

Fifteen

THE TAVERN LOOKED EMPTY WHEN JARED walked inside after leaving his horse with a slatternly postboy in the yard. The faded wooden sign outside proclaimed rooms for rent. Jared doubted many travelers made use of the accommodations, so much as a certain type of female intent on doing business on her back. The inn's location a mile from the village proper provided just the kind of privacy wayward husbands and other jackanapes that would visit such a place wanted.

Jared scanned the dim room, looking for some sign of life. Other than an old man nursing a mug of ale in the corner, there wasn't any. Very little light made it in through the soot-smeared windows high in the tavern's walls. Which undoubtedly was best for the patrons that frequented the rough establishment. Jared doubted the tables had seen a washing cloth in a sennight, and it would take either a man desperate for a drink or one totally unconcerned with grime to imbibe using one of the wooden mugs stacked haphazardly by the keg of ale.

Cali, with her unbending attitude toward cleanliness, would have a fit of vapors if Jared brought her into such a place. Not that he would ever make such a mistake. His sweet little wife belonged in a conservatory full of flowers, not this hellhole. He still felt guilty for taking her to the gaol to meet that bastard would-be kidnapper.

Jared had no problem imagining the puling coward frequenting a place such as this. But he could not picture the Duchess of Clairborne, or any other lady, coming inside for a word with him.

" 'Ere now, what can I get you gov'ner?" The small but rotund man had come in through a curtained doorway behind the long bar counter, wiping his hands on a cloth that might have been white at one time, but was now an uncertain shade of gray.

"I want information."

Unlike Ashton, Jared preferred the blunt approach to getting what he wanted, and had no doubt it would work with the proprietor and patrons of this seedy little tavern. That's why he'd sent his brother-in-law to question the squire's wife. Jared did not have the patience to soothe ruffled feathers, which would likely be required to get information out of Mrs. Jensen.

The barkeep stopped in the act of drying his hands. " 'Ere now, what might you be wanting to know?"

"A scoundrel by the name of Willem is known to drink his leisure here."

"Maybe 'e does and maybe 'e doesn't—"

Jared didn't let the man finish, but had him by the front of his collarless shirt and dangling in the air in a heartbeat. "There's no *maybe* if you want to keep what teeth you have left in your head."

The barkeep made a sound like a frightened pig and clutched at Jared's wrists, his balding head glistening with instant moisture. "What . . . do you . . . want to . . . know about 'im?" The words came out between gasps.

Jared lowered the other man slowly until his feet once again touched the floor. "A lady came in to meet Willem a little over a sennight ago. She was wearing widow's weeds and a veil."

The tavern keep nodded his head so fast, Jared was surprised he didn't knock himself out. "Aye, 'e said 'e met 'er, but knowin' Willem, I wasn't inclined to believe 'im."

"What do you mean? Didn't you see her?"

"Nay. Some boy comes in and asks for Willem. Next thing I know, 'e's gone out to the yard. 'e didn't come back for a bit, and I weren't sure if 'e 'adn't gone 'ome, like."

"What did the boy look like?"

The other man rubbed the stubble on his chin musingly. "Like most boys, I guess. 'e didn't wear no fancy livery like 'e would working for a toff. To tell you the truth, I didn't believe Willem because of it."

"What did Willem say?" Frustration at the realization that the tavern keeper would probably be able to tell him very little welled up in Jared.

" 'e said 'e'd met an angel, 'e did. Said she was fancy as could be and wanted to 'ire 'im for a bit o' work."

Bloody hell. It was nothing more than what the scoundrel had already told Jared and the others. "Did he describe this *angel* to you?"

" 'e said 'e couldn't tell me 'er name. It was a secret like, but 'e said she was an angel. To tell you the truth, that one would think a woman who didn't smell like pig swill and belch as loud as he did was an angel. 'is eyesight t'aint so good anyway. I didn't believe 'im when 'e said she was a real toff. No, I didn't. Be just like Willem to make it up."

"Did anyone else see her?" Jared asked, with little hope for a positive response. At least now he understood how the man could have been so mistaken about Cali.

He wasn't surprised when the barkeep shook his head. "She stayed in the yard in her carriage, she did."

"Did you see the carriage?"

"No. 'ow was I supposed to see the carriage in the yard

when I was busy serving my customers in 'ere, I'd like to know."

Jared frowned, and the man backed up a hasty step. "Did anyone else see it?"

"Maybe a customer or two. Me postboy should 'ave seen it. 'e's lazy as they come, but 'e would 'ave come forward to take care of it."

Like the boy had come forward to care of Jared's horse? Jared had had to yell for him twice before the lad had come out of the stable, rubbing his eyes like he'd been napping. "Call him inside so we can ask."

The postboy was called. He hadn't seen the woman, but he had seen the carriage. It was black, without markings, like a hired post chaise. Her servant boy was rude. He'd offended the postboy when he'd refused to come in the stable for a cup of ale and chat while waiting for the lady to conclude her business with Willem. Jared didn't find out anything more, even though he stayed to speak to the regulars that had been there that night. No one had seen the lady, and few had believed Willem's story of her beauty and fancy manners.

Those who had seen it described the carriage the same way as the postboy, dark and without any identifiable markings.

When Ashton came into the tavern several hours later, Jared's mood was as black as the mystery woman's carriage.

Ashton didn't look much happier as he sat down across from him. "If this table were any filthier, they'd have to take it outside and burn it as refuse."

Jared felt the corners of his lips tilt slightly. "What's the matter, Ashton? Have your proper sensibilities been upset by our host's lack of interest in cleanliness? I thought only women got upset about such matters."

Ashton's black brows came together in a pretty damn fine frown. "I've been in worse dives than this, but I'm hungry and my horse is being watered in a trough that looks as if it hasn't been washed out since the place opened."

Jared was hungry, too. He had convinced his host to wash an ale mug for him in fresh water, using soap, but he hadn't trusted the food that would come from the man's kitchens. "Your horse will survive. Caesar's there to keep him company, but I persuaded the postboy to bring a new bucket of water from the well for him."

Ashton grinned. "I should have used some of your methods of persuasion when I arrived. What about food?"

Jared shrugged. "I'm willing to wait until we get back to Rose Cottage."

Nodding, Ashton sighed. "It's for the best."

"I'm surprised Mrs. Jensen didn't feed you. Most ladies fall all over themselves being nice to you."

Ashton's eyes narrowed. "She offered me food."

Jared let out a bark of laughter. "That bad, huh?"

"Her cook rolls or sprinkles everything in colored sugar crystals." Ashton shuddered. "I couldn't stomach the thought of sweet rarebit."

Jared felt sympathy nausea at the thought. "What did you find out? Has she given her rose petal candy to anyone lately?"

The proprietor came rushing over with a full mug of ale and put it down in front of Ashton. He shot Jared a glance from the corner of his eye and then rubbed his hands down the front of his brown twill waistcoat. "I 'ad me wife wash it good and proper like you wanted yours, your lordship."

Jared inclined his head and gave the man a coin to cover the cost. Ashton eyed the mug suspiciously. "Proper like?"

"With soap and fresh water, heated on the stove."

"Ah." Ashton's expression lightened. He took a drink. "Well?"

"Not too bad."

Jared contemplated how his brother-in-law would look wearing the ale rather than drinking it. Ashton knew damn well he wasn't asking about the ale. "Who the bloody hell did she give her candy to?"

"Several members of the nobility, to hear her tell it. When pressed, however, she admitted that was over the past two years. Recently, she has only had occasion to share her little delicacy with another squire in the district, a countess she met at a house party in the north, and your wife."

"*My wife?* Mrs. Jensen's a bloody liar!"

All sound in the tavern ceased at the sound of Jared's roar of outrage.

"Calm down. I haven't told you the details yet."

Jared glowered at the other man.

"Just getting a little of my own back," Ashton said with mocking politeness that nevertheless reminded Jared that for all his fancy manners, Ashton was a man to be reckoned with.

He grunted his approval. "The details," Jared demanded.

"She said that your wife had sent a boy with a note requesting some of Mrs. Jensen's candy to use as comparison with her own recipe."

"What boy?"

"I asked and she didn't know. She didn't recognize him, but she wouldn't recognize Calantha's stable boy either. It's not uncommon for a woman of quality to hire local village boys to run messages for them."

"I know that, man." Jared hit the table, and the two mugs of ale shook precariously. "But it leaves us with nothing to go on. I suppose she sent the candy with the boy right then?"

She must have, because there was no way it could have been delivered to Rose Cottage without first Thomas, then Cali knowing about it.

"Yes."

"Damn." His gut told him the duke was guilty, but everything led back to Cali. She was going to be upset to learn that someone had used her name in procuring the candy for the attempt at poisoning Hannah.

"Someone is doing a remarkably thorough job of casting suspicion on your wife," Ashton said, mirroring Jared's own thoughts.

"When I get my hands on him, there won't be anything left over for the gallows."

"There's a woman involved somewhere. For all you know, the whole plot has been devised by her."

"But why, damn it? Hannah's no threat to anyone. All the duke has to do is deny Hannah's existence. There's no reason for him to attempt to kidnap and then kill her. It's too big a risk."

"Perhaps he is more concerned with his consequence than the threat of exposure. His brother committed an unconscionable act in begetting his daughter. Raping a servant is not unheard of, but it is damaging to one's reputation."

The laws of England gave practically no protection to the servant classes from a lord of the realm, particularly a duke, but society was not so forgiving. The nobility were expected to act with a certain amount of decency, or at least not get caught doing otherwise. Frequent affairs were not frowned upon amidst the *ton*, but *flagrant* affairs were. Still, as motive for such monstrous behavior, protecting the Clairborne family's name was a weak one.

"We'll know more after calling on him tomorrow."

"Yes." Ashton pulled a piece of folded notepaper from his coat. "I convinced Mrs. Jensen to let me take the note. I told her that someone had played a joke on your wife and we were trying to figure out who. I don't know how well the story will keep gossip down, but there aren't a lot of explanations for the types of questions I was asking."

Jared didn't care about gossip. He wanted to protect his daughter *and* his wife. "Let me see it."

Ashton handed him the paper. It was written on thick white parchment, scented with roses. It had been sealed with the Clairborne crest. Jared had to force his hands not to wad the note into a crumpled little ball at this further sign of the villain's perfidy. He read it, and it said just as Ashton had claimed. There was a stiltedness to the speech that reminded him of Cali when he'd first met her, all starchy and prim.

Remembering the way she'd reverted back to her prim little ways with him did not improve his mood. "I need to see something else she's written to compare the handwriting."

"Yes." Ashton took another drink of his ale. "I hope Thomas finds his list of instructions from Saturday as well. We can compare them, too."

Jared stood. "Your horse has had enough time to rest. We need to get back to Rose Cottage."

Ashton followed him without a word. Both men wanted to go home to their wives.

CALANTHA TUCKED HANNAH INTO HER NARROW BED and kissed the child's forehead. Inhaling the sweet scent of her daughter, she savored the moment. "Goodnight, love. God bless and keep you, and may your dreams be sweet."

Hannah's eyes drooped sleepily. She'd spent the day playing with her cousins and puttering in Calantha's conservatory, and now she was worn out. "Mama?"

"Yes, sweeting?"

"I want to kiss Papa goodnight, too."

Calantha stifled a sigh. She also wished Jared had returned. She was anxious to hear what he had learned. "I'll ask him to come in and kiss you when he gets home."

"What if I'm sleeping?" Hannah asked, and then yawned.

Calantha was sure the little girl would be asleep as soon as she let her eyes close. "He can kiss you anyway."

Hannah nodded, her eyelids dropping to hide her deep brown eyes. Her breathing turned shallow and even almost immediately. Calantha remained where she was, watching her daughter. She should rejoin the Drakes and Irisa in the parlor, but she could not pull herself away from the sight of Hannah's sleeping form.

She had thought never to be a mother, and now she had a four-year-old daughter who would perhaps one day be a big sister. Calantha laid her hand against the flat of her stomach and contemplated the miraculous possibility of carrying Jared's child. Even now, she could be pregnant. Unlike Irisa, the prospect did not frighten her. She wanted it more than almost anything in the world . . . except Jared's love.

Loving a man who doubted her honor hurt too much to contemplate, and yet she could not chase the knowledge from her head. She had thought he finally believed her that morning when she made her case about the color of candy, but then he had left his sisters and Drake to watch her. He had not trusted her to care for Hannah alone. That truth cut deep, another wound she did not know how to heal.

Just as it had hurt last night when he had not answered her question about taking their baby away. He had demanded she sleep beside him, had made love to her with reckless passion, and still he had not had an answer for her question. She had lain there in silence, hoping he would dismiss her worries, saying he knew she was not capable of such devious maliciousness.

He hadn't. He'd rubbed her back in a strangely soothing gesture until she'd felt herself falling asleep, his lack of verbal response a heavy weight between them.

She leaned forward and kissed the soft skin of Hannah's cheek. She understood Jared's desire to protect his daughter. Calantha would give her life to protect the child as well. What she could not understand, what she fought to forgive, was his distrust of her. She reminded herself that Jared had never claimed to love her. He did not know her well enough to trust her that deeply, and without the bonds of love, it would be impossible for him to do so.

Yet he demanded her trust without knowing of her love for him. She remembered their wedding night. He had ordered her to trust him, had insisted she tell him of that trust. She had given herself into his keeping, only to be betrayed the next day by his lack of belief in her.

At least no one had insisted on accompanying her to put Hannah to bed. That was something, she told herself as she stood and blew out the small lamp by Hannah's bed. She made her way to the door with the aid of the light spilling into the room from the hallway. She left the door cracked in case Hannah woke frightened, and then went downstairs.

The Drakes and Irisa sat at the small table, playing a game of cards. Thea had put her children to bed in the single guest bedroom when Calantha took Hannah upstairs.

Irisa looked up from the play and smiled. "Would you like to join us, Cali? There's room for one more and we've only just begun this hand. We can re-deal."

Calantha did not think she could concentrate on the cards while waiting impatiently for Jared's return, so she shook her head. "I'll just check on dinner with Cook. She was all in a pucker at the thought of serving a full table so late."

Drake smiled. "If the tea tray earlier is any indication, she's more than equal to the task."

"I'll tell her you said so. She's very proud of her rose hip scones. My mother taught her the recipe."

Cook had worked for her parents until their death and returned to Rose Cottage when Calantha moved in.

Thea smiled. "Does she use roses in her meal preparations, too? Jared's cook does some amazing things, and eating at Raven Hall is always an adventure."

"Yes."

She turned to go, when noise from the hall stopped her. Jared and Ashton had returned. Irisa tossed her cards on the table and jumped up with obvious eagerness at the sound of her husband's voice outside the door.

When Ashton walked into the parlor, she rushed across the room and threw her arms around him. "I was so worried. I hate the thought of you traveling after dark, particularly by horseback. I've been on tenterhooks this past hour, waiting for your return."

Ashton's face, which had been cast in grim lines upon his arrival, now relaxed into an intimate smile that made Calantha want to look away. She shifted her attention to Jared. He had been looking at his sister and Ashton, too. When he met her gaze, his eyes reflected a yearning she did not understand. Tense, she waited for him to tell her what they had learned about the person who had hired Willem.

She was destined to go on waiting, because Thomas came in to announce dinner at that moment.

Ashton broke away from Irisa. "I need to clean up."

Jared took him abovestairs, while Calantha instructed Thomas to wait dinner ten minutes.

Later, at the table, she waited until Jared had eaten his soup before asking the question that was burning inside her. "Did you find out anything?"

She'd asked the question quietly, but since they were at opposite ends of the table, the others all heard and stopped to listen to what Jared's answer would be. It was unheard of for a lady to address her husband during a meal, even if the table was small like the one in her unpretentious dining room. She should confine her discussion to the Drakes, sitting to her right and left. But she could not make herself care about decorum when she had waited hours to hear Jared's discoveries.

"The woman who hired Willem never went inside the Blue Goose. She waited in the yard in her carriage and sent a boy inside to fetch the scoundrel. No one else saw her." Jared sounded disgusted by that fact.

Calantha bit her lip. "Is that all?"

"No one knew the boy, so he wasn't a local lad," Jared's scowl deepened, "and everyone who saw the carriage thought it looked like it had been hired. There were no distinguishing marks on it, no coat of arms or anything else. It was dark. Probably black."

She could not hide the disappointment in her voice as she said, "I see." There was nothing to indicate the woman had not been her. She could have hired a carriage. She could have sent a boy to fetch Willem out of the tavern.

Jared met her eyes, his own sending a message she could not understand. "The barkeep says Willem has poor eyesight and would call most any woman dressed decently and smelling better than a barnyard an angel."

He was trying to comfort her.

"I didn't speak to him." She said the words, doubting they would have any impact on the others around the table, but needing to speak the truth anyway.

"I know you didn't." Jared's words of affirmation surrounded her like a comforting cloak, warming the edges of the cold that had invaded her heart the day before.

"Did you call on the squire's wife?" Drake asked.

"I did," Ashton replied, "while Ravenswood was talking to the proprietor and patrons at the Blue Goose."

"What did you find out?" Irisa demanded.

"Someone sent a boy with a note to Mrs. Jensen, asking for the candy on Calantha's behalf."

The warmth seeped out of Calantha, leaving her colder than before and she shivered. "I don't understand."

Jared's expression had turned murderous. "Someone, probably the bit—the biddy that hired Willem, wrote a note and signed it with your name asking for the candy."

"But no candy was delivered here." Thomas would have known about it if such an occurrence had taken place.

"The boy took it with him," Ashton said.

Calantha could not breathe. She was back to where she had been that morning, charged with a crime she had not committed, with no way to prove her innocence. She stood up and pushed her chair back. "Excuse me . . ."

She rushed around the table, needing to escape the room before the accusations started.

Jared's strong hands wrapped around her and pulled her

into his body. "It's all right, Cali. We'll find whoever is doing this to you. You've got to trust me."

She stared at him, his first words not penetrating the fog of despair clouding her mind. But she heard his admonishment to trust him, and something inside her snapped.

She twisted violently against his hold. "Should I trust you like you have trusted me?"

He wouldn't release her. "Calm down, angel."

"Don't call me that! You don't think I'm an angel. You think I'm a demon, someone capable of murdering not one, but three children. *Let me go*." She was practically screaming in her fury and desire to get away from him.

She would not remain in the room to be chastised again by his family. She *wouldn't*. Managing to get one arm free, she swung it in a fierce arc that connected with his cheek. The loud slap of skin against skin and the stinging sensation in her palm acted like a bucket of cold water on her senses.

What had she done?

She looked at him with stricken eyes, the entire room silent around her. The red imprint of her hand formed against his cheek, and she felt as if she were seeing it from a great distance.

"Please, release me." The words were quiet, controlled, completely at odds with her heated action and near screaming only a moment before.

She was once again in command of the emotions threatening to devastate her.

Jared shook his head. "No. Dam—I won't. Not until you explain why you're so upset."

He wasn't going to punish her for hitting him. That realization came at the same time as the understanding that he did not comprehend her anger. Was he so arrogant that he could not fathom her hurt at his lack of trust and the awful position she found herself in?

"Someone is trying to destroy my life and kill my

daughter." She spoke each word slowly, as if addressing a lack-wit, and Jared's eyes narrowed.

"I know, and I'm furious about it, but that doesn't explain why you're trying to get away from me. You're understandably distraught at the circumstances. You are a woman, delicate of feeling, but I'm not the one trying to hurt you."

His words didn't make any sense to her. Of course he was hurting her. He didn't trust her.

"I'm not a murderer." Once again, she spoke without tone or inflection as she'd learned to do when dealing with Deveril in one of his rages.

"I know that." Now he was looking at her as if her brains had gone to let.

"You said that I signed the note to Mrs. Jensen."

"I blood—I did not."

"I said that someone had sent a note and signed it with your name," Ashton inserted from behind her.

"It amounts to the same thing," she replied without turning to face him.

Jared tipped her chin upward until their eyes met again. "No, *mon ange*, it does not. You think that because we found more evidence of the conspiracy against you that we've changed our minds since this morning, don't you?"

Of course she did. The revelations of the day had given lie to the evidence that she had presented on her own behalf that morning. And Jared didn't fully trust her anyway, or he would not have left his sisters and Drake to watch her.

Jared shook his head. "No one believes you sent for the candy. We don't believe you hired Willem."

But he'd been so angry. They'd believed that very thing this morning, and the day's events had only served to substantiate it. "I cannot prove that I didn't write the note."

"Actually, you can," Ashton once again interrupted her discussion with Jared. "I brought the note from Mrs. Jensen. We can compare the handwriting, if it will make you feel better. I'd like you to look at it, regardless. Perhaps you will recognize the writing. I realize it's unlikely, but it's our only hope at the moment."

They didn't believe she'd done it. The truth sank into her consciousness slowly. Jared *did* trust her, at least a little. "But why did you leave Drake and your sisters to watch me if you didn't believe I'd done it?"

"I stayed because none of us was comfortable leaving our women unprotected with a madman threatening our family," Drake said.

"Really, Pierson. You talk as if we are incapable of defending ourselves." Thea sounded offended.

Calantha's confusion only increased. She turned finally and faced the others at the table. No one glared at her with accusation. Irisa's eyes were filled with tears, and she was looking at Calantha as if she wanted to hug her. Thea was glaring at her husband, and Ashton wore an expression of understanding sympathy. Drake looked irritated, but his gaze was directed at his wife.

They believed her.

Sixteen

CALI RELAXED MARGINALLY. "I AM SORRY FOR overreacting. Please, you may release me now," she said quietly, in that damn duchess tone again. "I am quite recovered."

She acted as if she had just now realized they believed her. Hadn't she heard a word they'd said that morning? He let her go, and she returned to her seat, her head erect, her carriage dignified. Damn it, the duchess was back in full form.

Cali sat down and allowed her gaze to encompass them all. "I apologize for allowing my emotions to get away from me. Please excuse the scene you were forced to endure. Lord Ashton, I believe you were discussing your visit with Mrs. Jensen."

Ashton's eyes widened a fraction, but he nodded. "Yes. She didn't recognize the boy, but that's hardly surprising. She believes you wanted the candy to make a comparison between the two recipes."

"How did you explain your questions on the matter?" Drake asked, ignoring Thea's continued scowl pointed in his direction.

"I told her that someone was playing a practical joke on Calantha, and we couldn't figure out where the candy had come from. I said that we were glad to have the confusion cleared up and my sister-in-law would be deeply apprecia- tive of Mrs. Jensen's ready generosity when she learned the truth of the matter. I implied it was the work of a vil- lage lad taken with the Angel."

"That was very clever," Cali approved, though her voice was monotone.

Jared wanted to shake her, only he never would. She'd suffered enough at a man's hand. He would never allow her to suffer at his.

"So, we're at the same place we were this morning," Irisa complained.

"No, my love, we aren't. We know that someone is def- initely trying to implicate Calantha in the villainy. We knew a woman was involved, but now we know she's hired a boy to run errands for her. Perhaps we can find him. We also have the note." Ashton sounded far too pleased considering how little the day's efforts had actually gained them. He took a bite of rosemary lamb from his plate.

"I'll look at it after dinner. I will also give you a few of the letters I wrote to my parents, my notes, and other papers to compare the handwriting." Calantha had not touched her meal since the soup course.

"That isn't necessary," Jared growled, his temper just below the surface. She acted like she had to verify every- thing, just as she had that morning. "We said we believe you. You don't have to prove yourself."

She stared back at him, her expression blank. "It is the logical next step to eliminate any uncertainty."

His temper boiled over. "There *is* no uncertainty, damn it! We believe you, and that's bloody well that."

Damnation, he'd been doing so well. She'd implied she didn't like his swearing, and he was trying to clean up his language in front of her. He'd start talking like Ashton if he thought it would get rid of that *duchess look* and bring a smile back to her face.

"What are you going to do next?" Thea asked, in an obvious attempt to change the subject.

He turned away from the distant look in his wife's eyes he hated so much, and focused on his sister. "I'm going to call on the duke tomorrow."

"Why?" Cali asked. "So far, the only thing we know for certain is that a woman is involved. There's nothing to implicate the duke in this."

"The duke is still our best suspect."

"But . . ."

"As we surmised before, he could be working with a female accomplice."

"Our conjecture hardly constitutes justification for interviewing the duke and possibly offending him."

Jared felt like cursing. This was the second time she'd argued with them about talking to Clairborne. The other man was just the type women found attractive—blond and gray-eyed with impeccable manners.

"I'm going to talk to him," Jared vowed. "I haven't forgotten he tried to talk you out of marrying me."

Cali's gaze met his. "Perhaps it would have been better for you and Hannah if he had."

Dinner went downhill after that. Jared was so angry that he had to stay silent or end up yelling, and he wasn't up to seeing Cali retreat further into her shell because of his anger. The rest of his family made small talk, but they were aware of the tension between him and Cali, and no one offered to linger to discuss any further plans after dinner.

Drake and Thea carried their sleeping children out to the waiting carriage, while Ashton tucked Irisa into a corner with a blanket. The air felt warm enough to Jared, but he supposed Ashton was feeling protective because of Irisa's pregnancy.

"I'll bring Cali and Hannah over in the morning before leaving for Clairborne Park," he said as Ashton's coachman took up the reins.

"We'll keep them safe while you're gone," Drake promised.

Jared nodded and waved the carriage on.

He accompanied Thomas on his rounds to make sure the house was locked up for the night and there were no open windows on the ground floor. When he was satisfied the house was secure, he went upstairs to face Cali, who had gone to their bedchamber directly after dinner.

He didn't know what he was going to say to her. He was still angry enough to shout the house down.

He found her brushing her hair, its golden strands shining in the lamplight. She hadn't put a sleeping robe over her night rail, and he could see the faint outline of her womanly curves through the sheer fabric. His body reacted despite his lingering fury.

"What the hell did you mean you wish you hadn't married me?" he demanded as he stepped into the room and shut the door.

She laid the brush down on the dressing table in front of her and met his gaze in the looking glass, her eyes remote. "I did not say I wish I hadn't married you. I said it might have been better for you and Hannah."

It was the same thing. He yanked at his cravat, removing it when the tie had come undone. "Why?"

She bent her head as if she were studying her clasped hands in her lap. "Maybe this is all my fault."

He tossed off his jacket and waistcoat in two jerky movements. "How?" He didn't understand how her mind worked.

"What if someone is angry with me, and this is their way of getting revenge? The one thing we know for certain is that whoever is guilty wants me to be blamed. If you and Hannah were not connected to me, she would not be at risk."

He unbuttoned his shirt and yanked it out of his riding breeches. "That's a dam— That's a bacon-brained thing to say."

Her head came up then, and she turned to face him, quickly averting her eyes when her gaze fell on his chest exposed by the open shirt. "It is not foolish. It's logical."

"Only a madman would think with that kind of logic," he grated, irritated by her arguments and her refusal to look at him.

"Only a madman would try to kill a child and risk two others to succeed."

He couldn't argue that point, but he didn't want to believe she was the target. "You aren't thinking rationally."

"I'm thinking the way I was taught to think."

"What do you mean?"

"Deveril would have thought nothing of using you or Hannah to hurt me."

She'd told him Clairborne had used others to hurt her, but he hadn't given it much thought. The man was dead, but clearly his influence on Cali wasn't in the grave with him.

Jared closed the space that separated them. He put his hands on her shoulders as she faced away from him. "The kidnapper was hired before you agreed to marry me, before anyone could know you would grow to love Hannah as you do."

Her gaze flew to his in the looking glass again, and he saw a spark of hope in her eyes. "But even then, the woman who hired the kidnapper took pains to implicate me. I can only think Hannah is an unfortunate target because of her convenient proximity to me."

Jared thought it over because her point was sound, but then shook his head. "We don't have enough evidence to speculate like this. It would be a grave error to dismiss the likelihood Hannah is the target, and you the convenient scapegoat."

"I just don't understand how someone could want to hurt our daughter."

"I don't either." He couldn't fathom the reasoning behind someone trying to make it look like Cali was the culprit, either. She was so gentle and caring, so kind. "But it isn't your fault."

She said nothing, but turned on the vanity chair until she faced him. "I'm sorry I slapped you."

She reached out and traced a delicate pattern on his stomach just above the band of his breeches. His sex, which had been semi-hard since he'd entered their room and found her in the diaphanous night rail, went rock-hard and pressed against the buttons of his fly.

"You were distraught." He still didn't understand why she'd been so angry with *him*.

He wasn't the one trying to frame her for murder and kidnapping. He was doing his damndest to find the real villain. Maybe her anger had just needed an outlet, and he had been it.

"So you said at the time." She trailed her finger down the ridge in his pants, and his entire body shuddered. "I've never struck another person, not even Deveril when he hurt me."

Jared didn't want to hear about Clairborne, not when Cali's touch was making him feel like he was ready to explode in his breeches. "I forgive you, angel."

"Thank you." One small thumb dipped into the waistband of his breeches and brushed the top of his shaft.

He groaned and thrust toward her, feeling completely helpless against the desire she set off in him.

She leaned forward and pressed her lips against his stomach. "I don't want to hurt you, Jared." She whispered the words against his skin.

"That definitely doesn't hurt," he said, his voice coming out guttural with his need. Did she have any idea what she was doing to him?

She tugged at the buttons on his breeches until they were all undone, and then she pulled them down his hips until his sex sprang free. Trailing her fingers along his hardened manhood, she let out an unsteady breath.

"You're magnificent, Jared. You're strong and so completely masculine in every way." She leaned forward and sipped at the end of his penis, making him feel weak at the knees. "I don't know how you do this to me. I'm so angry with you one moment, and then the next, I just want to feel your naked skin against mine."

Her words so exactly reflected how he felt that he groaned. "It's not me doing it, *mon ange*, it's you."

She didn't respond, but her mouth opened and slid gently over the head of his sex. His head fell back, and he reveled in the unbridled pleasure of his wife touching him so intimately. He bit back a shout, remembering just in time that Hannah was in the next room. Cali tasted him with all the delicacy of a cat licking at cream. He could see her in his mind's eye, her mouth opened wide around the thickness of his male flesh, her fingers gently massaging his length.

The fantasy combined with reality, and he felt the pressure in the base of his sex that told him he was about to come. He pulled on her head, forcing her to release him. "I need to be in you, now."

As he said the words, he went to step toward the bed and almost tripped. He still wore his breeches and Hessians. He wouldn't make it to get them off. He hobbled awkwardly to the bed and fell back on it. "Come here."

She came, tearing off her night rail as she crossed the distance from her dressing table to the bed. Her face and small, high breasts were flushed with desire. "I want you, Jared."

When she reached him, he begged, "Ride me, angel, please."

Her eyes darkened to the color of the sea with her desire, she climbed on top of him, prepared to do just that. With the last bit of his control, he reached down between her legs to make sure she was ready for him. He hadn't even touched her and she was slick with her desire for him. He used his finger to spread the honeyed wetness around her entrance and up to her sweet spot. She pressed herself against his fingers, whimpering with her pleasure.

"I need you *now*." He reached down and clamped his hands onto either side of her hips, then positioned her above his jutting sex and surged upward.

She cried out as he entered her. He stopped breathing. Damn, it felt good.

She pressed herself down until she'd taken his entire sex inside. "I feel so full when you are in me, as if I can't bear it, but I can't stand the thought of you withdrawing, even for a second. When you're in me, I don't feel alone."

He wanted to tell her it was the same for him, but even though he was breathing again, he couldn't speak. The pleasure was too intense. Her inner flesh gripped him like a warm, wet fist.

She lifted her body until he was on the verge of coming out, and slid back down his shaft. He growled. The low sound from deep in his throat surprised him and made her smile.

It was an utterly feminine smile of satisfaction. "I like it, too."

She closed her eyes, letting her head tip back and did it again. He didn't think he was going to last through another one of those sweet caresses and gritted his teeth. Damn. He wanted to feel her come with him. He reached down and put his thumb against her slick, hardened nub. He didn't move his finger, but let the rocking of her body slide her sweet flesh against it. Her mouth opened in a wide *O*, but no sound came out.

He reached up with his other hand and gently tugged on first one nipple and then the other. Her rocking started getting faster and faster, their bodies slapping together in a passionate rhythm until her entire body stiffened and then shuddered around him. He exploded, ramming himself into her with a final fierce thrust, as her inner muscles clenched his sex in several convulsions.

She let out a shuddering sigh and collapsed against him. They lay that way for a long time, neither speaking, and his sex still inside her.

He couldn't quite believe what had just happened. "Cali?"

"Mmmm?"

"Did you take me in your mouth because you were sorry for slapping me?" He had to know. It had been one of the most shattering moments of his life, and he didn't know if he could stand finding out she had done it out of guilt rather than desire.

"No." She nuzzled into his neck. "Is that the proper way for a viscountess to apologize to her husband?"

"Bloody hel— *No*."

"Good. That means I can do it whenever I feel like it and not wait until the next time we have an argument."

"Yes." Most definitely, yes. "Angel?"

"What?"

"Did you like it?"

"Couldn't you tell?" How could you feel your wife blushing? He didn't know, but he definitely felt Cali turn pink. "Did you like it, last night, when you did that to me?"

Her words came out hesitant and whispered against his neck. "Yes. Very much. You taste like honey and spice."

She licked his neck. "You taste like you. I can't describe it. It's like your smell. There's nothing else like it in the world, and I love it."

She loved his smell . . . and his taste?

He was a very, very blessed man.

He shifted under her and felt a stirring in his sex. "I think I should take off my boots now."

Her head came up at that, and she stared at him, her face contorting in a strange expression. Then laughter erupted from her, cascading over him like a warm waterfall of happiness.

She laughed so hard, she fell off of him and rolled onto

her side, grasping her stomach with both hands. He watched the spontaneous expression of emotion with almost as much pleasure as he had experienced making love to her.

"You are so beautiful when you laugh."

"You are . . ." She didn't finish, the laughter overcoming her again. "You are . . ." She rolled to her other side, her head bobbing up and down in mirth. "You are h-handsome when you are h-hard."

He stood up and yanked off his Hessians and the rest of his clothes before diving back onto the bed to join his giggling wife. "Then I must look like Adonis now." Because he was once again hard as a steel rod.

She rolled toward him, her eyes suddenly serious, her laughter stilled. She laid her hand on his cheek, against his scar as she'd done a few times before, and it affected him just as strongly. "You are far more attractive than a myth, Jared. You are the living, breathing fulfillment of dreams I thought dead when I discovered what kind of man I married when I was eighteen."

He didn't know what to say to such a declaration. There were no words for the tight feeling in his chest or the desire that was so much more than physical, spiraling through him. So he said nothing, and instead he used his body to show her the effect her words had on him.

IRISA SLEEPILY WATCHED LUCAS PREPARE FOR BED. HE'D insisted on carrying her inside once they reached home and helping her undress. She now lay snuggled comfortably in their bed. They hadn't slept apart in the entire fourteen months of their marriage, not since their *discussion* about the subject on their wedding night.

As her husband peeled away the layers of his gentlemanly veneer to reveal his sculpted body, the tiredness that had overwhelmed her faded away like the morning mist.

"You are an exceptionally fine example of masculinity, my lord."

She teased him with the use of his title, knowing it would spark more ardor than anger after the months of their marriage.

Lucas's eyes reflected the storm clouds of passion as he walked naked across their bedchamber. "And you, my lovely wife, are an exceptional judge of character."

She smiled. Finally. He was going to admit she was right. "I told you she wasn't capable of something so foul."

He slid into bed beside her, pulling her into the circle of his arms. He rubbed his chin against the top of her head in a gesture of affection. "A generous victor refrains from saying I told you so."

"Perhaps if the victor hadn't argued herself blue in the face, that might be true. But I feel a certain justness in saying the words."

His hand slipped down to curl around her thickened waist. "I would like to point out that nothing we discovered today encouraged me to change my mind about her."

"I wondered about that at dinner."

She hadn't said anything, because Calantha was already upset enough, but she had wondered at her husband's complete about-face. They'd gone to bed the night before arguing about it. His stubborn refusal to admit Calantha's innocence had so infuriated Irisa, she had yelled at Lucas. To no avail. He had simply repeated his intention to wait and see for the hundredth time. He hadn't let her go to sleep angry either. He'd insisted on kissing her, and, as usual, the kissing had led to something more.

She'd woken up in a better mood, but just as convinced of her new friend's innocence. Her mood had gone south that morning when everyone questioned Calantha so closely about the candy color. She'd wanted to shout that any fool could see the former duchess wasn't cruel.

She burrowed into his side, allowing her hand to drift over his chest and play with a small male nipple. "Why did you change your mind?" she asked, wondering if her arguments had finally gotten through to him.

He sighed with pleasure. "Several things Calantha said this morning, and her attitude."

Her fingertip stilled in its circling of his hardening nipple. "What do you mean?"

"If you go back to what you were just doing, I'll tell you."

She obeyed. As if she wouldn't have anyway, when she thought of it.

"She said she'd have to be muddleheaded to use her own servants to deliver the candy, and I realized she was right. She'd been here at the manor several times helping you with preparations for the wedding breakfast. She could easily have left the candy in the nursery for Hannah without anyone seeing her, but even simpler, she could have harmed Hannah easily when she was alone with her. She is too knowledgeable about herbs to have resorted to such an obvious poison as one that caused vomiting before death."

Irisa frowned. Her husband's arguments made sense, but she wished he were motivated by more humane considerations, like the fact that Calantha loved Hannah.

"But the biggest deciding factor for me was the way she wanted to protect Hannah, even if we still suspected her. I remembered all the times I'd seen the two together and frankly, can't believe that Calantha could fake that kind of affection. She cares too deeply for Hannah to ever hurt her. She was positively frantic that day Hannah was lost. The perfect Angel showed up to search, riding her horse in a morning gown and showing a good bit of leg. It just all finally fit together."

Irisa's frown faded. Her husband did understand, after all. She rewarded him for his perception by skimming her hand down his flat belly to let her fingers tangle in the hair above his manhood.

He made a deep sound of male desire. "Now you tell me why you were so sure from the very beginning. You never doubted her at all, even when the evidence looked irrefutable."

Irisa thought about it for a moment. "I'm not sure. Maybe it's the way she's changed since meeting Jared. She's opened up, somehow, and I realized she really was lonely before. I'd suspected it, but after seeing her with Jared and Hannah, I was sure of it. She'd made comments before that made me think she regretted not having children, and when she met Hannah, it all became so obvious. She was desperate to give love and receive it. I don't know if she realizes yet that she loves Jared, or that he loves her, but she's willing to give and receive love with Hannah."

Lucas's warm palm cupped her breast and gently abraded her nipple. Even the light touch elicited an overwhelming response from her. Her breasts had become very tender and sensitive during her confinement. "Do that again."

He did, and she arched into his hand. "Are those your only reasons for your unbending faith in Calantha?"

She had to force herself to think. "Well, no. Even if she didn't love Hannah, I don't think she'd be capable of hurting her. She's too kind. Look at what she did for Thomas and Timothy. Thomas is really older than a butler should be, but she won't let him go because of his granddaughter and her children. Timothy is a little young to have full responsibility for a stable, even one as small as Calantha's. However, after the rough treatment he received at Clairborne Park, she insisted on hiring him. I told Jared once that I think she cares, and she does. Deeply. Maybe too deeply. She's very vulnerable."

"Speaking of vulnerable." Lucas took her hand and placed it right on his hard male flesh.

She grinned and kissed his neck while squeezing the velvet hardness gently.

"Do you really think she loves Jared?" Lucas asked, his voice rasping.

"Yes. You should have seen her getting ready for her wedding. She positively glowed. I hoped my brother would one day meet a lady who saw beyond his scars and size to the wonderful man underneath, and I truly believe Calantha does."

Then she was lost in the wonder of her own love as Lucas pulled her under him and carefully pushed his thick manhood inside her welcoming heat.

A long time later, just as Irisa was going to sleep, Lucas whispered, "I hope he finds a way to convince her of his love after doubting her like he did."

So did Irisa, because she wanted both her brother and her friend to be happy. She wanted them to find the joy she'd found with Lucas, the pure bliss of knowing you are loved and free to love unconditionally.

Seventeen

"THIS IS RIDICULOUS. CALLING ON HENRY will serve no purpose but to make you a powerful enemy." Calantha tried to control the frustration she felt at Jared's stubborn refusal to listen to her arguments.

He'd woken her early that morning to make love. Then he'd insisted they get out of bed, bathe, and dress. He wanted her to spend the day at Ashton Manor with Hannah, while he called on Henry and questioned him in regard to the plot against the child. She wasn't going to do it.

Jared turned glittering eyes on her. "Dam— I mean, blood— Oh, the hell with it. Listen to me, Cali. I'm going on my gut instinct, and it's telling me the Clairbornes are involved in some way."

A few short weeks ago, his tone of voice and scowling disposition would have sent her running from the room.

She crossed her arms over her chest and glared at him. "The same instincts that told you I was guilty at first?"

Jared grabbed her and pulled her toward him, until their faces were only inches from each other. Instead of wanting to retreat, she wanted to scream at him. She settled for scowling.

He returned her look with a fierce one of his own. "My

instincts told me you were innocent, but I let the circumstances and your own admission that you resented Hannah convince me to go against them. I'm not going to make that mistake again."

She put his declaration away in her heart to take out and examine later. Right now, she had to convince the man she loved not to take such a foolish risk.

"Then give me one good reason why a duke of the realm would care enough about his dead brother's indiscretions to risk his own reputation and try to hurt a child," she demanded.

"I don't know, and that's why I'm going to talk to him. I want information."

"Then obtain it in some other fashion. Jared, you don't have a subtle bone in your body, and you're going to end up provoking Henry to nothing short of a duel." With Jared's lack of tact and Henry's monumental pride in the same room, something disastrous was bound to happen.

Jared's smile told her he wasn't at all alarmed by the prospect, and suspicion blossomed in her. "That's what you're hoping, isn't it? You *want* him to challenge you!"

Jared leaned down the few inches that separated them and kissed her softly before lifting his head so their gazes met. "I won't lie to you, Cali. Meeting your former brother-in-law over a brace of pistols at dawn is an inviting prospect."

She stared at him in appalled silence for several seconds, trying desperately to think of a rational argument to counter his male aggression. He truly thought risking his life in a duel was the solution to their problem.

In a desperate attempt to stop her husband from going, she used the only argument she could think of. "If you confront Henry about what has happened with Hannah, you'll give him a weapon to hurt me."

"What the hel— What do you mean?"

"Do you think I want the rest of the *ton* to know that I

stand accused of hiring a kidnapper and attempting to kill my daughter?" she asked, infusing her voice with more accusation than she felt. What she felt was desperate.

The Clairbornes were a powerful family, and she bitterly regretted that her connection to them had now put Jared at risk, and perhaps even Hannah.

Jared looked as if she'd slapped him again. His face wore that same stoic expression, while his eyes reflected hurt that had nothing to do with physical pain.

"You don't trust me to protect your name in this?" His voice was laced with both outrage and hurt. "You are my wife. Do you think I would expose you to the censure of the *ton*?"

Calantha wanted to reach out and comfort him, while at the same time part of her was glad that he was tasting the pain of distrust. He had dismissed his distrust of her as of no consequence.

That aside, she had to make him see that his present course of action was not the right one. "How can you help but tell Henry?"

"I'm not going to *tell* Clairborne anything. I'm going to ask him questions," he growled.

She could sense that Jared's frustration now matched her own, but there was still no give in him. "Can you guarantee that by bringing the matter to his attention, my supposed part in the ugly events won't come to light?"

"Cali, if he's behind the whole thing, he already knows."

"What if you are wrong? What if he isn't?"

"I'm not wrong. The Clairbornes are involved."

Mute with frustration, she turned her head away from him and tried to think of another argument to refute his overwhelming male arrogance. She hadn't thought of anything that would sway him by the time Jenny brought Hannah through the connecting door to her room.

"Good morning, Mama and Papa. I'm hungry."

Jared released Calantha and turned to smile at their daughter. "Then it's a good thing Cook has prepared breakfast for us, isn't it?"

Hannah nodded, tugging her hand from Jenny's so she could dash across the room and throw herself at Jared's knees. She hugged his legs and then turned to Calantha, who had knelt to the floor so she could receive a real hug. Hannah threw her arms around Calantha's neck, squeezing tightly. More and more of the little girl's natural exuberance was coming to the fore.

Calantha kissed the baby-soft cheek. "Did you sleep well, sweeting?"

"Uh-huh."

Calantha rose to her feet after another quick hug. "Jared, why don't you take Hannah down to breakfast? I'll join you shortly, when I'm finished getting ready." She counted on her husband's ignorance of things feminine to prevent him from noticing that she had already completed her toilette.

"All right, but hurry. I'm not leaving until you've eaten a proper meal. You barely touched your dinner last night. I don't like this tendency you've shown lately to miss meals."

"How do you know it isn't a long-ingrained habit?" she asked, irritated by his assumption he knew her so well.

"If it is, you can blood— You will break it." He swept Hannah up in his arms and turned toward the door. "Be downstairs in five minutes, or else."

She didn't ask or else what. She'd already pushed his temper far enough that morning.

As soon as he'd left with Hannah, she turned to Jenny. "Help me change into my habit. I've decided to ride over to Ashton Manor this morning."

She made it down to the dining room in just a little after Jared's five allotted minutes. He didn't grumble because she ate a full breakfast, keeping up a lively banter with Hannah all the while. Who would have known that a four-year-old child could have so many questions?

THEY ARRIVED AT THE MANOR JUST AS THE ASHTONS and the Drakes were finishing their breakfast. The butler led her, Jared, and Hannah into the breakfast room.

Irisa looked up from her meal and smiled.

Thea did, too, and said, "Good morning. The children have been waiting for Hannah's arrival since breakfast began."

She nodded at the nursemaid, and the girl stood.

"Is it all right with you if they go to the nursery? David found a new specimen just this morning for his bug collection that he wants to show Hannah."

Jared let Hannah down. "Stay in the nursery," he instructed the nursemaid.

She bobbed her head, her expression nervous. "Yes, milord. I wouldn't think of taking them out of the nursery, milord."

After that breathless promise, she turned to lead the children from the room.

Thea laid her fork neatly on the side of her plate. "She's positively terrified of you since the attempted kidnapping."

"Good," Jared said. "Maybe that will make her more cautious."

Irisa stood and walked over to Calantha. "It looks as if we will be spending the day together again."

Jared was busy nodding his agreement while Calantha shook her head, once, but firmly. "No."

He turned his head to glare at her. "You aren't staying at Rose Cottage alone. It's too bloody dangerous."

If she had doubted Drake's words the previous evening that he'd stayed behind the day before to offer protection, she couldn't any longer. Jared's eyes were filled with not only male arrogance and anger, but also undeniable concern that bordered on fear.

She patted his arm in reassurance. "I have no intention of staying at Rose Cottage alone."

"Dam— That's right."

"I'm going to go with you to call on Henry." It was the only thing she could think of to do. Maybe with her along, Jared would be more circumspect.

"No." Jared gave her a *don't you dare argue with me* look.

She ignored it. "Yes."

She deliberately turned away from him to face Irisa. "You don't mind watching Hannah for us today, do you?"

Irisa shook her head, a frown of concern puckering her brow. "Of course not, but are you sure you want to go with Jared? I don't think his interview with the duke is going to be pleasant."

"That's precisely why I am going. Perhaps if I am there, I can prevent the idiocy of a duel."

Irisa's eyes widened, and she turned to stare at her brother. "You plan to challenge the duke?" Her tone left no doubt how little she thought of that plan.

Jared said, "No."

Calantha gave him a sideways glance full of disapproval before turning back to his sister. "He won't have to. With his lack of tact, he'll have Henry challenging him within ten minutes of his arrival at Clairborne Park."

"Ravenswood isn't responsible for the duke's short temper," Drake announced as he stood up from the table as well.

Calantha turned her gaze to him. "How convenient. I suppose that, like Jared, you believe his meeting Henry over a brace of pistols at dawn is the solution to this awful mess."

Drake shrugged and helped his wife to her feet. "Well, it's one solution."

"It's a caper-witted one, and I can't believe you condone

it," Thea accused as she followed Drake to the door of the breakfast room.

He turned to her. "Your brother just wants to protect his family."

"You think he should risk a bullet to do so?" Calantha asked, not even trying to hide the outrage she felt.

Thea's glare made it plain she agreed with her.

"I'm not risking a bullet. I'm just going to talk to the bas— man," Jared denied.

"And I will be going with you to do so," Calantha said.

"*No*," Jared replied, his earlier temper returning.

"I don't think you should accompany your husband to-day," Ashton inserted as he led the rest of them to the hall.

Calantha gripped her riding crop tightly. "Why not?"

"Because you are clearly one of the villain's targets, and if the duke is responsible, your presence could make this confrontation even more volatile."

Calantha hated that Ashton was right, but that didn't mean she was going to let Jared go off on his own and end up in some terrible situation, like a challenge. "If the duke were going to try to hurt me physically, he would have done so on the two occasions he visited me alone at Rose Cottage." As she said the words, she remembered that he had tried, but she'd defended herself.

The memory must have shown on her face, because Jared snorted. "He tried to hit you, Cali. Just what do you call that if not wanting to hurt you physically?"

"That was different. I pricked his temper."

"You prick my temper all the time, and I don't try to hit you," Jared said. "The man's a threat, and it isn't safe for you to be around him."

"It isn't safe for you, either."

"I can handle it, damn it."

"So can I," she said firmly, not at all sure it was the truth, but hoping that her last two successful attempts at defending herself were a harbinger for the future.

"You're not going." Jared's words carried the finality of a man pushed beyond his temper's limits.

"Yes, I am." No matter how angry it made her husband, she was determined to protect him the best way she knew how.

Jared glared at her for a full minute before answering. "If he insults you, I'll do more than challenge him. I'll flatten him where he stands."

"No." The duke was insulting when he wasn't angry. After she had defied him to marry Jared, the man was bound to say something her husband would take issue with. "I won't allow you to take offense on my behalf."

"I can't help it. You are my wife. An insult to you is an insult to me."

Horror at the possibility that her accompanying Jared would actually precipitate a duel, rather than prevent one, kept her silent for several seconds. She couldn't go with Jared, and she couldn't stop him from going. "Promise me that you will not accept a challenge from the duke."

"I can't."

She would have to trust him. He didn't say the words aloud, but they shimmered in the air between them. She wanted to scream that it wasn't him that she didn't trust, but Henry. She didn't want Jared to take any risks. There had to be another way of getting the information they needed. The others were silent as she and Jared fought their battle of wills.

His gaze did not waver, the look in his eyes both demanded and pleaded she accept his plan. It was the pleading that swayed her.

"Very well." She dropped her head, so she was speaking to his waistcoat. She couldn't stand to look in his eyes and see the determination there. Determination that might very well get him killed. "Please, be careful."

He gently tipped her head up with a single finger under her chin. "I will."

He kissed her, long and slowly. She reacted without thinking and sank against him, absorbing his heat and strength. Her hands locked around his neck, and she opened her mouth for the invasion of his questing tongue.

When he pulled away, she swayed. He held her arms, preventing her from falling. His kisses weakened her knees and addled her wits. That was her only excuse for her complete loss of propriety in front of her new relatives. She could not believe that Jared had kissed her at all, much less so intimately, in the Ashton's hall. And she had responded. Her face felt on fire, and her heart still raced like a pony in a runaway gig.

Irisa and Thea gave her identical looks of commiseration. Perhaps Jared wasn't the only gentleman in the family that forgot propriety. Ashton's lips twitched, but he did not smile. Drake smiled knowingly and winked, causing her blush to intensify, but no one commented on the kiss. Thank goodness. She had no idea how she would have responded. A lady simply did not give way to such wanton behavior.

"I'll go with you," Ashton said, in a clear bid to draw the others' attention away from what had just happened. He grinned at Jared. "Calantha's concern over your lack of tact is well justified."

"And you think you can ease the effects of my blunt speech with your silvered tongue?" Jared taunted.

"I think I can watch your back," Ashton said, his smile disappearing.

Relief poured through her at the knowledge that Jared wasn't going to face Henry alone. She reached out to touch Ashton's arm. "Thank you."

He nodded in seeming understanding. Jared frowned, but did not argue any further.

"I had planned to go to London today. Thea suggested last night before we went to bed that we should investigate the money angle." Drake's words fell into the silence that had descended after her words of gratitude.

"Yes. People are willing to do a great deal of harm for money," Thea added.

"But Hannah doesn't have any money," Irisa said. "She's not an heiress. She's just a little girl."

"I think the best place to start is with the former duke's will," Thea replied. "She may not be an heiress, but her father was a duke."

"But she's not his legitimate daughter." Irisa's confusion matched Calantha's.

She did not see how Deveril's will could hold any answers to their present dilemma. Four years had passed since his death. Surely, if someone were going to threaten his daughter, it would have happened before this.

"A child doesn't have to be legitimate for a father to leave her something in his will. She couldn't be heir to his title or estates, but then, as a girl, she wouldn't anyway. However, that would not have prevented Clairborne from leaving Hannah an inheritance."

"I don't remember any mention of Hannah in the will."

"Were you there for the reading?" Thea asked.

"No. Henry insisted on going as my representative." And she'd been too spineless to argue back then. She'd also been delirious with joy at the prospect of freedom from the bondage of her marriage. She'd felt too much guilt over that fact to care overmuch one way or the other about the reading of Deveril's will.

"You'll have to wait to travel to London until tomorrow." Jared's voice once again brooked no argument.

Unlike Calantha, Drake chose to respect that.

Thea didn't, however. "Nonsense. There is no reason for Pierson to stay. We are quite safe here at the manor."

Irisa and Calantha both nodded their agreement.

Jared shook his head and frowned at his sister. "I've been thinking that you and Drake should take your children back to London anyway. David and Deanna have already been put at risk once because of the villain's plans to hurt

Hannah. It will be easier for me to watch over Hannah if I don't have to worry about them, too."

"Jared's right. You and Drake can investigate this money angle you are talking about while keeping your children safe. Please?" Calantha pleaded with her new sister-in-law, sensing that Thea would respond better to that then Jared's blunt instructions.

She was right, and Thea nodded. "I still don't see why Drake can't go to London today and begin the inquiries. The children and I can be ready to travel by tomorrow, or the next day at the latest, and can join him then."

Drake smiled, the expression not quite reaching his eyes. "That is not going to happen, my love. Even if there had been no attacks against one of our own, I would not allow you to travel unescorted to London."

Thea frowned. "You know how little I like it when you take that dictatorial tone with me."

Since his voice had been firm but gentle, and not in the least autocratic, Calantha found herself smiling.

"I know, but as in all good partnerships, compromises must be made," Drake informed his wife. "As I have been at pains to point out to you for the past five years, England bears no resemblance, in certain areas, to your former home in the West Indies. I want you safe."

"And therefore I am to do the compromising?" Thea asked, not sounding irritated anymore, so much as resigned.

"Exactly." Drake rewarded his wife with a swift kiss when she did not argue with him, thereby confirming Calantha's earlier thought that the gentlemen in her new family were more affectionate than strict propriety allowed.

Her former family's failings had run along opposite lines, which had resulted in both pain and fear. Calantha decided she liked the improper expressions of affection much better.

She wasn't so pleased with the arrogant stubbornness that appeared to be another common trait among the three men. Once Jared set a course of action, he refused to be swayed. She could not stop him from calling on the duke, but she did not have to like it.

She inclined her head to her husband. "I believe I will join Hannah in the nursery."

She turned to go, intent on dismissing her stubborn husband from her presence and her thoughts. She would not spend the rest of the day in a pucker over his decision to talk to Henry.

A large, heavy hand fell on her shoulder, and she found herself being spun around to face the broad expanse of Jared's chest. "You forgot to wish me farewell, Cali."

She curtsied as well as possible, considering she was hampered by his grip on her shoulder. "Good-bye, my lord. I pray your journey is both safe and pleasant."

He hauled her against him with rough swiftness. "Good-bye, wife." His mouth covered hers before she could protest his hold, or anything else.

Hard and intent, the kiss ended quickly, but nevertheless proclaimed his possession of her in an unmistakable manner.

JARED'S MOOD WAS DARK AS A MOONLESS NIGHT WHEN he and Ashton returned to the manor that evening. The duke and duchess had not been at home. Literally. Their butler informed him that they had gone to visit one of the Clairborne estates in the north and were not expected back for several weeks. It didn't feel right. He was missing something.

His Hessians clicked on the stone floor of Ashton's hall as he and his brother-in-law went in search of their families. A family. He, Cali, and Hannah were now a family. He would do whatever was necessary to protect them. If that meant meeting the Duke of Clairborne in a duel, then Jared would do it. And probably listen to Cali's nagging right up to the minute the pistols were loaded. His spirits temporarily lifted at the thought. Cali *would* nag him. She hadn't backed down from their argument this morning.

She no longer feared his anger.

He'd have to watch out, or he'd end up living under the cat's paw. He smiled to himself at the prospect. Cali made a very cuddly, warm, little feline.

He followed Ashton into the red and gold drawing room. Irisa had broken the immense room up into several smaller sections with furniture and exotic oriental carpets. His sister and Cali occupied one of the sitting areas. They were both sewing. There was no sign of the children, Thea, or Drake.

Cali noticed their presence first. Her head came up, and she shifted her attention from the round embroidery frame that held her concentration to him. Her eyes glowed with welcome for a scant second before she let her expression slide into that blank doll-mask she wore. Damn it.

The only time she responded to him with complete openness was in bed. She couldn't hide her need for him then. He wanted more. He wanted her to need something from him besides the pleasure he gave her. He wanted her to admit she trusted him to take care of the current situation, that he would protect both her and Hannah . . . in every way.

"You don't have to worry about the duke challenging me," he said, his voice harsh with his frustration from making the trip with no results.

Relief flickered in her eyes, but she said nothing.

Irisa's head came up from the tiny gown she had been sewing, and she leapt to her feet, letting the small froth of white fabric slide to the carpet.

She rushed forward and hugged Ashton and then Jared. "I'm so happy you have returned. The duke did not challenge you? Truly?"

"Truly," Jared replied, his eyes on Cali, who had remained seated, just like a proper duchess.

Irisa released him and stepped back. "What did he say?"

"Nothing." Jared waited for Cali to ask why, but she remained mute while Irisa peppered him with questions.

"Nothing? But why? Did he refuse to say anything?"

"He was not at home," Ashton replied when Jared remained stubbornly silent, waiting for his wife to speak.

"Oh dear. Don't tell me you are going to go back again tomorrow?" Irisa asked. "Thea and Drake are planning to leave for London in the morning. They've spent the entire day preparing for their return home."

"Jared will do just as he thinks best, regardless of other people's thoughts on the matter," Cali said, finally breaking her silence.

She was right, but bloody hell, he didn't like the way she said it. As if he didn't concern himself with what she thought, or how she felt.

He did care, but that caring couldn't prevent him from doing what was necessary to protect her. "We won't be going back tomorrow."

Cali's brows rose in faint inquiry, and he wanted to kiss her until that *duchess look* faded permanently from her face, until she was panting with her desire for him.

"He and his wife have gone north to visit another Clairborne estate."

"When did they go?" Irisa asked impatiently.

Ashton pulled her against his side and kissed her temple. "They left two days ago and aren't expected back for several weeks. Jared plans to take Calantha and Hannah to Raven Hall tomorrow. Now, does that answer all your questions?"

Irisa shook her head, even as she asked another question. "But what about finding out who tried to harm Hannah and make Calantha look guilty of the crime?"

"I'm going to hire a Bow Street Runner to follow the duke to his estate," Jared answered for his brother-in-law. "Drake is going to make inquiries in London, and your husband is going to continue questioning people locally. Once we have more information, I will make further plans."

He turned back to Cali. "Will you be ready to leave for Raven Hall tomorrow morning?"

"Would it matter if I said no, my lord?" she asked with polite formality, neglecting to answer his question.

Jared forced himself to use a reasonable tone of voice to answer. "I would, of course, take that into consideration, but I had hoped you would be packed by now."

When she said nothing, but responded with an inclination of her head, he added, "It will be easier for me to protect Hannah at home, where strangers are more noticeable. Whereas, if we stay here, those involved are clearly from the area and unlikely to arouse suspicion."

"I am ready to leave."

He didn't know if she meant she was ready to leave Rose Cottage, or to return there from Ashton Manor.

He chose to interpret it that she was prepared to travel to Raven Hall on the morrow. "Where is Hannah?"

"She and the other children are already abed." Once again it was his sister who answered him, while Cali busied herself putting her embroidery away in Irisa's sewing basket.

"I'll have the closed carriage brought around to take you home. We can tie your and Calantha's horses to the back. It will be easier to transport a sleeping child that way, I think," Ashton said.

"I had hoped you would both stay for dinner. You will be leaving on the morrow," Irisa said, her eyes full of appeal.

Jared waited until his wife looked at him again before answering.

When she did, he asked, "Well, Cali?" certain she would not demur.

She was too tenderhearted to hurt his sister's feelings, even if she did like to wear that bloody marble statue façade.

"I would be delighted to stay and visit a bit longer." Cali smoothed her skirts as she stood. "I will miss you when Jared takes me to my new home. I hope you and Ashton will come to visit before your confinement makes the travel impossible."

The genuine emotion in her voice left no doubt that her words were heartfelt, not a platitude spoken for the sake of civility.

Irisa pulled away from Ashton and rushed over to hug Cali tightly. "I will miss you, too."

"Then I shall have to make certain to take you to visit Raven Hall very soon, won't I? An intelligent man keeps his wife happy, particularly when she is increasing," Ashton said.

Irisa's smile for her husband cut through Jared like a sharp blade. The usual pleasure he felt at seeing his sister's obvious affection and joy in her marriage was absent. Would Cali's eyes ever warm with love for him? Devil a bit, where had that thought come from? He didn't need Cali's love.

He had her loyalty. She had defended him to the duke and insisted on marrying him even after finding out about his father's cowardly actions. He had her legally. She was his wife. He knew she would honor the tie that would bind them for the rest of their lives. He had her concern. Her upset at the prospect of the duke challenging him proved it. He had her body. She gave herself to him completely when they made love.

But it was not enough.

He wanted more than honor-driven allegiance. He wanted her emotions—but even if an angel could be convinced to marry a beast, would she ever give him her heart?

Eighteen

CALANTHA SLOWLY CAME TO CONSCIOUSNESS AS a warm hand rubbed her back.

"Wake up, Cali. We are almost there."

She nestled closer into the warmth surrounding her and mumbled a protest. After two grueling days of travel with a four-year-old, her eyes were too leaden to open even a crack. She'd had no idea how exhausting a journey with a small child could be. Jared had remained in the carriage, rather than riding Caesar alongside, to help her entertain Hannah, but he had set a pace that would have been tiring without the child's presence. Intent on reaching home as quickly as possible, he made the trip that could easily have take four days, in two.

Warm fingers slid under the hair at her nape and squeezed.

She rubbed her face against his waistcoat. "Mmmm."

Laughter rumbled low in his chest. "You sound like a content little cat."

She was content. She'd woken in her husband's arms. Having gone to sleep leaning against the interior wall of the carriage, she had known a modicum of surprise at waking up curled in Jared's lap. It had only been a modicum, however, because Jared seemed to like to hold her, and did so with the least provocation.

"Where is Hannah?" she asked without opening her eyes.

"Asleep on the other squabs."

Calantha tipped her head up until her face pressed into the curve of Jared's neck. Sniffing appreciatively at his warm, male scent, she allowed herself to revel in the intimacy created by their position and the darkened interior of the carriage.

She had found it more difficult than she anticipated, withdrawing into her old protective shell. Although Jared no longer appeared to doubt her innocence, he did not love her, and she could not risk exposing her emotions to him. They made her too vulnerable. So she tried to keep her distance from him when they were not making love.

She had no hope of doing so when he touched her intimately. Her body's betrayal of her was too complete. Though Jared did not seem aware of what it signified. He appeared to regard her response to him as purely physical, which only increased her conviction that his desire for her did not go beyond that of a male animal for his mate.

"Are you ready to see your new home?" he asked.

No. She wasn't ready to leave the intimacy of the carriage. She did not look forward to seeing the house where another woman had held such sway over Jared. Even if that woman had been Calantha's friend at one time and dear to her heart. She felt guilty for the jealousy she felt toward Mary, but could not rid herself of it. The prospect of living with a constant reminder of Jared's obvious tender feelings for another woman was a daunting prospect indeed.

"Yes," she said, knowing it was a lie, but unable to bring herself to say differently.

"We don't have many servants at present."

Calantha gave up. She was not going back to sleep. Opening her eyes, she sat up and then pulled away from Jared.

She tried to scoot off his lap, but his arms tightened around her. "Stay."

"I am quite awake now. You needn't feel obliged to hold on to me." She kept her voice even and polite.

In the dim glow of the single carriage lamp, she could see Jared's eyes narrow. "I like holding you."

"It isn't proper for you to hold me outside the privacy of our bedchamber."

"You knew I wasn't Town Polished when you married me, Cali. You are my wife. I'm going to touch you outside of our bedchamber, and you might as well get used to it, because that is not going to change."

"You say that a lot," she whispered.

"That I'm not going to change? That's not true. I'm trying my dam— best not to curse around you. You don't like it, so I try not to do it, but I won't give up touching you."

She had noticed Jared stopping mid-word on several occasions and wondered at the reason for his improved language. He was doing it for her.

A soft curl of warmth unfurled inside her. "I wasn't speaking of your changing. I referred to how often you remind me I am your wife. I assure you, I am not likely to forget."

"And I'm not likely to turn into a tame lapdog and touch my wife only in the privacy of our bedchamber."

Realizing she wasn't going to move without creating a major scene, she resigned herself to staying where she was.

She tried to act as if her bottom was not resting on the hard warmth of Jared's thighs. "Why don't we have many servants?"

"Nervous servants irritate me."

When he didn't add anything to that cryptic statement, she prodded, "And?"

"And I make most servants nervous. To tell the truth, I make a lot of people nervous. The *ton* did not name me Lord Beast because they find my looks and size charming."

She did not find his looks and size charming either. She found them enticing, irresistible, and exciting. *Charming* was much too tame a word for the response Jared's person elicited in her.

"You are an overwhelming man, husband. I think that were you several inches shorter and had a face unmarred by your heroic past, you would still spark a case of nerves in others. You live by your own rules and expect others to abide by them as well. That is not only unique, but unheard of, among the *ton*. I think it is the forcefulness of your personality that frightens others, rather than your looks."

"You aren't afraid of me." He sounded very satisfied by that fact.

"No. I am not. As you keep reminding me, I am your wife. Will you mind if I want you to hire more servants?" She assumed Raven Hall was quite large, and she did not wish to see only a few overburdened souls responsible for its upkeep.

"Hire as many as you like. You'll have to find a new housekeeper, too."

He hadn't been able to bring himself to replace Mary.

Calantha mentally pulled further into herself, not wanting him to see the hurt that knowledge caused her. "You wish me to hire the new servants?"

"You'll be in charge of them. It makes sense for you to choose them."

"Deveril did not trust my judgment in such matters." She regretted the words as soon as she spoke them. Deveril and his ugly opinions had no place in her new life with Jared.

Jared squeezed her waist. "The man was a fool. Don't expect me to repeat his mistakes."

"Is it safe to bring in new servants right now?" Could they be sure that their new servants were not in league with the villain trying to hurt Hannah?

"If you hire from the village, there won't be a problem. I know the people and their families, even if most of them will cross the street rather than walk by me." She was sure he exaggerated the villagers' reactions, but she could understand them being in awe of him. He was an awesome man. "If you want to hire servants out of London, we'll have to wait."

"I'm sure there are competent people locally." Contrary to what Jared seemed to believe about her, she was not particularly interested in Town Polish. She had been content to rusticate in the country these past four years and would travel to London with Jared when he requested, but he would never hear her ask to go. She was no longer interested in the Season, or its round of social obligations.

Her first Season, she had been shy and frightened by the *ton* and its ways, having never been out of the district in which her papa had been vicar. Her shyness had been taken as mysterious allure, and she had attracted Deveril's interest.

The next two Seasons had been a source of never ending strain in her life. She did not comport herself like a duchess. She spoke too long to one gentleman to be proper. She was too cold, too warm, too stupid, too talkative, too silent—a failure. The list had been endless, and each time she failed, it was an opportunity for Deveril to unleash his temper on her. She had no happy memories of her time in London and would not care if she never saw the huge city again.

As they stood in the entry hall to his home thirty minutes later, Jared watched Cali closely, trying to read her reaction to her surroundings. It was not anything like Clairborne Park, but it was much larger than the cottage she had been living in for the past four years. Raven Hall had been built two centuries ago along the lines of a castle fortress. He found the rough stone structure pleasing, but wondered if Cali would be similarly affected. Or would she dislike the old-fashioned, plain furniture, unadorned rooms, and sometimes drafty corridors?

Hannah lay sleeping in his arms, not having stirred when he lifted her from the carriage and carried her inside. Although the hour was late, his few servants had gathered in the hall to welcome their new mistress. Cali took time to greet each of them and find out their names, not showing by so much as a droopy eyelid how exhausted she was.

The trip had been difficult for both her and Hannah, but she had not complained once. She'd been patient, even when Hannah had grown fractious before falling asleep that night. Two days in a closed carriage had been one too many for their daughter.

He waited until Cali finished speaking to the servants before handing Hannah to a footman and instructing the maid that had helped him with the child since Mary's death to take her to bed. Cali insisted on going with them, to tuck their daughter in, and he took the time to inform his butler of the need for heightened security.

He and the servant made the rounds of the house, making sure all the doors and windows were shut tight and locked. After giving instructions to his butler to see to extinguishing the lamps, he followed his wife upstairs.

He found her in the nursery, sitting beside Hannah's bed and watching the little girl sleep. There was no light in the room, except for that coming from the hall through the opened door. The maid had already climbed into the other narrow bed in the room. He had no doubt that Cali had insisted she do so, not wanting to keep the servant up any later. His wife's tender heart toward others never ceased to amaze him.

He laid his hand on her shoulder. "Come."

Her head came up, and he looked into blue eyes, softened by her love for their daughter. "All right."

She followed him out of the nursery. Unlike in other houses, Hannah's nursery was on the same floor as the master and mistress's bedchambers. He thought grimly of the two connecting rooms and the smaller bed in the room adjacent to his own. Now that she was back to playing the detached duchess, would Cali insist on sleeping in it?

She had made that comment about improper touching in the carriage. Would she expect him to come to her, make love to her, and then leave like other proper gentlemen among the *ton*?

He damn well wasn't going to put up with it. Sleeping with his arms wrapped around her was too pleasurable. He needed to hold her at night, and she needed to be held, confound it. Even if she didn't know it.

He led her into his chamber, his gaze falling on his huge bed with grim satisfaction. The ancient four-poster was both wide enough and long enough for him to sleep comfortably with his wife.

"Do you want my help undressing?" he asked her, knowing full well she was accustomed to seeing to herself at night, but hoping nevertheless.

"I don't see my portmanteau or trunk." She turned her head to look at him. "I will need my nightgown."

"I prefer it when you sleep without a night rail."

Instead of getting all starchy, like he expected, she smiled. "I've noticed, but I should like to have it at hand in any case."

"Your things have been put in your room." He opened the door that led to the other chamber and waited for her.

She gave him an enigmatic look. "Are we to have separate rooms, then?"

"It is usual." But he didn't want it.

He hoped she would admit she liked sharing his bed, but if she didn't, he was prepared to demand she do so.

"Yes." She walked into the other room, and he followed her.

He saw that a maid had laid her night rail on the bed, probably intending to unpack the rest of Cali's things the next day. Jenny was supposed to arrive with the remainder of Cali's clothes in another week, or so. Until then, his wife would have to make do with whatever was packed in the single trunk and portmanteau. Knowing Cali, it wasn't all clothing. There were books and papers she insisted on bringing with them, while allowing her others to travel with Jenny and the rest of her things later.

She untied the ribbons from the stylish hat she had put back on after her nap. She pulled the straw concoction off and dropped it on the bed, along with her pelisse and gloves.

"Lise seems very nice," she said, referring to the maid that slept in Hannah's room. "Is she Hannah's nursemaid?"

"She's been acting as such since Mary's death. Before that, she helped in the kitchen."

Cali nodded and sat down to remove her short traveling boots. She managed to do so without showing so much as her ankle. "Is she good with Hannah?"

He had to repeat the question in his mind before it made sense to him, because she had gotten her boots off, and the sight of her pretty, narrow feet in nothing but stockings excited him as much as if she'd stood naked in front of him. Cali's high arches were kissable, and more erotic than he would have thought possible.

"Yes," he replied to her question about the maid being good with Hannah, "she's patient and lively."

"Does she prefer watching Hannah to helping in the kitchens?"

"How the devil should I know?" He couldn't read the maid's mind.

Cali began unpinning her hair, its silky, golden strands falling past her shoulders in long waves. "I take it you haven't asked."

"No." He'd needed someone to help him with Hannah. Lise had seemed the most logical choice.

"I'll talk to her tomorrow. If she's agreeable, I will keep her as Hannah's nursemaid and find another girl to help in the kitchen when I go into the village."

"Fine." Unable to stand the strain of waiting to find out

where she wanted to sleep, he said, "You can keep your things in here, but you will sleep in my bed."

Her head, which had been averted while she worked on braiding her hair, came around to face him. Her eyes were unreadable. "Will I?"

"Yes." He glared at her, prepared to argue all night over that particular dictate, if necessary.

"All right." She stood up. "Would you like to help me with the tapes on my gown?"

He couldn't believe she had given in so easily, but he wasn't such a fool that he would question his good fortune. He reached her in a few giant strides. Reaching down, he took hold of her arms and pulled her toward him.

"I'll help you with more than the tapes," he promised.

Although her face was set in serious lines, her eyes sparkled with mischief and warm passion. "And I'll help you with your breeches."

THREE DAYS LATER, WHILE JARED WAS OCCUPIED WITH estate business that had come up in his long absence, Calantha called for the carriage and a footman to take her to the village. Now that she had explored her new home, gotten to know the current staff, and assessed additional needs, she could begin hiring new servants. The house was much too big to be maintained by the small staff her husband currently employed, and she would need help preparing the conservatory for the arrival of her plants.

It was more like an atrium than conservatory, being located on the top floor of the castle-like house between the east and west towers. It had once been a roof walk, but an earlier occupant of Raven Hall had had the area enclosed in glass sometime in the previous century. She had been surprised to discover that Jared did not make use of it, and the long narrow room had become something of a storage area.

However, his interest in gardening appeared limited to

roses, and only those of the hardier outdoor varieties. He investigated new farming techniques for use in his own fields and those of his tenants, but he did not experiment with plant development in a nursery setting. Therefore, the glassed-in room had been neglected. As had much of the house.

The sparse staff had all they could do, keeping the used living areas presentable. That would change now. Calantha was intent on making Jared's entire house his home. She made a mental list of all the people she would need to hire as she waited in the cavernous hall for the carriage to be brought round. She'd already spoken to Lise and discovered the girl liked being a nursemaid. Watching her with Hannah, Cali had seen that Jared was right. The maid was very good with the little girl.

That meant Calantha needed a kitchen maid, an upstairs maid, another parlor maid, two more footmen, a chamber maid, and a housekeeper. She would call on the vicar's wife and ask for recommendations, and while she was in the village, she would pay her respects at Mary's grave. She wanted to say her good-byes.

MRS. FREELY, THE VICAR'S WIFE, SMILED WITH WARM approval at Calantha. "I'm so pleased the viscount has married. The good book says that it wasn't good for man to be alone, so God made woman. It will take a very special woman to help the viscount out of his solitude. He lives alone there at Raven Hall, with barely a servant to speak of, and I don't think he even realizes how isolated he is."

Calantha was not surprised by the other woman's insight. A vicar's wife was expected to know the people in her husband's congregation. Her own mother had been aware of far more than her father could fathom about what transpired amidst the people he'd been called to serve.

Calantha pulled out several sheets of foolscap from her

reticule and a pencil. "That is one of the reasons I've come to call today."

Mrs. Freely looked curiously at the blank paper. "Oh?"

"I need to hire several more servants. The scant staff we now employ simply will not do."

And Jared had given her permission to rectify the situation. He had not even reserved the right for final approval, but she had every intention of getting his opinion before making her decisions about who to employ. He knew the people and their backgrounds much better than she did.

Mrs. Freely nodded, her rounded face expressing serious consideration of Calantha's words. "I've wondered more than once how they get on at Raven Hall, now that Mary is gone. A gentleman can't do much without a housekeeper when he doesn't have a wife to see that things get done."

"Do you have any recommendations for a woman to fill the post?" Calantha asked.

"There's always the old housekeeper. She went to work for a local squire when Lord Ravenswood hired Mary to take her place. She'd be pleased to return to a viscount's household, I'm sure."

Calantha remembered Jared saying the woman had refused to let Mary work for her as a maid because the girl was pregnant and unmarried. "I think not. I should like someone who will fit into our household more easily than she could."

She didn't know if Jared's vicar and his wife knew that he had adopted Hannah, but the time had come to make sure they did. "Ravenswood and I are raising Hannah as our own. I could not hire a woman who had refused to work with her mother. I much prefer a housekeeper who will naturally show my daughter every respect due her."

The other woman's eyes widened. "I did not realize he planned to make the arrangement official."

Calantha smiled a polite, social smile. No doubt the locals believed that Jared was Hannah's real father. "I assure you, the *arrangement* is quite official. Can you think of a woman who would make a suitable housekeeper for Raven Hall?"

Mrs. Freely could, along with possible maids, footmen, and additional help for the stables if necessary. Fifteen minutes later, Calantha had a list of no less than twelve people to interview.

She stood, fully aware that the prescribed twenty minutes for a call had passed. "Thank you so much for your help in this matter."

Mrs. Freely stood as well, her short, rounded body bobbing in a half-curtsy. "Not at all. If I can be of service to you in any other way, please let me know."

Calantha returned the curtsy. "Thank you. You are too kind."

The other woman smiled, her eyes reflecting genuine welcome. "I hope you will return for tea soon."

"I should like nothing better." Calantha pulled on her gloves. "There is one other item, I could use your guidance concerning."

"Yes?"

"I should like to visit Mary's grave. Could you direct me to where she was buried?"

Shock and confusion shone on the older woman's face. Calantha did not understand it. Surely the question was not so odd. Or perhaps it was in the circumstances. No doubt Mrs. Freely found it strange that Jared's current wife wished to visit the grave of his supposed former paramour. She should have considered that possibility, but now that she had asked the question, she could hardly retract it.

"She's not in the church cemetery," Mrs. Freely blurted out.

Calantha had not expected she would be. It made her angry to think of Mary, that sweet innocent, buried among those the church considered damned. However, she refused to refine on it.

She wanted to visit her former friend's grave, regardless of where it might be found. "I am aware of that, but I assumed your husband would have officiated at the funeral and you would be able to direct me to Mary's final resting place."

Mrs. Freely frowned. "Have you asked Lord Ravenswood about this?"

"I assure you, I do not need my husband's permission to visit the gravesite."

Mrs. Freely opened and then closed her mouth, her agitation apparent. "I truly believe you should ask your husband about visiting his housekeeper's grave."

"Mary was more than his housekeeper. At one time, she was *my* friend," Calantha assured her.

If anything, her explanation appeared to upset the woman further. "This is most unfortunate. I had supposed you knew about Lord Ravenswood and Mary. You did say you intended to raise Hannah as your own daughter, did you not?"

"A word of advice, Mrs. Freely. Appearances are rarely what they seem, and perpetuating unsubstantiated rumor on the base of them is as likely to earn you enemies as titillate your friends."

Mrs. Freely blanched. "Of course, Lady Ravenswood. I would not want to be a party to feeding the rumor mill."

Calantha allowed a small smile to crease her lips. "I did not think for a moment you would." She tugged on her gloves and rose to leave. "About the other matter . . ."

"You did not ask his lordship, I take it?"

"No."

"That explains it. Mary is buried on Lord Ravenswood's estate, in a small grotto in the garden. Near the rosebushes, if I remember correctly."

At first Calantha could not accept the import of what the vicar's wife had told her. *Jared had buried Mary with his beloved roses?* She had always known of Jared's high regard for Mary, but this . . .

For the first time, she considered the possibility that

Jared and Mary had become lovers. Surely Jared would have married her in such a case, but perhaps even he had balked at marriage to a woman who had borne an illegitimate child. Or perhaps he'd asked, but Mary had refused.

Calantha's mind whirled with so many thoughts, no single one taking root long enough for her to reason out its practicality. Interwoven through all of them was the sense that even if Jared and Mary had not been lovers, he'd loved her as surely as he did not love Calantha.

If there had been the slightest doubt that her husband had loved the other woman, it melted away before such strong evidence of his tender feelings.

With a quick curtsy, a word of gratitude, and a smile that signified nothing, Calantha turned to leave.

She regained her carriage, guilt and jealousy at war in her already battered heart. Another woman had known Jared's love, and she felt so envious of that, she was vaguely surprised her skin had not taken on a green cast. But that other woman had been her friend, and deserved the love of such a wonderful man . . . thus the guilt.

Calantha wanted Jared's love, but he gave her his protection and his passion instead. He had not given her his trust, only his belated belief in her innocence.

It was not enough.

Nineteen

"WHAT THE BLOODY HELL DO YOU MEAN, SHE went to the village with a footman?" Jared roared.

His butler winced and took two steps backward, his hands fluttering at his sides like a woman with a fit of vapors. "I was unaware that her ladyship was not to leave the estate, my lord."

Jared glared at the other man. "She's not a prisoner, damn it. I'm concerned about her safety."

"But, my lord, she's only gone to the village, to visit the vicar's wife," the butler said, his tone implying no harm could possibly come of such an innocuous activity.

"Have Caesar brought round." When the butler didn't move fast enough, Jared said, "Now, damn it."

The usually dignified man went scurrying from the study. Jared's hands curled into fists at his sides. He ached to relieve some of his frustration at his independent wife's actions. She should never have left the estate without his escort, but she obviously did not realize that.

She had blithely called for the carriage and gone to the village without once considering the possibility that the bastard who had tried to hurt her and Hannah could have followed them to Raven Hall.

He stormed out of the study, into the hall, and toward the front door, stopping as it swung open to admit the source of his frustrated fury.

"Where the hell have you been, woman?"

At the sound of his voice, Cali, who had been walking as if deep in thought, stopped still at the other end of the hall. Roar, more like. He sounded like an enraged bear, the beast the *ton* thought him, and he could not help himself.

"I've been to call on Mrs. Freely, the vicar's wife."

He felt like exploding. He knew who Mrs. Freely was, damn it, and knowing she was the vicar's wife did not in any way diminish his anger. *"Why did you leave without telling me?"*

"Did not the servants tell you I had gone into the village?" she asked politely, in a quiet voice.

Her demeanor was serene, as if he had not bellowed like a berserker, but he noticed she came no closer.

He took care of that by continuing across the hall until he stood less than a foot from her. "They told me, all right. Is that supposed to make your brainless behavior acceptable?"

"Brainless behavior?" she asked, her tone frigidly polite, her eyes narrowed.

He was past caring if he upset her notion of proper behavior for a viscount toward his wife. *"Yes.* I can't decide if you are addled, or just plain foolish. What possessed you to travel to the village alone?"

"I didn't go alone. I took a footman." She spoke slowly, as if trying to hold in her own temper.

What good was a footman? "You didn't take me."

"I did not realize you expected to accompany me on all my calls. I had the impression that you preferred to avoid most social obligations."

He did. "That has nothing to do with it. This is about your safety."

She blinked, but that was all the indication she gave that he had surprised her. Her face wore that damned blank expression, but at least she wasn't backing away from him. "I was quite safe, I assure you."

"You aren't safe anywhere but at Raven Hall until the blackguard who tried to poison Hannah is caught."

"But the villain is trying to hurt Hannah, not me. There is no reason for me to be confined to the house."

"You yourself said someone wants you blamed for the villainy. That means they want to hurt you. You took a bloody stupid risk going off the estate without me. What was so blasted important that you risked your life going into the village?"

She pursed her lips. "I did not risk my life."

He just glared at her.

She returned his gaze, her own cool. "I went to ask Mrs. Freely about possible housekeepers and other servants."

"I would have taken you." He managed to say it with a semblance of control, his voice well below a roar.

She peeled her gloves off and put them in her reticule. "If I had known it would upset you for me to go alone, I would have asked you to."

No doubt she spoke the truth. Cali did not enjoy upsetting others. She did not play feminine games, like so many women among the *ton*. He reached out and gently pulled her against his body. Damn. He was going to have to apologize. He hated saying he was sorry.

"I shouldn't have yelled at you."

She stood, straight and stiff in his grip. "I shall not go into a brown study over the matter."

He sighed and tipped her head up with his finger bent under her perfectly shaped chin. "I'm sorry, Cali. I was so dam— deuced afraid, when I realized you'd left. It made me angry, and I took the anger out on you."

The mesmerizing blue of her eyes shimmered with moisture. Confound it, was she going to cry? He couldn't stand the thought. He lowered his head, taking her mouth in a gentle kiss. Her lips softened below his immediately, and he deepened the kiss, pulling her closer to him. Her response to him was so honest and overwhelming, he sometimes convinced himself it meant she had feelings for him.

Remembering they stood in the hall where the butler was sure to return any moment and not wanting to embarrass her in front of the servants by allowing the kiss to turn carnal, he lifted his head and pressed her face against his waistcoat.

"Do you forgive me?"

She was silent so long, he thought she would refuse. "Yes."

"Do you promise not to leave the estate without my escort until the bounder is caught?"

She pulled away from him. "What if he has gone completely to ground and you do not catch him? How long will you expect me to live confined to the estates?"

Didn't she think he could find the bastard? "You aren't going to be confined. I will take you where you wish to go. Now, promise me."

"Yes."

He pulled her back against him, and they remained like that for a long moment of silence.

"Jared?"

"Mmmm?"

"Will you show me where Mary is buried?"

TIME HAD TAKEN AWAY THE FRESHLY TURNED LOOK TO the earth that covered Mary's grave, but Calantha could still tell the outline of where her friend had been buried. Even if she had not been able to, the finely carved gravestone marked it well.

"Hannah wants me to plant a rosebush to mark her mother's grave. I planned to move one of my *Apothecary's* bushes in the winter when the plants go dormant."

So that was why he had responded so strangely to her

questions about his *Apothecary's Rose* on the night he had first kissed her. She now knew that at the time, he had blamed her for not protecting Mary from Deveril.

She looked at the pretty pink marble grave marker. It had been carved with a climbing rose that outlined Mary's name, her year of birth, and the year she had died. There were no sentimental words, but then, the roses said all that needed to be said. "I would have helped her if I had known. I would have tried to protect her."

Jared wasn't looking at the grave; he was looking at her. "I know, Cali. You're not at fault. It was all that bas— that bounder you were married to."

"I was a coward," she whispered.

Suddenly she was in Jared's arms, his eyes blazing into hers. "You were strong enough to survive marriage to a gargoyle. You did not betray Mary. That bastard you were married to did. But he didn't win in the end. She was happy here. She loved Hannah. You can be happy here, too, if you let yourself be."

Is that what Jared wanted, for her to be happy with him?

Calantha felt words welling up in her like the geyser of an underground spring. She had to ask the question. "Did you love her very much, Jared?"

His expression turned inward, and he released her. "Mary was my friend. She made me laugh, and she was Hannah's mother, and I loved the child. Since the moment I helped Mary give birth, Hannah's place in my heart has been assured."

"You delivered Hannah?" Calantha could not keep the shock from her voice.

"Mary didn't tell anyone she was in labor until it was too late to call for the midwife. I live on a country estate, I know the procedure, but Hannah was different from a new foal. She came out, her dark eyes open and solemn, and I fell in love with her on the spot."

Calantha had no difficulty imagining such an event. She had come to love Hannah too quickly for rational thinking as well. "She's a very special child."

"Yes."

"Her mother was special as well. I can understand how easy it would have been to fall in love with her, too."

Jared went still beside her. "You think I fell in love with Mary? Do you mean to say you believe she shared my bed?"

Calantha searched his features, looking for the truth of the matter. His words had sounded outraged and incredulous. "Did she?"

"She was my friend, Cali, not my mistress."

"You buried her in your beloved rose garden."

"I didn't want her buried next to cutthroats and thieves. Is that so surprising? She was my friend and Hannah's mother. She took care of my home. She took care of me. She never feared me. She made me laugh. Hell, maybe I did love her, but not the way you mean, and I bloody well never bedded her."

"I didn't mean to offend you."

Jared's mouth thinned in a fierce frown. "I'm not like the duke. I don't take advantage of the people under my protection. If I had wanted her in my bed, I would have married her. I thought you knew me better than that."

"I . . ." She didn't know what to say. He was right. He was nothing like Deveril.

"Dam— Confound it, Cali, do you think I'm such a monster I had to stoop to seducing a woman in my employ?"

He made it sound as if she had accused him of raping Mary as Deveril had done. "No, of course not. I . . ."

He turned to walk away, the expression on his face tearing at her heart. "I'll leave you to say your good-byes."

She wanted to call him back. She could tell she had hurt him, and that made her own heart ache. She had impugned his honor, but she had not meant to. She was well aware

Jared would never take advantage of someone in a weaker position than himself.

He was not Deveril.

It was as if the words were burning themselves in her brain. She had withheld herself from her husband because she feared his discovery of her love. Knowing he did not love her, she had not wanted to become vulnerable to him. *Why?* Jared would not use her love to hurt her. He would not try to manipulate her with it, or mock her feelings. He was too gentle, too caring, to do such a monstrous thing.

She had been hurt when Jared doubted her innocence, but by her own admission she had resented Hannah . . . at first. He'd had reason to doubt her. The evidence had been overpowering, and still he had been forced to fight his instincts that told him she was innocent in order to protect Hannah fully. At the same time, he had protected Calantha. He had insisted on sleeping with her, holding her, and comforting her when she wanted to curl into herself and hide.

She knew deep in her soul that he would not give up looking for the true villain until the blackguard was found. Jared wasn't so insistent merely on Hannah's behalf. He was concerned for Calantha as well.

He had warmed the cold places in her soul, given her back her womanhood, and she had repaid him with mistrust. She had withheld the one thing she could give him . . . her love. She had feared making herself vulnerable to him, not because he had ever shown an inclination to hurt her, but because she had judged his motives by old sins. Sins he had never committed. The sins of a dead man.

She had to find him. She had to say she was sorry she hadn't trusted him. She didn't know if she had the courage, but she wanted to tell him of her love as well. He'd given her so much; she wanted to give him her heart.

After saying thank you to a dead woman for taking care of the man Calantha loved, and giving her a daughter to love as well, she turned away from the grave. She had taken only a few steps toward the other part of the rose garden when the sound of a metallic click reached her ears. She turned her head to see the source of the strange sound and came face-to-face with the Duchess of Clairborne.

Dressed in widow's weeds and veil, she was nevertheless too familiar a figure to Calantha for her to mistake the other woman's identity. Ellen held a dueling pistol in her right hand, and it was pointed at Calantha's bosom.

"Lady Ravenswood." The duchess gave an abbreviated curtsy, maintaining a steady aim with the pistol.

Calantha found the sign of civility obscene in the present circumstances and refused to mimic it.

"I should like your company on a small jaunt in my carriage."

"No." She would be a fool to go anywhere with the mad woman.

"I really must insist. You see, my plans are quite set, and you are part of them. Besides, that little whelp you claim for a daughter will be very pleased to see you."

She had Hannah? Impossible. Jared would not allow Hannah out of the house unless both Lise and a burly footman accompanied her. "I don't believe you. You could not possibly have Hannah."

The duchess pursed her lips. "Really. How uncivil of you. Your rustication in the country these past four years has undone all the good work Deveril attempted on your behalf. I could have told him he would never make a proper duchess out of you. In fact, I did. He did not listen, of course. Gentlemen are so muddled in their thinking, are they not? So affected by a pretty face that birth and a proper bringing up are entirely overlooked, until it is too late. Do you not realize that a lady does not accuse a duchess of lying?"

The even tone of Ellen's voice was unnerving, but no more so than the steady hand holding the pistol.

"Perhaps a duchess should refrain from lying."

"In this instance, I have no need of prevarication. The rather large person guarding your little orphan and her feather-headed nursemaid has been dealt with. I'm sure someone will find their unconscious bodies eventually, but that is not important."

Fury welled up in Calantha, and her hands fisted at her sides. "*You're the one.* You've been trying to hurt Hannah, and now you've done something to Lise and the footman."

"Really, my dear. All this excessive emotion on behalf of your former husband's by-blow and a couple of servants. You never did understand who the important people were."

"I know who is important," Calantha bit out. "What I do not know is why a duchess would stoop to such despicable behavior."

Ellen's eyes narrowed. "Men can be very stupid, Lady Ravenswood. Just look at how your husband left you here alone and unprotected. He foolishly assumes that you are safe so close to the house. He underestimates me, of course. Men so often underestimate a woman."

"But why?" Calantha asked, her mind trying to wrap around the concept that the proper Duchess of Clairborne was a kidnapper and murderer.

"Deveril, that idiot, wrote a most improper will. Can you imagine leaving half your fortune to your child, and not stipulating whether or not that child was your by-blow?"

"Deveril left half of his fortune to Hannah?" Thea had been right. Money had been at the root of the terrible events, money due Hannah.

For a moment, unadulterated rage showed on the duchess's face. "He wasn't even that specific. He left half his fortune to a child, any child that was of his issue. One might almost forgive him, if one thought he had meant to care for a child not yet born to his proper wife, but we know differently. Deveril knew you could not have been increasing."

"How do *you* know that?"

"Come, Calantha, who do you think convinced him that you would lose your looks if he rushed you into childbed?"

"You?"

Ellen's laugh was as cold as a winter day. "Do not be absurd. Ladies do not discuss such matters with gentlemen. However, a few veiled hints to Henry, and he taunted his brother with the prospect. Henry was always jealous of Deveril's place as the eldest. He enjoyed goading Deveril with the idea that you would no longer be the *ton*'s perfect Angel if you grew big with child."

It made no sense. "What of an heir?"

"He would have taken you eventually, and that is why he had to die. I could not risk him impregnating you with a male child. I considered waiting until I had given birth to a son myself, and taking care of Henry and Deveril in one grand gesture, but that cad, Deveril, had begun looking at you with a certain lustful expression. It wouldn't have been long before he decided to consummate your two-year-old marriage. The thrill of being married to the ethereal Angel had begun to pall."

Even the thought of such an event taking place made Calantha's stomach queasy. She could not imagine being touched in the intimate way Jared used with her by Deveril. The thought was beyond disgusting, it was beastly. Then something else Ellen had said pricked her consciousness. "You killed Deveril?"

That wasn't possible. He had been shot by the jealous husband of one of his many mistresses.

Ellen looked bored. "Who do you think arranged for that slut's husband to find her with Deveril?"

The full import of the other woman's words hit Calantha. "You wanted the power of being a duchess. You planned to get it all along. You must have been furious when Deveril did not come up to scratch, but chose to marry a lowly vicar's daughter instead."

"I am the daughter of a duke. He should have married

me, but in typical male fashion, he was dazzled by your beauty and reputation as the Angel. There were bets on all the books at the gentlemen's clubs the year you came out, regarding who you would deign to wed. From the interest the gentlemen of the *ton* showed you, one would have thought you were royalty."

Instead she had just been a shy, frightened daughter of a vicar. "So, you settled for Henry."

"Yes." Ellen's hand squeezed dangerously at the trigger of the pistol. "I began making my plans the day your engagement was announced. Deveril would still be alive if he had asked me to marry him. I would have been content to be *his* duchess, but he was a fool, and he had to die."

"But why kill Hannah? We didn't know about the will. Surely you realized that. We didn't even think the Clairbornes knew of her existence. The issue would never have arisen."

"I knew what Deveril had done to Mary. When I learned of her pregnancy, I spread the rumors that Ravenswood had sired her. All would have been well if he had not brought her to the district, but I could not risk someone else guessing at the truth of her parentage."

"What of Henry? Is he a part of your dastardly plot to kill an innocent child?"

Ellen looked at Calantha as if her brains had gone to let. "Naturally not. Should he discover it, he might begin to suspect my other plans. Even a complete fool can have the occasional flash of insight."

"What other plans?"

"Why, to kill Henry once he's given me a male child, of course. I have decided that I do not wish to share the consequence of the title with a fool. Besides, he once struck me. He soon learned I would not tolerate that sort of behavior, but a gentleman that would treat a duchess like a common trollop does not deserve to live."

Calantha shook her head. "You're mad."

Ellen smiled, her face taking on a disturbingly evil cast. "Mad? I think not."

"Where is Hannah?" As morbidly fascinating as their conversation had become, Calantha wanted to make sure her daughter was safe.

"As I said, she is in my carriage. I'm sure the child is getting fretful with only my driver and helpers for company."

The thought of Hannah in the company of ruffians like Willem chilled Calantha's blood. But what if Ellen were lying? What if she did not have Hannah and her words were merely a trap? Could Calantha risk refusing to come? If Ellen did have Hannah, Calantha must go to her. And there was the gun to consider. She did not know if the other woman had the nerve to shoot her, but Calantha had no real desire to find out.

"Take me to my daughter."

Twenty

THE BLOODY, MERCENARY BITCH.

It took a full measure of control for Jared to bite back the shout of rage at the sight of the madwoman holding a gun on Cali. The pistol gleamed evilly in the afternoon sun, an ugly contrast to the early summer beauty of his rose garden. Feelings that he had not experienced since seeing his younger sister threatened by a wolf roared up in him. They were equal parts rage and fear. Cali could be hurt, damn it. Killed.

The same feral need to do whatever was necessary to protect his own thundered through Jared.

He'd been so angry when Cali had accused him of having an affair with Mary that he'd left her alone to say her good-byes to their dead friend, rather than stay and yell at her for her witless notions. Didn't his wife realize that she was the only woman he had ever loved? Mary had been his friend, but she had never elicited the kind of reaction in him his angel did.

He needed Cali like he needed his next breath. It wasn't just the passion he found in her arms, either. Oh yes, he needed her body. He craved her sweet, soft curves with a hunger that could never be quenched, but it was so much more.

He needed the gentleness that gave her such a sweet nature, despite the things she had suffered. He craved the strength that had kept her living in the face of pure evil. He desired her compassion, which was so strong, it made her offer comfort when she was hurting herself. He was in awe of her intelligence and hunger for knowledge. He needed everything that made her his angel, and he needed it for the rest of his life.

She made him feel like a man, not a beast.

And now she was being threatened by a duchess as half-baked as a loaf of bread with a sticky center. Thank God he had come back to set his angel straight on her confused thinking.

The two women were at the opposite end of the garden from him, and he could not see a way to overpower the duchess without giving away his hand. If the evil witch saw him, she might shoot Cali. Her hand was too firm on the pistol's handle, and her finger pressed too tightly to the trigger for his peace of mind.

He waited until the two women had left the small grotto before following them on silent feet, keeping to the shrubbery and trees so the gun-waving duchess would not see him if she chanced to look back.

The duchess directed Cali on a roundabout path to the road that led to Raven Hall from the north. Using the instincts of a hunter with his prey, he steadily closed the distance between himself and the villainous woman. He wanted to reach her before she brought them out into the open and his approach would be observed.

He could see the black form of a closed carriage through the trees and knew if he moved in now, she could call for help. He wasn't worried about dealing with the low-life bastards she might have hired to help her in her unconscionable plot, but he didn't want to risk one of them getting to Cali before he did. If they had Hannah, his daughter would be put further at risk, as well. There would be no way to predict what the duchess's men might do once they realized their plans were going awry.

They were closer to the clearing now, and he could make out the carriage with more detail. He saw no Clairborne crest on the doors, nor was the driver dressed in the livery of a servant to the nobility. The duchess was up to her old tricks, using a hired carriage and dressing in Cali's widow's weeds again. She must have gotten his wife's clothes from her attic at Rose Cottage in order to emulate the soft rose fragrance associated with the Angel.

He saw no sign of Hannah.

Had the duchess lied when she told Cali that she had their daughter?

As Cali and the duchess approached the carriage, the door opened. A heavy scoundrel who looked like he could be Willem's cousin stepped out of the carriage. The coachman lounged on the seat, chewing on a twig. As if he had no clue that he was aiding a coldhearted bitch in trying to kidnap Jared's wife and child.

Jared was poised, ready to spring at the duchess as Cali stepped into the clearing and the other woman was still concealed by the trees, when all hell broke loose.

The sound of a child's high-pitched scream came from inside the carriage, followed by the sound of a masculine yelp. Cali broke into a run toward the coach.

Hannah's dark head popped out through the open doorway, and the rest of her body followed. "Mama!"

She jumped down from the carriage, as a beefy hand reached out to grab her.

The duchess swore, using a most unladylike phrase.

Cali's entire body stiffened, and she waved her arms wildly in the direction of the forest. "Run, Hannah. Run and hide in the forest! Papa will find you."

Hannah did just that, dashing straight toward the trees

where Jared concealed himself. The owner of the beefy hand came stumbling from the carriage, rubbing at his shin and one hand covering an eye.

"Catch the whelp. She cannot get away," yelled the duchess.

She had turned from Cali, her gun now pointed toward his daughter's running figure. Cali threw herself at the duchess's back, knocking her to the ground. The pistol went off, its ball exploding into the earth and showering the two women with dirt. Cali had hold of the duchess's hair and was pulling with all her might. Jared came out of the trees at a dead run.

Hannah stopped when she saw him.

"Do as your mama said. Run and hide in the trees. Now, Hannah."

His daughter's eyes were wide and frightened, but she obeyed him and once again rushed toward the forest on her short but agile legs.

Jared veered toward the villain chasing Hannah and caught him a facer with an uppercut that sent the man flying several feet. He did not get up. Satisfied that he was no longer a threat, at least for the moment, Jared went after the man who had first stepped from the carriage.

The dirty bounder looked like he was ready to spring on Cali, but she and the duchess were rolling on the ground, locked together in deadly earnest. Jared grabbed the man and swung him around, bringing his free hand up to connect squarely with the villain's jaw in the same motion. The huge man staggered, but he did not go down under Jared's blow.

Jared did not give him a chance to recover. He brought his knee forward into the villain's groin. With another sharp jab to the stomach, he sent the man to the ground.

The coachman finally seemed to wake up and started the horses in motion. The duchess and Cali had broken apart and circled each other like contenders at a prizefight. The sound of the moving coach caught both women's attention, and they turned their heads simultaneously. The duchess's face turned livid with fury at the sight of her coachman leaving without her. She screamed very un-duchess-like invectives at the man as she chased after the conveyance, her torn and dirtied gown grabbed up around her knees.

The villain he had sent to the ground now lurched to his feet and rushed at Jared. He landed a blow that made Jared's head whirl. Jared growled and used the opportunity to land his own punch against his opponent's sternum, refusing to give in to the dizzy sensation assailing him.

He brought his other fist in for a blow against the man's nose. He felt bone crack, and blood spurted. Jared kicked the bounder's feet out from under him and then kicked the side of his head. The huge man remained in a heap on the ground where Jared had sent him.

He turned to make sure Cali was all right and saw her disappearing into the trees where Hannah had gone.

The duchess had managed to stop her coachman and was climbing into her carriage to get away. Jared couldn't afford to go after her right now. The first man he had felled was nowhere to be seen, and both his wife and daughter were out of sight in the forest.

"Put her down, you scoundrel!"

Cali's shout hit Jared more squarely than any of the bastard's blows during his fight moments before.

He ran into the trees, his senses heightened by the danger to his family. Following the sound of Cali's voice, he burst into a small clearing. The tableau presented made Jared's blood congeal in his veins. The bastard held Hannah in one arm, a knife in his other hand. Cali, her hair in wild disarray, clung to his wrist like a limpet, preventing him from getting the knife near Hannah.

Jared didn't waste time on words, but went forward in a silent rush. Grabbing the villain's hand and Hannah at the same time, Jared yanked his daughter from the filthy man's hold. He felt bones give under the steady pressure of his fingers as he tightened his grip on the other man's hand. The man screamed and swung his free arm, sending Cali flying.

Giving the feral shout of a male predator whose mate has been injured, Jared let go of the man's hand to bring his fist back and then swing it forward in a vicious blow to the other man's face. The villain crumpled to the ground.

Hannah hugged Jared's neck with a fierce grip. "Papa, is Mama all right?"

Jared did not know. *Oh Lord, let her be unhurt*, he prayed. He turned and found Cali sitting on the ground several feet away. Her feet stuck out in front of her like the legs of a porcelain doll and her torn skirts hiked up to expose one thigh.

She stared at Jared, her expression dazed. "It was the duchess. She planned it all."

He carried Hannah to Cali, kneeling on one knee by her side when he got there. He reached out and touched his wife's cheek. "Are you hurt, *mon ange*? Did you hit your head?"

Cali shook her head. "I hit my bum." She sounded bewildered by such an event. "It hurts."

He felt a grin split his face. She would be fine. "I'm sure it does, love. We'll look at it when we return to the house."

Her eyes widened. "I don't think—"

"You can't look at Mama's bum, Papa," Hannah interrupted, clearly scandalized.

He hugged her close, but didn't answer. He wouldn't lie to his daughter. He had every intention of looking at his wife's bottom, as well as the rest of her, at the earliest opportunity.

"Ouch, Papa, you're holding me too tight."

Jared eased his grip on his daughter and pulled Cali into the embrace. "You were very brave, poppet."

"I tried to hide, but the bad man found me." Hannah sounded aggrieved, as if a game of hide-and-seek had gone awry.

"You did very well, darling. Mama is so proud of you." Cali's voice was thick with tears.

"I didn't kick him like the other bad man in the carriage. I kicked *him* good. I poked his eye, too." Hannah's voice rang with satisfied triumph. "Aunt Thea says not to poke people's eyes 'cuz they could get hurt. I wanted to hurt that bad man, so I did."

"You did exactly right." Both his daughter and his wife had handled themselves valiantly today. He turned to press a kiss on first Hannah's cheek and then Cali's soft lips. "Can you walk, angel?"

"Of course," she said, as if she hadn't been through a brawl with a mad duchess and villainous snake.

He stood. "Will you be all right while I go check on the other bas— bounder near the road? I won't be gone long."

She nodded, her eyes still a little unfocused. "What of this one?"

Jared looked at the man who had threatened his daughter with a knife and sent Cali flying. "He won't wake up before I return."

If he woke at all. Jared felt no remorse at the possibility that he had mortally wounded the other man. The bastard had brought it on himself when he hired on to aid the mercenary bitch married to the current Duke of Clairborne.

When he returned to the spot where the carriage had been, he found it empty. The duchess and two of her cohorts were long gone, but Jared would find them. Later. Right now he had his wife and daughter to care for.

Four days later, Calantha paced the floor of Jared's bedchamber. It was after midnight and the entire house was abed, except the Bow Street Runner who guarded the hall outside the door. Hannah slept in the connecting room.

It had been this way for the past three nights, ever since

they had returned from their confrontation with the duchess
to find the Bow Street Runner Jared had hired to follow the
Clairbornes waiting at Raven Hall. He had informed them
that the Clairbornes had not traveled to their northern estate after all. The duke was in London, but the duchess was
supposedly visiting friends in the country. Calantha and
Jared had known better. A second attempt at kidnapping
could hardly be termed *visiting*, and it would be a snow-
bound day in Hades before Calantha would claim Ellen as
a friend.

The bounder Jared had felled in the forest had woken
from his unnatural sleep, pale and weak, but able to talk.
Jared had forced him to tell all he knew of Ellen's plans.
Although it was late afternoon by the time Jared had finished speaking to the runner and Ellen's cohort, he had insisted on going after the duchess that very day. He had
instructed the runner to stay and watch over her and Hannah, and had taken time to go to the village and hire two
ex-soldiers who had fought in the war against Bonaparte to
aid the runner in securing Raven Hall.

She and Hannah had not been allowed to set foot outside in four days. Thankfully, the servants recommended
by the vicar's wife had arrived the next day, and Calantha
had been kept busy supervising their work in the house.
Added to the burden of watching over Hannah and nursing
Lise and the footman, she should have barely noticed Jared's
absence. Her current inability to sleep was evidence to the
contrary.

She wanted her husband home.

Calantha stopped pacing in front of the connecting door
and quietly opened it. She slipped through the doorway and
went to the bed. Hannah and Lise lay still, their deep breathing indicating that both maid and child had found the oblivion of sleep. She said a silent prayer of thanks for their
safety, and soundlessly returned to Jared's bedchamber.

Hannah had overcome her experience and complained

more about her Papa being gone than the bad men who had tried to kidnap her a second time. She had woken with a nightmare the first night and climbed into bed with Calantha. The next night Lise had insisted she was well enough to sleep with Hannah. Calantha would have welcomed the comfort of her daughter's presence in the night as she lay awake worrying about Jared, but she forbore saying so. She would not allow herself to be so weak. A four-year-old child might need a nurse, but her mother did not.

She should find her own bed, but her mind was too occupied to sleep. Why hadn't she told Jared she loved him? What if the duchess hurt him? How long would he be gone? The questions whirled through her mind like the bits of colored glass in a kaleidoscope.

Someone knocked on the door. The runner must have heard her moving around and decided to check on her. She went to the door and unlocked it before pulling it open.

Jared stood on the other side. As their gazes met, his face, haggard with tiredness, softened with an emotion that made it difficult for her to breath. Her hand fell away from the door, and she threw herself into her husband's waiting arms.

"Jared." She hugged him with all her might, wanting to cling to him and prevent him leaving her to worry for his safety ever again. Her eyes burned with unshed tears of relief and happiness as her face creased in a tremulous smile. "I have been waiting for you, my love."

The look in his eyes scorched her, as his arms closed around her with strength and his ever-present gentleness. *"Mon ange."*

His mouth came down on hers in a ravenous kiss that spoke of his own ache at their separation, as he pushed her back into the room and shut the bedchamber door behind them.

She pulled her head back, breaking the kiss before her reason deserted her. "Did you find the duchess? What has happened? Have you spoken to Henry?"

Jared caught her beneath the knees and swung her high against his chest. "Later," he murmured against her lips, "I need you now."

He carried her to the bed, never letting his hungry lips leave hers, and passion kindled to a raging inferno within seconds inside of her. She tore at his clothes, making sounds of need that brought a deep, satisfied rumble in his chest.

He broke the kiss only to strip her of her night rail and finish tearing off his own clothes before joining her on the bed, where he resumed the consuming kiss. All of her questions, all of the fear she had suffered while waiting for his return fell away at the desire he kindled in her with his mouth and strong, sure hands on her flesh.

He touched her everywhere, as if memorizing the feel of her after a long absence. It had only been four days and three nights, but she understood the emotions she sensed in him, because she felt them, too. The raging need. The unquenchable desire. The fascination with his flesh. The essential oneness.

She caressed him, urging him closer, needing the experience of their shared flesh to assure her of his well-being. She opened her legs, making a place for his hardened flesh between them.

Tearing her mouth from his, she demanded, "Now, Jared. I cannot wait any longer."

Tilting her femininity toward him, she grabbed his buttocks and tugged his manhood closer. His breathing was labored, and his face wore the feral expression she had learned to associate with his passion.

"Yes, *mon ange*. I'll give you what you want, darling."

And he did. Oh, Heavens, he did. With one great thrust, he embedded his flesh in hers, and she shuddered with the sheer ecstasy of their union. He stilled above her, his body taut with sexual intent. In the soft candle glow of the room, his expression was shadowed from her gaze, and yet she could feel the intensity of his look as his eyes bore into her.

"Cali. *Mon ange.* My wife."

Her body craved his movement, but her soul reveled in the moment of communion between their hearts as his body linked to hers in utter stillness.

"Jared. My love. My husband." She whispered the words, unwilling to allow loud declarations to upset the atmosphere of spiritual union that surrounded them in the oversized bed.

He began to move, but it bore no resemblance to the frenzied rush that had marked their coming together. He leaned on his arms above her, his body blocking her view of the room. Her entire perception narrowed to the man making love to her with slow, tender care. She laid her hands against the muscled wall of his chest and absorbed the heat of his body through the sensitive skin of her fingertips.

He moaned. "I love your touch. I dream of your small hands running over my skin."

She circled his nipples with both forefingers. "Like this?"

Moaning again, he thrust deeply into her, but did not increase the pace. "Yes, just like that."

She allowed her hands to roam over the hair-roughened surface of his chest until she reached the area near his shoulder that had been wounded by the wolf. She reverently traced each line of raised flesh. "You are honorable in every way, husband. Thank you for marrying me."

He pressed a gentle kiss to her temple and continued his deep, unhurried thrusting. "Angel, there are no words for the gratitude and privilege I feel at being your husband."

Then words ceased as Jared finally increased the pace of his movements, bringing her closer and closer to that moment of sheer bliss that she had learned to crave at his hand.

She gripped his shoulders, and words exploded out of her as her body rocked in convulsions under him. "I love you, Jared. I love you. I love you. I love you . . ."

* * *

THE LITANY OF HIS WIFE'S WORDS OF LOVE ENDED ON A
loud moan of utter feminine surrender, bringing Jared to
his own release. He thrust himself into her one last time
and felt the warm explosion of his seed shoot into her body
as his entire body went stiff above hers. The climax felt
like it went on and on and on. She moved in tiny little convulsions under him and drew out everything his body had
to give until he collapsed on top of her, his sweaty flesh
pressed heavily into hers. He turned his face so his mouth
pressed against her cheek.

They lay that way in silence for several long minutes
until he felt her shift under him and realized she was probably having a hard time getting enough air. He rolled off
her, but pulled her against him, retaining their closeness.
She squirmed until her upper torso was resting on top of
his chest, her chin propped on her arms.

"Tell me what happened."

He didn't want to talk about that bitch, the duchess, but
he knew his stubborn wife would not rest until she had
wrested the details from him. He hoped he had the answers
she wanted. He didn't have them all himself, because the
duchess's final actions had prevented him from asking the
questions.

"I didn't find her where her cohort said she was going to
be, so I went to London."

"Did you talk to Henry and tell him her plans?"

Jared nodded, remembering the conversation. Henry
was a bastard and had tried to hurt Jared's wife, but the
duke deserved to be warned that his wife was a would-be
murderess and had plans to end his life once she'd given
birth to a male child. He had expected the duke's arrogance
to prevent him from believing Jared's claims, but that was
not what happened.

"He believed me. Every word. He must have sensed the madness that lurked beneath his wife's proper façade."

Cali traced a pattern on his chest with one fingertip. "Was the duchess there?"

"No."

"Did you find her?"

"Yes."

Cali's gaze caught with his. Incredible. One word, and she knew something was wrong. He could see the knowledge in her angel blue eyes. "Tell me."

"She was killed. By the time I caught up with her, both her hired coachman and the other bastard had disappeared. I could not tell if she was shot, or went completely mad and shot herself. The duke has put about the story that she was attacked by highwaymen on her way to visit friends."

Cali's eyes widened with apparent distress. "She's dead?"

"Yes."

"I can't believe it."

"Believe it. Dam— I mean to say, confound it, Cali. Don't tell me you grieve for the murderous witch."

Cali shook her head. "No. I'm relieved. It's over. Hannah is safe. You are safe."

Suddenly his wife was lying on top of him and hugging him with a fierce grip. He could feel her tears against his neck.

Wrapping his arms around her, he said, "We are all safe. Cali, tell me again that you love me."

He needed to hear the words, needed to know she meant them, and they had not been merely talk born of her passion.

She lifted her head and wiped at her wet cheeks with the back of one hand. "I do love you."

He couldn't respond because of an unfamiliar tightness in his throat.

She touched his scars again, as she had so many times and reminded him that in her eyes they made him a man of valor, not a beast. "When I was eighteen and realized what sort of person I had married, I gave up my dreams. You've given them back to me, Jared. I thought I would never be a mother, and you gave me a daughter. You've taught my body pleasure and my heart how to trust. How could I not love you more than my own life?"

He took a deep breath, trying to find the composure to speak, and the words, which at one time had seemed weakening, came out in a strong, bold rush. "I love you, *mon ange*. I love you with every beat of my heart." He kissed her. "You are my wife. Now and forever. I will always love you."

She buried her face against his neck. "Say it again. Please, say it again."

"I love you."

She kissed the underside of his jaw. "I love you. Today and always. I've loved you for the longest time, and it hurt so much to think your heart had been given to a woman now dead."

"I have never felt about another woman the way I feel about you."

She pressed her face into the curve of his shoulder, and he felt the wetness of tears against his neck. "I'm so glad. I thought you would never love me."

Her words stunned him. He couldn't believe she had doubted his feelings. Putting a hand on each side of her head, he lifted her face until their eyes met.

"Cali, you are the loveliest woman I have ever seen. Your blue eyes remind me of the summer sky; your hair is like a cascade of honey colored silk; your body is perfect in shape and form, but your heart is by far your most beautiful attribute. Your touch drives me wild. Your scent is the fragrance of Heaven to me, and I have known you belonged to me since the first time I kissed you in the garden at Ashton Manor. How could you have doubted it?"

She blinked her luminous eyes. "I thought after my first

marriage that I was unworthy of love. When you doubted my innocence, I believed you could not love me and think those things about me. I decided that Deveril must have been right."

Pain lanced through Jared at the knowledge that his actions had hurt her so deeply. "Deveril was a bloody bas— He was an idiot and a monster. You are so lovable that neither our daughter nor myself had a chance against your sweetness. I loved you then, but I let my head rule my heart." He hoped she could understand. "I wasn't used to the feelings you brought out in me. They scared me, at first. I felt vulnerable, and that made me angry and distrustful of my own instincts."

Her face softened with love that would last a lifetime. "My feelings for you are so strong and so overwhelming they frighten me. It is comforting to know I am not the only vulnerable party in this marriage."

"Your love is safe with me," he vowed.

"I know. I trust you, Jared."

Incredible. After everything that had happened, she did not hold his initial doubts against him. She trusted him, and he knew that for his wife that was a gift of incomparable treasure. He would never again allow the evidence of his eyes and ears to supersede his instincts about his wife's honor and compassion. "Thank you. I trust you, too, *mon ange*."

She pulled her head from his grasp and sat up. Then she wiggled down his body until her warm, wet heat pressed against his semi-erect sex. "I believe you, but I don't want to talk about that right now."

He arched toward her, causing her body to slide along his shaft in a tormenting caress. "What do you want to talk about?"

She rolled her hips in small arcs, making his manhood swell. "Nothing. I want to *do*."

"You're an insatiable wench."

Her eyes lit with humor, and her smile blinded him. "I

do believe I am. Will you mind very much being married to such a demanding wife?"

Mind? "Not bloody likely."

She leaned down until the tips of her breasts brushed against his chest and swayed from side to side, making her hardened nipples rub against him. "I'm glad."

"I'm happy you want me, too. Your love has rescued me from life as Lord Beast."

She pressed a heated kiss to his chest. "I believe we are even. Your love has rescued me from life as the Angel."

"You *are* an angel, *my* angel." He could barely get the words out, as her silken flesh against his brought a resurgence of the desire that rode him whenever they were together.

She raised her head and scooted up his body just enough to kiss his lips. "But your angel doesn't have to be perfect."

"I would much rather have your passion than marble perfection," he vowed.

So she gave him the passion he craved. They shared their love, their bodies expressing the depth of feelings too great for words. Afterward, he cuddled his wife's body close into his own and thought a lifetime with the love of an angel was like having his own slice of Heaven on earth.

Epilogue

JARED CARRIED CALANTHA INTO THE DRAWING
room and set her carefully on the fainting couch
beneath the window at the far end of the room. "I'm not
sure this is a good idea, *mon ange.*"

She smiled up at him, making no attempt to hide her
amusement at his overprotective attitude. "I will be quite all
right. Anna Elizabeth is a week old now, and I do not wish to
stay abed."

He snorted. "As if you stayed abed at all. I caught you
pruning roses in the conservatory the day after our daughter was born, wearing nothing but a night rail."

"That is hardly my fault. You'd given instructions to
Jenny not to allow me to dress."

"I thought that would keep you from getting out of bed
against the doctor's wishes, like you did with Marcus."
Jared's frown did not obliterate the warm love shining in
his beautiful dark eyes.

"I should have thought you would have learned by now

that your wife is every bit as stubborn as you," Irisa remarked, from her seat nearby.

In her second confinement, she glowed with joy and humor. Ashton stood behind his heavily pregnant wife, his hand resting possessively on her shoulder. Their three-year-old son played pick-up sticks with David, Deanna, and Hannah on the carpet in front of the empty fireplace, while Marcus played with blocks near his Aunt Irisa's feet. Thea and Drake shared a small sofa a few feet away.

The entire family had come to see Calantha and Jared's new daughter. Everyone except Lord and Lady Langley. Calantha had never met them, as their stay on the Continent had turned into a permanent exile.

"Do not call me stubborn. I am not the one who insisted on traveling to visit relatives only weeks away from delivering my second child," Jared said, sounding aggrieved.

"You, brother-dear, are incapable of giving birth." Thea smiled as she spoke.

Calantha adjusted Anna's blanket. "That didn't stop him from insisting on being in the room for Anna's delivery."

"At least he didn't faint during this one," Drake said.

Dull red stained Jared's cheekbones. "I didn't faint when Marcus was born. I had a moment of dizziness."

The moment of dizziness had lasted several minutes, if Calantha remembered correctly. She had screamed with pain as her son's head crowned, and her husband had crashed to the floor like a load of coal dropped from the scuttle. The doctor, who had been scandalized at the prospect of a husband being in the bedchamber during a birthing, had refused to administer aid in waking Jared.

She cuddled her new daughter.

Awed by the tiny features relaxed in sleep, Calantha felt her eyes fill with tears. "She is perfect."

Jared reached out and gently brushed the baby's forehead with his large finger. "Yes, she is."

"Papa, can we take Anna swimmin' wif us?" their two-year-old son, Marcus, asked.

"No, silly, she's too little." Hannah spoke with the authority of the eldest child, wearing her seven years like they were sixty.

Her sometimes too-serious mien enhanced the fine-boned beauty of Calantha's eldest daughter, but it was her status as an heiress that would give her papa heart palpitations when she was old enough to be introduced to society. She had indeed inherited half of Deveril's fortune.

Henry, in a move that had shocked both Calantha and Jared, had insisted on it after the debacle with his wife. Calantha had wondered at the time if it had been an attempt on his part to keep them quiet about his mad wife's actions. It hadn't been necessary. Neither she, nor Jared, wanted any reminder of that time, including gossip.

Marcus abandoned his blocks and sidled over to Calantha's side. He bounced on the balls of his feet. "Lise said we could go this afternoon."

Calantha smiled at her son. "I'm sure she will keep her promise to take you swimming, poppet."

The game of pick-up sticks ended with a crow of victory from Deanna. Hannah stood up and came to stand on Calantha's other side. She leaned her head on Calantha's shoulder and gazed at her little sister with an expression so sweet, Calantha wanted to cry. "I love you, Mama."

The tears that had threatened finally spilled over. "I love you, too, darling."

She had thought never to have children, and now she had three to treasure and cherish. Jared had given her the greatest gift imaginable, the gift of love.

Lucy Monroe is the award-winning author of more than thirty books. She's married to her own alpha hero and has three terrific children. The only thing she enjoys more than writing is spending time with them. Lucy loves to hear from readers at lucymonroe@lucymonroe.com, or visit her website at www.lucymonroe.com.

Lucy Monroe is
"an awesome talent."*

Tempt Me
0-425-20922-9

Lady Irisa Langley is at her wit's end. She has a secret that would shock even the world-weary denizens of the ton—and destroy any future she could have with her exasperatingly perfect fiancé. But then again, sometimes a little scandal is good for the heart and soul.

"A wonderful temptation for any reader."
—Bestselling author Susan Wiggs

Touch Me
0-425-20531-2

Together, Thea Selwyn and Pierson Drake embark on an extraordinary voyage from a tropical paradise to the glittering ballrooms of London. But will Thea's dark secrets destroy their illicit passion?

"Emotional, sexy, and romantic."
—*New York Times* bestselling author Lori Foster

*Best Reviews